PRAISE FOR NICOLE BYRD'S NOVELS . . .

Lady in Waiting

"Byrd's unpretentious writing style and sense of humor render this a delicious read."　　*—Publishers Weekly*

"Byrd sifts a measure of intrigue and danger into her latest historical confection, which should prove to be irresistible to readers with a taste for deliciously witty, delightfully clever romances."　　*—Booklist*

Dear Impostor

"Madcap fun with a touch of romantic intrigue . . . A stylish Regency-era romp . . . satisfying to the last word."
　　—New York Times bestselling author Cathy Maxwell

"A charming tale of an irresistible rogue who meets his match. Great characters, a plot that keeps the pages turning, and a smile-inducing ending makes this a must-read. Delightful, charming, and refreshingly different . . . don't miss *Dear Impostor*."　　—Patricia Potter

"*Dear Impostor* is the real thing—a story filled with passion, adventure, and the heart-stirring emotion that is the essence of romance." —Susan Wiggs, author of *The Firebrand*

continued . . .

"One of the most entertaining romances I've read in a long while. The story line is inventive, the characters are dynamic, and the pacing is lively . . . *Dear Impostor* is the rare romance that . . . never hits a false note . . . Readers who . . . are looking for a well-paced story that sparkles with originality are advised to run, not walk, to their bookstore and seek out *Dear Impostor*. I highly recommend it."

—*The Romance Reader*

"A terrific story with heartwarming, realistic characters . . . Do not miss *Dear Impostor* . . . The tale is beautifully written and enticingly romantic and is a Perfect Ten for me."

—*Romance Reviews Today*

Robert's Lady

"*Robert's Lady* is a most excellent debut."

—*The Romance Journal*

"Nicole Byrd has created a masterpiece . . . with the perfect blend of mystery, suspense, and romance. This is one romance story you hate to see end."

—*The Romance Communications Reviews*

"Highly recommended . . . more than a fabulous Regency romance. Rising star Nicole Byrd shows much talent and scope."

—*Under the Covers Book Review*

"Vivid . . . fully developed characters and a story set at a fast clip."

—*The Romance Reader*

"A very strong debut . . . I'll be looking for Ms. Byrd's future releases."

—*All About Romance*

Beauty in Black

Nicole Byrd

BERKLEY SENSATION, NEW YORK

BEAUTY IN BLACK

A Berkley Sensation Book / published by arrangement with the authors

PRINTING HISTORY
Berkley Sensation edition / June 2004

ISBN: 0-425-19683-6

BERKLEY SENSATION™
Berkley Sensation Books are published by
The Berkley Publishing Group,
a division of Penguin Group (USA) Inc.,
375 Hudson Street, New York, New York 10014.
BERKLEY SENSATION and the "B" design
are trademarks belonging to Penguin Group (USA) Inc.

PRINTED IN THE UNITED STATES OF AMERICA

10   9   8   7   6   5   4   3   2   1

Prologue

1817

The marquess of Gillingham traveled by night.

Everyone agreed that, in his dull black carriage with the faded crest on the door, bumping along a country lane by moonlight, the man whose face made babies cry appeared more comfortable with darkness. Some speculated he might feel uneasy with the stares his marred countenance evoked; others thought him indifferent to such vanity and suggested darker motives. Lurid rumors abounded as to why he preferred such a cloak of obscurity—tittle-tattle of devil worship and toasts made with virgins' blood—all of which had spurred the vicar of the local church to preach endless sermons about the dangers of superstition and idle talk, but such liturgical warnings did little to stem the gossip. If anything, they appeared in a backward way to support it. Since the marquess never ventured far, traveling only to survey his large estate in Kent and note how his tenants fared, the whispers did not seem to bother him, though errant children on the edges of his county were sometimes threatened with his name.

"Crack another egg by swinging your basket like that, Jemmy, and I'll feed you to the Black Beast of Gillin'am, I will."

And the child in question would gulp and cross himself, or finger a scruffy charm hidden beneath his smock, and pay more mind to his chores.

The marquess himself, his scarred face habitually shrouded by darkness, stayed close to home, ensconced in a large, dim mansion, ill cared for by the few servants who could be induced to stay with him.

Until that spring, when the chatter around the neighborhood took on a new note, incredulous and eager, whispered with lowered voices and wide eyes.

"The marquess is going to London!"

"The Beast is taking a bride!"

One

"I hear he is quite hideous," Louisa Crookshank said, her tone complacent. She bit into a plump hothouse peach. The juice dripped down her fair skin, and she rubbed it away, shaking back golden curls as she did so.

Any other female would have looked quite unkempt, Marianne Hughes thought as she watched, but Louisa, even with her hair straying into her face and juice stains on her chin, managed to look as beautiful as always. Among Bath Society, she had been dubbed the Comely Miss Crookshank, and it was likely her biggest misfortune.

"So why in the name of heaven are you contemplating his suit?" Louisa's aunt by marriage, Caroline Hughes Crookshank, asked, sounding as usual slightly harassed. "Evan, put down that rock, and do not throw it at your sister!"

The small boy tossed the missile, anyhow. His aim was off. The pebble hit the dove-gray skirts of their houseguest, but there was little strength behind the pitch, and it bounced harmlessly away. Marianne smiled and moved her feet away from the path of an even smaller boy, who was pushing a wooden carriage pulled by two wooden horses. As much as Marianne loved her sister-in-law and her children, Caroline's brood were a trifle unpredictable. Because the day was so fair, they were sitting outside by the rose garden, having tea on the lawn and letting the children run up and down the gravel walkways.

"Because Lucas Englewood jilted her, of course." Cara Crookshank, who was eleven, reached for another scone.

"He did not jilt me!" Louisa snapped. "And I shall box your ears if you again utter such a falsehood!"

"Only because he never proposed, but you thought he was going to." Cara plunged ahead, despite frantic signals from her mother to desist. But although she grinned at her older cousin, the child took the precaution of retreating behind her aunt's chair.

"Act your age, Louisa," Marianne murmured as Louisa jumped to her feet, seeming ready to put her threat into words. "You are approaching one and twenty, not twelve."

Louisa sat down again, but her perfect features twisted into a frown.

"I care nothing about Sir Lucas. He's barely more than a child—"

"He's two years older than you," Cara muttered, but this time, mercifully, her cousin did not hear.

"I should like to meet someone more mature. Anyhow, why should I settle for a mere baronet when I could have someone whose title is inferior only to a duke's? Perhaps I have a fancy to be a marchioness. And I'm told he's ridiculously wealthy."

"You don't need money. And you still have to look at him," the younger child argued.

"Cara, that is unkind," her mother scolded. "You know what the vicar says about beauty lying inside a person, not out."

But the vicar did not have to contemplate an ugly face over his morning tea, Marianne couldn't help thinking; she had met the vicar's plump, pretty wife, who was quite adorable with her round red cheeks and sweet smile. Then she scolded herself for being as shallow as Cara—besides, because of her tender years, the child had an excuse; Marianne did not.

Caroline finished her lecture, adding, "Since you have all finished your tea, I think it is time the children went back to the nursery. I shall check on them and on the baby before I change for dinner."

Cara pouted, but she turned toward the house. The next oldest sibling was made of sterner stuff.

"But I wanted to play another round of bowls with Auntie Marianne," Evan wailed, waving his handful of pebbles.

"Later, we will have another game," Marianne promised as their mother wavered.

Fortunately, the governess, Miss Sweeney, who had all the firmness their doting mother sometimes lacked, said, "Come along, now. And drop those stones, Master Evan."

She herded the children back toward the nursery suite. Their progress was reasonably peaceful—Evan only once reaching over to pinch his older sister, who shoved him away—until Louisa said while the young ones were still in earshot, "Thank heavens, infants make such a noise."

"I am not an infant!" Evan roared.

His younger brother, Thomas, took up the cry, bawling, too. "Not a 'fant!"

Caroline winced. "Louisa, please don't aggravate the children."

Still bellowing, the children disappeared into the house, Miss Sweeney's erect form just behind them. There was a moment of silence. A bird sang at the edge of the lawn, and a bee buzzed as it hovered above a nearby rosebush. The impassive footman offered them a selection of cakes from a silver tray.

Louisa looked innocent as she accepted a raisin cake. After "artless," it was her second most practiced expression, Marianne thought, trying not to laugh.

"But seriously, Louisa, why would you consider his suit?" her aunt Caroline continued. "You haven't even met the man. Looks aside, because he can hardly be judged on such a consideration, I have heard rumors that he is most unpleasant."

"If you haven't met him, how do you know he is interested in your hand?" Marianne asked, taking a sip of her cooling tea.

Louisa blinked. "He will be, when I do meet him. When I go to London!" The last was uttered in a rapturous tone, and she turned eagerly to their visitor. "It would be such an amusement for you, Aunt Marianne. I know your official mourning is long past, even if you do still wear such drab colors, and think how diverting it would be to chaperone me to all of the parties and amusements of the Season!"

Marianne glanced at her sister-in-law, who had the grace to blush. "So I'm to be waylaid, was that the plan? 'Diverting' would hardly begin to describe the role of chaperoning 'the Comely Miss Crookshank.'"

"Please, please, Aunt Marianne. I will be so useful, never a bother to you. And I have been longing to go to London and do a proper Season. You know how many times I've had to put it off! First, because Papa was sure that my little cold would turn into lung fever if I left home, then the next spring Aunt Caroline was increasing, and then the next year there was poor Papa's illness. Now that my own mourning is months past, as much as I miss dear Papa—" to her credit, the girl's voice wavered a moment before she finished— "I know he would wish me to go and enjoy myself."

The problem was, she was quite right. If her indulgent father had not pampered her so much, Marianne thought, Louisa might not be such a self-centered and naive young beauty. The girl's mother had died years earlier, and her father had felt compelled to deny his golden girl nothing. And this was the result.

Marianne wished she was as young as Thomas and could enjoy a proper tantrum. She glanced again at her sister-in-law, who put down her embroidery.

"Louisa, why don't you go and apologize to your cousins for calling them names while I have a chat with Marianne," Caroline suggested.

Louisa's brilliant smile flashed. "So you can plead my case? Oh, I will. I will be so good, you will see. Please,

please say yes, dearest Aunt. You will never be sorry!" She gave Marianne an impulsive hug that almost upset the teacup on the small table at her elbow, then floated off toward the house.

When the two women were left alone, Caroline waved away the servant and turned at last to face her guest.

"You might have warned me." Marianne lifted her brows.

"I know, I did mean to," Caroline said. "Please forgive me for thrusting you into this. I have tried to persuade her that she can enjoy a coming-out at home, but nothing will do for Louisa until she is able to taste the delights of London. And you remember that when she turns one and twenty, she will inherit that most respectable fortune, so I must entrust her to someone who will keep a sharp eye on her. I would not want her enthralled by the first fortune hunter she meets. And she has no aunts on her father's side, only a great-uncle who is a bachelor and not on good terms with the family, anyhow. And she is, indeed, somewhat vulnerable at the moment because, no matter what she says, I think she expected young Lucas to offer for her, and when he pulled away—and then, too, you are really the only person she actually listens to!"

The reasons tumbled out as if they had been often rehearsed. Marianne closed her eyes for a moment. The scene had seemed so peaceful, until now. In this quiet setting, she had hoped to escape the vague sense of frustration that had dogged her for months. And now—the prospect of having to ride herd on a high-spirited and somewhat self-centered young lady enjoying London for the first time—well, as she had said, diverting hardly described it.

"Caroline, why can't you—" Marianne began, then paused and asked bluntly, "I know you don't care for London, but—are you unwell?"

Caroline bit her lip. "I hated to beg off for such a reason, but the fact is I am increasing again, Marianne. I don't think Louisa has discerned my condition, although with her, you never know—one moment acting so childish and the next, putting on airs like a matron."

"Ah," Marianne said. The baby in the nursery was barely a year old. No wonder Caroline was looking a little wan. "My felicitations!" She leaned across to give her sister-in-law a quick hug. "How are you feeling?"

"Wretched," the other woman admitted. "I can barely keep anything down. And the thought of trying to negotiate a London Season in this condition—you know I much prefer the quieter pace of Bath."

Marianne sighed. It looked as if she was well and truly snared. How could she say no when she saw that Caroline, her late husband's sister as well as her oldest friend, was so pale and had barely touched her food as they had eaten? And in any case, who could blame her sister-in-law for wanting to delegate such a task? Louisa would be a challenge to a more resolute woman than the gentle Caroline, of whom Marianne was deeply fond. She still felt connected to her husband's family, by affection if no longer by the marital vows. In addition, she and Caroline had been intimates since they were girls, growing up on neighboring estates in the West Country.

"Then I'd best be prepared. Tell me about this notorious marquess," she said, giving in to the inevitable. "And why Louisa is so eager to captivate a perfect stranger."

Looking more at ease, Caroline leaned back into her chair. "It's all gossip, really, but you know how it is in Bath."

Marianne grinned and sipped her tea. No answer was necessary. Gossip was as common in the watering place as the ill-tasting mineral waters that visitors sipped at the Pump Room.

"The local squire's wife, in the village next to the marquess's estate, wrote to our Mrs. Howard that the marquess was on his way to London to look for an eligible bride. Apparently, after inheriting the title on his father's death, he feels it is time to set up his nursery. A perfectly normal decision."

"And there are no eligible ladies in his neighborhood?" Marianne asked.

"I'm not sure any would have him," her usually mild-spoken sister-in-law said.

Startled, Marianne looked up. "He's that ill-favored?"

"He contracted the small pox when he was a young man, as I understand it, and was left gravely scarred."

Marianne blinked in surprise. Most people of means, in the progressive years of the early nineteenth century, were inoculated to avoid the killing, maiming, much-feared illness that once had struck down so many. Most saw that their servants and farm laborers were also protected. Her parents had made sure it was done when Marianne was only little Evan's age. But she had heard the pricking of the arm did not work for everyone. And the phrase, "when he was young," was also ominous: the man was old, as well as maimed?

"Oh, dear," she muttered.

"And ill natured, I hear, which concerns me more," Caroline added. "I cannot allow Louisa to throw herself away on some rude boorish person, no matter if he has titles to spare."

Marianne nodded. Even if the girl was a bit vain, none of them wished her to be unhappy in a poorly conceived union, certainly not Marianne, who had had the rare choice of marrying her childhood sweetheart. It looked as if she would be forced, despite her better judgment, into the role of duenna.

She shook her head.

The other woman gave her a questioning look.

"Ironic," Marianne explained. "After Harry died, I always thanked heaven that I was left with enough funds not to be forced to hire myself out as a governess."

Caroline laughed. "Oh, come now. It will not be as bad as all that! You only have to go to parties with her and keep an eye on the men she meets."

"And theaters and parks and breakfasts and teas and balls and who knows what, and the men will gather around her like bees to a fragrant flower. I shall be beating them off with a cane," Marianne predicted. "Beauty and wealth, both? Despite her father's connection to trade, Louisa may be almost as big and successful as she hopes."

But at least, it might induce the girl to forget her goal of conquering the unknown marquess, and it should certainly ease the pain of her rejection by her first suitor. Marianne sighed. "I must tell my maid to start packing. I'm sure Louisa expects to leave for London with scant delay. And you should lie down for a time before you have to change for dinner."

Caroline, who had been trying to hide a yawn, did not argue. They both strolled toward the house, and inside, Marianne found her new charge lying in wait.

"Well?" Louisa demanded, jumping up from the chair where she had been sitting, apparently trying to look virtuous by stabbing the linen in her embroidery hoop with large, untidy stitches. "I have begged pardon of all my cousins, even Evan. Have you decided? Will you take me with you back to London, darling Aunt?"

Marianne barely had time to nod before the girl grabbed her in a delighted hug. "Oh, you are the dearest aunt in the world. You won't regret it! And you shall enjoy the diversions, too, you know. Aunt Caroline always says you should get out more. Even old people need some merriment."

Caroline protested weakly, "Louisa!"

Marianne, who was two years past her thirtieth birthday, blinked. What on earth had she committed herself to?

She sat with Louisa for a time, listening to the girl natter on about all the delights of London that she could not wait to taste, everything from a visit to Vauxhall Gardens to her formal court presentation as she made her bow before royalty. Finally, Marianne reminded Louisa of the approaching dinner hour, and they both went up to change.

In her guest room Marianne tried to convince herself that it would indeed be diverting to have a younger companion for several months. " 'Old' people need such young things around them," she told herself dryly, glancing into the looking glass as she changed into a dinner dress.

"The black with the silver trim?" her maid had inquired when Marianne came into the room.

Marianne shook her head. "Tonight, the lavender, I think. There is a concert after dinner at Sydney Gardens, and I know Louisa is set on going."

Her maid hurrumphed at the idea of her mistress's actions being directed by the younger woman's wishes, but she took out the other dress.

Louisa's comments had stung more than Marianne cared to admit. So she still owned several gowns of somber shades; gray and even black were perfectly becoming colors, and she was not so wealthy that she could replace her entire wardrobe every Season.

Did she look old? Her dark hair, which curved smoothly past her cheek, was not yet streaked by gray, and her gray-blue eyes had only a few laugh lines about their edges. Her complexion was clear.

If she had had a husband still, and a family, perhaps she would have given the passing years little thought. After her husband's death, when she had been only a few years older than Louisa was now, Marianne had had the appalling image of her life as a rosebud destined never to fully open, a bud not allowed to bloom. Sometimes in the middle of the night when she lay alone in her bed, the idea recurred, to be pushed away along with the self-pity that followed behind it like a doleful ghost. All those dreams she had had. . . . Not just the happy marriage, the children that would now never be born, but the other ambitions she had aspired to . . . musings she had rarely dared admit. Ladies of quality did not have such thoughts.

After all, she was luckier than many widows. She had a modest but adequate income; a small house in London; and the quiet pleasures of her books and her friends; as well as frequent visits to see Caroline and her family, and Marianne's brother and his brood, who with Marianne's widowed mother lived farther west in Devon.

Old.

Sighing, Marianne told her lady's maid about their new charge.

"She'll lead you on a merry dance, that one will," Hackett warned, her tone dire. But then, her abigail, who had

been with Marianne's family even before Marianne herself
had let down her skirts, was always a pessimist. "She
hasn't the wits God gave a gnat, I sometimes think."

"Please don't make unpleasant comments about Miss
Louisa, Hackett," Marianne responded, her tone firm. All
she needed was to see a feud set off between the girl and
Marianne's small household staff.

Her abigail sniffed, her long face twisted into a frown,
and brushed her mistress's dark hair back into a smooth
French knot at the base of her neck.

When Marianne went down to dinner, she found her
brother-in-law already apprized of the plan.

"And we shall start for town at once," Louisa volunteered, her voice eager.

"That depends on your uncle," Marianne warned. "It is
his carriage we shall have to beg the use of, you know, unless you plan to take the common coach." Marianne did not
have the funds to keep her own carriage, so her visits were
always planned to accommodate someone else's comings
and goings from London to the west. Fortunately, Charles
Crookshank was a noted Bath barrister who often had business in the larger city, so it was easily enough done.

Louisa made a face and looked toward her uncle, who
had become her guardian after her father's death. The ami-
able Charles laughed.

"I think we can manage that, on Friday or Saturday, if
not tomorrow."

Louisa pouted at having to wait three whole days, but
then she returned to her plans for her coming-out, which
seemed to become more ambitious with every hour.

"I shall need a whole new wardrobe, of course," she assured Cara, who looked sympathetic.

"I hope *I* can have a coming-out in London, too, when I
am of age," the child declared, throwing a glance toward
her aunt.

Marianne bit back a rueful laugh, but the comment reminded her of more practical matters. A coming-out would
require substantial expenditure. Apparently, her brother-in-

law had already considered the problem. After dinner, when Charles rejoined them in the drawing room, and the children, emitting their usual clamor, were brought down from the nursery to say good night, he drew Marianne aside.

"I shall have funds made available to you to cover the cost of Louisa's Season, of course," he told her. "She has a comfortable allowance, and you must make use of any sums you need, for your own wardrobe as well as hers, and for the cost of extra entertaining."

Marianne gazed at him with affection. "I do not wish to profit from this temporary guardianship," she protested.

He waved her qualms away. "Of course not; you know I trust you implicitly. But I do understand that such an upswing in social activity must increase your sartorial needs as well as Louisa's."

"Such wisdom from a mere man." She teased him gently.

"A mere husband! I have not been married for so many years for nothing," he assured her.

Marianne laughed.

Then the two boys barreled into their papa, begging for a ride on his knee before the governess took them off to bed, and Charles allowed himself to be led away.

It seemed that her in-laws would give her no excuse to change her mind about this plan, Marianne thought, just a wee bit cynically. She might as well put her mind at ease and enjoy the new charge.

It also appeared her chaperonage would begin at once, as Louisa was determined to attend the concert, and Caroline, yawning again, just as obviously wanted only her bed. So it was Marianne and Louisa who donned light cloaks and set off, in the Crookshanks' carriage, for the musical evening. Charles had volunteered to accompany them, but since Marianne knew that he had a tin ear and did not care for opera tunes, she waved away his polite offer.

So he saw them off with obvious relief, and Louisa chatted about her wardrobe plans all the way through the short drive into Bath, until Marianne thought that if she heard any more discussion of pleated sleeves and lace trim, she might scream. And she enjoyed fashion as much as anyone, anyone except perhaps a young lady on the brink of her long-delayed coming-out.

By the time they had crossed the bridge and the horses were straining to climb another of Bath's famous seven hills, Marianne was more than ready to be handed down in front of Sydney Gardens, the location of the night's concert.

Louisa, who had been discussing how much Bath's popularity, and thus its fashionableness, had declined over the years, seemed eager to step down, too, despite the "sad lack of the presence of people of real importance," which, she had just explained to her aunt, made Bath inferior to London.

They walked past the white columns and into the garden, where they found seats. Louisa sat for only a moment until she saw a friend, a younger lady with whom she was eager to share the exciting news about her imminent visit to London.

"Oh, Aunt Marianne, do you mind if I go over and chat with Amelia until the concert begins?"

"Not at all," Marianne said.

So Louisa moved away, and Marianne fanned herself and looked around her. The musicians were tuning their instruments, the famed soprano had not yet appeared, and the seats gradually filled with men and women. Many of them were somewhat inclined toward graying heads and paunchy silhouettes. Of course, Louisa would consign Marianne into the same category, she told herself, trying to laugh about it. Perhaps chaperonage was all she had left to enjoy, since her own girlhood was well behind her. Bad enough to feel the years slipping away, but to know her innermost dreams would never be realized . . .

This thought was so melancholy she gave herself a mental shake and turned to see who sat on her other side. She found two older women, one short and stout and gray, the other a tall, still-erect lady with lovely silver hair and a lorgnette.

Marianne smiled. "Good evening," she said to the shorter

woman. "I believe my sister-in-law, Mrs. Charles Crook-shank, introduced us at the Pump Room?"

"Yes, indeed, I remember." The other woman beamed at her. "I noticed the two of you when you sat down just now, and I thought I recognized your companion, the Comely Miss Crookshank."

Marianne managed not to laugh. Louisa would have been gratified to hear herself praised, but she was on the other side of the assembly at the moment, giggling and bending her head toward a short girl with reddish hair.

"I am Mrs. Knox, as you no doubt remember. This lady is Miss Sophie Hill, who has lately removed from London to Bath."

The silver-haired matron gave a slight inclination of her head. "How do you do?"

Marianne returned the greeting. "I reside in London, myself," she said. "But I enjoy Bath's quieter pace."

"Do you plan to stay long, then?"

"I had meant to," Marianne explained. "But I have been given the task of playing chaperone to my niece by marriage, so I find that I will be going back to town sooner than I had planned. She is eager to be presented in London."

Miss Hill gave a ladylike snort. "I have sustained that fate, myself," she said. "With a pretty girl, and one of means, you will find your time never your own and too many simpletons aspiring for her hand. Of course, my niece was well worth the inconvenience, but I am happy enough to have her safely married at last."

"I am sure that Louisa will not want for suitors." Marianne agreed.

"Many of them a bunch of vain popinjays." The older lady frowned. "One hopes she will not be disappointed in what she finds."

Obviously a lady of strong opinions. Marianne couldn't completely suppress her smile even as she gave a discreet signal with her fan in Louisa's direction. The concert was about to start; it was time to take a seat.

Louisa whispered one last comment into her friend's ear, then made her way back to Marianne. "I have told Amelia all about my wonderful adventure," the girl said, her clear voice easily heard even above the first notes from the orchestra. "And about the marquess of Gillingham, and his plans to take a bride, a design which I intend to aid."

"Hush," Marianne told her. The girl subsided at last into her chair with an expression of respectful attention on her lovely face as she gazed toward the musicians, although Marianne had no doubt her charge's expression simply concealed more daydreams of titled suitors and splendid new wardrobes.

"The marquess of Gillingham, you say?" The silver-haired lady on her other side inquired, for some reason frowning at the mention of the name.

"Yes," Marianne said in surprise. "Do you know the gentleman? I understood he comes seldom to London."

A pause as a violin trilled, then the other woman pursed her lips. "For good reason. You have undertaken a greater responsibility than you know, Mrs. Hughes."

Marianne blinked. "I don't understand."

"Your charge had best take care," Miss Hill murmured, so low that Marianne was not sure she caught the words. "The marquess is not a man to be taken lightly."

Two

In the spacious library of the large gray edifice
that crowned a low hill in the southern reaches of Kent,
John Sinclair, marquess of Gillingham, gazed out the window. He stood very still, his broad shoulders squared and
his hands clasped tightly behind him, and although the
view from the window was pleasing, he did not see it.

He had made up his mind; it was a necessary and logical
course of action. Anyone would have said so, and he had
put it off for months already. When his father had died,
John had known that this must be done.

So why did his heart sink at the thought of the trip and
the social scenes that awaited him at journey's end?

Some fears had to be faced, and he had no choice. But
even as he told himself so, he paced up and down the room,
his tall, long-limbed frame seeming to fill even this room
of handsome proportions. As he passed one of the smaller
bookcases, its glass doors standing open since he had removed a book earlier, he glanced up to see the small portrait, a miniature in a gold frame, that graced its top shelf.

And the pain of that sight made him utter an inarticulate,

almost savage sound. Without conscious thought he swung his fist hard. The small painting went flying, and, too late, he heard the splinter of breaking glass and felt the piercing pain.

The shattered glass had sliced the skin. Blood dripped down the side of his hand and stained his white cuff.

Blinking against the sting, he pulled a handkerchief from his pocket and wrapped his hand in the cloth to stop the bleeding. The slight wound ached, but nothing like the misery that lingered deep inside him.

And still, he must go to London. . . .

The women's departure was delayed for a few days, as Charles found he had need of the carriage. In the interim, Marianne's mother posted up from Devon for a brief visit with her daughter.

She had not been pleased by the letter announcing the news of Marianne's newly assumed responsibility. "Why on earth did you agree to do this?" she asked as soon as she and her daughter were alone.

"What, Mama?" Marianne asked cautiously.

"You know perfectly well what!" Mrs. Lambert, who was petite and only slightly more rounded than she had been as a bride, tried to glare at her only daughter, but the effort was not successful. She crossed the room and gave Marianne an impulsive hug. "Agree to chaperone this spoiled child, of course!"

"Louisa is quite sweet, really," Marianne argued. In the face of her mother's doubts, she felt compelled to push aside her own. "I'm very fond of her. She suffered the loss of her father hardly more than a year ago, so I'm sure this change of scenery will do her good. And she is certainly overdue for her coming-out; she has only enjoyed Bath society, which is somewhat limited in scope. It's time for her to meet more young people and have the chance to look for a possible suitor."

"And what about you?"

Marianne tried to look blank. "I don't know what you mean."

"What about your chance for another marriage? You deserve more than the role of duenna," Mrs. Lambert insisted, sitting down and regarding her daughter with a stern gaze.

Marianne shrugged. "I think I am past the age—"

"Oh, pooh! You are hardly in your dotage, and you are still most attractive. However, I fear that if you spend all of your time in the company of someone so young, who possesses such potential wealth—"

"Not to mention such ravishing good looks," Marianne murmured, but her mother affected not to hear.

"I am afraid that your own particular charms and sweet beauty could be overlooked." Mrs. Lambert gazed at her daughter with anxious affection.

Marianne went to kneel beside her mother and press her hand. "I am quite happy as I am, you know."

Her mother looked skeptical. "You cannot relish a solitary life, Marianne. I know how lonely widowhood can be. Since your dear papa died—"

"I miss Papa, and Harry, but I am content," Marianne tried to argue. "I am not languishing alone in some attic, unable to go out into company. I have my friends and my family."

Her mother made another rude noise. "As do I, and I have your brother's adorable offspring, who are a blessing, to pamper. But I wish to see you with your own children—I hate to think that you will be deprived of such a joy. Perhaps it would not be the same as it was with poor Harry, but marriages come in many forms, from giddy passion to quiet companionship. I'm quite sure you would receive an offer if you would just make the effort to meet more eligible gentlemen—"

Marianne shook her head. "Mama, please."

Her mother sighed, but she pressed her lips together. "Very well. But I speak only out of concern for you."

"I know that." Marianne reached for her mother's hand. "Let us go down—tea will be ready."

And as she followed her mother to the staircase, Marianne tried not to dwell on how depressing she found the thought of a marriage made for the sake of "quiet companionship"!

Marianne said good-bye to her mother two days later as Mrs. Lambert left for home. Then the following day Marianne and Louisa embarked for London, with their trunks tied onto the back of the carriage and with a dozen last-minute reminders from Caroline.

"Do not forget the heated bricks for their feet," she instructed her butler. "I know the day is mild, but there is a brisk wind blowing. Louisa, tie your bonnet strings securely, or your hat will fly away before you are over the first bridge!"

"She is not riding on the driver's seat," her husband pointed out. "I'm sure they will have a safe and uneventful journey."

He added more quietly to Marianne as she drew on her gloves, "If you need extra monies, just let us know. I have sent the letter of credit to your bank—there should be no problem drawing on Louisa's trust."

"Thank you," Marianne told him. "You have been very thoughtful."

"No, thank you for relieving Caroline of a burden she is not physically, or emotionally, able to bear just now," he said. His forehead creased with concern as he glanced toward his wife.

Marianne nodded. Caroline was easily tired and often overwrought these days as her pregnancy made its demands on her. She was certainly not up to sponsoring a young lady into the social fervor of a coming-out. "I'm glad I am able to do it," Marianne said, meaning her words.

Embracing Louisa for one last farewell, Caroline burst into tears. "Oh, dear, I shall miss you."

Louisa hugged her aunt. "Do not worry, I shall write you very often, and I hope to have such lovely tales to tell of parties and walks and balls that you will be amused, too."

Her cheerfulness was contagious. Caroline smiled as she gave one last sniff into her handkerchief. "No doubt," she agreed.

Charles gave Louisa a hug and patted Marianne's hand as he helped her into the carriage. Marianne's maid, Hackett, was already sitting primly in the opposite seat with her mistress's small jewelry box in her lap. Brown eyes big with excitement, Louisa's maid, a young girl named Eva, sat beside her. Charles nodded to the coachman, and the carriage lurched forward as the driver slapped the reins.

"At last," Louisa breathed, her excitement making her blue eyes gleam. "London!"

Marianne smiled. "I hope you are not disappointed," she said. "I'm afraid you are considering London in the light of some earthly paradise—it is not quite that, you know."

"Oh, but the parties and the parks and the balls—I cannot wait." Louisa sighed in pure happiness.

Marianne gave up and settled down to listen to Louisa's chatter as they rolled across a bridge and turned east, toward London, the goal of all Louisa's dreams.

John set off the next day, frowning at the bright sunshine as his groom swung open the door of the chaise. Unfortunately, this journey was too long to be made by moonlight.

The butler, whose long jowls gave his face a look of perpetual gloom, had supervised as the luggage was tied on. "Likely will be a fatiguing drive, your lordship."

"I trust I am up to the exertion." John raised his brows. "Try to keep the cook from drinking up all the best port. You have the keys to the wine cellar."

"I think he's learned how to pick the lock," Pomfroy answered, his tone glum.

And on that dismal note, John stepped inside the carriage, the driver flicked the reins, and the journey began.

He arrived in London in late afternoon when long blue shadows stretched across the innyard. He chose a quiet inn on the edge of the city. Leaving his coachman and groom to see to the horses, John pulled his hat low on his forehead and, taking a deep breath, strode with his usual long steps into the building. The host, a short man with a balding head, hurried to greet him. Eyes wide, the innkeeper stared at the marquess for an instant, then pulled his expression back into one of polite welcome as he bowed low.

"You wish rooms, my lord?"

"Yes, a bedroom and a private parlor," John said, his tone brusque. "And space for my servants and my team, of course."

"Of course, your lordship," the man said, obviously forewarned by one of his servants, running in when the carriage with its faded crest had rolled onto the cobbled yard. He bowed again, then paused to exclaim, "Here, you mangy mutt, get out of my inn!" He waved his arms toward the small dog following behind the new arrival. It barked in protest.

"Leave off—the animal belongs to me," John snapped.

Startled, the other man stared down at the undersized black-and-white spaniel with the drooping ear. "Of course, my lord, excuse me."

The dog pattered across the wood floor, catching up with her owner as the innkeeper led him up the stairs to show him the best bedchamber and the parlor adjoining it. John glanced around the room. "This will do."

"We are honored to have you, your lordship. Shall I serve dinner at eight?"

John frowned. He was empty from the long ride, yet he knew that in town he would need to dine at the "fashionable" hour, absurd as it was.

"Six," he said, deciding that fashionable could wait till another day.

"Of course, your lordship. Umm, is your man with you?"

He meant a valet, of course, not the servants who accompanied the carriage.

John shook his head. "I am without a manservant just now."

The last valet had been a deep drinker, and John had discharged him, although with regret, because at least the man had not wrung his hands and fussed over his master as most valets were wont to do once they regarded John's un-fashionable attire and careless habits.

"I see, one of my servants will be available to assist you, my lord, if you should need it."

John nodded, and at last the man took himself away.

John pulled off his cloak and wide-brimmed hat. He had seen the man's stare, of course. John told himself he didn't care, hadn't cared for years, what people thought of his ap-pearance. But somehow, it still rankled—that moment of surprise when people first gazed upon his pockmarked countenance. At least in his own home everyone knew what to expect, and he did not have to brace himself for his first encounter with outsiders.

What was he doing here?

London, England's largest city, full of strangers who would gawk and whisper. And he would have to attend so-cial events, just the thing he hated the most—he, who could not dance, had no polite discourse, and felt at ease only in the countryside with a fishing rod in his hand or strolling through a field of ripened grain.

He must be mad.

But he needed a wife. And he had seen all of the women of marriageable age and suitable estate in his own neigh-borhood, and none had caught his interest; not one had seemed to him a female whom he could bear to spend years with, much less stir his passion enough to allow him to engender a child.

And he must have an heir. Else, the title he had so re-cently inherited would pass to his younger brother, and that indignity could not be borne.

The little dog whined. She had an uncanny ability to read his mood, and she was right; just now his temper was as dark, almost, as it ever had been.

"I should have stayed at home, Runt," he told her,

dropping heavily into a chair stout enough to hold his solid frame and scratching the small spaniel behind her ears.

Wagging her tail, she regarded him with adoring eyes. She was the only female who did so. Was that why he had saved her life when his gamekeeper was about to drown the runt of the litter, a tiny pup who'd been born with a misshapen ear, besides?

No, he thought he had been drawn by the spirit of the little dog, the courage so much bigger than her small frame. At any rate, her loyalty unfailing, she had followed him from that moment, ready to scrap with dogs twice her size to make sure she had the favored place at his feet. And how many creatures fought for the favor of his attention?

"I could have married Miss Gunter," he told her. "She grimaces when she looks at my face, but darkness covers a multitude of misfortunes."

The dog whined.

"Yes, I know," John agreed. "Her laugh sounds like the screech of a pen hen. That would be a trial. And there was Miss Allan, the vicar's niece, with her sour frown. But she browbeats her servants, and they say she's a terrible miser, though I suppose that would save on the housekeeping bills."

The little dog licked his hand.

"But none of them made me anxious to be a husband," he admitted. "Yet, in London, how shall I expect to impress a strange lady? As if anyone would want to be my bride. Oh, I know, I have money enough, and a respectable estate, and an ancient title to share, but still—"

She would still have to look at him, his unknown and undiscovered bride. John frowned again, catching a glimpse of himself in a small looking glass across the room. He picked up his wide-brimmed hat and tossed it toward the glass. It landed in front of the frame, hiding his reflection.

John sighed and put one hand across his face.

When they brought up his meal, he ate his dinner alone, tossing bits of the best meat to the spaniel lying at his feet. When he retired to bed, he slept poorly. The noise of the street—the rumble of carriages and wagons passing, the staccato beat of horses' hooves, the babble of people talking and shouting to each other—all seemed to reverberate through his bedchamber. The clamor sounded very loud after the quiet of the countryside.

It was early in the morning before he dropped into a restless doze, and then he woke soon after, when the first rays of light shone through the polished windowpanes.

He lay there, his head aching dully, knowing what awaited him. He had to call upon two perfect strangers, and he dreaded the prospect. But how else would he be able to find introductions to polite society? He could hardly ride into Hyde Park, pick out a likely looking lady, throw her over his horse's neck, and ride off with her like a Tartar.

Too bad—it would have been much simpler.

John pushed himself out of bed, washed, and dressed in clean linen. One of the chambermaids had unpacked for him last night, putting away his small supply of clothing. After donning buff-colored pantaloons, he tied his cravat with the carelessness which had driven away many a valet within weeks of initial employment, then shrugged into one of his customary black coats. Since his illness, he had always worn black, disdaining the niceties of fashion as too petty to merit his attention. With a clothespress of black coats and capes and cloaks, he never had to make a choice. And why should he worry about his appearance, when it was a hopeless case?

He took the spaniel out for a short walk in the innyard and made sure that his horses, and his groom and coachman, were being properly tended to. Then he returned to his rooms and called for food.

He was standing with his back to the door when the servant knocked.

"Come in," he called without turning and continued to gaze out the window while he waited for the table to be laid.

"You may go," he said when he could tell that the servant had paused. Then at last, he returned to take his seat. But although the beefsteak was tender, and the eggs fresh enough for town produce, he found himself with little appetite.

It had to be done. He was no craven, so he must take this

necessary first step to find someone to reintroduce him to the polite society he had ignored for so long. He had come armed with the names and addresses of two of his father's old cronies. John picked up his hat, adjusted it to shadow his face, and then spoke sternly to the small dog.

"Stay."

She whined, but she sat obediently, with the doleful expression of one who will, despite being so abandoned, wait patiently for her lord and master to return.

He shut the door, speaking to the maid who waited in the hall. "Do not allow the dog to wander outside. She is not used to city traffic."

The servant nodded.

John found his carriage waiting. He had told his servants to be ready at nine, and his groom had obtained the necessary directions.

Climbing into the carriage, John tapped on the door. The coachman flicked the reins, and the vehicle moved off into the congested London streets. Ahead of them a coal cart rolled with annoying slowness, and two carriages passed so close they almost scraped the wheels of his chaise.

He was not accustomed to moving at such a sluggish pace, and he sat well back in his seat, refusing to stare at the crowded street and the houses and shops that edged the pavement, but even so, they eventually reached their goal. John climbed out and went up to the front door, lifting the brass knocker.

The footman who appeared blinked at him. "Tradesmen go round to the back."

John grimaced. He knew his appearance was unfashionable and his face unsightly, but still—he quelled the servant with the kind of look that had sent grown men a step backward.

"I am the marquess of Gillingham."

The footman gulped. "Beg pardon, sir, eh, my lord," he said. "You're here to see Mr. Laughlin? He's at his office in the city."

John frowned. Had he gotten the direction wrong? "No, I'm looking for Lord Eschon."

The servant's chagrin faded into a puzzled frown. "Lord Eschon? He's been dead these ten years, my lord. The house was sold to my master long ago."

"I see." John turned abruptly and stomped back to his carriage. So much for this contact.

He would hope for better luck with the next man, old Sir Silas Ramburt. At the next house, a large structure which nonetheless managed to look somewhat shabby, he found Sir Silas still in residence. But the footman looked at him oddly when he asked to see the old gentleman.

John was shown into a morning room, where he paced restlessly up and down. When the door opened, he turned quickly. It was not a gray, bent older man who entered, as John had anticipated, but a slip of a girl. She was well dressed, but her shoulders sagged and her expression was one of great weariness. He bowed, and she made a slight curtsy.

"I regret that it is impossible to see my grandfather," she said without preamble.

"But this is important," John protested. "I need—"

"Why is it important? You cannot possibly know him; he has not gone into Society these several years."

John blinked, but he was willing to be blunt, as well. "My father, the marquess of Gillingham, was a friend of Sir Silas. They spent much time together in their youth. I have just come to town and wish to pay my respects."

The girl—he suspected she was barely old enough to be out, but the wrinkled brow and dark hollows beneath her eyes made her appear older—stared at him, and for a moment he thought she wavered on her feet.

He gestured toward a chair, but she ignored his motion and took a deep breath. "Your father was the marquess of Gillingham?" she repeated slowly.

Wondering if she was dim-witted, John nodded. "As I have said. He died last year, and I have inherited the title."

"Was it an easy death?" the girl demanded. Again, her tone seemed curt, and she hardly seemed to be offering condolences.

John frowned. "It was a sudden illness," he said. "His

heart failed him. Why do you ask, Miss . . . Ramburt?"

Silence stretched, and although she looked at him, she seemed to stare right through him. At last she answered, "My grandfather is alive, but his wits are gone, as well as his health. He is dying by inches, and I have to watch his pain and confusion get worse every day."

Relieved to have some explanation for her odd behavior, John nodded. "I am sorry to hear it. Do you not have help? You're young to carry such a burden."

She shook her head. "My parents are dead. There is only me, and the servants, of course, but . . ." Her words trailed off as she seemed to forget the rest of the sentence.

Feeling compassion this time instead of irritation, John bowed. "I am sorry to have intruded. You have my sympathy."

"Do I?" She sighed.

"If there's anything I can do to assist you . . ." He told her where he was staying, not sure if his words penetrated the fog of melancholy that seemed to bemuse her. "I will not trouble you further."

John made his way out. A house full of tragedy, he thought, though illness and death came to all families. Still, this situation seemed even sadder than most. He pitied the girl, though he knew he was still glad to hear the footman shut the door behind him.

Drawing a deep breath, he got back into his carriage and discovered he did not know where to go next. How was he to achieve entry into the Ton now? Who would perform introductions? His two leads had both come to naught. There had been no point in explaining his request to Sir Silas's granddaughter. Even if she had been not been consumed by more important matters—he was still not sure if she was a bit slow or just overwhelmed by her sad situation—a girl could not sponsor a grown man. Damnation.

He told his coachman to drive on, without any idea where to go. The traffic was dense and held the horses to barely more than a walk. The city seemed to press in upon him. John suddenly wanted out of the confines of the carriage. He knocked on the panel and when the coachman pulled up the horses, said, "I am going to walk for a while. Find a spot to wait."

Pulling his hat down, he strolled along a walkway that was almost as crowded as the street. Wincing at facing such mobs of people, John tilted his head and tried to avoid meeting anyone's gaze. But he had gone hardly twenty feet when a child's clear voice penetrated the chatter of the other pedestrians. "Mama, Mama, what's wrong with that man's face?"

John frowned. Several people turned to stare, even as the matron tried to shush her little girl. He felt an urgent need to avoid the curious looks. Turning abruptly, he opened the door of the nearest shop and bolted inside.

Within the shop the atmosphere was hushed, with only a few customers contemplating shelves of merchandise. One woman in a gray walking outfit and dark bonnet stood at the counter examining gloves with the assistance of the clerk on the other side.

"Yes, that will do nicely. And the two tan pairs, and one maize. And when will the rest of Miss Crookshank's new gloves be ready?"

"We'll have them sent to you by the end of the week," the clerk promised. "I'll just wrap these up for you, ma'am. I'll be with you in a moment, sir."

John nodded and turned quickly away. His head tilted to hide his face, he glanced sideways from beneath his hat brim and stared at the shelves. Good lord, this was a woman's shop! He should not have come in. He would slip out, locate his carriage, and return to the inn. But as he retreated in disorder, head still down, he trod on something, then collided with an appealingly soft figure and lost his balance.

In his confusion he had not noticed the woman step away from the counter. She exclaimed in annoyance and pain—he had trodden on her foot—and now both wavered.

Red-faced, John grabbed at her as she fell. But as he tried to grasp her upper arm, he brushed the tender curve of her breast instead, smooth and soft beneath its light fabric covering.

She gasped and pushed him back.

But she still tottered, and he tried again to seize her, even while he felt a wave of embarrassed chagrin, and—yes, something more—a spark of attraction. It made him, somehow, even more clumsy as he tingled with a surge of unbidden desire. She felt so rounded, so touchable, so intensely womanly.

She regained her footing first and this time pushed him away with all her strength. "How dare you, sir!"

He reeled backward, hitting a small table with a display of gloves and a small vase holding a sprig of flowers. The table went flying with a crash of breaking china, but at least he had his balance again.

He tried to bow, but his hat started to fall and he paused to grab it. "My apologies, ma'am, I was only trying to—to—"

"It was quite obvious what you were trying to do," she retorted, her tone cold. "And if you touch me so intimately again, I shall summon the clerk and have you ejected!"

He swept off the hat, as he should have done in the first place, and gave her a more-or-less-proper bow. "It was unintended. I was only trying to stop you from falling."

"I would not have fallen in the first place if you had not knocked me all asunder!"

How her eyes sparkled when she was angry, he thought in some corner of his mind not totally benumbed by embarrassment. They were blue-gray, the color of a smoky autumn sky, and intelligence glimmered in their depths. She had a straight nose of just the right size and two full lips beneath it. He even liked her voice, which was mellow, its tone just now decisive.

"Well, yes, that was my fault, too," he admitted. "I offer my regrets once more."

The clerk came running up. His expression was startled. He had thin, mousy brown hair, and he stood barely as high as John's shoulder. An image of the little man trying to eject his bullish customer made John fight a grin.

For the faintest instant he thought the unknown lady might feel amusement, too, as if the very same thought had crossed her mind. But she conquered the slight lift of her lips and regarded him with a frosty gaze.

"The table, oh my, oh my." The clerk waved his hands in dismay. "Mrs. Hughes, are you all right?"

John felt an irrational surge of disappointment. Of course she would be married. How could a woman with such a lovely rounded figure and trim waist, such glowing eyes and creamy skin, not be married? She was also limping just a little, he saw, and guilt now overlaid the confusion of emotions within him. Was there any other gaffe he could commit?

The woman nodded to the clerk, but she spoke to John. "I will accept the possibility that it was an accident. But I would suggest that you look what you are about before you trample another person's foot. You are not the most delicate of persons, and your weight is quite painful when inflicted on an innocent spectator."

John felt even deeper chagrin. "Are you hurt? My carriage is outside—"

"I am bruised but not maimed, and I would not think of getting into a stranger's carriage!" She tucked a straying lock of dark hair back beneath her hat. She was an enchanting sight, John thought, wishing he were not the one who had incited the flush of anger which tinted her creamy cheeks. At least, in her ire, she seemed too distracted to have noted the imperfections of his face.

"Still," he tried to argue, "I am responsible for your injury. I will summon someone, your husband perhaps, to aid you if you should require assistance?"

For some reason, this seemed to irk her even more. "I can take care of myself, thank you."

"I am only trying to help," he told her. Was every woman in London this hard to please? Heaven help him, if so!

"I believe you have 'helped' enough today," the lady retorted, her blue-gray eyes turning dark with annoyance. "Now, if you will excuse me—"

She limped toward the door, her head high.

"Mrs. Hughes." The clerk hurried after her. "Your package!"

She paused long enough to accept the small parcel, neatly wrapped in brown paper and string, and this time John had the sagacity to keep his thoughts to himself. She was appealing but stubborn; he told himself that he did not envy her husband dealing with such a strong-willed woman. No, that was not true . . . perhaps he did. Her lovely eyes bright with intelligence, the smooth curve of her hips, and even the moment when they had seemed to share the same private jest—they all evoked longings he seldom allowed to surface.

He waited till Mrs. Hughes had marched out of the shop, then he handed the clerk a guinea, muttering, "For the table," and made a quick exit himself. When he found his coach waiting by the side of the street, he climbed in and sat far back into the seat, keeping himself out of view.

Presently, his heart slowed to a normal beat, and he could draw a deep breath and try to think.

Damn it, he still needed a sponsor, or this whole trip had been a wasted effort. There was only one other person in the city with whom he had a connection. Could he bring himself to apply to his younger brother?

Gritting his teeth, John sent his groom into several shops to make inquiries as to the address, and when the servant found someone who knew the name and direction, they proceeded slowly to a handsome square in the west of London. There, John told the coachman to pull over; he was still not sure if he could debase himself by approaching a brother neither he nor their father had spoken to for years.

John stepped out of the coach and told the driver to wait, then walked a few feet, staring up at the town house before him. It was a large residence and well maintained, unlike the last house he had visited. But to grovel before his brother . . .

No, he would not do it. He would have to think of something—someone—else. John turned on his heel, but before he could take more than a step, he heard someone call his name.

"Gillingham? What in God's name are you doing here?"

His shoulders tense, John looked around. There stood a tall fair-haired woman of striking beauty, and by her side, a stripling with brown hair and merry eyes, his hat pushed a bit too far back on his head.

"Westbury?" The young earl, whose estate ran alongside John's own, had inherited his title very young. John had heard he was something of a rakehell, and the young lord seldom visited his country home. Having met Westbury's mother, John did not blame him. But even though they had not conversed for years, the earl had not forgotten John's face. Mind you, with its disfiguring scars, how could he be expected to?

"What are you doing in London?" the handsome youngster repeated, raising his brows.

John tried to control his irritation. "I am no longer under quarantine, Westbury. Despite what you may have heard, I am quite well. Am I not allowed to travel?"

"Course, but everyone knows you never leave home. Good God, are you here to see your brother and make peace at last?"

John hesitated. Before he could disabuse the young earl, the woman, who had been watching them both with keen blue eyes, exclaimed, "You are the new marquess of Gillingham? And you've come to see Gabriel! Oh, you must come in."

Three

He could not find the words to explain that he had not really meant to call. Unable to withstand her enthusiasm, John was swept into the house.

The woman, who John soon realized was his unknown sister-in-law, Lady Gabriel Sinclair, led them inside. A footman opened the door, his expression lofty, and though he blinked when he glanced at the visitor, his countenance did not reveal any sign of repugnance. Well trained, indeed, John thought sourly.

"Allow me to remove my wrap—I shall return momentarily," Lady Gabriel told him. The footman took his hat and gloves and showed John into the drawing room.

John sat down on an elegant gilt chair, then in a moment found himself too restless to remain still. He stood and paced up and down the room. Sweet heaven, he had made a muddle of it now.

From the hallway outside, he clearly heard Westbury say, "I'm not sure Gabriel will be pleased about this, Psyche."

"But they are brothers!" the woman argued.

"If you say so," the young man answered. "I don't think I shall stay to see the happy reunion, however. You may escape unscathed, but I'm not his new bride! Just as soon stay out of it."

John gritted his teeth. He had to get out of here. But the door opened again, and Lady Gabriel entered. She was truly a vision, a tall woman in blue with lovely classic features and blond hair pulled up at the back of her head. She regarded him thoughtfully. John kept his own expression stoic, waiting for her to exclaim in revulsion or retreat in embarrassment, now that she had a good look at his face.

Instead, she came into the room and, as calmly as if this was a normal social call, sank into a chair. "Please accept my condolences on your father's death. I was surprised when I heard of it," she said. "He seemed well enough the last time I saw him."

Reluctantly, John sat down again and stared at her in surprise. A virtual hermit, his father had not ventured into London in years. "You had met my father?"

"I had occasion to encounter him, once. It was a sudden illness?"

He nodded. Annoyed to find himself as tongue-tied as a boy, he tried to pull himself together. "There was little warning."

"I tried to—that is, I suggested to my husband that he should go down for the funeral, but he was unable to do so."

John could just imagine what Gabriel had said to that! "It was a quiet affair," he said. His father had feuded with all of his neighbors and had not bothered to keep up contact with former friends. John had a sudden memory of the desolate graveyard, with only himself and the vicar and a few curious villagers standing around the grave in the drizzling rain, John's own emotions a confused turmoil of shock and loss . . .

He pulled his attention back to the woman sitting across from him. Gabriel had always been the fortunate one, John thought, and now to have a wife with such flashing blue eyes, such elegance of person, and such—hell's fire!—enticingly womanly curves. Damn Gabriel, anyhow, the lucky bastard!

"But you have come to see Gabriel?" Her tone seemed warm. Did she care that he and his brother had not spoken in years?

John braced himself. He was here, despite his qualms—he might as well take the last step. *In for a penny, in for a pound,* he thought grimly.

"I have—I have something to ask of him," John said, finding the words hard to get out. "If he is willing to receive me."

"My husband is not at home just now, I'm afraid." She seemed to make up her mind. "If you do not have plans, perhaps you will return and dine with us tonight?"

John hesitated, then at last he nodded. "I will come."

Psyche, Lady Gabriel Sinclair, canceled a luncheon with a friend and waited impatiently for her husband to return. When he did, in the middle of the afternoon, he looked startled to find his wife pacing the drawing-room floor.

He walked forward to gather her into his arms—they had been married for over a year, but the honeymoon fervor had not abated in the least—but she returned his kiss for only a moment, then pulled back to gaze up at him.

"Have you had any word from your brother since the note last year about your father's death?"

He looked at her in surprise. "Of course not. The new marquess has little interest in me, and I none in him."

Sighing, Psyche shook her head. She knew how bitter Gabriel's feelings were about his family, but still . . . "Do you not think that he might regret the gulf that exists between the two of you?"

He led her toward a cushioned settee. "Never. You know there is little love lost between me and my family. So be it. It does not trouble me, nor them."

Taking her seat, she picked up the glass of lemonade

she had been sipping. Lately, wine seemed to turn her stomach, so she had switched to lighter beverages. "You might be surprised."

He walked across to pour himself a glass of burgundy. "I very much doubt it."

"No? You have had a visitor." She paused deliberately, then, when he did not answer, continued. "The new marquess of Gillingham came to see you this morning."

His hand wavered as it held the decanter, and a drop of wine spilled onto the side table. Then Gabriel's famous self-control reasserted itself, and he turned, his expression as guarded as it had once been when he had spent his time as a gamester.

"My brother? You must be mistaken."

"I admit, I have never seen him before," Psyche agreed. "But he looks a little like your father, though better looking, I think. And why would he claim to be the marquess—"

Gabriel raised his brows, and Psyche laughed out loud. She had once invented a fictional title for a so-called fiancé, but— "That was different," she protested, knowing that he would understand.

Gabriel still looked skeptical. "Perhaps. But I very much doubt that my brother, who never leaves his home and who would certainly have no desire to see me, would actually travel to London and knock on my door. It must be some kind of ruse. If this person calls again, have the butler deny him the house."

Psyche gazed at her husband thoughtfully. "I'm afraid I cannot do that, my darling."

His expression was inquiring, but instead of challenging her comment, he waited. Oh, he did know her well. After such a tumultuous courtship, she should not be surprised.

"I have invited him to dinner," she said, her tone innocent.

"Psyche!" Gabriel set down his glass so abruptly that the wine sloshed onto the much-abused table, then he came forward to grasp her hand. "Why would you do such a thing? You know how I feel about my father. Well, that's a—you'll pardon the macabre pun—dead issue now, but my brother was just as condemning when I was sent away. Why would you even consider asking him into our home? I thought you understood!"

Psyche touched his arm, her contact gentle. "Gabriel, I am always on your side, you know that. But I am concerned for you. You will never be able to find peace with your father—the chance is gone forever. And yes, I saw what a bitter, angry man he was, so intolerant and punitive and unloving. I would never fault you for your feelings, or your decision to have nothing more to do with him. But your brother—he has come to you, Gabriel. Perhaps he regrets the support he gave your father when you were disinherited."

"You think he has come to offer me a share of the estate? I don't need his money," Gabriel retorted. "I have done well enough on my own!"

Psyche nodded. "Indeed, you have. With you handling our investments, our worth has soared, not to mention the acquisition of the country estate, which was your doing."

Her husband, who no longer had to resort to a good hand of cards to ensure a roof over his head, as he had for years after his family's expulsion, looked scarcely assuaged. "So why should I forgive them now?"

"As I said, he has come to you," Psyche repeated. "At least, give him a chance to speak. He's your brother. When my parents died, my sister and I became even closer . . . I could not have endured life without her."

"That's different," Gabriel muttered, his countenance still dark. "Circe is a darling, although somewhat—unique. But that is only part of her charm," he added quickly before Psyche could defend her younger sister. "And the two of you were always devoted. John was a bully when I was younger, and he was intensely jealous of me."

"Why?"

"He thought our mother favored me, and even though my father certainly preferred him, he took it amiss."

"And you are much the handsomer," Psyche pointed out matter-of-factly. "That may have rankled. Gabriel, when did he contract the pox?"

He had frowned; she knew that he did not care for anyone to comment on his extraordinary good looks, but he glanced up at her last words.

"When I was a child. They feared he would die. My mother sent me away so that I would not catch it, too."

"You were not inoculated as children?"

"My father thought it unnecessary, but after John fell ill, I was, yes. My grandfather took the precaution as soon as I reached his house."

"What carelessness," Psyche exclaimed. "What a poor excuse for a father the late marquess was! I know you could never be so imprudent." She touched the slight swelling of her belly without thinking. Gabriel's expression softened when he saw the gesture.

"You really wish to entertain my beast of a brother?"

She smiled at the exaggeration. "Yes, dearest, I think you should give him an opportunity to be heard."

Gabriel sighed. "Very well, but only because you wish it."

Psyche smiled with the serene confidence of a woman who knows she is adored. This time, she held up her arms without reserve, and he bent to pull her into a strong embrace.

The day stretched on for what seemed a small eternity. John stayed in his room, wondering what insanity had led him to begin this mad venture. In late afternoon one of the male servants knocked on his door.

"Come in," John snapped, as his small dog gave a small warning bark.

When the servant opened the door, he bowed. "Do you desire any assistance changing for dinner, my lord?"

"No."

The servant looked surprised, but he nodded. Then, glancing around the room, he took a step forward. "I'll just light more candles for you, my lord."

"Leave it," John said, his tone still abrupt.

The servant paused. "As you wish, my lord."

John had been sitting in the biggest chair, which was the most comfortable for his tall, big-boned frame, with only one candle lit on the table beside him as he glanced through a book he had brought with him. The curtains had been pulled across the windows, and the room was comfortably dim.

Outside, the streets teemed with traffic. He could hear people shouting and talking in the courtyard below. London had many attractions, no doubt, but they could wait for a later time. At least that was what he told himself, trying not to admit that all he really wanted to do was pack up and return home, where he did not have to face strangers at every turn, did not have to witness—a hundred times a day—the surprise and dismay which his disfigured countenance elicited.

He was no coward; he would stay the course. But his heart felt leaden, and too soon it was time to call again for his carriage.

He wore the same black coat he had worn for his morning call. If his precious brother, with his usual elegant ways, took offense that John had not changed for dinner, that was his misfortune.

When he arrived, John braced himself, stepping out of the carriage and walking slowly up to the front door. What if his brother refused to honor his wife's invitation? What if—

But this time an elderly butler with a keen, respectful gaze admitted him and showed him the way to the drawing room. There, John found Lady Gabriel, looking even more beautiful in a gold-hued gown. She sat in a brocade-cushioned chair while across the room Lord Gabriel Sinclair, the man whose family name he shared, if perhaps little else, stood very still, his expression grim.

John knew his own face must reflect the same reserve. He hesitated for a moment on the threshold as the butler announced in an impassive voice, "The marquess of Gillingham, my lord, my lady."

The servant withdrew, and for a moment there was

silence. The woman turned to her husband and seemed to be waiting.

Gabriel spoke, his voice gruff. "Come in, then. I shall not threaten to put the dogs on you, as my father did me at our last meeting. Not that we have any guard dogs at the moment, nor did he, but the menace was genuine. At any rate, there's no need to stand in the doorway."

He had not meant to reveal so soon his lack of enthusiasm over this visit. Grimacing, John advanced into the room.

His newly met sister-in-law smiled at him and gestured toward a chair. John made her a polite bow, awkward as it likely was, but he remained on his feet, like a warrior unwilling to chance a sudden attack from his enemy.

"I am—ah—amazed to see you in London," Gabriel said. His face was still blank, revealing nothing at all of the emotions he must be feeling.

But John could guess at them accurately enough. "Circumstances forced me to come."

Gabriel lifted his brows. "What incredible occurrence necessitated such a radical change of habit?"

John swallowed hard. "I have few acquaintances among Polite Society. I find that I am in need of some introductions."

This time it was easy enough to glimpse Gabriel's amazement, as well as his skepticism. "You wish to enjoy the Season in London? Why on earth? I don't recall you having any taste for Society."

"I don't, but it seems I am forced into it," John admitted, trying not to grit his teeth. "I need—"

His brother and sister-in-law watched him, both apparently at a loss. "I need to wed," he forced the words out. "I must have an heir."

"So that, if you die as suddenly as our father did, the title does not fall to me?" Gabriel's tone was almost choked. Was he on the verge of angry denunciation?

But they were interrupted before he could continue.

"Dinner is served, my lord, my lady," the butler said from the doorway. He withdrew, but the silence lingered.

Lady Gabriel looked startled, but it was her husband whom John turned back to observe. He stared at the younger man and felt his bile rise as he recognized, from years past, the wicked gleam in Gabriel's sea-blue eyes.

The bastard was laughing!

~⁊~

Dinner seemed interminable, and although the food was excellent, John found it hard to get down. He had swallowed enough of his pride for one day; perhaps that was what lessened his appetite.

He was surprised to find a schoolroom miss joining them for dinner. The child, who was thin with straight brown hair pulled out of her face, had unnerving green eyes and a concentrated gaze, which she fixed on his face through the whole of the first course. Had she never seen a pox victim before?

He glared at her while the footmen were taking away the dishes and bringing in the next course, and she met his look without flinching. That was unusual enough, but he tried again, speaking to her in a low voice.

"I'm sorry if my countenance offends you," he said, his tone grim. "However, if no one has informed you, it is rude to stare at people."

Lady Gabriel made a sound deep in her throat, and his brother looked up, his own expression icy. "It is also rude to correct a child in whose home you are being entertained."

His wife added, "Circe is an artist, you see," as if that explained everything.

But the child with the unlikely name did not seem abashed. She simply raised her brows, for a moment looking more like her sister. "Oh, no, I am not offended. The pox marks are not that bad, and you have excellent bone structure. I was thinking that your face would be interesting to draw."

He was so disconcerted that he did not attempt to speak to her again, and it was a relief when the ladies withdrew.

Although then, he was alone with his brother.

Gabriel, who had maintained a facade of cool civility in front of his wife and her sister, dropped the pretense when the door shut behind the females.

"You haven't changed, have you, John? Still like to browbeat those younger and weaker than yourself?"

John bristled, even as he thought that the child hadn't appeared intimidated in the least. "She's an odd thing, you must admit. And you obviously indulge her too much—no wonder she sounds so little like an ordinary schoolgirl."

"Circe will never be an ordinary schoolgirl. And you will not criticize my family in my own house!" Gabriel's perfect features were rigid with anger, anger that had been simmering for years, John suspected. His sibling had always been a whiner, running to their mother when he'd taken a cuff from his brother.

So be it. John had not come here to apologize for imagined and ancient wrongs. He took a deep drink of his wine. "I was the older brother. Boys get into scrapes. What did you expect? Don't be such a craven, crying over every little smack."

Gabriel's blue eyes narrowed. "You were as cruel as our father, if that is possible, taking any excuse to knock me around. Why in hell do you think I should help you now? So that some other woman will suffer your rudeness, some future child your vicious handling?"

"You prefer that I remain single and childless, so that you can someday come into the title and the estate?" John thrust back. "You'd like that, wouldn't you?"

"I don't want your precious title! Nor one guinea of your inheritance, and I certainly would never live in that house again! If it were mine, I would burn it to the ground."

"I would burn it first, if I thought you were going to inherit! Even if I left no other heir, you wouldn't deserve it, if the truth were told—"

John paused as Gabriel pushed back his chair so suddenly that it tilted and hit the wooden floor with a bang. Gabriel jumped to his feet, and John sprang up, too.

They faced each other, a scant three feet between them, three feet and years of antagonism, as well as the family secret which Gabriel was so loath to admit. Tension charged the air, but for an instant no one spoke.

John felt his own anger swell; he, too, harbored grievances from the past. Why had he been so foolish as to come here, to give his wretched brat of a brother the chance to turn down his ill-considered request? He should go soak his head in the Thames, it would do him as much good. No, he would go home.

If one of them did not die right here. He glared back at Gabriel, finding that, just like his brother, his own hands had curled into fists. The silence sizzled, and neither man relaxed his stance. If there had been a weapon at hand, John could not have said who would have reached for it first.

When the door opened suddenly, they both jumped. John pulled his gaze away to see who stood there. Her expression concerned, Lady Gabriel hesitated in the doorway.

"Circe has gone up to bed. I thought you two would join me in the drawing room?" She glanced at the overturned chair, but did not comment on it.

"I'm afraid that will not be possible. Our guest is leaving," Gabriel answered, by the sound of it through gritted teeth.

John nodded. He tried to speak evenly. "I must thank you, my lady, for the excellent dinner. I fear I will not be seeing you again."

"Why not?" Lady Gabriel demanded. She glanced from one to the other. "I thought you had come to London for the Season?"

"It was an ill-advised plan," John said, as brusque as his brother. "I will be leaving town shortly."

"Nonsense," the woman said, surprising him one more time. "You will join our excursion to Vauxhall Gardens on Saturday. It will be an easy way for you to make some acquaintances in London, and the evening will be relaxed and not at all formal. It will be the perfect occasion for you to test the waters."

Did she perceive just how unaccustomed to polite company he was, how poorly equipped to navigate the complicated seas of Society? John hesitated, and his brother spoke.

"Psyche, I need to speak to you."

She smiled. "Of course, my dear, in a moment." To John, she continued, "I shall send you a note with all the particulars. At which inn are you staying?"

He told her, wondering if Gabriel would command her to rescind the invitation. Was anyone able to command this woman? He was beginning to doubt it; she was as singular, in her own way, as her strange little sister.

Still, John had no desire to linger. He gave his hostess a stiff bow and glanced toward his brother.

Gabriel nodded. "We shall not stand on ceremony."

In other words, John could see himself out, a major concession, since he knew perfectly well that Gabriel longed to forcibly eject him by the seat of his pantaloons. As if he could! Gabriel might have grown into a height of over six feet and could now meet his brother eye to eye, but he lacked the width and breadth of John's physique. Although John, too, would relish the excuse for a good set of fisticuffs. Whine about mistreatment, would his pampered little brother? He'd show him mistreatment!

John stomped down the hall, was bowed out by the footman, and found his carriage waiting. The butler must have summoned it. The whole household seemed to run as evenly as a calm stream through a meadow. He thought of his own home, its patchy housekeeping and indifferent meals, and frowned. That was what came of not having a mistress for his household. Surely that was reason enough to stay a few days more in London, as much as he still longed to tell the coachman to turn the carriage and gallop south, toward home and refuge.

John leaned against the seat and shut his eyes for a moment. Why not admit it? He envied his brother his beautiful bride, his elegant and well-managed dwelling, his no-doubt countless friends among the Ton. Gabriel was as good-looking, as charming to the ladies, as cunning as he had been as an angelic-faced child, and John felt much the same emotions as he had then.

Damn Gabriel, anyhow.

And why was his sister-in-law so determined to help

him? John hadn't a clue, but he might as well take advantage of her strange benevolence.

When he reached the inn, he hurried up to his room. Runt whined when he opened the door, and he bent to scratch the dog behind her ears. "Yes, we'll go out for a walk," he promised her.

Yet she waited for his petting before barreling toward the open door. Someone, at least, was happy to see him.

John thought again of his brother's wife, considered what a pleasure it must be, making love to a woman who could love him back. Unlike the quick, joyless unions John sometimes had with the occasional village girl who was willing to share his bed, always in darkness, and the woman nearly always a little stiff with fear. . . . What would it be like to have a woman feel real passion for him? He had almost given up hope of finding out.

Just a few more days, he told himself. He could stomach a few more days.

They had reached town without incident. Marianne was a bit afraid that Louisa might be disappointed in her aunt's modest town house, but Louisa seemed determined to like everything that met her eyes. She exclaimed over the buildings and the parks and even the traffic all the way in from the outskirts of the city. The tall, narrow house, which sat side by side with its neighbors, met with her full approval, nor did she cavil when she found that the guest room was two flights up.

Instead, she pronounced the bedchamber charming, with its rose-patterned draperies and bed hangings, and set her young maid to work unpacking.

Marianne had greeted her footman and the housemaid and kitchen maid, heard about the squirrel that had got into the attic and made such a mess before finally being driven out, and conferred with her cook about meals to plan for the following week. Then she sat down to look through the correspondence that had piled up during her absence.

Scanning one gilt-edged card, she told Louisa when the girl joined her in the small but elegant drawing room, "I am invited to a luncheon tomorrow with a party of my women friends, most unexceptional, and you will enjoy it. Then tea with the countess Sealey on Wednesday next, an old friend. And a visit to Vauxhall on Saturday evening, no, I think we should postpone that till another time—"

"Oh, no," Louisa cried. "That is one of the places I most want to visit! I have heard so much about the amazing array of lights, and the fireworks, and the dancing, and—"

"But you have not yet been formally presented, Louisa," Marianne reminded her. "I'm not sure how much you should be seen about town until you can make your bow at court."

"But that will not happen for weeks, you said," Louisa protested. "And then we will have my coming-out party, just a small affair, but tasteful and with music, you promised! But Vauxhall, oh, please, please, I will wear a domino if you like! But I must go."

Marianne laughed despite herself. "It is not a masquerade, just a group of friends going for dinner, a concert, and the fireworks afterwards."

"Then, you see, it is quite an unpretentious affair and just the thing for me," the younger woman argued.

Marianne sighed. If she said no, she would never hear the end of it. And it was true, it was only a small informal party.

"Very well, I will write and convey our acceptance," she agreed. "And now, I think we should both retire—the journey was fatiguing, and we have much to do tomorrow."

"I'm not sure I shall sleep a wink," Louisa declared. "I am so excited—London, at last! I could almost fall down and kiss the cobblestones!"

Marianne laughed at such an absurd idea. "I beg you will not," she said. "You will have a face full of mud, if you do."

Louisa giggled. "I didn't really mean it. Oh, Aunt Marianne, you are so good to me! Thank you, thank you for bringing me to London."

She gave Marianne a hug, and then they went up the

staircase together. In her own room, Hackett helped Marianne shed her traveling costume and put on her nightgown, then brushed out her dark wavy hair.

"I think Louisa will be a pleasure to have with us," Marianne told her maid, remembering her dresser's earlier warnings of dire consequences. "She is so happy to be in town that she is quite amenable to my suggestions."

"It's early days, yet," her dresser replied, her expression as dour as always.

Marianne waved away her maid's pessimistic reply and retired to bed with an easy mind.

The next day she spent the morning writing notes, answering invitations, and making plans for Louisa's presentation, and after lunch she took Louisa off to see her own dressmaker. The next few days were filled, to Louisa's great delight, with shopping, fittings, and visiting friends. Louisa had her hands measured for new gloves, her feet for riding boots and delicate dancing slippers, and even her supply of underthings and lacy nightgowns and nightcaps had to be replenished. The first of the new gowns arrived just in time for the expedition to Vauxhall, and Louisa's excitement was almost impossible to contain.

They took a hackney to the famous garden just after sunset, since the pleasure park appeared to best advantage after dark when its hundreds of lights could dazzle newcomers.

Louisa was suitably impressed. "Oh, it's heavenly," she cried. "I have never witnessed such a spectacle! I have dreamed of this for so long, Aunt Marianne. You are such an angel to allow me this pleasure!"

Marianne, who knew what went on in the more secluded glades of the gardens and the tree-lined walks that were deliberately less well lit, thought that *heavenly* might not be the right metaphor. But she kept these reflections to herself, vowing to keep a sharp eye on her charge so that Louisa did not discover, too soon, just what worldly debaucheries sometimes were enjoyed among couples in the garden's darker corners.

As usual, the garden was crowded, but they met Marianne's party of friends at the arranged table and enjoyed a dinner of the finely sliced ham, roast chicken, and other delectables for which Vauxhall was famous. Then after eating and chatting, they enjoyed listening to the concert from the rotunda, with its dazzling lights and impressive facade.

Afterward, there was dancing, and Louisa begged to see more of the gardens.

"We can take a stroll along the pathways," Marianne agreed. "But you will have to stay beside me, Louisa. This is a public place, please remember, and some of the rougher elements are often present, eager to take advantage of a young woman alone."

"I will," Louisa promised.

But as bad luck would have it, they had hardly risen from their table when a matron, who was an acquaintance of Marianne's, appeared and greeted her with enthusiasm.

Mrs. Mendall was full of news, since it had been a whole two weeks since they had met, and Marianne had to pause and listen to the woman's chatter.

Trying to hide her impatience, Louisa turned a little away. Marianne sensed when the younger woman stiffened. What was it?

While Marianne made automatic responses to Mrs. Mendall about a somewhat dull party she had missed because of her sojourn in Bath, she scanned the crowd to find out what had upset her charge.

There, the good-looking young man with the brunette in pink on his arm who moved so smoothly on the dance floor, that was whom Louisa watched, though she tried not to make her attention apparent. Obviously, he was someone Louisa knew, and, since her acquaintances in London were few, could it be the young baronet from Bath whom Caroline had mentioned, Sir . . . Lucas Englewood. Marianne dredged the name from her memory. If so, oh dear.

Louisa's color was high. As the couple circled on the dance floor, the young man, who had brown hair and appealing bright brown eyes, glanced up and met her gaze. His expression altered in a quick and almost comical succession: first pleasure, then guilt, then alarm, and finally even more complicated emotions impossible to read. Then he swung back into the dance pattern, and his face was hidden from them.

Louisa wheeled abruptly to face the two older women. "They do seem to let just anyone into Vauxhall, do they not?" she interrupted, her tone brittle.

Marianne winced for her charge's manners, but Mrs. Mendall did not seem to take the sudden comment amiss. "So true, my dear, which is why one must not be unchaperoned."

"No, indeed," Louisa agreed. "Why, in Bath, where they called me the 'Comely Miss Crookshank,' I was most careful whom I acknowledged. I can see that in London, one must be even more circumspect."

Marianne looked at the younger woman in astonishment. Louisa never boasted of her own charms, she was much more adept in Society than that. But of course, up to now, she had not had to. In London, no one knew her, as yet. And if—

But Mrs. Mendall was still talking. "And speaking of odd creatures, you will never guess whom I met earlier!"

"Who is that?" Marianne asked, less because she really wanted to know than in the hope of diverting Louisa's mind. If the girl broke into tears right here, it would cause gossip. Louisa's feelings for the young baronet must be deeper than anyone had suspected; Marianne must speak to her about this as soon as they had a private moment, but not now.

"He has come to town for the first time in anyone's memory, and he is—well, the poor man cannot help it—but really, he is hardly a sight for delicate eyes." Mrs. Mendall fanned herself.

Marianne frowned. She recalled that she did not care much for this shallow-natured woman. "What on earth do you mean?"

"The marquess of Gillingham, of course. Gossip says he is looking for a bride, but with his looks so destroyed—"

"The marquess?" Louisa interrupted.

Really, Marianne was going to have to talk to her charge about proper manners. The girl rushed on.

"He is here, tonight? Oh, where is he?"

Mrs. Mendall raised her thin brows. "He's wearing an ancient black morning coat and his cravat is untidy. He looks positively disheveled, and one would think he is on his last shilling, though I have it on good authority that he is wealthy as Midas. He talks to few people, but he is indeed here with his brother, Lord Gabriel Sinclair, who apparently got *all* the looks in the family. If Lord Gabriel were not so charming and his wife such a beauty, or, one might as well say, if Lord Gabriel were not so devilishly handsome and his wife so engaging, I cannot think that the marquess would have any hope of acceptance from the Ton, title or no. But if they bring him into Society, well, what can one do?"

Louisa hardly seemed to hear the last part of the speech. She was scanning the crowd, obviously in hopes of detecting the mysterious marquess. Oh, dear. She was going to turn this poor man, who might be quite dreadful in character as well as appearance, into some fairy-tale prince, Marianne thought. Louisa was so naive that—

Then she saw the girl brighten. "Is that him, there, at the corner of the crowd?"

Mrs. Mendall nodded. "Indeed, that is the man. You cannot tell from here, but—"

Marianne ignored the rest of the woman's no-doubt unkind observation. From this distance, she could see no obvious disfiguration, but the man wore a hat with a brim wider than usual, and, his head down, he stood in the shadows at the very edge of the assembly.

Louisa had already plunged into the mass of people, and her objective was obvious. Oh, dear, oh, dear.

"Excuse me, I see someone I must speak to," Marianne said hastily, then she hurried after her ward. What harebrained scheme was Louisa up to? One did not just march up to a man to whom one had not been introduced—Louisa was overdue for a strong lecture about propriety and correct social etiquette, Marianne thought grimly.

Although she quickened her steps, she did not reach them soon enough. By the time she had caught up with

Louisa, the girl had dipped a curtsy and was smiling up at the mystery man, whose response seemed to be to turn even farther into the shadows. With a sinking heart, Marianne heard the younger woman speak.

"How do you do? You are Lord Gillingham? I am Miss Louisa Crookshank. I believe you know my aunt, Mrs. Harrington Hughes."

He hesitated, as well he might. Marianne found herself blushing, as Louisa—impudent child—should have been doing for her dreadful solecism and was not!

"I beg your pardon, I fear my niece has mistaken—that is—" she murmured. "Come, Louisa, we must not trouble the gentleman."

Then he lifted his head, and she got her first clear view of the enigmatic marquess.

Four

To her shock, Marianne realized she had seen this man before. What—of course, the glove shop, he had stepped on her foot and grabbed her in—in a most inappropriate place. She had tried to give him the benefit of the doubt when she did not know his name, but now—could the marquess be as rude and unmannerly as Caroline had feared?

And here was Louisa making a cake of herself, just to—Marianne had no doubt—make the young Sir Lucas jealous.

"You are mistaken, Louisa." Marianne tried to pull herself together. "I fear that I have no acquaintance with this—with this gentleman."

"On the contrary," the man said, his deep voice familiar and his tone much milder than on their last encounter. "We have met, but somewhat irregularly. Your servant, Mrs. Hughes. If you like, I shall summon my sister-in-law, Lady Gabriel Sinclair, to perform a proper introduction." Removing his unfashionable wide-brimmed hat, he bowed to them both.

Marianne found herself unable to give him a direct snub. Something—but before she could identify the feelings that hovered at the edge of her mind, Louisa interrupted.

"Oh, we don't mind that."

"Yes, we do." Marianne glared at her charge. "Louisa!"

The younger woman returned a smile so dazzling that it was hard to remember to be angry. No wonder the scamp had gotten away with so much with her papa, Marianne thought ruefully.

Louisa breezed ahead. "If you would introduce me—properly!—perhaps the marquess would enjoy a turn on the dance floor?"

This was unsuitable for so many reasons that Marianne drew a deep breath. Yet, if the marquess was willing to overlook such audacious behavior, Marianne had little hope of stopping her ward. And, in fact, the man seemed stunned beneath the force of Louisa's beauty and brimming good spirits, so Marianne was sure she could hope for little help from him.

Gritting her teeth, she said, "My husband's niece, Miss Louisa Crookshank, newly arrived from Bath."

He bowed to the younger woman. "John Sinclair, marquess of Gillingham, at your service."

"Then you do wish to dance!" Louisa flashed her brilliant smile again.

She had taken a commonplace remark for an invitation—really, this was too much. Marianne opened her mouth to utter a scathing censure, but she found that Louisa had already put her hand on his arm and was drawing the marquess toward the dance floor.

She was going to lock Louisa in her room for the next month! There was obviously no other way to control her. Marianne told herself she had been much too harsh on her sister-in-law. She should never have scorned Caroline's lack of authority over her niece. No one could keep a rein on this spoiled, impetuous girl.

It served Louisa right that the marquess seemed ill at ease on the dance floor. Although it was only a simple round dance, he still managed to make several mistakes. Regrettably, it did not appear to dim Louisa's obvious happiness; she gently directed him back into the proper form. Why did he not know the steps? Perhaps the marquess was simply overcome by her beauty. Was he smitten by Louisa already?

Marianne grimaced. If that was true, she could foresee a labyrinth of possible complications ahead.

At least, watching the pair, she could take a closer look at the man's face. Yes, his countenance was marred by half a dozen pockmarks, but really, the effect was not the horrible disfigurement she had expected. The scars had faded somewhat through time, and he had a strong chin and well-formed nose, and his eyes, a deep dark brown, were quite pleasing . . .

But his hair, brown with glints of gold, was overlong and badly cut, and his apparel was a disgrace, his coat ill fitting, and his cravat clean but awkwardly knotted. In addition, his manners were as atrocious as Louisa's, trying to pretend that their accidental contretemps in the glove shop constituted an acquaintanceship . . . Was he so desperate to have an opportunity to speak to Louisa? Perhaps he and Louisa deserved each other!

No, she had promised Caroline, and, anyhow, Marianne did not wish Louisa to rush into some improvident connection just to avenge the suitor who had abandoned her. And speaking of him, where had the young Sir Lucas gone?

Marianne looked farther across the dance floor and the many couples parading up and down, dipping to the measured flow of the tune, bowing and curtsying to each other. In a moment she located the young man, with the same partner on his arm, completely ignoring the other couple—so completely that she suspected he was indeed aware of Louisa and her highly ranked partner.

Oh, Lord, what a Season it was going to be!

John gritted his teeth and tried his best to remember the steps. They were not complicated, and he had danced this tune as a boy, he was sure of it, but those elusive memories were impossible to grasp. An alluring young woman with sparkling blue eyes and pale hair smiled up at him, and the radiance of her beauty made him feel a little light-headed. He was only human. And how long had it been since a woman had looked at him without a trace of repugnance or fright? The sheer surprise of it had knotted his tongue, not to mention his wits, or else he would have made an excuse to avoid dancing.

So here he was, stumbling around the floor, doing his best to ignore the surprised glances of other dancers when he moved the wrong way. He felt beads of sweat on his forehead from the sheer effort of putting the correct foot forward, as he tried not to look like a total imbecile in front of this angel who seemed, inexplicably, to be drawn to him.

She was unlike her lovely chaperone, with the smoky gray-blue eyes and the brows drawn together, as if she did not approve of his having the temerity to claim her ward's hand. Not that he could blame her. For that matter, over-seeing this high-spirited beauty must be a singular charge. And Mrs. Hughes did not look that much older than her niece.

Perhaps because of his fervent, if unspoken, prayers, the music ended at last. John could bow one last time and offer Miss Crookshank his arm to escort her off the floor.

She batted her lashes. "Thank you so much. You do not wish to join the next set?"

But this time he was prepared. He shook his head. "I fear I am not the most polished dancer," he told her, hoping she would not laugh in his face at such an understatement. "I will retire to the side, instead, and allow you the oppor-tunity to be guided by a more practiced hand than mine."

"No indeed," she said at once, fanning herself with her free hand. "I am quite warm—in fact, I'm sure I must look a sight, with my face so flushed."

A seasoned man-about-town would have inserted a quick compliment here. John felt as raw as uncooked mut-ton. "Uh, no, not at all," he mumbled.

But despite his awkward response, her smile did not fade. "In fact, sitting out for a time is just what I would like."

He was surprised that she did not accept his polite withdrawal—this beauty would have no trouble acquiring another, better-favored and smoother-footed partner.

"Perhaps you would like a glass of lemonade?" he amazed himself by asking.

"I should love a glass, if you will sit with me and tell me about Kent. I have heard it is a most scenic county. What is your favorite spot?"

She really wanted to spend more time with him? Incredulous, but not one to refuse such a gift from the Fates, John escorted her to a table at the side of the dance floor and summoned a waiter to order refreshment. Then he wondered if he had erred again. Should he have included Miss Crookshank's chaperone in their party? He glanced about, sure that Mrs. Hughes would not have gone far, unless she had rejoined her husband and was dancing, too.

Sure enough, her gaze somewhat suspicious, she was regarding them from a few feet away. When she saw him staring, she inclined her head slightly but did not smile, then turned her head to continue her conversation with another matron.

He would like to make her smile, John thought, not sure from whence the thought had come. No, it was obvious; he'd like to convince her that he was a proper escort, even for an innocent, lovely girl like this one. Of course, first he had to convince himself. He was not sure which would be more difficult.

Sighing, he found that Miss Crookshank was waiting for him to expound upon the beauties of Kent. And why did his loosely tied neckcloth suddenly seem too tight?

His command of easy conversation was barely more polished than his skills on the dance floor. Trying to think, he drew upon memories of his favorite fishing spot. "Kent? You might imagine it as a thick green carpet of grass. The land rolls down toward the marshes that edge the salt water. Seabirds call overhead, and waves pound against the shore. It is an ideal place to be alone with one's thoughts."

Her expression guileless, Miss Crookshank regarded him. "Are you often alone, then, my lord?"

He hesitated, unsure just how to respond. She was too innocent to intend to suggest any undertones. "I enjoy walking my estate with one of my dogs at my heels. It is easier to focus on matters at hand, especially if one's meditations tend toward melancholy."

Now why had he said that? He was much too unnerved by the unaccustomed presence of a lovely young woman.

Miss Crookshank opened her blue eyes wider. "Surely you are not inclined toward melancholy, my lord? You have everything you desire, do you not?"

He blinked in surprise, and she blushed.

"Forgive me, I spoke without thinking! It is one of my besetting sins. You have recently suffered the loss of your father; of course, you must have pensive moments."

John considered explaining that he and his father had not been close, but that might sound insensitive, and, anyhow, the lady had rushed ahead.

"I lost my own beloved father a year and two months ago, and I miss him dreadfully," she told him, blinking away a hint of moisture that made her eyes glisten.

"I am so sorry to hear of it," he said.

"You're very kind." She reached forward for an instant to touch his hand, then, as if remembering her manners, pulled her gloved hand back. But his skin tingled from the slight contact.

If she were not so young and naive, he would think her the most brazen flirt, he thought. Likely, she had no idea how such a soft contact could inflame a man's passions. And he had no business thinking of passion in connection to an innocent girl. On the other hand, such ardor was what he had sought, had he not, coming to London to find a wife?

Not love, of course, never that, but enough simple desire to enable him to tolerate a stranger as his wife, to father the children he needed. He had promised himself he would offer his wife, whoever she should be, courtesy and politeness, but there had to be a touch of something more; if not—if not, the emptiness inside him would ache forever. And it would not be such a bad bargain—his wife would have the adoration of her children, and she would share a worthy title and all his wealth. Many women accepted less in a marriage.

Was it possible that Miss Crookshank would consider his suit? Would her parents consider it, that is, her current guardians—would that be the stern-faced Mrs. Hughes and her husband?

John noted a young man with a fashionable appearance, his shirt collars appallingly high, eyeing them from a few feet away.

"I fear I am monopolizing your company," he told his companion. "You should dance with a more urbane partner. But perhaps you would allow me to call upon you in a day or so?"

Her lips lifted into a wide smile. "That would be delightful, my lord. I should very much enjoy seeing you again."

At least she did not pretend to be coy; he hated playing games. They stood, and the young man visibly gathered his courage and approached.

"M-Miss Crookshank? We were introduced earlier," he stammered. "May I have the pleasure of the next dance?"

"Of course, Mr. Blaton. I should be most pleased," Miss Crookshank agreed. The young man gulped and led her back to the dance floor.

John took a sip of his wine and looked about him. If he meant to pursue this fortuitous acquaintanceship, he had best make some overtures to the young beauty's chaperone, who did not seem to regard him with any great warmth. So he looked about the room till he found Mrs. Hughes, still chatting with another woman, and he bided his time.

When the other matron turned aside, John strode toward Mrs. Hughes. "I hope you are enjoying the evening?"

She looked up at him, and for a moment he feared she might spurn his greeting. Then she answered slowly, "Yes, indeed. And you? Do you come to London often, Lord Gillingham?"

She had a most pleasing voice, he thought, smooth and melodious. "Not at all. This is my first visit to Vauxhall," he told her. "It is quite as amazing as everyone has said."

Mrs. Hughes nodded. "My niece has been most anxious to see it, though I had some qualms about the less than refined company she might encounter. This is her first visit to town. I have been newly entrusted with her care, so you will understand that I am very careful about what I allow her to do."

It was a clear warning, he thought, but perhaps a bit extreme. He was not, after all, a penniless Captain Fortune, hanging out for a wealthy wife. Was the young woman wealthy? It hardly mattered; he had little concern about the riches or lack thereof that accompanied his future bride. If she was, he would face more competition, however.

"I believe I am reasonably refined," he asserted, his tone mild. "I will admit to a lack of town polish, having spent most of my adulthood on my country holdings, but doubtless that can be remedied. My name and estate are all that anyone could wish, even if my face is not the most pleasing. Surely I am fit to be received by polite company?"

She blinked, and her cool facade wavered, if only for an instant. "I did not mean to suggest otherwise, my lord, that is—"

Direct assault on the enemy often gained one an advantage, he reflected. It had always been the best way to deal with his father. Careful not to reveal his satisfaction over her small retreat, he continued.

"Oh, I do not fault you for being a conscientious guardian—even a mother hen will attack a fox if her chicks are threatened. But you would not object if I were to call upon Miss Crookshank?"

Trapped, she hesitated a moment as if unable to think of a reasonable objection, then inclined her head. "No, indeed." She gave him her address, though her smile seemed forced.

John noted it, then, bowing, took his leave. He was not willing to risk forfeiting the progress he had made. The younger lady had smiled upon him, and her guardian had agreed that he could pursue the acquaintance. He did not wish to risk the redoubtable Mrs. Hughes regaining her quick wits and conceiving an excuse with which to put him off. So he made his way back across the crowded room and located his sister-in-law. She sat at a table chatting with several friends as she took small bites of the thin-sliced ham they had been served for their supper.

So many people thronged the popular park that John's brother, though doubtless not far away, was not in sight, which was just as well. After an awkward greeting earlier, they had avoided each other as much as possible all evening.

"Leaving already?" Lady Gabriel asked as John thanked her stiffly for the invitation. "I hope you have enjoyed the evening."

"I believe it has been profitable," he answered. "You've been very kind."

Her gaze thoughtful, she considered him, but she nodded. "I realize that it is a small step, but it is a start, you know. You and Gabriel are bound by blood and familial memories—you may yet come to improve your connection."

On a chilly day in hell, perhaps. But it was rude to contradict a lady, so he bowed and did not answer. When he lifted his head, he saw by the understanding in her clear blue eyes that Lady Gabriel was not fooled, but at least she did not appear angry.

An intriguing woman, he thought, making his way toward the park's entrance to find a hackney. Would the lovely and exuberant Miss Crookshank gain something of his strong-willed sister-in-law's strength of character as she matured? Or equally, might she grow to resemble her exacting guardian? John would wager that Mrs. Hughes had courage and heart to spare, the kind of bottom that one wished to find in a fine horse . . . not that it was suitable to consider her in such equine terms. And really, her fine figure and her sparkling eyes made him—made any onlooker—only too glad that she was human, female, a lady of character and spirit . . . not that she was in any way within his reach.

Although John had often heard how common affairs were

among the Ton, he was not one of those rakes who desired an easy, brief coupling with another man's wife. So it was foolish to dwell on the older woman's attractions. He tried to focus his thoughts on the pleasing memory of the winsome Miss Crookshank, instead, to remember how easily she had smiled up at him, how unaffected she was, and how seemingly blind to his scarred face.

Yet somehow, on the ride back to the inn, it was the guardian instead of the possible bride whose image lingered in his mind's eye.

When Marianne, ignoring Louisa's protests, insisted that it was time to withdraw—if one remained at Vauxhall too late, the crowd became rougher and more unpredictable—she made her farewells to her friends. Then she and her charge allowed a servant to hand them into a hackney. They rolled through the darkness toward Marianne's London home.

Louisa's high spirits had faded just a little after the marquess had made his strategic retreat, but, nonetheless, she declared that she had a wonderful time.

"It was a dream; thank you so much for taking me. We will go back, won't we, dearest Aunt?" she insisted. "Although I know London has so many more amusements to offer, as well. We have my coming-out ball to plan, and I must obtain vouchers to Almack's. Every young lady of any substance goes there; I have heard all the stories about the famed 'Marriage Mart.' Do you have acquaintance with any of the patronesses, Aunt Marianne?"

"I know Lady Seton slightly, and one or two others; we shall see what we can do," Marianne answered absently. Her own thoughts tended to linger on the mysterious lord who had surprised her with his rush to courtship. Really, she should have thought of some excuse to avoid his call, Marianne reflected. What had slowed her usual quick responses? Would Louisa truly hook such a big fish on her very first foray into London's social scene? It was ridiculous.

And why was she feeling almost jealous? No, no, she would not admit to such an undignified response, Marianne assured herself. Of all the other men, young and old, who had sought out Louisa tonight, none of them had sparked any unseemly desires inside her; it was only the marquess who—

Shaking her head, she refused to finish the thought.

"Do you not think pink is a good color for me?" Louisa sounded anxious. She looked up at her aunt in concern.

Marianne had not been listening; the girl was discussing clothes again. "Pink is most becoming," she assured her. "With your fair hair and pale complexion, I'm sure it would suit." She allowed Louisa to chatter on about the new clothes that were ordered, and where they would next venture out so that Louisa could look over some of London's more fabled sights.

Only after they were home, and her footman had let them in and locked the door behind them, did Marianne broach the subject that had been troubling her through most of the evening.

"I noticed Sir Lucas Englewood taking part in the dancing," she said, following Louisa into the guest bedchamber and sitting on a side chair as Louisa's maid unbuttoned her mistress's gown.

"Umm . . . the thin-shaven ham was quite delicious, didn't you think?" Louisa answered, but she kept her gaze directed down toward the gloves she peeled off.

"Did you not observe him?" Marianne persisted. "I believe he is an old friend of yours from Bath?"

Louisa shrugged. "A childhood friendship, nothing of significance." Her voice sounded a little shrill.

"I see," Marianne said dryly. She thought she saw all too well. "So you do not mind that he seems to have a new attachment?"

"Of course not!" Louisa's voice rose for just a moment, then she had it back under control. "I am happy for him."

The girl was trying, Marianne thought, but . . . "Louisa, if you have some—quite understandable—feelings of chagrin at the parting of the ways with an old, umm, friend, just be aware that it would be most unkind to encourage another man to court you simply to show Sir Lucas that you are unaffected by his loss."

Louisa drew herself up to her full five feet and sought to control her bottom lip, which seemed to want to pout despite her best intentions. "Really, Aunt, I would not be so petty."

"Mind that you do not," Marianne said, her tone serious. "It would be ill served in the long run, both for the marquess and for your own feelings."

"How can you suggest such a thing?" Louisa blinked hard. "If I were a bit distressed that Sir Lucas most rashly broke off his friendship for no reason that I know of, would it not be only natural to seek to make new—new friends?"

"I suppose so," Marianne agreed. "But do not rush too soon into any commitments, Louisa. It would not be wise, and as your temporary guardian, I would not allow it. I'm sure your uncle would listen to my concerns."

Louisa's face was hidden as she turned to divest herself of her clothing. As the maid took the dinner gown to put away in the clothespress, Louisa pulled on a robe. When she turned, her expression was innocent. "Of course not, dearest Aunt. I would not trouble you for the world."

Somehow, Marianne did not feel reassured. But she kissed Louisa's cheek and bade her good night. What else could she say?

Perhaps she was anxious for no reason. But she had seen that sparkle in Louisa's eyes before.

Louisa retired in a terrible mood. After she said good night to her aunt, Louisa took to her bed with a pounding head and a mind full of thoughts as helter-skelter as the squirrel's nest in the attic they had heard described at least three times from different members of her aunt's small household staff.

She was finally in London, had actually danced at Vauxhall and listened to melodies floating from the orchestra on the rotunda. She was beginning to live her life, at last, instead of wasting away while confined to Bath along with its collection of elderly invalids. It was a dream come true, and she should be ecstatic. She had been, she had been thrilled and happy and untroubled, she told herself, thumping her pillow.

A small feather escaped the linen case and floated to land on her cheek; frowning fiercely, she shook it away. At least she had until Lucas had had the temerity to walk into her long-awaited London fantasy—how dare he! And with some sallow-faced brunette on his arm, in a dress with entirely too many flounces, and no doubt the spaniel eyes she made at Lucas had only inflamed his already too-pompous sense of his own self-worth. Serve him right if he married the silly girl!

Louisa tried to smile at the thought, but, instead, she found her eyes brimming suddenly with bitter tears. Oh, no, not again. How many times had she cried herself to sleep after Sir Lucas had so suddenly broken off his attentions? And then had to send her maid to sneak up cold slices of cucumber to lay upon her swollen eyes until she could be seen downstairs without exciting suspicion. She would not be pitied over a broken heart! If the servants noted it, gossip would seep out to other families, other Bath society . . . and then there would be no end of the tales.

She pounded her pillow once more and blinked hard, determined not to succumb to the dismals. She had come to London to escape all those recollections—why did Lucas have the gall to be here just when she did! Never mind that a good proportion of people of worth gathered in London for the Season, he could have stayed at home! He had stayed in Bath last spring . . . but then, so had she, and they had still been courting, then. No, she could not dwell on those memories.

Louisa gulped hard, trying to find comfort in the extraordinary good fortune that had led her to an introduction to the mysterious marquess she had been brooding over. He had danced with her, he had gazed at her with obvious interest. He had told Aunt he would call; Aunt Marianne had reluctantly admitted as much. So Louisa's plan, born of the bitterness of Lucas's abandonment, was bearing fruit already. And the comment Lucas had thrown at her once during a quarrel, the painful observation that she might be—imagine!—somewhat self-centered, would be proven false.

All the world would see that she was not so base. If she loved a man whose face was marred by scars of old illness, if she could see past that to his obvious nobility—and she did not doubt that such high character would be there—would not that prove to Lucas, to everyone, that she was not as shallow as he had so foolishly judged her to be?

Louisa felt a small wave of warmth that almost filled the cold hollowness inside her that had lingered since Lucas's departure. The marquess would adore her; she would minister to his ailing health and sit by his side, admired by all much like an earthbound angel. Hadn't she sat with her father in the sickroom through his long illness, till the physician himself had ordered her away for more rest and fresh air?

Louisa, selfish? Never!

Sighing, she tossed and turned until at last she drifted to sleep.

On Sunday, Aunt Marianne took Louisa to St. Paul's for morning service, so that Louisa could admire the fine dome and remarkable architecture of the church. They spent the afternoon quietly, and their attendance at St. Paul's made a safe topic for a long letter to her aunt Caroline in Bath.

Dipping her pen into the inkwell, Louisa filled two pages with her fine, small script. She said little about the more exciting excursion to Vauxhall, not wanting to incur any more lectures on propriety; she'd had enough of that already from Aunt Marianne! But privately, she thought that her "too forward" behavior had been well worth the risk. She'd met the marquess, and she was eager for Monday to see if he did, indeed, come to pay a call.

And when she woke the next morning, with sunshine streaming through the polished windowpanes, she felt much better. She was in London, at long last, and her life would brighten just like the sunshine, she had no doubt of it.

She rang for her maid. The girl appeared shortly, with a tray of tea and toast and porridge flavored with honey, just as she liked it. While Louisa ate, she eyed the windows with longing.

"Is my aunt up yet?" she asked Eva.

The servant girl shook her head. "I don't think so, miss."

Louisa considered. A walk in the small park in the center of their square would be unexceptional, if she took her maid along. She told Eva her plan, and when the girl moved her breakfast tray to a side table, Louisa hurried to wash and dress. She chose a fresh new sprigged muslin and a matching maize-colored spencer, in case the breeze was fresh, then a new straw bonnet trimmed with spring flowers, and she drew on her gloves and skipped down the staircase, with Eva behind her.

The little fenced area held a swatch of green, some low trees, and a few flower beds, whose sickly blooms seemed to be struggling amid the smoky London smog. But today, a fresh breeze kept the gray haze to a minium, and Louisa could draw a deep breath and stride along.

She walked three times around the patch of greenery, somehow feeling overflowing with energy, or perhaps simply impatience. She had waited so long for this coming-out, dawdling away her time stuck in Bath with the widows and the invalids. Now that she was here, Louisa longed for excitement, for balls and parties and theater outings, for a romantic courtship, for a splendid wedding in a lovely dress and a wedding trip to the Continent, perhaps, and then to return to a grand estate, where she could manage a household with the sweet-natured firmness of her mother, and someday there would be babies. . . . And she would always return to London for the Season, of course, with a devoted husband by her side. And if her future spouse's face was a bit hazy in her daydreams, that would resolve itself in time.

Lost in dreams of marital bliss and social acclaim, Louisa marched around the park until she noticed that her maid was panting and lagging behind. Taking pity on the girl, Louisa slowed her steps. The sun was higher now, perhaps her aunt would be up and about and they could discuss what interesting excursions would fill the day. Shopping, perhaps, there were many more shops on Bond Street she had not yet examined, and then a luncheon; she wanted to taste the ices at Gunter's and peek into Ackermann's print shop, where all the Ton browsed. And perhaps they could call on one of the patronesses of Almack's, so Louisa could obtain vouchers for that hallowed assembly. And was there a party to attend tonight? Louisa did hope so.

She returned to her aunt's town house. Inside, when she had taken off her bonnet and her gloves, Louisa looked up to find the footman, a stout man of middle years, regarding her with fatherly indulgence.

"You have received flowers, miss. I've put them in the drawing room."

Louisa drew in a deep breath of delight. "Really? Oh, how splendid. Who are they—I mean, thank you, I shall go and see."

She kept her steps measured only with great self-control, going on into the small but elegant chamber, where she was thrilled to see the handsome bunch of lilies and tulips and other spring blossoms, which graced a side table. She hurried across to read the note.

"With respect, Gillingham."

Not exactly a loverly sentiment, but perhaps he was old-fashioned, she told herself. And he had thought to send flowers, which was very proper, and most promising from a man she hoped—and planned!—would pay her suit.

The footman, Masters, came in behind her with a tray and a small pot of tea, which she had not ordered. "I thought you might be dry, miss, after your walk," he explained. He glanced covertly toward her, as if curious to see her reaction to the flowers. Was the staff whispering to each other already? So be it, she didn't mind them knowing that she had so promptly attracted an admirer of such rank. Putting down the tray, Masters poured the tea into the cup that sat beside the pot and offered it to her.

Louisa found herself smiling as she accepted the cup and saucer. Why should she not show her happiness? Life was good, and as for Sir Lucas, pity on the poor boy who didn't recognize true devotion when he had had it!

Humming to herself, Louisa sat down and drank her tea.

Marianne slept poorly. When she finally woke, the morning was more advanced than usual. She glanced at the sunshine slanting through her windows and pushed herself up on her elbows, feeling a moment of alarm. Gracious, she must get up. Louisa would be impatient to be on the go again.

Then she drew a deep breath and deliberately lay back against the pillows. The girl could wait; she would not make herself a serving lady for Louisa's convenience. However, Marianne rang for her dresser, and when Hackett brought her breakfast tray, she didn't linger over her tea and raisin cake.

When Hackett opened the clothespress and surveyed the contents, she said over her shoulders, "The gray morning dress, ma'am?"

"No," Marianne said firmly, startling herself as much as her dresser. "The new blue silk, I think."

Hackett glanced at her in surprise.

"I have calls to make later," Marianne explained, not that she had to justify her choices to her maid, of course.

And drawing on the new gown, she felt a flicker of pleasure as Hackett buttoned up the line of tiny buttons and straightened the skirt. Taking a quick glance at herself in the looking glass on the wall, Marianne thought the shade of clear blue became her; her eyes looked brighter and her skin softer.

Not that she intended to succumb to vanity at her age,

but still, it was pleasant to have new clothes. Louisa was not the only one who had been busy in the shops and dressmaker's salon last week.

Hackett brushed out her thick dark hair and coiled it into the usual knot on the back of her head, although Marianne decided to leave free several wisps of curls at the sides to soften her aspect. A mother hen, eh?

When Marianne went downstairs, she found Louisa in the drawing room, eager to talk about plans for the day. Masters brought a fresh cup and saucer and poured tea for his mistress. Marianne listened to Louisa's chatter as the young woman bubbled over with ideas for their mutual amusement.

"Because I know you will enjoy it all, too," Louisa told her after listing enough excursions to fill the next half year.

"No doubt," Marianne agreed, trying not to smile. They discussed which of Louisa's suggestions they should pursue first, but in the end, they did not even get so far as heading upstairs for their wraps before a knock sounded at the front door.

"Oh, who is it?" Louisa looked up eagerly.

"Someone come to call, perhaps." Marianne kept her tone level, but her curiosity jumped, too. Unless it was only more flowers for Louisa; Marianne had duly admired the large bouquet sent by the marquess. The sight of the flowers, again, drew a curious mixture of emotions. She certainly did not begrudge Louisa her suitors, but the marquess did not, perchance, appear to be the best-suited husband for a girl so young and lighthearted.

They both sat quietly and sipped their tea, and Marianne knew that Louisa listened eagerly for the sound of a male voice in the hallway. Sure enough, a deep mellow voice spoke quietly to the footman, so it was no surprise when the servant came to the door, pausing to announce with a suitably impassive face, "The marquess of Gillingham, madam."

They both stood and curtsied as the marquess made his bow.

"Please sit down," Marianne said, keeping her voice

cool. If her pulse jumped when this man entered the room, it would be foolish indeed to show it. And she was only concerned for her ward's sake, Marianne tried to tell herself. It was not that she had any personal interest in the man!

At least, unlike some chaperones, she did not have to worry about her ward being tongue-tied with shyness. Louisa smiled sweetly toward their caller and spoke at once. "Are you enjoying your London stay, my lord? You are up betimes this morning."

He looked taken aback. "I hope I did not call too early?"

"Oh, no," Louisa assured him. "My uncle is always about his business while the day is fresh—I am accustomed to it."

For some reason, the marquess glanced at Marianne. "Your uncle puts aside his own pleasures very promptly— some men might be tempted to linger at home. But as long as I am not upsetting the household—"

"Your calls could not be too early for me, my lord." Louisa smiled.

Her brow raised, Marianne glanced at the younger girl. Avoiding coyness was one thing, being unsuitably forward was another.

As if realizing that she might have gone too far, Louisa colored slightly. Regrettably, it only made her look more appealing.

"I only meant that I woke early, myself. The sun was shining into my window, and it is such a lovely day it seemed a shame not to be up and about."

"That is true—I was hoping that you might enjoy a stroll in the park?" he suggested.

"That would be most pleasant," Louisa said, only a shade too quickly. She kept her tone prim this time, but her sparkling eyes betrayed her.

No, no one would ever accuse Louisa of being too retiring, Marianne told herself. She pressed her lips firmly together. She, on the other hand, was no blushing ingenue, so she could certainly not afford to appear obsequious, no matter how high the caller's rank and consequence.

Fortunately, he had no inkling of her thoughts. He added, "If you and Mrs. Hughes would join me, we could drive to Hyde Park and take a stroll?"

Louisa jumped to her feet. "Oh, that would be delightful. I shall get my wrap." She hurried out of the room almost before he had finished his sentence.

Raising his brow, he watched her sweep out of the room. "Miss Crookshank is a lady of decision."

Marianne felt a regrettable impulse to laugh, but she controlled it, keeping her expression—she hoped—suitably bland. She would not suggest to the formidable marquess that she favored his suit; it was much too early to decide if he merited her approval.

"That is true," she agreed. Too true; her main worry right now was that Louisa would rush into a precipitous engagement with this man before taking time to find out more about his character or his habits.

Since she was the girl's sponsor, she must do some delicate probing of her own, Marianne decided. Besides, they had to talk about something! The man who sat across from her, his gaze on the patterned paper on the wall and his thoughts seemingly far away, seemed remarkably devoid of small talk.

"Why have you come to London so seldom?" Marianne asked, then, afraid she herself had been too blunt, added, "I mean, most of the Ton come to town for the Season every year. Do you not enjoy parties and theater outings, balls and galas?"

John felt his heart sink. How could he keep up this charade? He already felt like a total impostor; simply conversing with ladies of good breeding was taxing his limited social skills. He considered telling this lovely, if somewhat cool-mannered, lady that he would give a thousand pounds to be back on his own estate right now, strolling through the grounds that surrounded his home, checking a field of ripening grain or watching a bird spooked by Runt or one of the other dogs soar up into the blue sky. With an inner sigh he put away that vision of solitary peace and pulled his mind back to the rigors of a London drawing room.

"I am a plain countryman," he said, hearing the stiffness in his tone. "I lack those easy manners with which to please people I do not know, and also—I fear—the patience to accommodate the stares and curious whispers of strangers. Not that I care about such things, of course."

Despite his disclaimer, he feared he had said too much. The cool gaze of the woman sitting across from him had warmed into a look of sympathy and—something more. He did not wish for pity! But when she bent and touched his arm lightly with her hand, he felt a spark from the slight contact that reverberated through his whole being.

God, she was tempting, and the curve of her breasts as she leaned forward made his stomach go hollow with unbidden desire. Her eyes seemed bluer today, like a deep smoky sky in autumn, and he wished he could read the thoughts she guarded so carefully. No, he must not think these things—except he suddenly ached with wanting to reach for her, pull her closer . . .

John blinked and gave himself a mental shake.

Sensing his retreat, Marianne drew back. Had she offended him? She had not meant to seem patronizing—nor pitying—she could sense his fierce independence of spirit and knew he would abhor such treatment. But she had suddenly realized that his scarred face must be a trial for him. He did care, no matter what he said, that people found his pockmarks disconcerting. Yet, only an ignorant lout would stare at such small imperfections; they were overall a trivial part of his appearance, did he not realize that? His well-shaped brown eyes, with their arching dark brows, his strong nose and firm chin with the hint of a cleft, all gave him a look of such vigor, such decision, that no one who looked closely could fail to grasp his strength of will.

The question was, how did he use that inner strength? How would he treat a wife as young and untried as Louisa? It was vital that Marianne discover his private tendencies before she allowed this courtship to go too far.

Now Louisa floated back into the room, a wispy shawl tucked around her shoulders, and smiled at the marquess. "I am ready!"

Standing, he had the manners to look at Marianne before offering Louisa his arm. "Do you not wish to also don something against the wind?"

"I'm fine," she said and motioned for them to go ahead. But he waited for her to preceed them down the narrow staircase and outside, where his groom handed the ladies up into a dark carriage, to Louisa's ill-concealed disappointment. Marianne mentally scheduled another lecture on the proper conduct of a lady—not that all her earlier ones had made much dent in Louisa's boundless naivete, but as a proper guardian, Marianne had to try—and took her seat inside the carriage.

It was of good quality, but perhaps somewhat out of date. Her thoughts too obvious, Louisa gazed about at the leather cushions and wood paneling. Marianne hoped the marquess could not read her ward as easily as she herself did, but when he took his seat, he remarked, his tone mild, "It has excellent springs and rides well, though it may not display the most current fashion."

Marianne said quickly, before Louisa could speak, "We do not expect gentlemen to follow the latest fads like the ladies sometimes enjoy doing, my lord."

This was not precisely correct, of course. Many men of style were quite as interested in fashion's trends as were their wives and sweethearts. But she did not wish to embarrass him.

The marquess raised one brow. "Only to keep their footing?"

She was almost surprised into a laugh. While Louisa gazed at them both in surprise, Marianne conquered her sometimes irreverent sense of humor. "Of course."

When they reached Hyde Park, the coachman pulled up, and the three of them stepped out and strolled through the walkways. At this early hour of the day, the park was lightly peopled, mostly with nursemaids or governesses shepherding small children or sitting on benches and watching their charges at play. As she watched Louisa flutter her long lashes toward the gentleman who gallantly offered her his arm, Marianne thought the neatly uniformed women had the lighter responsibility. Too bad she couldn't trade places with one of the serving girls! That small girl toddling about dragging her doll behind her would be much easier to mind than a rash and impulsive young lady. . . . No, that was nonsense. Marianne had no wish to be a servant, and chaperoning Louisa was not so onerous.

Avoiding one young lad who rolled his hoop down the walk, Marianne tried to hang back just a little, but the marquess slowed to wait for her. He seemed determined to include her in the group, and the three of them chatted about the flowers, the pale blue sky overhead, and similar matters of high import.

The man seemed to be trying very hard, Marianne thought. While she knew she should approve, in a way it seemed a poor use of his time. His big frame, broad shoulders, and towering height seemed suited to bigger venues. Of course, at least out in the open air, there was no furniture for him to upset.

"Have you ever gone abroad, my lord?" she asked suddenly. Louisa had paused to examine a particularly pretty clump of daffodils, and Marianne and the marquess waited a few steps farther on.

He shook his head. "No, when I was younger, the war prevented it, and then—since then I have not had the inclination."

With all the wealth and time at his disposal, she thought it a pity. He must have read something of her disapproval, because he lifted his brows.

"And you?"

Marianne grimaced. "My husband would call travel a waste of good money, and, as you said, the peace that would allow it came only recently."

She paused, but her thoughts continued wistfully as she recalled old dreams long deferred. It was, of course, more difficult for single ladies to journey alone. Wealthy women could do it, with a suitable female companion and lots of male servants to protect them, but she did not have the requisite funds. But she would never speak of her comparative penury. Marianne was thankful for the small income she did have, and if she minded her budget, it had always sufficed to keep her comfortable.

"But you have considered it?" To her surprise, he seemed interested enough to pursue the topic.

She glanced down at the tulips lining the path, not ready to expose so much of her inner self. "I heard a lecture recently by a sojourner just back from Egypt," she said. "It was a fascinating talk, all about pyramids and deserts and whirling dervishes."

"And the great Sphinx," he suggested. "With the body of a lion and the head of a man—ancient mysteries there, indeed."

"Oh yes," she agreed, delighted to find a sympathetic spirit. So many of the Ton yawned if she spoke of faraway lands. "Only think of the wonders that await the traveler brave enough to venture so far."

But now his expression reverted to that familiar shuttered look; what had she said? While Marianne searched for her misstep, Louisa rejoined them in time to join in.

"Aunt is right—only consider Paris, with its wealth of fashion! The Gothic beauties of Notre Dame, and Versailles, where queens once danced! A trip across the Channel would be divine. I should love a honeymoon on the Continent."

She paused, and, this time, the younger woman blushed for real. Marianne said, making her tone as repressive as any proper gray-haired chaperone, "Plenty of time to think of that, Louisa. Let's walk a little farther this way, those beds of tulips look most pleasing."

Mercifully, Louisa confined her comments to the flowers for some time and barely even fluttered her lashes. The marquess murmured polite responses to her small talk.

With Louisa temporarily abashed into propriety, Marianne tried to make out the puzzle of this guarded, rather withdrawn man, as enigmatic in his own way as some ancient monument. At least, he did not make fun of Louisa's impulsive blunders, and so far, she did not sense the mean-spiritedness or malicious impulses that had been her biggest fear. Perhaps he would turn out to be a suitable candidate for Louisa's hand, after all.

For some reason, this did not raise Marianne's spirits. So it was a somewhat subdued party that rounded the curve of the walkway and paused when another couple blocked their way.

Marianne, who had been lost in her own thoughts, glanced up and knew that her eyes widened. The young woman in the green pelisse and sprigged muslin gown smiled politely, but the young man's expression appeared arrested. It was the gentleman from Vauxhall, Louisa's onetime suitor, Sir Lucas Englewood.

He bowed, looking down at the gravel path and not meeting their gaze. "Excuse me."

Louisa lifted her chin and took a firmer grip on the marquess's arm. "Of course," she said, her tone cold, and immediately broke into animated chatter directed pointedly at her companion. "Shall we return to your carriage, my lord? I believe the wind is becoming colder. I would not wish for my aunt to become chilled."

Very considerate, Marianne thought a bit sourly, trying not to watch the play of emotions that flashed across Sir Lucas's face. If that was indeed Louisa's only motive for wheeling the marquess about and marching smartly back toward his carriage, her fashionable bonnet turned resolutely away from the couple they had just encountered, she was being solicitous, indeed. But somehow, Marianne had her doubts.

Five

*W*hen they returned home, Lord Gillingham escorted them to the door. Louisa made her thanks with her usual guileless charm. "It was so good of you to favor us with your company. I hope we can do it again, my lord."

He nodded. "Of course. Tomorrow morning?"

"Or perhaps in the afternoon, around five?" Louisa fluttered her lashes, and her smile would have melted butter.

Had she already learned that this was the fashionable hour to be seen in the park? Marianne tried not to allow her cynical thought to color her expression.

The marquess hesitated. "You don't think the park will be unpleasantly crowded?"

Marianne opened her mouth, about to argue for the morning, since he so obviously did not care to stroll with too many people about, people who might stare at his blemished face, but Louisa was too quick.

"Oh, but my lord, I am so new to London, I enjoy seeing the lovely ladies and impressive gentlemen. Not that any man could be more splendid than you, of course."

Marianne stared at their escort's unfashionable clothes and careless appearance and swallowed hard. Only Louisa could make this artless speech sound heartfelt.

He hesitated again, then bowed. "As you wish."

He made his departure, and the ladies went into the house, pausing in the hall to take off their bonnets and gloves.

"That was not very considerate, Louisa," Marianne told her ward, annoyed with the girl's usual determination to get her own way.

"What? I am not allowed to see the same gentleman two days in a row?" Louisa opened her light blue eyes very wide.

"You know what I mean!" Marianne restrained her irritation with effort, aware that Masters hovered nearby, listening to every word.

"Luncheon is ready, madam," the footman said.

"Thank you, we shall be there directly," Marianne told him. He withdrew, and they proceeded to the dining room. When the ladies had both been seated and the first course served, the footman withdrew for a moment, and Marianne was able to proceed.

"You know that the marquess does not enjoy crowds— he's very conscious of the scars on his face."

"But I wish to help him overcome his excessive sensibility," Louisa said, her tone earnest and her expression quite free of guilt. "I have no abhorrence of his appearance, and he must be made to see that any well-meaning person will not regard such minor imperfections."

This was hard to argue with, though Marianne still felt qualms. She was not sure that the marquess's dread would be so easily assuaged. She sensed darker emotions beneath the man's guarded demeanor, scars from a hurt deeper than those that lingered from his illness.

"And you will enjoy seeing all the fashionable people, and being seen in the company of a man of such high rank?"

"Of course." Louisa's smile was sunny.

Marianne stabbed her fork into a piece of chicken, but

though it was tender enough, she somehow found it hard to swallow.

"After luncheon, may we go out to the shops?" Louisa asked. "I have in mind a new bonnet to go with the violet walking dress I ordered from the dressmaker last week."

"Perhaps later," Marianne said. "I think you should have a short rest before we venture out again."

The picture of boundless energy, Louisa lifted her head. "Oh, do not worry, I'm not in the least tired."

"But I am," Marianne said, trying to keep her tone even, but wishing she could shake her irrepressible charge. "And my head aches. Perhaps the sun was too bright."

"Oh, poor Aunt!" Louisa exclaimed at once. "I shall make you a tisane that Aunt Caroline favors. And I can come up and rub lavender drops on your temples, that might help."

Marianne rubbed her forehead. "Thank you, Louisa, but truly, I only wish a few minutes of quiet. I'm sure I will feel better shortly."

Louisa had tried hard to offer her aunt aid, but she was determined to retire unattended. So Louisa took a copy of *La Belle Assemblée* up to her own room to study, too restless to lie down, and in an hour, she was pleased to see her aunt reemerge, apparently in better spirits. They strolled down to the shops to inspect the bonnet that Louisa had noted on their last shopping excursion, taking Aunt Marianne's footman as escort. They returned home in time for tea, the servant's arms laden with hatboxes and other bundles, and later a quiet dinner for just the two of them.

Louisa had never lived without the convenience of a private carriage; she wondered if she should propose to her aunt that they should hire one for the duration of Louisa's visiting. But when she suggested it, Marianne shook her head.

"I have no stable in which to house a pair of horses," she reminded her niece. "And no groom, so there would be

many extra expenses. I do not wish to make such a charge
upon your funds, Louisa."

"But I do not mind—"

"We shall be fine with an occasional hired vehicle." Her
aunt's tone was firm, so Louisa was silenced, though she
thought she might bring the subject up again, perhaps on
the next rainy day.

At the moment, however, she was pleased enough with
her progress. The marquess seemed suitably taken with
Louisa's charms. Now, if she could convince him to venture into a broader section of Society—he would have her
nearby at all times, ready to bolster the poor man's dam-
aged pride, and he would be happier for it. She was sure he
could not be content in such self-imposed isolation—and
if others, such as a certain oafish young baronet, should
note Louisa's impressive new conquest, so much the better!

The next morning, Louisa woke early once more. Since
coming to London, she had been brimming with energy,
and it was hard to lie abed as most fashionable ladies did.
So she rose and dressed, and after toast and a coddled egg,
she and her maid ventured back to the tiny park in the middle of the square.

But this morning, in addition to a nursemaid and her
small charges playing on the grass, Louisa was startled to
see a young man of fashionable appearance and resolute
expression awaiting her.

"Sir Lucas?" she exclaimed. "What on earth are you doing here, and at such an early hour?"

"Miss Crookshank." He bowed, the model of a correct
gentleman. Was this the young man she had known for
so many years, the lad she had played games with when
they were children? The man who she would have sworn
so recently had had feelings for her? Louisa bit her lip in
chagrin.

"I—ah—I called yesterday afternoon while you were

out, and the footman told me you seemed to enjoy early strolls," he admitted.

Louisa stared at him. "You left no card."

"No, I only—I just—well, it seems to be awkward when we meet, and since in London, one is always running into some—um—acquaintance, I thought we should talk. I do not wish you to feel constrained."

Louisa exclaimed, a little too loudly, "Constrained—why should you imagine such a thing? You are too quick with your assumptions, sir! I am quite unaffected by your presence, or lack of it!"

The nursemaid glanced their way, and Louisa paused. When Lucas answered, he kept his own voice pitched low, but his formal tone had disappeared.

"Oh, come off it, Louisa," he retorted, with some of their once-familiar ease. "You bristle like a gamecock whenever you see me, especially if I have—well—a young lady with me."

"I do not!" she argued hotly, then with an effort moderated her voice. "If you wish to escort any person of your choosing, why should I care?" She thought that this time, she had managed to sound lofty and disinterested, although she spoiled the effect by adding, "While I might wish to warn the young lady not to expect any great constancy from you, I will, of course, refrain."

"Unfair, Louisa!" He met her angry gaze without blinking. "I might, with much more purpose, say the same about you."

"Me? I am not the one who disappeared without a word, ignoring a sweet—an old friend whom you had known since childhood, and all because I laughed when you took a small tumble down a hill, and your pride was injured. After that afternoon, I waited and waited—"

Louisa swallowed hard against the rest of the words she wished to hurl upon his head. He had not returned to her uncle's house, not called, not appeared at the next dance at the Pump Room to provide his usual escort, not arrived in his chaise to drive her about the streets of Bath. She had felt surprise and dismay and a terrible humiliation, wondering how many other young ladies were laughing behind their fans at his sudden and unexplained abandonment.

"Louisa, it was not merely my pride that was injured," he told her, his voice suddenly grim. "By the time I took you and your maid home that afternoon and returned to my own house, my foot was swollen to twice its normal size. I had to have two footmen help me out of the carriage."

Shocked, Louisa stared at him. She did remember that he had limped after he had tripped on the loose rock on their walk along the riverbank, but she had thought it was only a touching play to gain her sympathy, especially as she had giggled at his misstep and sprawling fall; he had indeed looked very funny. But she had never dreamed he'd actually been injured.

"My mother summoned a physician, who probed the swollen limb—most painfully!—and decided that I had broken a bone in my foot. I was not allowed to leave the house for over a month. I had to linger in my room with my foot propped up, helpless as a babe; it was a most trying time."

"Why did you not send word?" Louisa demanded. "I had no idea!"

"You never asked," he told her, and beneath the lingering anger, she thought she could detect hurt. "You knew that I had taken a misstep, you might have thought—"

"But I didn't." Louisa tried to push aside stirrings of guilt. "How was I to know? And I never heard a word of gossip about it. Usually, one hears of the slightest ailment among Bath society."

"I hardly wanted it noised about! I forbade my mother to speak of it to anyone. Proper fool I should look," Lucas retorted. "Breaking my foot on a simple stumble. But you were there, you knew I had taken a fall."

"You are always so healthy and strong, Lucas, I never conceived that you had truly taken harm. I thought—I thought you were angry at me. I could not understand why you suddenly ceased to call."

They stared at each other, their faces only a foot apart, and she had a sudden memory of a quarrel when she was eight and he ten, over an abandoned bird's nest that both had wanted to claim. But this was much more important. Had she thrown away her first love over such a ridiculous misunderstanding?

"But now that I know that you were truly hurt, Lucas—" she began, her tone tentative, prepared to make a proper apology. But she did not have the opportunity to finish; he pulled back, and she paused.

"It's not as if it were the first time you have only thought of yourself, Louisa, always expecting to get your way."

She flushed. "And you should not be so quick to take offense. Gentlemen are supposed to be courteous to ladies!"

"Courteous, yes, but you have always been so indulged that—if your father had not given in to your every whim—"

"Don't you speak of my dear father in such a way!" She stamped her foot and glared at him.

Sir Lucas paused, then plowed ahead, his expression stubborn. "I do not speak ill of your father; you know I was most grieved at his passing. But now that I realize at last just how shallow you are—"

It was her turn to jerk back; she felt as if she had been slapped. "How could you say such a hurtful thing!"

"Francis always said it was so—he cautioned me about you often enough, warned me that you would break my heart, but I would not listen." Lucas looked away, his mouth pressed into a thin line.

"Mr. Lackland? He's a lack-wit!" Louisa protested. "You would take his word on my character?"

"He is my friend, and only concerned for my well-being. And he had grounds to base his opinion upon. He wrote you a poem once detailing his devotion, and you told him it did not scan well," Lucas reminded her.

"I was fifteen!" she flashed back. "I am older now, more mature, and I would not be so unkind."

"It's no matter. He will not make that mistake again, nor will I," Lucas said. He sounded calm again and entirely resolute.

She felt a sinking feeling inside. She had driven Lucas away; it had not been his lack of constancy, as she had thought. But it had been an accident, a mishap of circumstances; he was reading too much into small arguments in their past; if only he would listen—

But he showed no inclination to hear her rebuttal. "Now that you understand, I'm sure you will not regard my presence as of any consequence, and we can meet in Society without further awkwardness."

"To be sure," Louisa lied, trying hard to compose her features. "You need not be concerned about me, Sir Lucas. I have new friends who have more faith in my character, and doubtless I shall soon form an even more permanent connection."

"My felicitations," he told her, but his tone was dry.

Louisa wished she could slap him. But instead she drew herself up to her fullest height and gave him a dignified curtsy. "I must get back before my aunt wonders at my absence," she said. "Good day to you, sir. I wish you only good fortune."

Without waiting to hear his farewell—he had certainly said enough—she turned on her heel and hurried back to Aunt Marianne's door. Behind her, Eva had to run to keep up. Once Louisa was safely inside, and the door had shut behind her and her maid, she put her hands to her face, feeling the tears already beginning to flow.

Masters hovered in the hallway, but she ignored him and hastened up the stairs until she reached the solitude of her own chamber.

"Miss," Eva asked, coming in after her. "Does your head ache? May I fetch something for you?"

"Yes—no," Louisa blurted. "I just want some quiet."

So, after drawing the draperies, the maid slipped away, shutting the door behind her. Louisa fell upon the bed and pressed her face against her pillow so that no one would hear her sobs.

Much later, after she had cried till the last tear had been drained from some deep part of her soul, she fell, exhausted, into a restless sleep. When she woke, she found that Eva had brought her a cup of tea and some sliced cucumber.

Once again, she would have to try to hide the swollen

eyelids and mottled cheeks, Louisa thought. Her head still ached, and a leaden weight seemed to have settled inside her.

Broken his heart, Lucas had said. Could it really be true? And had he set himself against any feeling for her, so that no hope of reconciliation was possible?

It seemed so.

She took a sip of the tepid tea and had to force the liquid down past the lump in her throat.

So, she had a much more eminent suitor now, one mature enough not to take offense where none had been offered or feel slighted by some stupid misunderstanding. Why should she care if a silly young man misread a lady's perfectly proper reaction to an apparent rejection . . .

Louisa felt one more tear slip down her cheek and dashed it angrily away. No, she would not allow another torrent of useless regret. Steeling herself, she reached for the cucumber slices.

When Marianne went downstairs, after dressing and lingering over her breakfast tray, she was surprised to find Louisa still up in her room. However, it gave Marianne a chance to look through her mail. Two more invitations, a note from a friend to answer, and a bill for some of Louisa's dressmaking excursions. Marianne put the last away to pay from Louisa's account and sat down at her desk to write an answer to the friend, who was, for her health, spending a few weeks in the south of France. The invitations she considered briefly after checking her calendar, then, knowing that Louisa would welcome gaiety of any form, she penned acceptances to both.

When Louisa appeared, looking a bit wan, Marianne told her ward of the dinner and the opera party, but the girl did not seem as excited as Marianne had expected.

"Yes, that's nice," Louisa agreed, but without any of her usual sparkle.

Only when Marianne mentioned today's planned drive

with the marquess did Louisa lift her head. "Oh, yes. I'm so glad we found a hat yesterday to match the new green dress—I must try it on again to be sure it is the right costume to wear to Hyde Park. I've heard that everyone in Society visits the park at the fashionable hour."

"Very close to everyone," Marianne agreed. "And that also means that you must remember to be on your best behavior, Louisa. With so many eyes sure to be on you, you must not suggest any hint of forward conduct."

"Has Sir L—has someone suggested that I do not conduct myself properly?" Louisa demanded, her eyes flashing. "Because if so, I must protest—"

"No, nor would I listen to specious gossip," Marianne assured the girl. "But your contriving a meeting with the marquess was not really the thing, and I should not like you to repeat such a ruse."

"But I simply had to meet him," Louisa argued. "And to have him appear right in front of my eyes—how could I resist?"

Marianne shook her head. "Trust me, it would not do to give the Ton a bad first impression of you."

Louisa subsided, though her expression was still stormy. "Of course not. I promise to be on my best behavior, Aunt."

Marianne hoped her ward's resolve would last through the afternoon. Something was not right with Louisa, though Marianne could not put her finger on the change. But she sensed emotions tightly suppressed beneath the younger woman's lovely surface, like a volcano ready to erupt, lava seething unseen beneath smooth green meadows. If so, Marianne only hoped that the eruption would not occur in a public place!

Her sense of unease was such that she wondered if they should cancel their expedition or postpone it. Surely the marquess would understand. But when she hinted at such, Louisa protested angrily.

"But why? I am not overly tired nor am I agitated. I am perfectly calm!" Her voice rose dangerously.

Marianne gazed at her. She didn't believe Louisa's

statement for a moment, but without a better reason, it would be too unkind to deny the younger lady an outing so obviously important to her. Perhaps Louisa was only overexcited by the stimulation of London's merriment. Although heaven knows, they had done little enough. Could it be that she was losing her heart to the marquess, already? This could not be wise, but again, Louisa reacted angrily to Marianne's reminder about the dangers of rushing into a commitment.

"My heart is my own," the younger woman said stubbornly. "I am not a child!"

Marianne decided to let it go, at least for the moment. But she would keep a close eye on Louisa until she had some hint of what new plot was being concocted behind those guileless blue eyes.

So when the marquess arrived promptly at five, they were both ready. Louisa wore the new green dress and matching bonnet, and Marianne had donned an older, but still pleasing, plum-colored walking costume.

The marquess bowed. "You look as lovely and bright as two spring blossoms," he declared.

Louisa's smile broadened. "You're too kind," she said, her tone mild and not at all forward. She glanced at her aunt as if to say, *There, you see? I can be proper.*

Marianne was thinking that Lord Gillingham's praise sounded a bit forced; he was not the kind of man, she thought, to go about spouting compliments. But he was obviously trying, and she admitted to a moment of secret satisfaction that she had not worn the drabber dun-colored walking dress. Not that she was the one he had come to see, of course. Perhaps he was as smitten with Louisa as she was with him. To hide her frown, Marianne lingered as Louisa sailed out the door, only to pause in surprise upon the doorstep.

"Oh, how splendid!" the girl exclaimed. "A new carriage? And it's a barouche, very much the thing!"

"I hired it this morning for my stay in London," the marquess explained. "I thought it was a more proper vehicle for rides in the park, one that would ensure a lady's pleasure."

A lady with less than sedate tastes, at least.

Marianne blinked. This barouche was certainly in the latest mode, if not downright gaudy. It had a collapsible top, which had been pushed down to allow its occupants the opportunity to enjoy the pleasant day and to be easily seen when they rolled along the avenues and into the park itself. Its bottle-green body was accented with touches of gilding and high gold-painted wheels, and the horses which pulled it were well-matched cream-colored steeds. What a picture they were going to make! Marianne tried not to giggle at the thought; she put her hand in front of her face and turned the incipient laugh into a cough.

Then she caught the marquess's eye; he had lifted one brow in a quizzical glance that seemed to read her sentiment perfectly, and even, perhaps, to agree. For an instant, understanding flashed between them, and Marianne allowed her smile to show.

Then he stepped forward to hand them both into the carriage, while his groom stood at the horses' heads. No one could say he was not doing the thing properly, except perhaps for his own attire, which was as casual and out-of-date as ever.

The barouche had two seats. He handed the ladies into the forward-looking bench and he himself took the one behind the coachman, facing them. Louisa, Marianne suspected, would rather have sat beside the marquess, but, after her aunt's lecture on conduct, apparently did not dare to push her luck. So she kept her yearnings to herself and smiled as the marquess nodded over his shoulder to his coachman. The groom took his position at the rear of the carriage, and the driver flicked the reins and edged the flashy equipage into the thick London traffic.

When they reached the park, the lanes were almost as crowded as the city streets. They joined the other carriages and riders who made their way slowly about the Ring, circling the park. As predicted, they found a multitude of fashionable people to gaze at, and occasionally Marianne saw friends or acquaintances to wave and nod to. A few times, she directed the marquess to pull up his vehicle so that she could perform introductions. Louisa smiled and greeted the new acquaintances sweetly. The marquess received some curious stares, but he held up stoically, inclining his head and speaking politely if briefly.

Between introductions Louisa chatted about London's amusements and hinted at another visit to Vauxhall. She also could not keep from glancing toward any younger man with brown hair and medium height, which, Marianne was thankful, the marquess didn't seem to notice. But as far as she could tell, Sir Lucas was not among the park visitors on this afternoon.

Still, Marianne was relieved when Louisa suggested they stroll a while in the park. The marquess directed his coachman to pull up the carriage and then offered his hand to the ladies to help them down.

Louisa went first, flashing her wide smile and taking a few steps up the pathway, where she paused to unfurl the parasol she had brought with her.

As she stepped down, Marianne felt the strength of the marquess's hand, and it seemed almost as if he allowed his grip to linger. Marianne looked up at him as they stood, for a moment, very close; she felt a little breathless. His shoulders were so wide, and he had an air of great strength closely contained. She could see his chest rising and falling beneath his outmoded jacket; did he breathe quickly? Beneath his wide-brimmed hat, his hooded dark eyes were hard to read, and yet—

Then Louisa called merrily, "Come along, Aunt," and the spell was broken.

No doubt, Marianne told herself, she was putting too much emphasis into a common courtesy. She could hardly act like Louisa; she had no excuse in a lack of social experience. Refusing to meet his eyes again, she gazed resolutely at the flowering shrubs and blooms they passed as they strolled along the wide walkways.

For a time they walked three abreast. Louisa chatted about the flowers, Lord Gillingham nodded agreement, and Marianne simply listened.

Even though it was for Louisa's best interests that she was forced to play chaperone, Marianne did feel, at times, a bit de trop. So when Louisa paused to chat with another young lady she had met during their evening at Vauxhall, Marianne dropped back a little. But the marquess, to her surprise, lingered near her. Perhaps he did not wish to speak to yet another stranger.

"Do you miss the quiet of the countryside?" she asked on impulse.

His dark eyes lifted. A mistake, she had not meant to allow her gaze to linger on his. There seemed to be too much understanding between them, as if their thoughts were attuned, with meanings that passed easily even without words. He was not *her* suitor, Marianne told herself sharply and turned to study the top of a distant tree.

"An oak, I believe," he told her, sounding amused. "And yes, I admit that I do. I lack the polish—"

For some reason she felt a stab of annoyance. "You mentioned that before, my lord. The polish on my silverware comes from hard rubbing. It was not acquired without effort."

"You think I need more—ah—rubbing?"

To her fury, she found that she was blushing as furiously as any girl in her first season. But perhaps with more reason. Louisa would likely have read no double entendre into his comment. Which he—surely—had not meant the way her unbridled thoughts seemed to be leading her.

"I meant that with some effort, even if it does not come naturally, you could be as cultured as you should wish."

That was the real question, however. What did this man really want? Why had he come to London and plunged so quickly into courtship of a girl he hardly knew? No, she knew the answer to that, gossip said he wanted a son to inherit the title.

Again, he seemed to understand her too well. "Surely you do not fault me for wishing to set up my nursery? I have an old name to protect, and I need an heir."

A reasonable motive, and yet, his voice held an urgency

she did not understand. Once more, his words rang with undertones of meaning, and this time he showed no hint of humor to lighten the mood.

"You are not ill?" she said before she thought.

He shook his head. "I am quite well, Mrs. Hughes."

Now she was the one to feel foolish. So much for being the dignified chaperone. Where was Louisa? Let the girl deal with this dratted man herself, Marianne thought. She looked about for Louisa, who was still chatting with her new friend.

And indeed the path was becoming more crowded. Three gallants walked side by side, chins high behind even higher collars, jackets all that the most florid of tailors could deliver. One held a lorgnette with which to peer at the ladies, and they all openly ogled any personable woman within view.

Behind them an elderly lady ambled with slower steps, her companion holding a parasol over her to shade the wrinkled, powdered face from the sun. A simply dressed younger woman followed, her eyes downcast. Then another lady of middle age and great fashion strolled and chatted with a friend, while the small dog she held in her arms surveyed the scene like a royal personage making the tour. Marianne saw faces among the crowd that were known to her and debated whether the time was right for introductions. Turning her head, she was able to catch Louisa's eye and make a subtle motion.

Louisa said good-bye to the other young lady and wheeled to rejoin them. Then, Marianne caught sight of another familiar face. *Oh no, not him,* she thought. It was Sir Lucas and, of course, the man must once more be escorting a damsel. Marianne prayed that Louisa would not notice her old sweetheart, but the two young people seemed as connected as two magnets drawn always by their invisible bond. Louisa's head lifted and she gazed straight at Sir Lucas.

He nodded his head gravely and looked away. Marianne held her breath.

Except for a slight flush, Louisa maintained her composure. Marianne thought with relief that there would be no social gaffe for others to remark upon. And so it might have been, except that the small dog in the nearby matron's arms suddenly spied a pigeon loitering too invitingly upon the grass. His ears pricked, his head lifted, and he leaped out of his mistress's grasp.

"Heros! Come back!"

The animal paid no heed. Making a mad dash for his feathered prey, he crossed the path just as Louisa stepped forward.

Treading on the little dog's paw, the girl tripped. The dog yipped in distress as Louisa struggled for her footing.

Marianne knew that Louisa must feel foolish, especially with Sir Lucas and his new amour still within easy viewing of her awkward posturing as she flailed her arms, dropping the parasol, and struggled to keep her balance.

The lightweight parasol came down upon the beast's head; the dog yelped again.

Louisa, who was usually as fond of animals as anyone, snapped, "Oh, do be quiet!"

This did not appear to endear her to the dog's owner, who waved her handkerchief in alarm.

"Oh, dear." Marianne hurried forward. But her progress was impeded; a crowd was gathering around the principals, and she found it hard to push her way through. At least she could see that Louisa was once again steady on her feet. The girl bent to console the dog, which lifted its lips and snarled at her.

"Here, now," Louisa scolded. "I did not do it on purpose. Let me see your paw." She tried to touch it, but the animal growled once more.

"Will you attack my dog again?" the dog's owner shrieked, rushing up to reclaim her pet. A scarlet ostrich plume that adorned her hat now dangled over her forehead, and she was flushed with alarm.

"I did not mean to—"

"And then to rebuke my poor baby! How can you be so insensitive? Heros, *mon petit,* are you injured?" She scooped up the small dog.

"But," Louisa protested, "really, you must see that it was not my doing. The dog ran in front of me—"

"If you had been looking where you were striding, you would not have trodden upon his tiny feet! Such clumsy manners, my dear, really—a milkmaid would have more grace." The woman's voice was high-pitched and all too audible; the interested group around them grew denser with each passing moment.

"I am hardly a milkmaid, madam!" Perhaps aware of all the staring faces, Louisa lost her temper with a flourish. "I am a lady of quality, and to suggest that I lack grace is hardly decorous behavior on your part!"

"You would impugn my conduct? A lady of more experience of the world than you, and, I am sure, of higher position?" The woman's tone sounded truly dangerous now, and Louisa had the wit to hesitate.

Marianne pushed past a stout woman in puce who had been most unwilling to give up her view of this interesting bit of drama. "Louisa!" she said, her tone a warning. "I'm sure, Lady Jersey, that my niece did not intend to harm your dog. We are so sorry that such a mishap occurred. I hope your pet is uninjured?"

The stylish matron still glared. "Let us hope so, indeed, Mrs. Hughes. I shall summon my personal physician to have my *chéri* examined when I return home. In the meantime, you would do well to give your young relation some lessons in deportment, especially when pertaining to ladies of higher rank."

Louisa had gone pale. "My lady, I am truly sorry. I only—"

But Sally, countess of Jersey, who could hold a grudge when it suited her, was not interested in belated apologies. She cuddled her pet to her bosom and swept away.

Louisa's eyes had reddened; she looked ready to cry. But the fashionable crowd gathered around them still watched and listened, and Louisa's hysterics would only add fuel to the already too combustible spark of gossip that would, without a doubt, soon sweep through the Ton. Marianne took her ward's hand. "Let us go back to the carriage," she said gently.

For a moment it looked as if they could not even move,

but then the marquess made his way through the press, parting the well-dressed onlookers like a scythe, and offered his arm.

At last, they could make their way back toward the barouche.

Marianne was pleased that Louisa kept her chin up, and if her lips trembled, a curious bystander would have to have been quite close to have noted that detail. Still, it was a relief to see their barouche just ahead on the side of the park circle. Its bright colors no longer seemed pleasing, only as gauche as Louisa appeared now to feel.

Marianne waited to allow Louisa to be handed up first, but just as the younger woman stepped into the road to approach the carriage, someone shouted behind them.

"Look out!"

Six

A riderless horse galloped toward them, and Louisa stood squarely in its path.

Marianne gasped, too frightened even to shout. The steps had not been put down; there was no time for Louisa to clamber into the carriage, no time for her to evade the horse's lumbering trajectory. Moments they had, that was all.

As Marianne watched in horror, time itself seemed to slow. She saw Louisa's eyes widen and her mouth open in a silent scream. The horse's eyes were wild, its reins slapped loosely about its neck, and it seemed heedless of obstacles ahead.

But the marquess moved swiftly, running toward the panicked steed instead of away. Without regard for the thundering, heavy hooves, which could easily have trampled him into the earth, he jumped to grab the horse's head.

Marianne held her breath.

In a moment he had hold of the bridle. A smaller man would have had no hope of controlling the runaway. Even though he was much lighter than the horse, which must weigh five times as much as he, Gillingham, with his solid frame and strong arms, managed to pull the animal aside. It dragged him several feet, but the marquess did not release his grip, although his hat flew off and he seemed to have ripped his jacket.

He clung grimly to the horse's neck until the animal slowed, tried to toss its head, then blew through its nostrils and came at last to a halt.

A garishly dressed young man ran up behind them, his neck cloth somewhat disordered and his expression distressed. "So sorry, so sorry, what a narrow escape! Good God, but what a save, my good man, well done!" He put one hand in his pocket as if to fish out a coin to reward Lord Gillingham. Good heavens, did he take the marquess for a servant?

If so, he was soon disabused. The marquess turned a stern gaze upon the errant rider, and his tone was icy. "You should control your animal, sir!"

The younger man flushed. "I had only dismounted for a moment to speak to a lady friend. Somehow, it just dashed off and I couldn't stop it in time." He pulled out a mauve-tinted handkerchief to wipe his brow and babbled on. "Something must have spooked it, had no reason to bolt like that. Mind you, it's a hired hack, so I know little about its temperament."

Her legs wobbly with relief, Marianne turned to see about Louisa. The girl looked very pale. "Here, get into the carriage, my dear," Marianne murmured as the groom hurried to put down the steps. She had glimpsed the marquess's expression, and she was content to leave the hapless, and careless, young man to his rebuke.

After a low-voiced dressing down which turned the rider of the runaway almost as white as Louisa, the marquess picked up his hat from the pavement, joined them inside the carriage and signaled to his coachman to drive on. "Probably rides as witlessly as he speaks," he muttered. "Miss Crookshank, are you recovered?"

Louisa made no reply, but she gazed at him, her aspect truly pitiful, and drew a long ragged breath.

"She must have a glass of brandy when you are returned to the house," he suggested to Marianne.

"Yes, we must go home at once." Marianne pressed her charge's hand. "Lean on me, my dear, if you are faint."

Louisa still didn't answer. Marianne tried again to reassure her. "Louisa, we shall have you home soon, and you can lie down. I know it was a terrible fright, but thank heavens you are not hurt."

Louisa shrugged, her thoughts apparently elsewhere. "Was that—" she asked in a tremulous voice. "The woman—the lady whose dog I trod upon. Is she *the* Lady Jersey?"

"One of the patronesses of Almack's? I am afraid so," Marianne agreed, realizing the direction of her ward's thoughts.

Louisa burst into tears.

The marquess looked bewildered, and Marianne made no attempt to explain. She felt both sympathy and vexation. The girl could have died there, and Lord Gillingham—who could have been injured or killed himself—had performed the most amazing rescue that Marianne had ever seen. She herself was still breathless from the sight, and the image of the powerful man grasping at the runaway steed, refusing to release it even when the animal tossed and dragged him bodily along, the muscles in his arms and shoulders visible even through his poorly cut jacket—the vision would linger in her mind's eye a very long time, Marianne thought.

And while it was a social setback for a miss in her first Season to anger one of the women who controlled access to Almack's, it hardly compared to a narrowly averted maiming or even death.

She could tell that Louisa, dabbing her eyes with her wispy handkerchief and sniffing back more tears, did not agree.

They rode silently back to Marianne's town house, and the marquess came inside with them, offering his arm to the still silent Louisa and being all that was polite and solicitous.

For once, Louisa hardly seemed to notice. She smiled wanly as he advised her to rest and recover and only fluttered her lashes when he promised to check on her the following day.

"Go upstairs and lie down, Louisa." Marianne had summoned her ward's maid as soon as they'd entered. "I'm sure our guest does not expect you to stand on ceremony. I shall be there to check on you in a moment."

Lord Gillingham bowed. "No, indeed," he agreed. "I will take my leave. I'm sure you are both fatigued. I had not meant our excursion to be so tumultuous."

Marianne grimaced at the understatement. She left Louisa to Eva's solicitude and walked with their guest to the door.

"My lord," she said on impulse, and he paused to look down at her.

He had the deepest brown eyes she had ever seen; she thought that stronger emotions lingered in their depths than he ever allowed anyone to glimpse. The moment stretched, and she forced herself to remember what she wished to tell him.

"Since Miss Crookshank is—understandably—not herself, please allow me to thank you for such a miraculous rescue. She could have died beneath that horse's hooves. It was incredibly brave of you to jump in front of the runaway as you did."

"Anyone else would have done the same," he muttered, shrugging off her words.

"Oh, no, I don't think so," Marianne insisted. She put one hand on his arm in emphasis. Yes, his biceps were as firm as an oaken rail, and the strength he projected—

Something changed in his expression, and he took a step forward. They stood now very close.

Marianne found it hard to breathe. He was so tall, his shoulders so broad, his eyes so deep and dark that she felt she could dive into them and lose herself entirely. And the warmth that flooded through her, she had not felt this way since—had she ever felt this way?

She felt dizzy, and she knew she should step back. But she wanted the touch to linger, she wanted—

He seemed to be breathing quickly, and something primal sparked in his eyes. She had not been a married woman for very long before her husband died, but she knew the look of a man's need when she saw it.

Heavens, what was she doing?

A light voice from behind them broke the spell.

"Lord Gillingham?" Louisa had followed them.

John felt Mrs. Hughes jump. She moved quickly to put a more respectable distance between them. He cursed it, every inch of it.

But she was not the one he was pursuing, and he forced himself to recall the fact. She was spoken for, irretrievable, not within his grasp, even if he had not already made open court to her ward.

And as if his thought drew her, Louisa Crookshank came to stand next to him. She smiled up at him, her blue eyes wide.

"I have been remiss, my lord. I could not let you leave without thanking you. You saved my life!"

"Not—not at all," he stammered.

She put one hand on his arm, much as Mrs. Hughes had done—Louisa's guardian had retreated and turned her back. She seemed to be giving orders to her footman, effectively ignoring them—but somehow, this young woman's touch did not produce the same effect. He wanted to pat Louisa on the head and make her smile, but his first infatuated reaction to her had long since passed. Now when she stood near him, her presence stirred nothing in his blood. The treacherous pounding of his heart, the ache in his groin—if they lingered, it had nothing at all to do with this engaging child, lovely as she undoubtedly was. His reaction had been to another woman, a woman with smoky eyes and darker hair, a woman with spirit and—and one he could not have. Of course, physical longings were not everything; he must remember why he had come to London.

"But you saved me from the runaway horse, like a knight swooping down to slay a dragon!" Louisa smiled at him, her adoration patent.

John almost groaned. He had never meant to steal her

heart or awaken schoolgirl fantasies which, as a husband, he could not possibly fulfill. Good God, what a fix. Having a complaisant and agreeable wife was one thing; trying to pretend to a romantic love that he would never be able to maintain was something else, a tragedy in the making.

He had been clear and rational in his design when he had begun this quest, and he must remember his original plan. He thought briefly of his brutish father and unhappy mother, memories he dwelt on as little as possible. In his youth he had seen enough of domestic calamity, of pain that endured for years and left everyone in its wake bitter and unhappy.

While she continued to extol his heroic virtues, he felt a most cowardly impulse to flee. "You must rest," he said with as much firmness as he could muster. "You have suffered a most shocking experience."

"You will call tomorrow?" she asked, her gaze worshipful. "You will not fail me?"

"I will come," he agreed.

"I knew I could depend on you, my lord."

"I should hope so," he said, a bit absently. "Always."

"Always?" She opened her blue eyes very wide. "Do you mean—oh, my lord. I am honored beyond words!"

If he had not still been distracted with yearnings for the wrong woman, perhaps he would have realized what he had suggested, or had seemed to suggest, to an impressionable young lady. "Think nothing of it—I mean, what did you say?" He saw that her eyes had brightened and her cheeks now showed a deeper blush.

"Nothing? It's everything, my lord. To spend my life by your side—oh, you will not regret it, I promise you!"

"Good God," he muttered. "That is, I don't—I mean—" Then he hesitated. Would it be this simple, after all? He had not even had to get down on one knee and dream up flowery speeches of the type young ladies seemed to expect, and he had been dreading that bit of playacting.

Still, he sputtered, "I just—I mean, I'm sure you would please any man honored by your—your favor."

"Oh, thank you, my lord. You have made me so happy!" She stood on tiptoe and kissed his cheek.

And John realized, to his shock, that he had done just what he had set out to do—arrive in London and secure a betrothed bride within the shortest possible span of time. He waited for a sense of satisfaction to grow, but somehow, he felt instead only a vague disquiet.

Louisa was talking; he tried to take in her words.

"Can you come to dinner tomorrow, my lord?"

"I do not wish to presume upon your aunt's hospitality. Perhaps I can escort you and Mrs. Hughes—and her husband, of course—to a good hotel for the evening meal?"

Miss Crookshank smiled sunnily. "As you like—as long as you are with us. We must celebrate this happy event!"

Why did his mouth feel dry? "I shall make plans for a party of four," he agreed.

"Oh, only three," she corrected.

He lifted his brows.

"My aunt is a widow, you see," the girl said, her tone bright. "But we will both enjoy your escort amazingly."

Mrs. Hughes was a widow? "But earlier, you mentioned your uncle," he reminded Louisa.

"Oh yes, you will need to speak to my uncle—he lives in Bath with his family. He has been my guardian since my dear father died. But I am sure he will raise no objection to our match."

John glanced toward the woman who stood, her back turned to them, conversing at surely unnecessary lengths with her servant. She was a widow. No husband, no marital bond, no impediment to another man who might want—

He felt the small hand on his arm, its grip as firm as an anchor which could immobilize a great sailing ship. His expression surely arrested, he looked down into the smiling face of the comely Miss Crookshank.

"We shall expect you at seven," she told him.

After the marquess left, looking as weary as she herself felt, Marianne rang to request a soothing cup of tea for Louisa, with a dollop of brandy added. Marianne walked up

to the guest chamber with Louisa and told the girl, "I want you to lie down for an hour. You've had a great shock."

This time, Louisa did not argue. "Yes, it has been a most fatiguing day," she agreed, sighing. "A perfect day, if I had not been so stupid. To think that of all the women in London, I should insult one of Almack's patronesses!"

"No, no, I meant the runaway horse." Marianne didn't know whether to laugh or to groan with exasperation. "I want you to put away all thoughts of the afternoon's calamity and think of something pleasant."

"Oh, I shall do that! Thank heavens I still have the marquess." Louisa sighed heavily. "Without his proposal, I think I could not bear to go on living."

"Don't be ridiculous!" Marianne snapped, with more vigor than she'd intended. The girl would be ordering her bridal clothes, next. "You must not read too much into his rescue. He would hardly stand by and watch you be run down. But that does not mean that he is certain to offer for you . . . you must not depend on it, not yet."

Louisa looked determined. "But he did, Aunt, just now."

Marianne's patience snapped. "You cannot be serious! I turn my back for five minutes and you manage to secure an offer of marriage?"

Louisa's ready tears brimmed her big blue eyes and threatened to overflow again. She looked anxiously at her aunt. "Don't you think he cares for me? He would not jest about such a serious matter, surely?"

Marianne gave herself a mental shake—she felt downright dizzy with shock.

"Are you telling me that Lord Gillingham has asked for your hand?"

Louisa nodded.

"Oh my God." Marianne sat down upon the edge of the bed. "I don't mean to—that is, really, Louisa, you've only just met Lord Gillingham. It's much too early to be thinking of accepting an offer from the man. Your uncle will never agree."

"He must!" Louisa interrupted. "It's a wonderful match—how could Uncle Charles not approve?"

"Perhaps he will, in time, but it's too soon, Louisa!"

"But I am ready to accept him. Surely, you cannot mean to forbid me." Louisa lifted her chin with the stubborn look that Marianne knew only too well. And the girl would be twenty-one before the end of the year; she would need no one's approval, then. Trying to think, Marianne stalled for time.

"Of course I will not forbid it. I will write to Charles and seek his counsel—he is the one who is really your guardian, after all. But I think he will agree with me . . . you must spend more time with Lord Gillingham to be sure of your feelings. I do not want to see you hurt, my dear."

Louisa smiled. "I will not be."

Marianne had a sudden sense of déjà vu; this was just how she had felt about Harry. Oh yes, she remembered being that young and that certain. Eons ago. She sighed. "I hope not. But in the meantime, we will make no public announcements yet, no puffing it off in the *Times,* agreed?"

"Oh, very well. But we shall celebrate tomorrow. He is taking us to dinner."

"Dinner?"

"Yes, at a nice hotel, so he doesn't presume upon us, he said. But we should invite him to dinner here, soon, dearest Aunt, don't you agree? Perhaps plan a real dinner party."

"Perhaps," Marianne agreed, her voice suddenly sounding as hollow as she felt inside. She pulled the curtains across the window and left her ward to her musing; she wasn't sure the younger woman even noticed her go.

Then, at last, she could go to her own room and lie down upon the coverlet, and stare up at the pale blue curtains that hung about her bed. She tried to think of commonplace things, as she had advised Louisa to do. It had been a most fatiguing day; she was very glad they had no engagement for dinner.

Louisa. Engaged. To the marquess.

The man wasted no time in his pursuit. Was he truly in love with Louisa? And, why not? If not in love, at least smitten with her beauty and youth and bubbly charm—which would be more than enough for most men. In addition, she had a handsome fortune to bring with her. There was no reason for any sensible man not to desire her hand in marriage.

What man would pass up a beautiful young lady with a fortune for an older one with a smaller purse, with more lines upon her face and more cares upon her soul?

Marianne remembered the moment of attraction between them—she was sure she had not imagined it—in the front hall. It had been so—so intense, so amazing, so unexpected. From the beginning, she had—despite her better judgment—admired his aura of strength and his restrained intensity. But she had not expected to feel so drawn, so hungry for his touch, to dream of seeing the man shed that unfashionable coat and ridiculously threadbare linen so that she might gaze upon a torso that, judging by his handling of the runaway steed, must be as firm and well muscled as a blacksmith's . . .

She bit her lip. No, no, this would not do. She had a clear obligation in the matter. The man was courting—had actually proposed to—her niece by marriage. Marianne was the older, wiser woman; she could not allow herself to be distracted by an instant of carnal appeal. After all, how much did such things matter, in the long run? Marriage involved so much more. This would be a most advantageous match, because even if Louisa did enjoy wealth and beauty, her family lineage was not distinguished, and to snare a marquess, of all things, would be considered by the world as an amazing coup.

Marianne tried to imagine Louisa as Lady Gillingham, to picture the girl at the altar while the marquess smiled down at her and reached for her hand. . . . The image was so painful that she pushed it aside.

Trying to distract herself, Marianne reflected more deeply on the marquess' shabby appearance. Why would he pay so little heed to his apparel? Was it possible that the man was not rich, after all, despite all the rumors of great wealth? Could he possibly be attracted to Louisa's tidy fortune? Legally, a husband controlled all his wife's assets.

She could not see him as a fortune hunter, but as a conscientious guardian, even a temporary one, she would have to make some discreet inquiries before this engagement became official, Marianne told herself. She had to remember her duties.

Duty, yes. She was duty-bound to aid Louisa, and that was that. She no longer had any real qualms about Lord Gillingham's character; she had seen no hint of cruelty or selfishness or vice in him, although his rush to marry puzzled her a little. His deep reserve hid something, yes, but she did not think he was an evil man. In fact, she thought he was a better man than he knew, and she was puzzled by the unusual contradiction.

The fact that she herself might feel something unexpected for the marquess—it was shameful, it was improper, it was downright pathetic! What a fool she would look, at her age, if anyone fancied that she was setting her cap for a man of such rank!

Even if his dress did make him look like a common tradesman . . . at least, until one met those deep dark eyes and commanding gaze . . .

They must do something about that. Louisa was too entranced to realize it, just yet, but eventually she would, and Marianne had no wish to see her young charge embarrassed by the marquess's lack of town polish. As she had told him, it was simple enough to acquire; she was sure he had the wit, the good sense, the taste to accomplish it. Perhaps with a little help . . .

And thinking of tailors and haberdashers, Marianne put aside her own feelings and tried to believe, lying alone in her solitary bed, that all was well and she had no wish for anything more.

Seven

Being unhappy in a large house
is little better than being unhappy in a small one,
even if the service is better.

—MARGERY, COUNTESS OF SEALEY

The next day Marianne made sure that
Louisa spent a quiet morning, but after a light luncheon, as they planned their dress for dinner, Louisa suffered
a sudden setback of nerves. It was not a delayed reaction to
the near accident of the day before; instead, it had to do
with the delicate question of ribbons.

"I thought I could wear the pink ribbons that I bought
last week, but when I look at my new dinner dress—and I
do wish to look well tonight, this is my betrothal dinner, after all, at least until we make a formal announcement and
can hold a ball—it is not at all the same shade of pink,"
Louisa insisted.

They were in the girl's room staring at her bed, which
was almost hidden beneath layers of gowns, petticoats, and
various items of a delicate nature, as Louisa wasted no effort in assembling the perfect outfit.

Marianne found herself heartily sick of discussions
about clothing. "Then wear the white ribbons," she suggested. "You have the pink rosebuds which his lordship
so generously sent over this morning. You can tuck a few

of those into your hair, and it will be quite perfect."

"But it will be even more perfect if the ribbon were pink, and the correct hue," Louisa insisted.

Marianne tried not to gnash her teeth. "Louisa, we were going to the countess of Sealey's house for tea."

"But it would only take a few minutes for a quick trip to the draper's shop on Bond Street," Louisa begged.

Marianne frowned. She was, by now, familiar with Louisa's shopping trips, and they were never a matter of minutes. She had been looking forward to meeting some old friends at the countess's weekly tea.

"Please, Aunt? I do so want to look quite perfect."

The girl's blue eyes were clear, with no betraying laugh lines around them, and her complexion completely flawless. Marianne considered pointing out that the bloom of youth and good health was much more guaranteed to please a gentleman than ribbons of any shade at all. But she knew that Louisa would not heed her.

"You may go to the shop. You can take Eva and Masters with you," she decided suddenly. "I will keep our commitment to Lady Sealey."

"Oh, thank you, dearest Aunt." Louisa beamed.

So, after summoning a hackney, they set out in different directions, Marianne on foot with her own lady's maid, and Louisa with her entourage of servants. While they strolled toward the countess's large house in a square a short distance away, Hackett sniffed.

"Always in the shops, that girl is," she muttered.

"She's young," Marianne said. "And she has an ample allowance—she might as well enjoy it."

Her maid sniffed again, but Marianne turned her head to gaze at a handsome bed of daffodils and pretended not to notice.

When they approached the countess's front door, flanked by its white columns, Marianne felt her spirits lift. Inside, she nodded to the footman who had opened the door, allowed Hackett to take her pelisse and gloves, and then made her way up the wide stairs to the drawing room.

When she entered, her hostess—lovely in a lavender

gown with a trim that matched her silver hair, dressed high today in a somewhat old-fashioned style that still became her—smiled.

"Marianne, my dear, how lovely to see you. I had thought you were settled in Bath for several more weeks."

"That had been my plan, but I was given a charge to carry out, so I came back to plunge into the gaiety of the Season." Marianne made her curtsy, then accepted a kiss on the cheek.

"And this is why you sound so grim? You are forced into merriment, and it displeases you?" the countess inquired, her tone severe but her faded blue eyes sparkling with her usual good humor.

Marianne managed a laugh. "Of course not. I mean, I do not usually care that much for the Season, but—"

"But that is because you do not take full advantage of it." Lady Sealey gestured to her guest to sit. Marianne took the chair next to the countess and accepted a cup of tea and a plate of small cakes from a footman, resplendent in crimson livery.

"I've been telling you for years, dear girl, that you should take more advantage of the men who cast admiring glances your way."

Marianne rolled her eyes. "And there are so many of them."

The countess shot her a mock-stern glance. "You would have much greater enjoyment of the balls and parties if you had a man or two with which to flirt."

"Or three or four? Why stop there?" Marianne took a bite of cake. "I could enlist a whole regiment."

"Be serious, my dear," the countess scolded. "I am a firm believer in discretion, but nonetheless, there are sweeter things in life than petit fours."

Swallowing her pastry, Marianne took a sip of tea. "No doubt, but cakes are much easier to come by."

"Now, Marianne," the older woman admonished. "I am sure that you are ignoring many interesting gentlemen."

"Like old Sir Roderick, who stands on his tiptoes to peer down my neckline whenever I am nearby? Or what's his name, the stout poet with the fractured verses and round belly who followed me around after Harry died?" Marianne quipped. Sometimes it was a relief to be quite honest with another woman; men required such tactful handling, or at least, her husband had. And his sulks had been such a nuisance, she had tried not to upset him. "I felt little temptation to dally with such as he!"

"Of course not, I would not suggest that you waste your favors on inferior persons, but there are better men out there," Lady Sealey promised, sipping her own tea.

Unbidden, the image of the marquess came into her mind's eye. Marianne pushed it hastily away. "Not for me," she murmured.

The countess raised her brows.

"I mean, I have been entrusted with a young relation to chaperone for the Season; it is her possible suitors I have to pay heed to," Marianne explained. "She was called elsewhere this afternoon, but I will introduce her to you, if I may, very soon."

"Ah, I see." Lady Sealey nodded. "I shall look forward to it. One has responsibilities, of course. But do not forget your own needs, my dear. You are too young to forswear pleasure entirely and spend *all* your time doing charitable deeds. You need a good man beside you."

"I had a good man," Marianne reminded her. "And I mourned his death sincerely."

As the countess knew well; Marianne had met Lady Sealey several years ago after Harry's death. She had found the older woman, a widow herself, very much in sympathy with others who were bereaved, and helpful in advice and support as the new widows gathered their courage and remade their lives. Some of Marianne's deepest friendships had been made inside this salon. Not all of the women here were widows, of course, but many were or had been, and the women who assembled at the countess's weekly gatherings were sometimes called, jocularly, the Merry Widows.

"But I had to go on, and to be truthful, life is much more easily arranged when one has only oneself to consider."

"I said a good man, my dear. You had a nice boy, I think," the countess argued gently. "You married young, did you not? I do not think you really know what it is to have the love of a man."

Marianne blinked and for a moment was not sure how to respond. Should she confess her conflicted feelings for her own niece's fiancé? No, that would make her sound totally devoid of principle. Fortunately, another guest entered the room, and Lady Sealey turned to chat with the new arrival.

Marianne moved across the room to speak with several friends. Therese LaSalle, a vivacious redhead who had been one of the party at Vauxhall the night of Marianne and Louisa's excursion, asked about Louisa.

"How is your charming niece doing, Marianne? Still in raptures over London's urban delights?"

"Oh, yes," Marianne agreed, thinking, *over his lordship's courtship, especially,* but she could not remark upon that . . . "Though she has suffered a sad setback, sad at least, on Louisa's part." She described the episode in the park with the dog—it was not as if it was not surely being talked about, anyhow, and she might as well get a version more favorable to Louisa circulating—ending with, "It's a shame, and it really was not Louisa's fault. The poor dog ran right beneath her feet, and fortunately, it was not injured."

Therese, who adored animals, nodded. *"Le pauvre chien!* I am relieved to hear it. It's a shame that it had to be Sally Jersey. I know some people do not like her, she does chatter incessantly, and there are times when she can rush to judgment. However, I do not believe that she is truly hard-hearted. When I was newly come to London, she was most welcoming."

A tall, fair-haired beauty with classical features who stood nearby had apparently overheard; she moved closer to join their tête-à-tête. "But she does hold a grudge, I fear. If my aunt were in town, she might persuade her to relent. I think Aunt Sophie is one of the few females that Sally does not dare to contradict. But as it is, I fear your niece will have to be patient if she wishes for the opportunity to obtain vouchers to Almack's."

Marianne nodded. "I agree; it would not be prudent to apply to one of the other patronesses just now. Lady Jersey would think we were trying to go behind her back and become even more incensed. She might never forgive poor Louisa. And for new applicants, it takes two of the patronesses to agree, if I remember." Marianne tried to recall the name of this elegant blond with whom she was speaking; Marianne had chatted with her briefly at previous teas. Not a widow, Marianne remembered; not every woman here was bereaved. The countess had many friends. The name came suddenly to her mind—Lady Gabriel Sinclair. *Sinclair?*

Of course, the marquess had mentioned her name at Vauxhall. Marianne studied the woman with more interest. "I believe I have met one of your, that is, your husband's relations," she said.

Lady Gabriel lifted her perfect brows. "Really?"

"Lord Gillingham," Marianne explained. "We were—ah—introduced the night he was part of your party at Vauxhall Gardens, and since then he has been to call and has been most attentive to my niece."

Why did the newcomer's expression turn so thoughtful? But after a pause, Lady Gabriel nodded.

"Of course, I was only surprised—that is, he is newly come to town and has not yet made many new acquaintances. I am happy to hear that he has ventured out a little," the other woman said.

"Lord Gabriel has a brother?" Therese's eyes sparkled. "Is he as handsome and charming as your so-amazing husband, Lady Gabriel?"

The other woman hesitated. "He has his own particular charms, I believe."

Therese interpreted this correctly. "Ah, a shame if he has not Lord Gabriel's so beautiful looks, but it's often so with siblings. One gets all the cream at the top of the milk, and the rest must make do. At least, he must have the same polished appeal? But I should not ask you such a thing; how could you compare the two, when your own still-new husband is so dear to you?"

Lady Gabriel smiled. "In truth, I don't know my brother-in-law very well. He has not come to London in the past, but I am hoping to become better acquainted with him this Season."

"No doubt Lord Gabriel is pleased to have his brother in town," Marianne suggested. She handed her teacup to a passing servant and accepted one more scone from a silver tray.

"Umm . . ." Lady Gabriel paused, turning to gaze at the servant's offering. "No doubt. What wonderful pastries Lady Sealey's cook concocts."

"Of course, he is French," agreed the outspoken Therese, who was also, but she would not be diverted. "Are the brothers not in sympathy?"

"My husband spent several years abroad, so they have been separated for some time. I am hoping to see them become closer," Lady Gabriel said.

Therese seemed poised to question her further, but a conversation among another knot of ladies chatting nearby caught her attention.

"Lucy, do not tell me that your husband has really declined the offer of a greater title from the prince regent," one lady said, her voice carrying. "I hear the prince is still so grateful to your husband for—you know—the whole affair with that cursed ruby that he's eager to shower him with honors."

"Hush, Julia, you know that Richmond would never be so rude to his future monarch," the petite blond answered, but her eyes twinkled as if there was much more to the story.

"But surely, you have something to say about it, too," her friend argued.

"Do you think that I am not perfectly content to be a viscountess?" The fair-haired lady chuckled. "In fact, just being Nicolas's wife is quite enough honor—and delight—for me."

Therese's brows lifting in ready curiosity, she turned to join the other women and hear the rest of the chat.

Now Marianne could speak quietly for one woman's ears, only. "I don't wish to be inquisitive, Lady Gabriel, but I believe—that is—my niece sees Lord Gillingham in the light of a serious suitor."

Lady Gabriel raised her light-hued brows. "Really? My felicitations. His rank and estate should please any lady."

"I am more concerned with his character." Marianne could be blunt, too, when the occasion demanded. "I do not wish Louisa to regret her choice. You have heard Lady Sealey speak on unwise choices."

Lady Gabriel looked thoughtful. "She is quite right that one should choose carefully, Mrs. Hughes. To be equally candid, I know nothing to his discredit except that my husband says that his brother bullied him as a lad. And that is not unusual among small boys."

There seemed something more hanging at the edge of her tongue, but she paused.

Marianne hesitated. "And now that they are men, does Lord Gabriel still feel that his brother is overbearing? I would not ask, except for concern about my niece."

"I'm not sure," the other woman said slowly. "They have not been close for years, and only recently have they spent time together."

Marianne knew that her own brows had knitted. What could have brought such a falling out? Although she felt the question too personal to ask; even when unspoken, it hung in the air between them.

"It was their father," Lady Gabriel explained. "He was not the most exemplary of men, and he was not an affectionate parent. When my husband committed a youthful transgression, Gabriel was disinherited. His brother, the present Lord Gillingham, did not support him, and the rejection still rankles."

"That is understandable," Marianne agreed. She sighed. "I don't know. We have spent a little time in his company, and the marquess does not seem to me a vicious person. But I also feel that there is much beneath the surface that he does not wish to share—and Louisa is truly naive, even more so than most young ladies in their first Season."

"At least she has your guidance," Lady Gabriel pointed out. "Some mothers, or aunts, would be interested only in

Lord Gillingham's estate, wealth, and title. If you will forgive me for speaking frankly, I am glad that he has made
the acquaintance of a young lady who is not ruled only by
greed or a desire to improve her station."

Marianne smiled a bit ruefully. "Louisa has her faults,
like all of us, but she is not greedy, nor does she need to
marry for money." She thought it might be best not to delve
into Louisa's expressed interest in the man's title. "And to
be equally candid, Lady Gabriel, I think a good many of
the world's ills, and many a family misunderstanding,
could be avoided by an honest talk."

"A commendable sentiment." The other woman nodded.
"And please, call me Psyche. I have a feeling that we may
be seeing more of each other, and the prospect pleases
me." Her clear blue eyes sparkled.

Marianne found that she liked this woman's intelligence
and directness of manner. "And you must call me Marianne."

By the time Marianne made her farewells to the countess,
she felt that the afternoon had been profitable. She had no
more worries about the marquess's lack of wealth, or that
he might be interested in Louisa only for the fortune she
would soon inherit. Which only led her back to the central
question of his character. She still wondered a little about
that, even though she did not think him mean-spirited. But
something dark hung over him, and Marianne would much
like to know what it was that sometimes, out of nowhere,
shadowed his face.

Did she wonder for Louisa, or for herself?

A nonsensical question, she was only concerned for her
niece, of course. What did her own feelings have to do with
it? If there was no obvious impediment to the proposal, she
was duty-bound to aid her niece in securing such an advantageous match. But only in time, and she would not allow
Louisa to rush into a hasty marriage.

So she steeled herself to a cool propriety as they prepared for the dinner. Louisa's shopping expedition had

been successful, even if she had had to visit three shops before locating the exact shade she desired. The younger woman merrily described her arduous pursuit of the perfect ribbon, and Marianne nodded and maintained her air of interest. At least the girl was no longer moping over the Lady Jersey debacle.

When the marquess arrived in his fancy barouche, they were both ready. This time, the top had been raised, since the air had cooled with sunset. They rode to the hotel that the marquess had selected—he had obviously been inquiring about fashionable meeting spots—and were shown into a private parlor, where a fire burned merrily on the hearth and the linen on the table was spotless, the host obsequious as he bowed them into the room.

Allowing the servant to take her wrap, Marianne pulled off her gloves before accepting a glass of wine. She sipped it as she listened to Louisa being her most charming and well-mannered self and the marquess responding appropriately. He had greeted Marianne politely but otherwise said little to her, and if she felt somewhat bereft, she scolded herself for it.

It was only proper that he would direct most of his attention toward her niece, the woman he had just offered for. Nor would Marianne respect him if he tried to court both women! Rakes and Lotharios she had absolutely no esteem for, so she was most pleased that he behaved with choice and discretion, she assured herself. And if he seemed a bit distant with her tonight, it was understandable. It was not easy for one man to entertain two women at one time, especially if the man himself was quiet by nature and obviously unused to his role as host.

At least indoors, in the softer glow of candlelight, he had put aside the wide-brimmed hat with which he often shielded his face from strangers' too observant eyes. But his costume was still as unfashionable and ill fitting as ever. Did the man not realize how well his wide shoulders would look in a properly cut coat? She had to find a way to convince him to refurbish his wardrobe, now that she was sure he had the funds for it.

Although the food was well prepared, the dinner seemed interminable. Sighing, Marianne accepted a helping of roast goose and thrust her fork into the crisp browned skin.

John watched her from the corner of his eye, then pulled his attention back to Louisa, who seemed unable to stop chattering. When did the child pause long enough to swallow a mouthful of food? Would this dinner stretch on till the spring flowers outside turned brown and spare with winterly chill?

John thought it likely. He had afforded the manager complete license to produce a meal suitable for two discerning ladies of quality, and the man apparently had determined to lavishly uphold the honor of his chef, not to mention inflate his bill as much as possible. The courses were many, and the side dishes alone ample for feeding a small cavalry troop.

And meanwhile, John had to focus his attention on Miss Crookshank, undoubtably alluring in palest pink, with some of the rosebuds he had sent her now beribboned and tucked into her fair hair. While she smiled and blushed and rattled on, he was duty-bound to pay heed to her ramblings on shops and amusements and coming balls.

To his alarm he found that what he really wanted was to gaze upon her companion, whose calm demeanor hid more interesting thoughts, he was somehow sure, and whose appearance, her darker hair and lovely face flattered by a gown of deep ruby-red, made his pulse beat faster. But he could not regard her as closely as he would have wished because the girl at his elbow, the young lady he had so rashly chosen with such precipitate haste, gazed up at him in patent adoration. He cursed his own need to escape the rigors of the capital, with its keen-eyed, sharped-tongued Society, and the speed with which he had, even if inadvertently, bound himself to a stranger.

Louisa had come in with more thanks and praise to offer. To his great discomfiture, she had called him her hero.

"No, no," John said. "The merest trifle."

Her blue eyes widened. "To jump in front of a charging steed? It was the most gallant, the most intrepid thing I have ever seen. A knight saving a damsel from a dragon could not have been more brave. To risk your life for me—"

John shifted restlessly. "I assure you, I took little risk."

Louisa smiled at him, her expression angelic. "It was a marvelous feat of courage, and I shall never forget it! I know that I will be perfectly safe with you, always, my lord."

He wished she would direct her soulful gaze back down at her plate of roast goose and boiled lobster. But Louisa had eaten little; she seemed much more anxious to keep his attention riveted. She had explained earlier her aunt's request for a delay in the announcement.

"We must write to my uncle and seek his blessing," she told him. "But I'm sure there will be no objection made."

"Of course," he agreed. "I should have spoken to him first. I did not realize that your guardian was—was not Mrs. Hughes's husband."

Still smiling, Louisa nodded. His new fiancée seemed to read nothing additional into that statement, although John was beginning to suspect it was the biggest blunder of his life.

Instead, she chatted about wedding plans. He tried not to wince.

Almost absentmindedly, he leaned forward as if to pay more heed to her comments. In so doing, his wineglass tipped a bit too far. The ruby-colored liquid spilled upon her pale-hued gown.

Miss Crookshank squealed in dismay.

"My apologies," John said quickly. He pushed back his chair and waved to the footman hovering nearby. "Fetch a maid, at once, who can take this lady to a private chamber and see to her gown."

His betrothed had at last lost her sweet smile; she frowned down at the stain on her skirt. "It is ruined!"

"It was entirely my fault," he told her. "A moment of inexcusable carelessness—I was listening too closely to your comments. You have my deepest apologies, Miss Crookshank. You must allow me to replace the gown."

Louisa shook her head, though she still struggled to

regain her usual cheery serenity. "It is of little import, my lord. Please do not trouble yourself."

A maidservant had appeared, and the marquess turned to her. "See what you can do to aid this lady," he directed.

The servant curtsied quickly. "Oh, miss, let me sponge that with soda water—we'll have you right as rain in no time, we will."

Mrs. Hughes had pushed back her chair and seemed ready to follow her ward out of the room. John put out one hand, assured that the others were too absorbed to notice, and murmured, "No, stay, if you please."

She looked at him in surprise, but, happily, she seemed as quick-witted as ever and made no comment to attract attention. But when the younger lady, with the servant still chattering of what could be done to alleviate the damage to the muslin gown, disappeared through the doorway, Mrs. Hughes drew back just a little, her expression wary.

What on earth was this about? Marianne watched the marquess as he strode back to his chair at the head of the table. He hesitated for a moment as if unsure of how to proceed.

She broke the silence first. "You did that deliberately."

He looked up at her.

"Spilling the wine, you did it on purpose. Why? I mean, Louisa's praises might have become a bit tedious, but that was an extreme reaction."

He gave one of his rare smiles, but he did not deny her charge. Instead, he reached inside his coat and pulled out a glove, holding it out to her.

She stared at it, still confused. "What?"

He nodded toward a stain on the dark leather. "Look closer," he suggested. "I didn't note it until I had returned you and Miss Crookshank to your home. But if you examine it carefully, you will detect what disturbs me."

Marianne touched the glove; the dark stain felt sticky against her fingertips. She gasped. "Is it—blood?"

Eight

*B**lood?*

He didn't answer, but he didn't have to; his expression was grim.

Marianne's eyes widened. "Did you injure yourself when you grasped the runaway, my lord? I am not surprised—I mean, I feared as much when you jumped at the charging beast—but I do hope the wound is not serious?"

He held out his hands, palms up, for her to inspect. She saw no sign of a cut or scratch.

"I have some bruises from the encounter, but nothing of import," he said. "No, I think the blood that stained my glove came from the horse. I think the animal was hurt by some sharp object, perhaps a tossed stone or even a blade."

She wrinkled her brow, trying to follow his logic. His tone was grave, something of more significance than a wounded steed disturbed him.

"You think that a child in the park tossed a stone and that caused the horse to bolt?"

"Perhaps. Or perhaps the horse's injury was deliberate," he told her. "I am most likely being too cautious. I admit that is my nature. But can you tell me if anyone would wish to harm Miss Crookshank?"

Her first impulse was to laugh. This was too nonsensical. But then the seriousness of his expression subdued her first moment of disbelief.

Marianne shook her head, but her knees felt a little weak. She sat down in the nearest chair. "Oh, surely not! She's hardly more than a child, how could she have any enemies? Some girl her own age who envies Louisa's beauty might make a spiteful remark over a cup of tea, but an attempt on her life? Oh no, it's impossible to imagine."

"I would agree with you," he said, pulling up a chair and sitting close enough to easily meet her eyes. His own expression was still troubled. "But I saw the horse charging toward her at the park, and now that I suspect the beast was incited to its panic, it all seems too convenient to blame on a youngster throwing a stone. Besides, I don't remember seeing any children in the immediate area just before the horse bolted, do you?"

Marianne tried to think. No, nor did she, although the park had been crowded enough that perhaps they had not noticed a lad weaving through the crowd. "But it was only an accident—" She paused, and he must have read the change in her expression.

"What?"

"I just remembered. It seemed of no significance at the time. A few months ago Louisa and her uncle and Sir—and a friend had been walking in the hills near Bath. A large boulder fell from the top of the hill, narrowly missing Louisa and her friend. They were alarmed, briefly, but suffered no more than bruises when her friend pulled her out of the path of the falling rock. We put it down to a natural slippage of the earth. The area had recently had rain. Surely it was only—" Her voice faltered.

"Another accident? It seems that Miss Crookshank is encountering more than her fair share of fortuitous perils." His voice was grim.

Marianne swallowed hard. "But there is no reason for anyone to wish Louisa harm."

The silence stretched, and she heard a coal pop in the fireplace. When the marquess spoke again, he said, "I do not wish to inquire into her personal affairs, because it matters little to me, but—what is Louisa's financial condition?"

Marianne blinked. "In less than a year, when she turns one and twenty, she will inherit her father's estate."

He raised his brows.

She continued, a bit reluctantly, "Over fifty thousand pounds."

The marquess nodded. "A respectable sum."

That was putting it mildly. It was a tidy fortune to most people's eyes, and, Marianne supposed, people might have been murdered for much less. Heavens, you could venture into the wrong part of London and have your throat slit for a few shillings in your pocket. But this was not a chance encounter with a murderous thief. And that led to the next question.

Lord Gillingham voiced it. "And if Louisa were—not able to inherit—who would receive the money?"

Marianne considered. "I do not know the exact terms of her father's will, but I suppose it would go partly to my brother-in-law, her father's younger brother. And Charles would never consider such a terrible crime—he is in no need of money!"

"He's wealthy, himself?"

She bit her lip. "If he is not exactly wealthy, he is certainly comfortable. He has a house outside of Bath, and Charles is a successful barrister." Uneasily, she thought of the large family he had to support, daughters who would need dowries and sons who would need to go to university or—could Charles possibly have been tempted?

Shaking her head, Marianne exclaimed, "I cannot credit it. You must be mistaken, my lord. I have been friends with my sister-in-law since we were children—she would never consider such a thing. And I've known her husband since they began courting, over a dozen years ago. I cannot accept such a suspicion."

The marquess did not argue. "Putting aside your

brother-in-law, what about someone else who might have a claim on the inheritance?"

She tried to think. "There is another relative of her father's, an uncle, I believe, but I have never met him. There was some kind of estrangement. He lives somewhere in Scotland."

"You don't know his name or location?"

Marianne put one hand to her lip. "No," she said, her voice almost a whisper. "I don't recall."

Could it be true that somewhere, a faceless man plotted to endanger Louisa's life, hoping to inherit some of her wealth? It was a horrifying thought. Marianne felt a chill run over her, and she shivered.

The marquess leaned forward to take her hand. "I may be quite wrong, you know," he said, his voice soothing. "Perhaps I have simply allowed my imagination to run amok. If so, I have distressed you for no reason."

But he was not a fanciful man, Marianne told herself. And she believed him; if he had not been truly worried, he would never have brought up the possibility.

"It's just that Louisa is here in London for the first time in her life, and I am the only one she has to look out for her. It was a big charge to begin with, and if there is even the faintest chance that she is in danger, I—well, I feel inadequate—" She stopped.

It was not his fault that she felt suddenly overwhelmed. Nor did she want the man to think she was imploring his help, even though the touch of his hand was enormously comforting. How did she sense his strength, his energy, even through such a light touch?

"I don't suppose she could consider returning to Bath?" he asked.

Marianne laughed a little wildly. "You have no idea how fervently Louisa wanted to come to London. She would never consider leaving so soon. And we have only the merest suspicion—besides, if these accidents are not chance events, as they most likely are, then the first one occurred in Bath, so I do not see how returning there would help."

She shut her eyes, feeling a tremor of concern.

"I am no doubt being overcautious," the marquess said. "I am sorry to have alarmed you."

"Any danger seems most unlikely, but we cannot dismiss it out of hand," she said, sighing. "I will write to my sister-in-law and ask for more details about the uncle." And if he turned out to be some elderly, frail cleric living in Edinburgh, then what? she thought.

Most of the time, Marianne found her single state acceptable. She could handle her household without a male's guidance, she could travel through England as far as her funds allowed, she faced the usual small annoyances of life calmly. The bigger dreams she had once dreamed—those she had put aside, and, really, they seldom infringed upon her contentment, or so she tried to tell herself.

But in a moment of crisis, she was reminded of how much she would like to have another adult with whom to share such crucial decisions. Not that Harry had ever been much help in a domestic crisis, and they had never faced any serious emergency during their short marriage. But still—

She was annoyed to find that her eyes had dampened; she blinked hard against betraying moisture. But he must have seen her moment of weakness, because, her eyes still closed, Marianne felt a light touch on her cheek as he wiped away the one drop of liquid that had escaped her control.

Marianne's eyelids flew open. The marquess had leaned even closer, bringing his face only a few inches from her own. His expression was troubled, and his brown eyes seemed as dusky as a bottomless pool, their center reflecting the flickering light of the nearby candles. She thought she saw solicitude and perhaps some other emotion inside them, but no sign of scorn for her frailty.

His grip on her hand had tightened; she felt the warmth of his skin against her own ungloved fingers, and suddenly it was hard to breathe. He was so close . . . she could smell just a trace of his masculine odor, not at all unpleasing, a blend of soap and clean linen but with a hint of healthy male skin beneath his ill-fitting apparel.

She could lose herself in his eyes . . . forget the rest of the world and sink into their deep brown darkness, the warm comforting darkness where, the poets said, a man's soul dwelt. . . . What would it be like, the soul of a man whose spirit, she felt instinctively, had been wounded long ago? Would she find him bitter in his heart of hearts over the hurt he hid so carefully, or did he hunger for a loving touch from a woman who—no, this was madness!

With an effort, she pulled her glance away from the mesmerizing dark gaze and allowed it to travel over his well-shaped brows and high forehead and the dark brown lock of hair that had fallen over it, hair that in the sunlight showed glints of gold. Her gaze slid back down past the strong nose, and the lips which looked so firm—how would they feel pressed against hers? She found that—without any conscious decision—her own lips had parted. She shut them at once.

Afraid she was blushing, she dropped her stare even lower; his chin was strong, with a hint of a cleft, suggesting an equally strong will and a man used to taking charge. After scanning his face, Marianne realized she had hardly noted the scars left from his old illness; when one became accustomed to his face, they were such a small part of the whole. His skin, somewhat browned by his habit of spending time outside, was clean shaven, though she suspected that his beard would have the glint of gold if he ever allowed it to grow.

These thoughts were entirely too personal. Trying to distract herself, she lowered her eyes again, glancing at the broad shoulders and the upper arms that she knew held such strength. No, this was dangerous, as well; she moved her gaze and saw his chest rise and fall. Was he breathing quickly, too? She felt an unusual tightness in her chest, and farther down, an unaccustomed ache deep in her belly that made her heart pound and the air in the dining parlor seem overheated. She suspected that it was not the fire that warmed her now, but the well-made frame, covered so fittingly by toned muscle, of the man who leaned so near to her.

She wanted to touch his face. She wanted his hand to stroke her cheek again, to caress her lips. She wanted him to lean even closer and touch those lips with his own. She wanted to throw her arms about his neck—

A coal popped again in the fireplace, and Marianne jumped.

"My dear," the marquess murmured, in a tone she had never heard from him. By some small miracle he lifted his hand once more toward her face.

Marianne shook her head, trying to emerge from this strange spell. "We must think of Louisa," she said, a bit too loudly, trying to bring the specter of her duty between them, to remind him of the lovely young girl he had chosen to offer for and whom he could not have forgotten so quickly. "With so little to go on, I do not think we should tell her that her life might be in danger."

He dropped his hand, but before he could answer, another sound made Marianne turn.

Louisa herself stood in the doorway, holding a napkin to the damp spot in her gown, which the servant had cleaned. Her expression was alarmed.

"I am in danger?"

Marianne jerked back, trying to put more distance between herself and the marquess. He stood quickly, and she hoped they did not both look as guilty as she felt. It was not what it seemed, she thought wildly. If Louisa thought—

But the girl threw herself forward, running across the room to cast herself into the arms of the startled marquess.

"Oh, my lord, you must protect me! Who would wish to harm me?" She hid her face against his chest and sobbed.

The expression on Lord Gillingham's face twisted, as he glanced from her to Marianne. Marianne took a deep breath. Standing, too, although her knees still felt like butter, she hurried to comfort her ward while the marquess awkwardly patted the girl's back.

"Do not be alarmed, Louisa," Marianne told her. "It is most likely nothing, and we will look after you."

And she would remember just what her own duties were, Marianne told herself. That moment of insanity was only—well, she had been disturbed, and the marquess had felt sympathy for her, that was all. She had no right—no right at all—to read more into it than that.

"You are the dearest aunt in the world," Louisa blurted, reaching out one hand to Marianne, while still clinging to the marquess. "I know you will—both of you—never fail me!"

Marianne swallowed hard.

And the man Louisa clung to so tightly looked over her head to meet Marianne's gaze, and what she saw in his eyes this time, she really could not have said.

Soon afterward, since none of them seemed to have an appetite for dessert, the marquess saw them safely home. Louisa was unusually subdued. Marianne wished for the dozenth time that she had not spoken so loudly, that the girl had not returned at such an inopportune moment . . . inopportune in more ways than one! But Louisa seemed not to have noticed how close the marquess had been leaning, nor the heat that had flushed her aunt's cheek. Marianne told herself that such an awkward scene would never happen again; she would see to it.

Perhaps the marquess struggled with some guilty thoughts of his own; at any rate, no one spoke more than barest civility allowed. When he walked them to their door and said good night, Louisa clung to his hand.

"You will call again soon, my lord, will you not?" She sounded so forlorn that Marianne felt another stab of guilt.

He patted the girl's hand. "I will call tomorrow, I promise." Then the door shut behind him, and the marquess was gone.

Louisa sighed, and Marianne had to bite her lip not to do the same. Shabby clothes or not, he carried such an air of substance about him. She felt safe when he was there, and that was an indulgence she had not allowed herself in years. It did not do to depend on another person's strength; sometimes, the strength was only an illusion, as it had been with her young, feckless husband. No, she could take care of herself, she would take care of herself. But Louisa was another story. Marianne had taken on an immense responsibility when she had accepted the temporary guardianship of her niece, and now it looked even more vast than she had imagined.

Could it be possible that someone wished the girl harm?

Shaking her head, Marianne took one look at the younger woman's wan expression and made her tone deliberately brisk and matter-of-fact. "A warm glass of milk, I think, to help repose your mind before bed."

Louisa gave a reluctant giggle. "I'm not ten years old, Aunt."

"No, but warm milk is helpful at any age," Marianne insisted. "With a dash of nutmeg, you'll find it very soothing."

"Only if you come up and talk with me for a time," Louisa said, and her voice trembled a little.

"I will," Marianne promised.

Giving Masters the request for the milk, Marianne slowly climbed the stairs to change into her dressing gown. Hackett helped her out of the tight-fitting evening frock and pulled the pins from her hair. Marianne nodded a dismissal. "Will you check on the warm milk, please, Hackett?"

By the time Marianne reached the guest room, Louisa had also shed her evening dress and was sitting before the looking glass while her maid brushed out the shining blond hair. Marianne waited, and soon Marianne's dresser entered with two glasses of milk on a silver tray.

"I took the liberty of bringing one for you, ma'am, as well," she told her mistress, allowing a hint of concern to show through her usual impassive facade. Did Marianne look as weary as she felt?

"Thank you, Hackett," Marianne said. "You don't have to wait up."

Hackett nodded and made her exit. Louisa thanked her own lady's maid, who slipped out of the room, too, and in a moment, the two were alone.

Marianne—feeling like a coward—put off the moment of truth by gesturing toward the tray. "Do try the milk while it's still warm, Louisa. It's quite pleasant and will help ease your nerves after a trying day."

Louisa took a long drink of the milk as she was bade, then set down the glass. "Aunt Marianne—" Louisa began.

Marianne braced herself.

"Why do you think I am in danger?"

Marianne released the breath she had, without realizing it, been holding. The waver in the younger woman's voice revealed genuine concern, perhaps even fear.

"I don't know, Louisa. His lordship is concerned about the runaway horse. And there was the falling rock in Bath. Perhaps it was only an accident; such things do happen."

"But two accidents—" Louisa argued.

"They were almost three months apart," Marianne countered. "And they were very different. It may be nothing. I would not refine too much upon it."

She would write to her sister-in-law before she retired, and the letter would go out by special post tomorrow. In the meantime they would certainly be vigilant, Marianne told herself as she watched Louisa sigh. Just in case the unthinkable might be true, and someone, somewhere, lay in wait to harm Louisa.

The thought troubled her sleep, and Marianne woke early, going over some of the ideas that had sprung up during her long intervals of sleeplessness, when even the remotest suggestion of danger somehow took on nightmarish proportions. Some she discarded, though reluctantly. Hiring a Bow Street Runner to watch her modest town house and to shadow Louisa—even though she did have the finances as long as she had access to Louisa's trust fund—would only call attention to them and incur more gossip, which would distress Louisa. Besides, the idea of a burly bodyguard stalking about outside a tea party seemed insane. In the warm light of day, such measures seemed like obvious overreaction. Nor could they keep Louisa shut up inside the house forever, although Marianne would try to keep a close eye on her.

But at least Marianne could find out about this unknown

uncle. She sent the letter to Caroline on its way as soon as she rose.

When Louisa came downstairs, Marianne obtained the girl's reluctant promise to stay indoors for the morning.

"But it's a nice day, I thought perhaps a walk in the park—" the younger woman said, sounding wistful.

"Not today," Marianne said, her tone firm. "Stay inside and look through the latest edition of *La Belle Assemblée*— you might find some ideas for your next evening dress. We are going to plan a dinner party."

"Really?" Louisa brightened at once. "How many people?"

"As many as my small dining room will hold," Marianne promised. "You will be able to meet more of Society."

Louisa looked more cheerful at once. "Oh, I was so afraid you would postpone our social engagements," she confessed. "And all because of this possible threat, which on reflection, I cannot believe to be real. It is such a far-fetched notion. I know the marquess only means to protect me, and I am delighted by his solicitude—he will make a wonderful husband, don't you think? But his concern must be exaggerated."

Marianne nodded, though she dodged the central question. "We will certainly not imprison you for the entire Season, Louisa. You came to London for a purpose, and we shall see that it is not forgotten—you shall enjoy your stay."

Louisa looked appeased, and she promised to stay indoors while Marianne ran some errands of her own.

So Louisa took her second cup of tea to the drawing room and settled down with the book of fashions, calling her maid to her with her sewing basket full of snippets of fabric, threads, and laces so that they could compare hues and textures, and she could have someone to listen as she pondered the choices aloud. Marianne knew that the two young women would easily lose the morning in a long discussion of fabric, lace, trim, and matching accessories.

A discussion Marianne was just as happy to miss. She tied her bonnet snugly beneath her chin—from her bedroom window she had noted the tops of the trees tossing in a spring breeze—and drew on her gloves.

But as she walked outside, ready to set out on foot with Hackett dutifully in tow, a familiar, overly bright barouche pulled up.

The marquess!

She waited while his groom pulled open the carriage door, and Lord Gillingham stepped out. He bowed to her, and she made her curtsy in return.

"Good morning, Mrs. Hughes," he said, his tone a bit formal.

John knew he could not, must not, reveal how his pulse jumped when he saw her, her cheeks flushed from the wind, a few tendrils of dark hair escaping the confines of her brimmed bonnet to frame her face most pleasingly. And beneath the snug-fitting pelisse and morning dress, her full breasts swelled with promise . . .

He pulled his thoughts together in time to hear her explain that she had been about to pursue some errands.

"But I can put them off till later if you are calling on Miss Crookshank," she told him. "I have nothing urgent requiring my attention."

Of course, the girl should not be having male callers without her chaperone present. But John found that he was shaking his head. "I can see Miss Crookshank presently. She will be safe at home. Perhaps I should escort you on your expedition," he suggested. "It's breezy today for a lady to be out on foot."

"I would not wish to take up your time," she began, but John overrode her.

"It would be my pleasure."

She looked thoughtful. "Hackett, you may stay here—I have an escort now who will look out for me."

The maid pursed her lips in disapproval but did not contradict her mistress. "Yes, ma'am."

John helped Mrs. Hughes into the carriage, its top was up today, since the wind was brisk, and then took his place, daringly, beside her, instead of sitting opposite.

She glanced at him and did not move away, nor, of

course, did she slide closer. He should dream of such a pleasure! He reminded himself that he had come to London hoping to find, as quickly as possible, an amenable, proper young lady to take for his wife, to carry back to his secluded estate and live together without obvious discord but also without any real tenderness, as long as she would share his bed occasionally and bear him a son. That had been his plan, and he had been successful, so why did it now seem such a pale and joyless vision? The lovely Miss Crookshank was all that he had hoped to find, but that had been before he'd come to know Mrs. Hughes. Now, somehow, the dream had lost its appeal.

It did not do to dwell on the irony of it. He would marry the girl soon, just as he had originally planned, but today, this moment, he was sitting beside Marianne Hughes, smelling just a hint of her rose scent, hearing the rustle of her skirts as—avoiding his gaze—she arranged them more carefully. Could it be possible that she was nervous, too?

She cleared her throat. "I—ah—sent my maid back because I did not wish the servants to hear of our fears."

As if he would complain about being gifted with a rare chance to be alone with her! "You have thought of something new?"

"No, but I have written to my sister-in-law, asking for the name and location of the unknown relation who is in line to inherit some of Louisa's fortune, if—if something unthinkable should happen to her. I did not tell Caroline the whole of our concerns—she is increasing and already in a fragile state of mind. I do not wish to alarm her when she can do nothing from a distance."

He nodded. "Do you think she will find the request odd?"

Marianne bit her lip. "I hope not—I told her I am planning a small but select coming-out ball to take place as soon as Louisa is presented at court. And it would be only natural to include any of her relatives, even those hardly known to her, if the man should happen to be presently in London."

It made sense; many people came to the capital for the

Season, he knew, and it would not be unheard of for some-one to travel even from the wilds of Scotland.

"I shall be interested to hear her reply," he agreed, trying to pull his thoughts from the delightful curve of Mrs. Hughes' cheek. Perhaps he sounded absentminded, because her tone became more insistent.

"It might be useful to us."

"I agree—pinpointing the man's name would be help-ful." He still found his focus too inclined to linger on the soft curve of her lips, the delightful arch of her brow. And as for the swelling bosom that led down to a trim waist and womanly hips—his body threatened to reveal his too per-sonal interest.

John crossed his legs and looked away, trying hard to think of something innocuous. Outside the carriage a dog barked at a team of lumbering oxen pulling a wagon filled with coal.

"My lord," Mrs. Hughes said. "May I make a sugges-tion?"

"Of course." He fixed his attention on her face, deter-mined to look no lower and to keep his mind off her per-sonal attractions.

"I am planning a dinner party for next week. I—we—that is, Miss Crookshank, will certainly hope that you are able to attend."

He nodded, although the thought of facing their other guests, strangers who would stare at him, gave him little pleasure. "I am honored by the invitation."

"In that case, for your own ease, may I take the liberty of suggesting—" she hesitated.

John waited, not sure where this was going.

"Since you are new to town, perhaps I could suggest a good tailor? You would have time to have a new set of eve-ning clothes run up before the dinner."

John winced. "Are you implying that Miss Crookshank will be embarrassed by my lack of refinement?"

Mrs. Hughes answered quickly, her tone conciliatory. "I am sure that normally, it is of little matter, living in the coun-try and dining only with your friends and neighbors—"

Perhaps just as well she knew little about his hermit's life, John thought sourly. He suspected that Miss Crookshank was accustomed to a continuous round of gaiety. How would the young woman like living a quiet life in the country? He pushed away his misgivings and tried to focus on Mrs. Hughes's words.

"But in town, you might be more at ease with more—ah—fashionable apparel. I hope I have not offended you, my lord." She sounded anxious.

John drew a deep breath. "I will admit that I pay scant attention to fashion. It has always been of little interest to me." He rubbed his chin, absently touching the old pockmark that disfigured it, only one of those that scarred his face, then regretted the too telling gesture.

He knew she watched him, and he braced himself, afraid to look back at her and see pity, damning pity, in her smoky blue eyes.

But when he turned to face her, he encountered something else, something he had rarely dared to expect: the genuine warmth of her smile, her eyes full of easy acceptance and free of censure.

It was so intoxicating that he drew a deep breath.

The barouche pulled up. They must have reached Bond Street and too soon for his taste. A tailor fussing about him; the idea displeased him, but for Mrs. Hughes—no, no, for Miss Crookshank—he supposed he would have to make the effort.

She nodded toward the establishment. "Would you like me to come in with you, or would you prefer for me to do my errands and rejoin you in a while? I am going to my dressmaker to check on the order Louisa put in few days ago."

"I will face the rack alone, thank you," he told her, his tone dry.

She did not try to argue, wise woman! Instead, they set a time to meet again.

His groom opened the door and John stepped out, then handed down his passenger himself, relishing the momentary touch of her hand. She smiled, but with an impersonal friendliness that, after the moment of closeness inside the carriage, only made him hunger for more.

He had the ridiculous impulse to hold on to her hand, to call her back as she turned down the street. *Nonsense, get a grip on yourself, man,* he told himself sternly. John set his shoulders and entered the shop.

A dapper young man hurried up, but he frowned, looking John up and down with as much disdain as if he were a beggar asking for alms. "Perhaps you have the wrong establishment, sir? There is an ironmonger's two doors down."

John held his temper, but barely. Perhaps Mrs. Hughes was right; he was tired of being mistaken for a servant, or at best, a farmer come to town for the day.

"Please tell your employer that the marquess of Gillingham is considering bringing his trade to this shop. *If* the work done here is up to his standards—" John fixed the calfling with a steely glare, daring him to point out the disgraceful state of this new customer's existing wardrobe— "and *if* the shop has attendants who are becomingly civil."

The young man gulped. "Ah, yes, sir—that is—your lordship. I will inform him right away, your lordship. If you would care to come into a private room and take a seat? May I fetch you a glass of wine, my lord?"

John followed the man into a small fitting room, sat on the padded chair, sipped the mediocre wine that soon arrived on a silver tray, and waited.

The tailor himself, when he appeared very shortly, was even more obsequious. If he repressed a shudder, he nonetheless did not remark on his new patron's current attire. Instead, he eyed John's form with obvious appreciation.

"My lord, you are wise indeed to come to me. With such a straight posture and such shoulders, a fine chest, and, ah, such calves to your legs, oh yes, no padding will be required there, either! You shall not regret your decision, my lord." Tapping his cheek, the man appeared to lose himself in a delightful daydream, perhaps of ambitious schemes for a whole new wardrobe for a customer who had the means to pay.

"Just come to London, are you, my lord? Yes, yes, obviously. You will need evening dress, and morning coats, pantaloons and trousers, riding dress, cravats—oh, dear, oh, dear, such a travesty—" He eyed the carelessly tied neckcloth that John wore as if it were a personal offense. "And good linen shirts—I shall send you to a shirtmaker, next."

"He can come to me," John snapped. At least neither of the men had stared overlong at his face; they seemed too appalled by his costume. "Or send him my measurements—I do not care for tedious fittings."

"We shall arrange it, my lord," the tailor agreed. "All shall be done to your liking, and you will have new, well-fitted attire, all wrought with taste and style."

All certain to guarantee the new client's modish appearance and lighten his pocket, John thought, wryly. Not that the size of the bill mattered, and if it would please Mrs. Hughes—Miss Crookshank—so be it.

Measuring tape in hand, the assistant waited, like a serpent poised to strike.

John sighed and gave himself to the gods of fashion.

❧

Louisa found that after an hour of perusing the fashion periodical, she had tired of its contents. She was about to send her maid off to look for another volume when she looked up to see Masters in the doorway.

"You have a gentleman caller, miss. Shall I inform him you are not in, to visitors this morning?" His tone implied that this would be correct behavior, with her aunt not here to chaperone.

But Louisa was suddenly even more aware of how bored she was, and, besides . . . Her tone hopeful, she asked, "Is it the marquess?"

"No, miss. It is Sir Lucas Englewood."

Louisa felt her heart miss a beat. "Then show him to the drawing room at once, if you please."

When the footman hesitated, she frowned. "My maid is

here," she pointed out, daring a mere servant to give her lectures about propriety.

"Yes, miss." Masters bowed and turned smartly on his heel.

"Eva," Louisa said quickly. "Take your sewing basket to the chair in the corner and busy yourself with something."

"What, miss?" the servant asked. "I finished all your mending yesterday."

"I don't care," Louisa pleaded. "Just look busy!"

The young maid took her basket and moved to the far side of the room, and Louisa stood as Sir Lucas was ushered in.

He bowed, and she gave him a dignified curtsy.

"How nice to see you, Sir Lucas," she said, her tone formal. "Please sit down."

He looked somewhat ill at ease, perching on the edge of a narrow chair. "I simply wanted to be sure that you had recovered from yesterday's fright," he told her.

"That's very kind of you," Louisa said, careful not to allow her flicker of pleasure to show. "My nerves were greatly agitated, I admit, but the marquess and my aunt were all solicitude, and I am feeling much better today."

"Good."

Heavens, he was standing already? What kind of call was this? Something like panic lanced through her, and the aching emptiness of his loss. The grief that had dogged her after he had walked out of her life ballooned again inside her. Louisa gazed up at him, trying to hold him with the intensity of her stare.

"And do not concern yourself about me. I do not place too much importance on the marquess's suspicions," she added quickly.

"No doubt," Sir Lucas was saying. "If you will excuse me, I must be on my way. Things to do, you know."

"He thinks someone may have tried to kill me!" Louisa finished, speaking a little too quickly.

At least this startling statement made Sir Lucas hesitate as he was about to turn. "What are you talking about? That's nonsense, Louisa. The man's not senile, is he?"

"Of course he's not senile!" Louisa snapped. "He's not *old*!"

"Looks it to me," Sir Lucas argued. "But if you want an elderly husband, none of my concern, of course."

"And you're the one to judge? You're barely out of leading strings."

"Cutting it too thin, Louisa! I am two and twenty," her erstwhile suitor argued, assuming an attitude of great dignity.

She frowned. "For your information, Lucas, Lord Gillingham is in his prime—his form is superb, and his wits are as keen as anyone's. He found blood on the horse's neck—he thinks someone incited the steed to run away."

"Awkward way to kill someone; the beast could just as easily have run the wrong way," Sir Lucas pointed out.

Louisa sniffed and put her lacy handkerchief to her eyes. "It may have been an assault planned against me! How can you be so unfeeling?"

"Oh, snuff it, you can't pull your tricks on me, Louisa," her unfeeling visitor objected. "I know you too well."

"I don't think you know me at all." This time the moisture that dampened her eyes was both real and unsought.

Perhaps he detected the change in her tone because the look Sir Lucas cast her was uncertain. "Now, don't take a pet."

"I thought you cared for me, once," Louisa said. "I know, of course, that is all in the past, but still, if someone is trying to harm me, I thought you would at least feel an ounce of compassion."

He sat down again and leaned forward to catch her eye. "You know I do, Louisa. Now, don't take on. Why on earth would anyone want to hurt you?"

"I do have an inheritance coming when I turn one and twenty," she explained, pleased by the increased attention he was at last paying to her suggestions. Some of the lingering unhappiness inside her eased. Perhaps Lucas did still feel something for her. Perhaps despite his hurtful words, despite his new feminine companions, he did not despise her totally.

She explained the marquess's concerns in more detail, and Lucas listened. And, although he still discounted any notion of a conspiracy, he stayed for tea, and Louisa felt a glow of happiness she had not known for months.

Marianne returned at the appointed time and found Lord Gillingham waiting for her. He motioned to his groom to take the packages she carried and put them into the barouche. She smiled, glad to be relieved of her burdens, and he suggested, "I am told there is a place called Gunter's not far from here which has very nice confections. Could I interest you in a light repast?"

She hesitated. What would Louisa say about her aunt having a tête-à-tête with the marquess? Errands were one thing, but—

"Unless you do not care to be seen with me until I am outfitted with my new finery?" he suggested, his tone mild.

Stung that she might appear so superficial, Marianne said quickly, "Of course not! I only thought—that is, I would be happy to sup with you, my lord."

He gave instructions to his coachman, and then offered Marianne his arm. They strolled down to the pastry shop and were ushered in and seated at a small table.

"Now, there is someone whose outfit no doubt would earn your approval," the marquess suggested. "In a few days, I shall doubtless outshine the poor fellow, putting him totally into the shade."

As the serving woman brought them steaming cups of tea, Marianne drew off her gloves and managed to glance unobtrusively over her shoulder. The man who had caught Lord Gillingham's eye was a stripling adorned in a morning coat of bright green, with a striped waistcoat of broad cerulean stripes and shirt collars so high he could not turn his head. His cravat was tied into a fearsomely complicated knot that barely allowed him room to swallow his tea.

Marianne bit back a decidedly unladylike snort of laughter. "Certainly not! I sent you to a reputable tailor, my lord, not a circus costumer. I would never wish to turn you into such a jackanapes!"

He raised his brows. "I am relieved to hear it."

"If you think me interfering, then I apologize," she told him, her tone dignified. "I only wished—"

"For your ward not to be embarrassed by my unkempt appearance," he finished for her. "Quite understandable."

"No, no, I never said such a thing," she protested. "Only that—that—"

"Yes?" He fixed her with what she was certain was a deliberately bland gaze.

"Most people new to London can use a little town polish," she tried to explain. "You said yourself—"

"Ah, I'm afraid I know little of polish, though I can describe a quite good poultice for a swollen fetlock, made with oatmeal and Epsom salts."

"My fetlocks—my ankles—are quite satisfactory," she retorted.

"Oh, I agree."

This was a most improper subject. She glared at him, but he grinned into his teacup.

"You may have your revenge, my lord," she told him, refusing to be baited further. "My only aim was to make your stay in London more pleasant. Was the tailor's fitting really that troublesome? Or do you prefer to go about looking less than you are?"

He raised his gaze, and she was able to look into his deep dark eyes. "You do tend to get to the heart of the matter."

"I don't wish you to think that I judge men—people— merely by their outer appearance. I would hope I am not so shallow. I know perfectly well that the real measure of a man is on the inside, and although I do not know you well, I am coming to believe that in the most important aspects, you would not disappoint." Her words had come out in a rush, and now Marianne paused, not sure she should have said so much. When had it become so easy to talk to the once formidable marquess? The serving woman brought them an array of dishes, and they both paused. Marianne stole a glance at his face.

He did not seem offended; he gazed at her with an expression so guarded, and yet at the same time so vulnerable, that her breath came a little faster. Had no one ever told this man that he was worthy of respect and admiration?

"But—" she added, determined to explain once and for all, her interference into his personal habits, "you cannot expect everyone to take the time to get to know you well enough to see past first impressions. And there is no need to put people off—you have the funds, you have the social standing, you have health and good sense. A well-fitted coat is like a well-chosen horse, my lord. It serves its purpose. It makes your life easier."

"There is good reason to expend effort selecting good steeds. My horse carries me where I wish to go," he argued.

"So does a respectable costume," she threw back.

He smiled. "Touché. I am bested again."

Marianne laughed. "And I am finished making speeches, my lord, so you may do just as you will about your clothing. If you wish to turn up at our dinner party in a sultan's robes, I shall say nothing more."

"A pity," he murmured. "I find I rather enjoy your lectures."

This was such a backward commendation that she ignored it completely. "The pastry is quite good, my lord," she pointed out.

John hardly noticed what he ate. The pleasure of the meal came with the company, he found. And whether she was admonishing him with her usual blend of candor and tact or telling him of new exhibits in town that he might enjoy visiting, he simply enjoyed her presence, the unaccustomed privilege of being able to concentrate solely on her words and her face and her pleasing form. The time passed too quickly. When they walked back to the absurd barouche he had rented and were driven back to her home, he felt his private joy fade, yet he knew he was duty-bound to go inside and call upon Miss Crookshank.

The younger lady flew down the steps when she heard

them in the front hall. "There you are, Aunt, I have had—oh, Lord Gillingham! How delightful to see you."

She sank into a curtsy, and John made his bow.

"Won't you come into the sitting room, my lord. It is so kind of you to call."

She seemed to assume that he had just arrived. He felt Mrs. Hughes's glance on his face, and with no conscious decision—much less collusion—for duplicity, neither of them mentioned that they had shared a shopping expedition.

Instead, when Miss Crookshank playfully reproached him for being so late to call, he explained that he had been to visit his tailor.

Wincing a little at the way her face lit up, John went on. "I wanted a new evening coat for the dinner party your aunt is planning."

The girl flashed her sunny smile. "Oh, you are coming, then. That is lovely. Which night have you chosen, dearest Aunt?"

"Next Friday," Mrs. Hughes said, her voice quiet. "I must send out the other invitations right away. If you will forgive me, I shall write some notes just now."

She chose a seat at a table at the edge of the room, and John was forced to direct his attention toward the younger woman.

Perhaps encouraged by the news of his shopping trip, Miss Crookshank launched into a description of her planned wardrobe and its newest additions. It was not that much different from the conversation that he had with her aunt, yet John felt a strong sense of tedium steal over him.

Somehow, it had been much more stimulating to trade words with Mrs. Hughes; somehow, with her he never felt bored. She never looked at him with a slight look of bewilderment, as Louisa sometimes did; she always understood his jokes . . .

Was it because beneath her gentle manner he caught the hint of deeper emotions, more complex motivations, thoughts she did not trust him enough, perhaps, to express? He sensed that Marianne Hughes was a woman whose pleasing aspect hid more than it revealed, and he longed to know her better, somehow sure that he would not be disappointed.

Hadn't she said much the same about him? Her positive comments had pleased him deeply, he realized, thrilled him, and if he had not already plunged into his too precipitous courtship of her niece, he would very well consider—

John realized that he was gazing blankly at Miss Crookshank, who had paused in her chatter. She seemed to be awaiting his response. But he had no idea what she had said.

"Really?" he ventured.

"Don't you think another visit to Vauxhall would make a delightful evening?" she said, her tone hopeful.

"Of course," he agreed, trying to make up for his most uncivil inattention. "After your aunt's dinner party, perhaps?"

Louisa beamed.

Marianne tried not to notice the easy relationship between the two. Gritting her teeth just a little, she bent over her writing, pulling her thoughts back to the dinner party and possible guests. She had jotted down the names of a couple of friends, and she would invite Lady Sealey, although Marianne knew that her more socially prominent friend was so popular that she had few available evenings unless one planned well in advance. However, if she was not careful the dinner table would be unbalanced; they were going to be short of men. She added a male friend who, if he were not already engaged for the evening, could be counted upon for unexacting company.

The main thing was to allow Lord Gillingham—and Louisa, of course—to enjoy the evening. Now, who could she invite that the marquess would be comfortable with, since he knew so few people in London?

Of course! Inspired, she added the names of Lord and Lady Gabriel Sinclair. A family member should make the party easier for Lord Gillingham, she told herself, pleased with this brainstorm. Even though she was not well acquainted with Lady Gabriel and had never met her husband, they would likely be happy to come, for the marquess' sake.

After the turmoil of the past few days, it would be an uneventful, pleasant evening, Marianne told herself. She picked up her pen.

Nine

A family is as hard to predict as a bowl of fruit:
some apples have blemishes, some are bruised,
and some are tarter than others.

— MARGERY, COUNTESS OF SEALEY

During the next week, Marianne made sure to keep Louisa under her watchful eye. They shopped, called upon female friends, and spent an evening at the opera in a friend's private box, but Marianne kept a careful lookout upon their surroundings and took her footman along whenever they went out. No further alarms were raised, and as the days went by Marianne felt her tension slip away as she again considered how unlikely that anyone would really wish to harm an innocent girl.

Caroline's reply to her letter had not been very helpful. The great-uncle's name was Alton Crookshank, he was the youngest son of his generation and not much older than Louisa's father, which dispelled Marianne's image of him as old and frail and harmless.

Caroline had no idea if he ever came to London or not. No one had been in touch with the man for some time, although Caroline did not remember the details of the family dispute. "He was a wild young man, I believe," she had written. "He was supposed to be quite dissolute, going through a good deal of his father's money, and then he crowned it all by running away with a tavern girl. I think they parted later, and he married a Scottish merchant's widow with some money of her own, so he ended up with a modest estate near Edinburgh."

All in all, not a very sterling character, Marianne thought. Still, it did not mean that he was a murderer.

During one of the marquess's calls, Marianne managed to share this news with Lord Gillingham. He took note of the name and the location. "I will make some inquiries," he told her, then, to Louisa's disappointment, firmly declined to drive them back to Hyde Park to join the masses of the Ton in that fashionable meeting place.

"Not just yet," he told his young fiancée, who sighed and nodded.

Louisa's agreement seemed a bit forced. Marianne knew the younger woman was beginning to chafe at the abridged social activity, and especially the lack of male companionship. The marquess had called upon them twice, but only stayed a brief time, and when Louisa tried to cajole him into accompanying them on their jaunts, he pleaded other commitments.

Marianne did her best to amuse her niece, although the evening at the opera was not as successful as Marianne had hoped. The soprano was in good voice, but the music had barely begun when Marianne saw Louisa stiffen and glance to the side, then bite her lip. Worried, Marianne looked, too. She soon found the familiar face that had produced the reaction in her ward. Sir Lucas sat in another box farther along.

Marianne looked back at Louisa, but the girl did not comment, although she blinked hard. The opera proceeded through several passages before Sir Lucas caught sight of them. When he did, he bowed, but he did not come along to their box to chat. He was with a different girl tonight, a young lady of petite stature and ruddy cheeks, along with a matron who was probably the girl's mother, and two other couples.

Marianne braced herself for a scene, but Louisa seemed to have learned something from the mishap at the park.

She nodded politely when her old suitor made his bow and then kept her gaze pointedly turned away, her attention ostentatiously fixed on the performers, and after the curtain came down she chatted spiritedly with her aunt on the merits of the drama.

But once they were in their hackney and on the way home, she fell into a dismal silence that made Marianne feel genuine sympathy.

"Louisa," she said quietly, "it will get easier, you know, with time."

"What, understanding the Italian in the arias?" Louisa asked absently, gazing outside at the carriages passing by.

"No, I mean forgetting your first love. It's normal that some feelings might linger, but they will not last forever."

She paused, alarmed to see real tears glisten in Louisa's eyes.

"I am not mourning his loss!" the younger woman said, a little too loudly. "He had no confidence in me. Why should I want a man who does not value me or trust me?"

"You should not," Marianne agreed.

"No, I will not be such a ninny." Louisa ruined the effect of this pronouncement with a noisy sniff.

"Of course not," Marianne agreed, reaching to pat the girl's hand. Perhaps Louisa was beginning the difficult journey to genuine maturity. "In time, it will only be a memory, replaced by more satisfying attachments."

"Yes, I have the marquess," Louisa said, though her voice quivered a little. "He, at least, values me."

Marianne hesitated again. "As to that, you are not just using the marquess as a crutch to get over Sir Lucas? That would be fair to neither of you, Louisa."

"Of course not!" Louisa declared. But her tone was guarded.

"You must think of the marquess's happiness as well as your own," Marianne continued. "Or else, your engagement would be selfish, indeed."

Louisa opened her blue eyes even wider. "But I am quite sure I can make the marquess happy, Aunt. I will work very hard to do so!"

Marianne sighed, wishing she could make out what lay inside the young woman's heart. Did Louisa already have, or was she forming, a true attachment to the marquess? If so, it would be infamy for Marianne to separate the two, if indeed she had the power. No, she could not consider such a thing. . . .

The preparations for their dinner party continued.

Lady Sealey, as Marianne had feared, was unable to come and had declined with pleasingly sincere regret. Marianne's other friends had sent notes of acceptance, but she had not yet heard from Lady Gabriel. Perhaps the couple already had a prior engagement, Marianne told herself. She did not think that Psyche would deliberately snub her, but it stood to reason they must have a busy social schedule.

So she did not mention to Louisa, or to the marquess, that his relatives might be coming, unwilling to excite Louisa's anticipation, or his, without cause.

When she visited the countess on Wednesday, Louisa dutifully in tow, she was able to chat with Lady Sealey. Louisa found another young lady to talk to, and Marianne had a few moments of quiet conversation. Unfortunately, Psyche was not present at this week's tea.

The countess repeated her regrets. "Such a shame I have already promised the evening to Mrs. Cowling," Lady Sealey said, sipping her tea. "But I am sure your dinner party will be a most enjoyable event."

"I hope so," Marianne confessed. "My cook is trying out new recipes upon us every night, and my footman has polished all the silver twice, which, since my collection of plate is not extensive, didn't really take long." She laughed. "I suppose it has been a while since I have entertained at home—one can get complaisant when one is alone."

The countess fixed her with a thoughtful gaze. "Yes, you must not turn into a hermit, my dear Marianne. You're much too young to sit in front of your own hearth every night. And if you socialize, you may yet find a gentleman whom you find appealing."

They had had this conversation before. Marianne was not inclined to discuss it again. To change the subject, she mentioned her invitation to Lady Gabriel and her husband. "I have not yet heard from her, but if they are able to come, I had hoped it would make Lord Gillingham's evening more enjoyable."

The countess paused with her cup halfway to her lips. She set it down. "Ah, as to that . . . with brothers, one can never know." She hesitated.

Marianne had the feeling that the older woman, for once, was not sure what to say. "Is there something I should know?" she asked.

Lady Sealey pursed her lips. "I cannot break a confidence," she began.

"No indeed," Marianne said quickly. "I should not expect it." The fact that Lady Sealey was so discreet was an important reason that her many friends felt so safe in confiding in her.

"I will simply caution you not to expect too much."

Marianne raised her brows, not sure how to interpret this cryptic warning. "I don't understand."

"Some families are close, some are not," the countess said. "And if Psyche must decline, I'm sure she has good reason."

"Of course," Marianne agreed, although she suspected that the countess had more in mind than a previous social engagement.

It had seemed so simple, merely a quiet dinner party, with nothing more to worry about than her cook becoming overly ambitious and ruining all the sauces. Why did Marianne now experience a nervous feeling in her stomach?

On Thursday she received a short note of acceptance from Psyche. Relieved, Marianne stared at the gilt-edged piece of paper. No doubt she had worried too much about the delay, and even upon the countess's puzzling pronouncement.

So she went down to the kitchen to tell the cook the final number of guests. When she entered, she smelled smoke in the air and the acrid scent of scorched butter.

"Is everything all right, Mrs. Blount?" Marianne asked, after giving her servants the total to expect.

The cook stood squarely in front of the cookstove, her wide hips blocking any view of the modern innovation, which Marianne had had installed in her kitchen a few years before. In the corner the housemaid fanned her apron, as if to dispel the strong odor. "Oh, no, ma'am, just trying out a new sauce for the custard."

"Ah, yes," Marianne agreed. "I have total confidence in your abilities," she told the servants. "It is only a simple dinner, you know, so no need for nervous qualms."

The cook wiped her brow. "Of course not, ma'am. But it's a marquess! First time we ever had such to sit down for dinner in this house."

She spoke as she might about a wild tiger, Marianne thought, swallowing a smile.

"So, I still think we should add more side dishes." The cook sounded determined to uphold the honor of the household.

"Very well," Marianne agreed. "But don't put yourself out concocting new sauces, please. Your usual caramel sauce is quite delightful."

"Thank 'e, ma'am," Mrs. Blount said. "Very well."

Marianne thought it best to make a tactful departure and to hope that things in the kitchen would return to some semblance of normalcy. She went back upstairs and found Louisa waiting for her in the hall. She had promised the younger woman they would take a turn about the park in the center of the square.

"It's such a pretty day," Louisa pleaded. "And we have been inside so much, Aunt."

"Yes," Marianne agreed. "Let me get my hat and gloves."

When they set out, with Masters a few steps behind them, Marianne told her companion about the new addition to the party.

"Oh, that's lovely," Louisa exclaimed. "I shall much enjoy meeting Lord Gillingham's brother and sister-in-law. I'm sure the marquess will be delighted."

Marianne nodded in agreement.

John was walking, too, with his disreputable spaniel at his heels. When they had first arrived in London, Runt had displayed an unhappy tendency to bark at all the traffic and fellow pedestrians. She was finally becoming inured to the carriages and wagons that thronged the streets, and even to the herds of cattle that weekly flooded the roads on their way to market.

Today she trotted along obediently and only sniffed at the unusual odor of a coal wagon that rumbled past them.

"Good dog," John told her. "You'll become city wise yet. I wish I could say the same about myself." He tugged his wide-brimmed hat farther down to shade his face. It was the only part of his old costume he still wore every day. He now had, it seemed to him, a whole room full of new clothes, shirts, and new boots as well as all the different outfits the tailor had deemed necessary. A lot of fuss for nothing, he thought, and worse, now he had to have one of the inn's servants help him into the close-fitting coats.

When he bothered. Today he had shrugged on an older jacket to take his dog out for a stroll, and the people who passed spared them barely a moment's glance. Which was just how John preferred it. He certainly had no desire to be singled out, either for his raiment or his disfigurement.

Yet his longing to retreat to the countryside was not as pressing as it had been when he'd first arrived in town. His brief visits to Mrs. Hughes's house were always pleasurable, and if he enjoyed the conversation with the chaperone somewhat more than Miss Crookshank's artless chatter, well, that was something he chose not to dwell on. No, London was not quite as bad as he had expected. And as for Mrs. Hughes's personal attractions, perhaps he was only too long without a woman . . .

While his thoughts wandered, a cab veered into the side of the road and came alarmingly close to John. He jumped out of the way, whistling to his dog. The animal yelped.

"Watch what you are about," he yelled toward the driver.

"Here, Runt." He ran his hands over the trembling dog, but could not find any injury. Perhaps the hackney's nearness had scared her.

"Sorry, sir, the foreleader shied, weren't my fault," the man on the box called back as he hauled on the driving reins.

Runt turned her back on the offending vehicle and barked sharply toward a pedestrian a few yards away, as if to regain her pride and show how unimpressed the little dog was by the potential dangers of the road.

"Yes, I know," John told her as the cab got under way again. "Come along. We'd best get back to the inn. I have one more evening of quiet before I have to face the social whirl once more."

The dog barked, and John grinned. "You can say that; you don't have to go."

As they approached the inn, a slight figure stepped out of the alley that ran behind the houses. "Like a good time, sir? Only a shilling."

Pulling his hat farther down to hide his face, John stared at her. She was a prostitute, her form skinny beneath her slatternly gown, her brown hair bedraggled. She had been pretty once. Now her eyes looked old before her time, though he doubted she was out of her twenties.

"I can give you a good time, sir," she repeated, stepping closer as if encouraged by his hesitation. She smelled like unwashed clothes and cheap gin.

He had been reflecting on his body's need, but despite her smile of invitation and her low-cut gown, he felt a curious absence of desire. No, it was not this woman, it was not just *any* woman, he longed for.

"Sorry, no," he told her.

Her thin face fell. She was likely hungry, he thought. But if he gave her money, would she only buy more gin?

He saw a hot-pie vendor at the corner of the street and beckoned the man closer. "Two of your best for this—this young person," he told the man, taking coin from his pocket.

She looked puzzled, but she licked her lips at the succulent scent of the pies. "Thank 'e, sir."

And John, not altogether pleased at what he had discovered about himself, went quickly into the inn.

On Friday Marianne woke with a sense of tension. Blinking, she tried to think what worried her, then she remembered. Tonight's dinner!

She sat up, her mind at once reverting to the list of details she had been mulling over when she went to bed. The napkins and linen tablecloth had been pressed, the silver polished, the house cleaned from top to bottom—not that anyone would be inspecting her bedchamber. She paused, pondering an impossible scenario that somehow did away with all the other guests, Louisa included, and had the marquess leaning over her in this very same chamber, his dark eyes glinting in a way that made her heart beat faster . . .

Good heavens, what was she thinking? She hastened to direct her thoughts toward more acceptable channels. She'd ordered fresh flowers. She'd finally cajoled Cook into a reasonable menu. And she needed to check that the fresh fish had been delivered, and that it was indeed fresh.

Marianne rose and rang for her maid. She was already half dressed before Hackett appeared with her breakfast tray.

"Here, ma'am, let me." The maid put down the tray and hurried across to fasten the remaining buttons on the back of the morning dress, which Marianne strained to reach.

"Have the flowers arrived, Hackett?" Marianne asked as her dresser picked up a brush and nodded to her mistress to sit.

"Yes, ma'am. The primroses are in good shape, and the hothouse blooms, but I tossed half the daffodils, as they was a bit brown about the edges."

"Oh, dear," Marianne said, already turning.

"Sit still, if you please, ma'am," her maid commanded, as if Marianne were still a fidgety child in short skirts.

Marianne obeyed. "I don't wish the arrangements to look skimpy."

"No need to worry," her maid said. "I already sent Masters out to fetch more, and Miss Louisa is working on the flowers right now."

"Oh, good," Marianne said, hiding a smile. At least the dinner had led Louisa to do something of which Hackett approved. Which meant that whatever happened, the evening would not be a total loss.

And why did she keep thinking something untoward was going to happen? It was a quiet dinner among friends, she reassured herself, just as she had the cook, and she could not put her finger on the source of her disquietude. Was it the countess's hesitation, that comment she had not made?

No, all would be well. Determined to hold on to that thought, as soon as her maid finished brushing and pinning up her hair, Marianne hurried down the staircase.

She stopped in the dining room to commend Louisa's efforts with the flowers. The girl was sitting at the table, three vases on its polished top, and what appeared to be a whole field's worth of flowers and wildflowers in tubs on the floor beside her.

"That's looking lovely," Marianne told her.

Louisa beamed. "Thank you, Aunt. This one is for the table, this one for the sitting room, and this small one for the front hall. We had to send for more daffodils, but the rest of the flowers and greenery are quite fresh. Do you think I need more pink in this one?"

"Perhaps just a little, on the side. You're doing a fine job," Marianne told her. "Excuse me, I'm going down to the kitchen."

"Good luck," the younger woman said, wrinkling her nose. "I put my head in this morning and Cook almost tossed a pot at me."

"Oh, dear," Marianne murmured and headed for the lower floor.

But when she entered the kitchen, all seemed well. A large pot bubbled on the stove top, and the housemaid was at a side table scrubbing vegetables. The cook herself had flour up to her elbows and looked a little flushed from bending over the stove, but nonetheless, her nervous qualms seemed to have settled into a comfortable optimism.

"Yes, ma'am," she said in answer to her mistress's query. "The fish is just what we should want, scarce out of the water, and the turtle, too. The turtle's already in the soup pot, cooking up nicely. And the beef roast is in the cold-safe steeping in marinade, and the hen is stuffed with herbs and ready to go into the oven, when the time is right."

"Excellent," Marianne told her. "It already smells heavenly in here."

"This pastry is almost ready to put into the oven, and though I may be only a good plain English cook, not one of them hoity-toity French fellows, if I do say so, pastry is my strong point." The cook gave the dough a resounding slap and smiled grimly at the large bowl of flour and dough in which she had immersed her hands.

"No one makes a better fruit tart than you, Mrs. Blount," Marianne agreed quickly. "I see that all is in order, and I can rest easy with you in charge."

The housemaid smiled just a little from her vantage point behind the cook, but Mrs. Blount swelled with pride. "Yes, ma'am. We never had a marquess dine at our table before, but he shall have nothing to complain about tonight, on my honor."

Marianne made another soothing comment, and then, leaving the reputation of the kitchen, and the cherry tarts, in her staff's capable hands, went back upstairs.

By the time she reached the ground floor, Louisa called her to come and inspect her progress with the flowers. Or lack of progress. In her anxiety to achieve the perfect grouping she had pulled the first arrangement almost to pieces.

"Is this too top-heavy? It should suggest a pleasing balance." Louisa worried. "Or so Aunt Caroline always says."

Marianne sat down to help with the flowers. After another hour, the vases and urns were filled, and Louisa had been persuaded to the pleasing aspects of each. Just in time, too, as the housemaid was waiting to set the table for a light luncheon.

Masters brought in the post and Marianne glanced through the letters. One from her sister-in-law Caroline in Bath she scanned quickly, but it was all family news, with no new information about Alton Crookshank.

She and Louisa carried vases into the sitting room and the hall. Then lunch was served, and she persuaded the girl to eat a few bites, although Louisa chattered so much about the evening that she barely had time to swallow.

"I'm sure all will be well," Marianne tried to tell her ward, "and everyone will enjoy the company as well as the meal."

"Oh, I do hope so," the younger woman said, picking up a slice of pear and then putting it down again. "I have such butterflies in my stomach that I am not even hungry."

"You shall have to do better tonight," Marianne warned, smiling. "Or else, after all her work, Cook will be highly offended."

Louisa laughed.

When they rose from the table, Louisa's maid came in to report that she had a cleansing cucumber mask ready for her mistress, and Marianne sent her ward away to lie down with the gunk on her face, secretly happy to see the girl kept occupied for a while.

The rest of the day whirled by in a succession of small tasks, and before she knew it, the sun had dropped in the sky and it was time to change before their guests arrived.

Marianne had chosen a simply cut silk gown of soft blue, which she knew became her. It was Louisa who was the star of the evening, but she herself did not wish to look too drab. Did Louisa's artless comment about dull colors still sting? Marianne shook her head at herself as she reached for her pearl necklace.

Louisa was still in her bedchamber when Marianne came downstairs to inspect the rooms one more time before the first guest arrived. The dining-room table was resplendent in snowy linen, the china plates and crystal goblets ready to receive the results of Cook's labors. The flowers were graceful, and the whole room seemed to shimmer with an air of pleasant anticipation. Marianne nodded in approval and went up to the sitting room.

She sat down in one of the slender chairs just as, almost in unison, she heard the knocker at the front door and Louisa hurried into the room.

"Oh, Aunt, is it the marquess? I didn't wish to be late." The younger woman sounded breathless.

"Whichever guest it is, Masters will show them up," Marianne said. "Take a long breath. You don't want to look flustered."

"Oh, no," Louisa agreed, throwing herself into a settee with her usual impetuousness. "I do not wish to look overeager. That would be gauche."

Marianne swallowed a smile and said, truthfully, "You look lovely, my dear."

Louisa beamed. Her maid's cucumber mask, or simply her own youth and good health, had added a rosy glow to the porcelain fineness of her skin. Her eyes were bright. Her fair hair was swept up into a riot of curls, and the white dress with pink ribbons was perfectly suited to a young lady in her first Season. Marianne had no doubt that Louisa would enjoy the evening thoroughly and be admired by all who saw her—especially the marquess.

Which was just as it should be, Marianne told herself as Masters announced, "Mr. and Mrs. Denver, ma'am."

Marianne stood and went to greet the first guests.

"Marianne, how lovely to see you," Roberta Denver said as her husband bowed to the ladies.

"I'm delighted you were able to come," Marianne told them both. "This is Miss Louisa Crookshank, who is visiting me for the Season. You met her at Vauxhall."

"Of course. Are you enjoying your time in London as much as you hoped?" Mrs. Denver asked, sitting down beside Louisa.

The housemaid offered glasses of wine, and Mr. Denver accepted a glass. "Just got back to town, myself," he told his hostess. "Had to post to Salisbury for a few days."

"I hope all is well," Marianne asked politely.

"Colic in my favorite mare," he explained, and plunged into a discussion of equine remedies that lasted until the next guest was announced.

"Mr. James McNair," the footman said.

Behind him a man of middle age with a merry smile, his slightly widening girth almost disguised by his well-cut coat, paused in the doorway.

Marianne excused herself and went to say hello.

"So, my dear, you have been dragged into the Season," the gentleman said, grinning. "About time, I say. If you won't marry me, the least you can do is get out into Society a bit more."

Laughing, Marianne put out her hand. "Jamie, you know perfectly well you have no serious interest in marriage. You would faint dead away if I made any indication of accepting your suit. Besides, you 'proposed' to at least three different women last year, and none of the offers were serious."

"Ah, but it brightens a lady's day, don't you know," her old friend suggested, taking a glass of wine. "Nothing like an offer of matrimony to make a lady feel desirable."

"And what will you do if someone takes you up on your kind proposal one of these days?" Marianne asked.

"No, no, that's why I make my offers very carefully," Jamie answered. "Otherwise, I might have to disappear into the wild northland, and that would never do. I mean, a spot of fishing is one thing, but I would miss my tailor if I had to go into real exile."

"Just your tailor?"

"And your company, of course," he corrected hastily, lifting her hand to his lips for a showy salute.

Marianne laughed again. Jamie was a middle-aged dandy, and totally self-centered beneath his easy charm, but he was excellent company.

Someone else stood in the doorway, and Masters announced in a deep voice, "The marquess of Gillingham."

Marianne glanced up. Oh, how well he looked in his new evening clothes! The well-cut coat emphasized his broad shoulders and fitted smoothly across his muscled chest. He had even made an effort to tie his cravat more smoothly. But when she gazed at his face, she saw that Lord Gillingham looked unexpectedly stern.

She stepped forward to welcome the newest arrival. "My lord, I am so glad you were able to join us."

He bowed, but his expression still seemed somber; his lips were tight. Before Marianne could say any more, Louisa hurried up.

"Oh, Lord Gillingham, you look so dashing. And I am so pleased to see you. It's been an age."

"Two days at least," he agreed, his tone dry.

Marianne raised her brows. What had caused this asperity in his tone? Surely, he was not bothered by Jamie Mc-Nair's flirtations? But that would mean—aware of a slight increase in her pulse, Marianne pushed the thought away. But there was no doubt that the marquess's glance toward Mr. McNair was less cordial than the polite welcome he made to the other guests as Marianne performed introductions.

Fortunately, Mr. Denver brought up his sick mare again, and this apparently was a topic with which the marquess was well acquainted. The two men discussed horses while Louisa lingered nearby, and Roberta Denver added the occasional word. Jamie McNair accepted a glass of wine, and Marianne glanced at the clock on the mantel. What about her other guests? No doubt they were simply fashionably late, but she didn't want to upset the cook by holding dinner back too long; the chicken would be dry and the beef overdone.

But no, now she heard the knocker at the door again, and Masters slipped away to answer it and show the last arrivals up.

All should be well, now, Marianne assured herself. Soon the footman reappeared, to announce in clear accents: "Lord and Lady Gabriel Sinclair."

There was a moment of silence. Lady Gabriel entered the room, looking as beautiful as always, her fair hair swept up in a simple twist behind her head, diamonds flashing at her throat and ears, and her gown an elegant column of pale

green silk that made Marianne feel almost underdressed
And Lord Gabriel, whom Marianne had not met, was just as
amazingly handsome as she had heard, even with his lips
set into a grim smile and his deep blue eyes hard. He had
dark hair and, though tall, a slim build. This was the marquess's brother? They did not look at all alike.

Marianne glanced back at the marquess and saw
something in his expression that chilled her. The tempera-
ture in the room seemed to have dropped, despite the fire
dancing on the hearth. With a sinking heart, she wondered if
she had made a dreadful error in judgment. A happy family
party? The two brothers looked as elated as two rivals meeting on a battlefield.

Automatically, she performed introductions to the earlier arrivals, and when she came to the marquess, she had
to steady her voice. "And Lord Gillingham, of course, you
already know."

Lord Gabriel gave a slight bow, just short of being of-
fensive in its briefness, and did not answer. Lady Gabriel
was more gracious. "How nice to see you again," she told
the older brother, offering her hand.

He bowed over it. "An unexpected pleasure," the marquess agreed, his tone dry.

Marianne felt a stab of guilt. Oh dear, why had she not
discussed her plans with Lord Gillingham before inviting
his relatives? It had seemed so simple.

Lady Gabriel smiled and joined the marquess and
Louisa. Lord Gabriel took a glass of wine offered by the
footman and seemed to ponder the painting over the side-
board.

"What hornets' nest have you stirred up, my dear?"
Jamie McNair came closer to Marianne and spoke in a low
tone. "Have you blundered into a family feud?"

"If so, I did not know it," Marianne retorted. "Do you
think I am trying to ruin my own party?"

"No, but I sense a distinct lack of camaraderie," he

pointed out. "This may be a most interesting evening. I'm so glad I accepted."

"You always accept," she replied, glancing toward the others in the room. "You dine out every night, as we both know."

"Of course, I keep no cook. You know how tiny is my income," he agreed, not in the least insulted. "Plus, my rooms offer no scope for entertaining. But I love to be able to offer a tidbit of gossip to my hostesses, and this evening promises potential for some interesting anecdotes."

"Jamie, if you dare!" Marianne glared at him. "I shall tell Mrs. Carabell who spread that terrible joke about her daughter's performance on the pianoforte."

"I'll keep that in mind," he promised. "But for now—"

"For now, behave and help me keep my guests from each other's throats!" Marianne pleaded. "Go and be civil and tell funny—but not scandalous—stories."

"Are there any other kind? Very well, I will attempt to spread oil on roiled waters," he agreed when she frowned at him. "Although I warn you, with some torrents, the attempt is useless before it begins."

Hoping his words were not prophetic, Marianne gathered her courage and walked over to stand beside Lord Gabriel.

"I am so pleased to meet you," she began. "I have had the pleasure of conversing with Lady Gabriel at the countess of Sealey's teas."

"So Psyche said. Lady Sealey is a remarkable woman," he agreed. "With a fine wit, a sharp mind, and somewhat advanced views. She was a friend of Psyche's late mother, I believe."

Feeling slightly more at ease, Marianne nodded. "Lady Sealey is most benevolent. She was very kind to me after I was widowed."

"My condolences," he said. "Is this your husband?"

Marianne glanced at the portrait, which showed a pleasant-looking young man with brown hair and hazel eyes, an engaging grin and perhaps a slightly weak chin. "Yes, that was Harry. He died at a young age."

"I don't believe I ever met him," Lord Gabriel said, sipping his wine and continuing to contemplate the portrait. "But then, I was away from England for quite a few years."

"My husband's family is from the West Country," Marianne explained. "Although Harry spent time in London after he came of age."

She might have wondered about her guest's interest in a man he had never met, except that she suspected it gave Lord Gabriel the excuse to keep his back turned to the rest of the company. Heavens, what an evening it was going to be!

She saw Masters appear once again in the doorway. He caught her eye and she gave an almost imperceptible nod.

"Dinner is served, ma'am," he announced.

"Shall we go in?" Marianne suggested.

She waited for her more socially prominent guests to lead the way. Lord Gabriel offered his arm to his wife, who had come to stand beside him.

The marquess, who of course outranked them all, hung back. What was he waiting for?

"Do not stand on ceremony," Marianne said firmly, and his brother and wife led the way out of the room and down to the dining room.

Mr. and Mrs. Denver followed.

"Ah, I see it falls to me to take in the newest beauty to make her debut into Society." Smiling, Jamie McNair offered his arm.

Louisa, who had obviously been hoping for the marquess's escort, did not possess the social skill to deflect the invitation, so she was swept up by Mr. McNair and led away.

So it was Lord Gillingham who remained to lead his hostess into dinner.

"My lord," she said quietly. "I had thought you would be pleased to have your relatives join us this evening."

"A natural assumption," he agreed.

She felt an irrational relief that he did not seem to be angry at her. But his expression was still guarded, and she could not shake her feelings of apprehension.

They descended one flight of steps and entered the dining room, where, as the guest of honor, the marquess was seated beside the hostess. Marianne knew that this would not thrill Louisa, but it couldn't be helped; to do otherwise would have been to slight the marquess. At least Lord Gabriel was seated at the other side of the table, next to Louisa, and she could certainly not complain about her proximity to such a charming and handsome man.

The first course was served, and the food seemed to be all that Mrs. Blount had hoped to achieve. Conversation fell into a comfortable hum, and the brothers were able to ignore each other without being too obvious.

Marianne chatted first with Lord Gabriel, on her other side, then turned back to glance at the marquess.

He had apparently directed all his attention to his soup. Marianne hoped that Lady Gabriel, on his other side, would not take offense.

But he seemed to feel her gaze, because he glanced up as the footman took away the soup dish and served him a portion of fish.

"Is Mr. McNair an old friend?" he asked.

Marianne glanced toward the foot of the table, where Jamie sat in the host's position.

"Yes, you could say so," she agreed cautiously, not sure of the tone of the question. "He was a friend of my husband's, so I have known him for years, and he often serves as host when I entertain. Mr. McNair is a social creature and is happy to join almost any party, if he is not promised elsewhere."

"But you are not betrothed?" he asked.

She blinked at the bluntness of the question. "No, of course not, we are only friends. I doubt that Mr. McNair will ever marry," she said. "I suspect he has not the constitution for it." She looked at the man beside her. Surely, it could not matter to him just what her relationship to Jamie might be?

"And he has no estate to concern himself about?"

"Needing an heir, you mean, as you do?" She watched his face, wondering if she dared ask why his relations with his brother were so strained. But the tautness of his expression made her hesitate.

"Just so," the marquess said, but, to her disappointment, he did not offer any added enlightenment.

"No, I believe not." She answered absently, still puzzling over the hostility evident between Lord Gillingham and his brother. "Lord Gabriel tells me that he has spent a considerable time away from England."

"My brother's journeys were not voluntary," the marquess said, his voice low.

And what did that mean? Marianne broke off a piece of bread with unnecessary force, wishing she could toss it at the man seated next to her.

"And you have no wish to travel?" she noted.

"Why should I? I find my own home the most comfortable venue."

"No doubt, but there are so many marvels to see . . ."

"Yes, you said that once. You would enjoy traveling?" His glance was too discerning for her comfort.

Marianne realized she had, indeed, sounded wistful, and quickly turned the conversation to a less personal aspect, making her tone more brisk. "Of course, there are more ways than one to see the world. I understand there is an exhibit of Italian and French landscapes at the art institute this week."

"Would you like to see it? I should be happy to escort you, and Miss Crookshank, of course."

Down the table, Louisa lifted her head; had she caught the mention of her name even from a few feet away? No doubt.

Marianne said, "I'm sure she, and I, would enjoy the excursion." And at least, they would likely not run into any unwanted relatives!

John allowed himself to show only polite interest, and the dinner stretched on for what seemed like an interminable length. At least he had Mrs. Hughes beside him, and he could ignore the unwanted presence at the other side of the table.

But eventually, it came time for the ladies to withdraw.

He detected the anxious glance that his hostess sent him be-fore she stood, but custom ruled, and she gathered the other ladies like a flock of elegant and comely hens and took them away to the drawing room. The men were left to their port and their exclusive male company. This was the time for frank conversation, if ever there was any, but John stared into his glass of deep ruby wine and ignored the rest of the men as Mr. Denver and the dratted McNair did their best to carry on a conversation about a recent racing day. The younger Sinclair was also unusually quiet. Where were his usual wit and funny stories, where was the charming and debonair Gabriel, whom John so heartily despised? With good reason, he told himself, with good reason.

After a few minutes of somewhat forced conversation, the other two paused, and the silence stretched.

McNair took a deep gulp of his wine. "Much as I hate to leave such good wine unfinished, I think you and I, old man, are a bit de trop. It appears that our fellow guests have a—family discussion—that seems to be unfinished." The man's bright eyes gleamed like a curious magpie's, John thought, his resentment surging again. Damned interfering bastard.

Yet he knew that it was not really this man who had in-cited his anger, even though McNair's easy familiarity with Mrs. Hughes was damned annoying. It was the other man at the table, the silent man who bore his name, whose throat John wanted to put his hands about . . .

John pressed his lips together and didn't answer. With a shrug the short man nodded toward his fellow guest. "What say we join the ladies? And I'll take my glass with me, by God." He poured more port into his goblet and took it with him as he led the way to the door, throwing one more com-ment over his shoulder. "No bloodletting, mind, it would stain the rug." He closed the door ostentatiously behind them.

Now there was only Gabriel and John, sitting a few feet apart at the polished table. The servants had removed the linens before the dessert course, and John leaned one arm on the tabletop.

He had nothing to say to his brother. Or perhaps he did.

John stared into his own wineglass. "I promised myself I would not suffer through another dinner in your company," he said without looking up.

"As did I," Gabriel agreed dryly.

"So why are you here?" The question sounded like a challenge. John took a deep breath and got his voice under control once more before he continued. "You, at least, must have known who your fellow guests would be. I did not."

A pause, then Gabriel answered, "I have a wife."

"And she has you so well trained that you follow, like a faithful spaniel, wherever she goes?"

It was an unworthy response, and he knew it, but John could not contain the bitterness that surged inside him. Gabriel had a wife . . . a beautiful, intelligent, desirable wife of whom any man could be proud. Not that John coveted his elegant blond sister-in-law, it was just that Gabriel always got what he wanted, always had females falling at his feet, always gained the love and the approval that John—he wrenched his thoughts away and waited for the answering snarl from his little brother. John would relish a quarrel, just now, an excuse to throw angry words like daggers toward the smooth, unmarred, too perfect face of his sibling.

But the younger Sinclair spoke slowly, his words measured. "I have a wife who loves me, who believes in me, who is so sure that I will always behave only with the utmost honor that I find myself striving to live up to her expectations. It obliges me to find depths of integrity inside myself that I had never believed existed. Someday, you might understand."

Stung, John flung back, "Might? You think I cannot find a wife?"

Gabriel regarded him, those dark blue eyes which had charmed so many females now hooded and impossible to read. "You can find a female who will accept your hand, of course. Many women would wed a donkey to gain your title and wealth—"

"Damn your cursed hide!" His anger surging out of

control, John slammed down his glass so hard that the wine inside sloshed onto the smooth tabletop. "You think that no woman will have me just because I am not—that I have not—" He could not finish, the words were too bitter to spit out.

"I was about to say, the question is not whether you can find a wife, but do you have the wit and the heart to find the right one," Gabriel finished. "A wife who makes a man hurry home, no matter how enticing the other pleasures that might be found abroad, a wife who makes every day a pleasure and every night a singular joy. A wife who makes you feel at home for the first time in your life."

He paused, looking as if he had said more than he meant, but John was in no mood to analyze his brother's soul. His own ached with an old pain, and the misery consumed his thoughts till he heard Gabriel's comments only through a cloud of anger and gall.

There was too much truth in the words. Hadn't John already made a botch of this whole business, rushing too quickly into an engagement that now hung about his neck like an ox's yoke? He thought of the sweet, lovely Miss Crookshank and wanted to groan.

Gabriel was still watching him. "And I cannot even wish you the felicity of finding that woman," he said. Could it be pity that John glimpsed for the briefest instant in those usually mocking eyes?

John felt his fury rising again and tried to control himself. He could not distress Mrs. Hughes by committing murder in her dining room, though he thought that was the only constraint which held him back from irrational action. "I do not need your good wishes!"

"Because," Gabriel went on. "I have no trust at all in your ability to treat her well, and I would not wish on any woman the hell that our mother suffered!"

John half rose from the table, then took a deep breath. The door to the hall opened, and the footman—who was extraordinarily brave or simply amazingly foolish—put his head in. "Do you require anything, my lords?"

A broadsword with which to sever his infuriating sibling's head from his body, John thought, closing his eyes with the fervency of his wish.

"No, thank you."

He would not lower himself to expose his feelings in front of a servant, nor air the ugly discord of a family twisted asunder by simmering resentment.

The footman bowed and shut the door.

John stood, refusing to even look toward his brother—not that Gabriel deserved that designation! "I shall rejoin the ladies. You can go to hell."

"Your kind regard is duly noted," Gabriel pointed out, his tone dry. "Believe me, I feel just as you do. Unfortunately, civilized conduct, as well as a regard for our hostess's feelings, require me to treat you with a semblance of courtesy. You may believe how fervently I wish it otherwise."

John grunted but did not trust himself to answer. Without waiting to see if the other man followed, he pulled open the door and stomped up the stairs to the sitting room.

It was further infuriating to find McNair sitting close to Mrs. Hughes, making her laugh a little over some no-doubt clever anecdote. For an instant John hated all these men with easy ways who could charm their way through Society—who could make a woman smile. What good did new clothes do, when a man lacked grace and ease?

His face must have revealed too much because there was a silence when he came into the room, and even Miss Crookshank, who had risen as if to cross to his side, hesitated.

It was left to Mrs. Hughes, who had the unceasing courage of a warrior riding into battle, to come and speak quietly to him. "Is there anything I can do for you, my lord?"

He should be angry at her, it was her misguided invitation that had forced him into another encounter with his wretched brother. He should have been, but somehow, gazing into her anxious blue-gray eyes, knowing that she was quite aware of his own agitation, he found that he could not turn his fury toward her. Some of the acridity that burned inside him eased a little, and as long as he could stand close to her, catching just a hint of her rose scent, observing the softness of her cheek and wishing he could touch it—

One of the other guests spoke, and Mrs. Hughes had to turn. John walked away to gaze into the fire, as if he needed its warmth, when the reality was just the opposite. The anger that burned inside him was more than enough to fire his blood.

But Gabriel had been conversing quietly with his wife, and now Lady Gabriel came forward to claim her hostess's attention. "I hope you will forgive us, Marianne, but I find that I have a bit of a headache. I think we must make our farewells. Thank you for the delicious dinner and a delightful evening."

Delightful? John managed not to snort. He glanced back to see his brother bowing smoothly to Mrs. Hughes, and then in a moment, blessedly, they were gone.

And since he had little hope of any private words with Mrs. Hughes, the only thing that might give him pleasure and ease the torment that raged within him, and as he really could not summon the resolution to make polite conversation to the group, John decided he should follow their example.

He said good night with as much savoir faire as he could manage, and pretended not to see the disappointment in Miss Crookshank's face. Mrs. Hughes's expression was more difficult to read, but he thought her eyes reflected her worry.

"I will call tomorrow," he promised, and then he walked into the hall and accepted his hat and gloves from the footman. The hired barouche had been called and was waiting on the pavement. He climbed inside, able at last to scowl into the darkness without worrying about what anyone else would think of his rudeness.

Gabriel could take his lovely wife home, could spend as

much time as he wished with her . . . and John would go home alone, as always, with no one to greet him except his faithful Runt.

The anger inside him, the aching loneliness—he seemed destined to endure it all his days. Even if he married—after he married—Miss Crookshank, would he ever know real contentment? John took a deep breath. He would bear his fate like a man and not succumb to self-pity. Gabriel had been blessed with the good looks and the charm, and John, who had never even before his illness had the ease in company of his engaging younger brother, had been struck down by the scourge which had left him a trial to look upon, disfigured for all time, the object of pity perhaps but not of love, hardly a fit match for any woman of taste and sensibility. And the self-loathing that lived inside him was even more toxic . . .

The ride back to his quiet hotel seemed long, and the darkness teemed with ill spirits, with memories more potent than a ghost conjured out of a late night tale . . .

When the carriage pulled up to the inn, John climbed out and sent the barouche on to the stables. He waved aside a servant who looked out of the main tap room and continued up the steps to his room.

At least Runt rushed to greet him, jumping upon his clean stockings with slightly less than clean paws and barking in delight.

"Down, girl," John commanded, then bent to rub the little dog's head. "Yes, I missed you, too. Come along, we'll take a short walk before bedtime."

The dog had been confined for hours, and she padded happily down the staircase and out the door. John followed along the dark side of the street; at least traffic was infrequent at this time of night.

He leaned against the side of the next building and waited for the dog to do her business; then they would go inside and he would have another glass of wine, maybe two—who cared if his head ached tomorrow. The pain inside him, contained so long as he had resigned himself to his fate, had been reawakened by the sight of his brother happily married, and even more by the tantalizing figure of Mrs. Hughes, whom he wanted—with body and soul— more every day, and yet whom he could not even court un- til he resolved his complicated entanglement with her ward. How could he jilt an innocent young lady? That would hardly endear him to her aunt.

John shut his eyes for a moment, trying to push away the lowering thoughts that hung over him like a cloud of dark smoke. He heard his little dog bark sharply.

"Stay here, Runt," he commanded. "No chasing after stray cats at this time of the night."

Something moved in the shadows past the innyard wall, but it was too large to be a cat. John narrowed his eyes. He heard his dog growl and patter forward on the cobble- stones. He strode after her, bending his head a little to call his spaniel back.

He heard a whisper of movement and smelled just a hint of—

Something crashed down against his head, and the dark- ness swirled around him.

Ten

"*Yes, indeed,*" *Jamie McNair said.* "*That was most entertaining.*"

Marianne glared at him. After half her guests had departed, she had asked Louisa to play upon the pianoforte to amuse those remaining. Louisa agreed with her usual good spirit, and, seating herself at the instrument, ran her fingers along the keys and delivered a sprightly tune. Lord knew they could all use a lighter mood.

But Marianne had a strong feeling that Jamie, who loved to create mischief, was not referring to Louisa's musical accomplishment.

"Take care," she murmured to him as he sat in the next chair before she turned back to join in the applause. "Nicely done, Louisa! Play another, please."

"Perhaps a ballad?" Jamie began. "I know one about two brothers who fight to the death over an old feud—"

Marianne cut him off without compunction. "Perhaps the new Handel air we bought at the shop last week? Or if Mr. McNair wishes a ballad, you must ask him to sing with you. He has a lovely tenor."

Jamie looked self-conscious. "Ah, as to that—"

But Louisa smiled at the middle-aged man. "Yes, do, I should love someone to share the song."

Preening just a little, Jamie walked over to pick out a ballad from the sheet music spread before Louisa, and Marianne sighed in relief. Lord, what a night it had been. Why had she not warned the marquess about inviting his brother to dinner? It had seemed such a simple thing to do. But families were not always simple. Families could be complicated, families could tie one in knots like a tangled thread.

Louisa and Jamie sang a duet, and Marianne tried to pay attention. Eventually the evening wound to a close, and the Denvers and Jamie both said good night.

"Be sure to invite me again the next time you have the Sinclair brothers to dine," Jamie told her, looking arch as he bent over her hand. "I do so love family quarrels— they're so much more intense than the nonfamilial kind."

Marianne rapped his knuckles with her fan. "You remember what I said about being discreet," she warned.

He chuckled and accepted his hat from the footman.

When the door shut at last behind him, she made a rude face he could not see, although Masters looked startled. Feeling unusually weary, she climbed the steps. Louisa hurried after her.

"Aunt Marianne, why was it so uneasy between the marquess and his brother? Lord Gillingham looked quite grim. I was not sure what to say to him."

"I wouldn't say anything about his brother," Marianne warned. "I don't know what the problem is, but obviously there is some bad blood between them."

"Lord Gabriel is so handsome he takes one's breath, but even though he talked with me during dinner, whenever I tried to ask about their childhood, he always changed the subject. He told me funny stories about his travels, but I wanted to hear about Lord Gillingham as a boy. Perhaps Lord Gabriel is not as charming as he seems. If there is a problem there, I'm sure it is not Lord Gillingham's fault," the girl insisted, loyal to her chosen swain.

Marianne felt too weary to try to make sense of a puzzle of which they possessed so few of the pieces. She shrugged.

"At least the marquess promised to come back tomorrow, did he not?" Louisa said as she paused at the doorway to her room.

"Yes, he said he would take us to see the new exhibit of Italian paintings," Marianne agreed, her spirits lifting at the thought. "Sleep well, Louisa."

"Oh, I will," the girl agreed. "Thank you for planning the dinner party, dearest Aunt. You're so good to me." She gave her a quick hug.

Louisa was a sweet girl, Marianne thought as she went into her own bedchamber. She deserved a good husband. But why did it have to be the marquess she had set her heart upon?

With unnecessary force, Marianne pulled the pins out of her twist, pulling a few hairs painfully with them. Rubbing her abused scalp, she took a deep breath and allowed her maid to unbutton her dress.

John opened his eyes to find his face pressed into a muddy patch of dirt which smelt unpleasantly of horses' urine. Runt licked his cheek with wet sloppy enthusiasm.

"Yes, yes, enough." John pushed himself up. He felt groggy, and his head ached like the very devil. What—had he stumbled?

No, memory came rushing back. There had been a blow, and he remembered his spaniel barking and growling with every ounce of her small body. There had been someone in the darkness, though he had not had the time to make out the form . . .

His heart beating faster, John lurched upright. Someone had hit him. Was his attacker still here, still a danger?

He had been foolish not to pay more heed to his surroundings. This was not his quiet secluded estate, but the outskirts of London, a city rife with criminals ready for any opportunity to prey upon the unwary. This was what he got for choosing a small inn in an out-of-the-way location. All his senses now alert, John looked around. But he heard nothing except a lone cart trundling along the street; otherwise, the street and the innyard seemed empty.

He pulled out his handkerchief and wiped the mud off his face. His fashionable new evening hat lay at his feet. John stooped, suppressing a groan as the movement made his bruised head spin. He straightened slowly, the hat in his hand battered past repair. The fashionable shop from which it had come would not claim its creation now. But the stiff hat had softened the blow for him, which was much more important.

And Runt had played a part. He had a dim memory of the dog growling and snarling at the unknown assailant. John reached inside his jacket and patted his pockets, but nothing seemed to be missing. Had his small dog with her heroic mettle frightened away the would-be thief? John walked a few feet into the darkness and looked about him. Runt followed eagerly, pausing to sniff a scrap of thin cloth.

Despite the vertigo his movement triggered, John picked it up. It felt wet and he smelt the tang of blood. Yes, Runt had sunk her teeth into someone's leg.

"Good girl," he told her, hoping the thief ached as badly as John himself did. "Now, inside. We've had enough adventure for one night."

It was a fitting end to a bad evening, he thought. He walked back to the inn and considered reporting the incident, but there seemed little to be gained. The criminal was surely long gone, and John had no stomach to listen to long apologies and commiserations from his landlord.

A glass of wine, a cold cloth for his aching head, a bath and bed, that was all he wanted. Or at least, that was what he could manage to obtain. What he wanted was a winsome woman with dark hair whose blue-gray eyes seemed to look inside his soul . . . but she was out of reach, at least for the time.

He snapped his fingers at his dog and led Runt back to their chamber.

The next day Lord Gillingham arrived at their door as promised. Louisa, who had been waiting all morning for him to appear, rushed up to the sitting room to tell her aunt.

"He's here," she said, sounding a little breathless. "Come along, Aunt."

Marianne looked into the glass and adjusted her hat, then followed more sedately down the stairs. But although she might look serene enough on the outside, she could not keep a flush of happiness from surging through her.

The marquess handed them into his hired barouche. He looked somewhat pale, she thought; she hoped it was not the result of the unpleasant evening.

"Good morning, I hope you are well?" she said, meaning the question as more than just the usual pleasantry.

"A slight headache," he admitted. She thought that he winced a little as he adjusted his usual large-brimmed hat.

"Should we postpone our outing?" she asked, concerned.

Louisa's eyes widened in protest, and Lord Gillingham shook his head. "No, I shall be fine," he assured them. He called to the coachman, and the carriage pulled away and into the traffic.

When they arrived at the exhibit hall, they were handed down by the groom. The hall itself was crowded, and Marianne hung back a little to allow Louisa and the marquess to talk as they joined the mass of people who all seemed called to meditate upon the beauty of Italian villages and rustic landscapes.

The scenes were lovely, and gazing at them, Marianne felt the long-repressed pang of old dreams never fulfilled. As a girl, she had vowed to see Venice before she died, to contemplate the beauties of French valleys once the eternal war with Napoleon ended. She had longed to gaze upon the great pyramids and to explore China's fabled wall. They were unlikely, perhaps even unseemly, dreams for a well-brought-up young lady, she knew. They were rarely spoken of because they would earn her the usual lecture from her mother. But like her quiet father, who pursued his reveries in his books, she longed for more than village teas or even fashionable London assemblies.

Marianne allowed her thoughts to wander into the painted scenery, while for the next half hour Louisa smiled up at the tall man at her side, chatting about the scenes portrayed in oils and waterpaints and framed in carved gilt frames. The marquess nodded and answered politely. But presently Louisa spied a young woman she had met at Lady Sealey's tea, and she paused to speak to her.

Lord Gillingham fell back to stand closer to Marianne. "Shall we sit down for a moment?" he suggested.

"Where?" Marianne asked practically.

But the marquess took her arm and guided her to the side of the hall, and somehow procured two chairs for them, then caught the attention of a waiter and sent the man to bring them tea.

"Does your head still ache?" she asked, a little worried about his lack of spirits.

"It's nothing," he told her, his tone dry. "Perhaps a surfeit of artistic-looking peasants."

"I do wonder if they can be as happy as they sometimes appear in paint," she agreed, laughing a little. "I suspect that rustic cottages are not quite so appealing as they often look here, dry and snug and framed in gilt."

"With no inconvenient rain to creep about the eaves," he agreed. "Though my tenants have little to complain about with their roofs, I promise you. I would see to their repair at once."

"I'm sure you would," Marianne agreed. She felt he would be a responsible landlord. Beneath his sometimes brusque manner, which already seemed to be somewhat smoothed as he spent more time in company, she increasingly believed he had a kind heart. He was the kind of man one could depend upon when times were bad, and celebrate with when times were good.

She thought for a moment of her late husband. During difficult times, poor Harry had shrugged and waited for others to act. Waited for Marianne to placate an angry creditor, when Harry had lost too much of his quarterly allowance at the gaming tables, left it to Marianne to discharge an inefficient servant. She had sometimes felt more like his mother or older sister than his wife.

Marianne sighed. Since she'd left her own home to marry, left her patient, bookish father and efficient, bustling mother, she'd never been able to depend on a man to come to her aid. In the beginning, she'd been dismayed to find her husband so reluctant to take charge, so indecisive and so ready to shrug off any responsibility. But marriages were made for better or for worse, and she had scolded herself and put aside her disappointment, telling herself that real life was not the same as a fairy tale, that sagas of gallant knights who always rescued their ladies were only a poet's invention. Those strong heroic men were the stuff of stories for young girls to dream about, not a pattern for real life.

Yet, perhaps some part of her still wondered if a man could be both strong and kind, understanding and resolute.

Lord Gillingham seemed a man one could count on, even if it were only for a cup of tea when one was thirsty, or an arm to lean on if the way were rough. And the way he made her feel when he touched her hand or took her arm—now, that was not in the least brotherly!

"Thank you," she said when the servant came with their tea, but it was the marquess she glanced toward.

She had promised herself not to mention the difficult evening just past, but to her surprise, he was the one who brought up the subject.

"I hope I did not spoil your gathering," he said, a bit gruffly. "I fear I am not very practiced in a lady's drawing room."

She was about to reassure him when a stout matron passed just in front of them and paused, her expression changing as she glanced at the marquess's face.

He flushed and pulled down the brim of his hat, and the woman walked on, whispering something to her companion.

Pursing her lips in anger, Marianne put one hand, without thinking, upon his arm. "Do not regard it," she said.

He gazed into her eyes. Before he put up the usual barrier, for an instant she glimpsed just how much it bothered him, the stares and inquisitive looks from too curious strangers.

"I can't blame them," he said bluntly. "I know I am not an object of beauty."

"I blame them!" she retorted. "They are rude and judgmental to consider such a trifling aspect of a stranger's appearance." It had been so long since she had considered his scarred face that when she gazed upon him now she hardly noticed the pockmarks. She saw instead his dark eyes and his strong nose, the mouth that tried to hide all emotion but could not always mask his hurt or his rare moments of humor.

"Trifling?" He looked at her in what seemed to be surprise, and she was prepared to explain to him just how little he should regard the marks left by the illness when he put his hand on top of hers, where it still rested on his arm.

What a strong grip he had. Even through his gloves she could detect the warmth and the energy that flowed through his whole body, an energy that seemed to spark an instant response inside her. Her belly ached with longings she had put aside long ago, with a hunger she had, in her brief marriage, barely learned to feel.

But somehow Marianne sensed that it would be different with this man, that if he leaned forward and pressed his lips against hers, she would feel a masculine power, a potency as different from her boyish husband as night from day. Her skin rippled with sensation, and the ache inside her deepened. She found herself bending closer . . .

A woman tittered, and with a start Marianne remembered the mobs of people all about them. The crowd that chatted and laughed and thronged the hall made this no place to indulge in dangerous fantasies. How could she have forgotten? Blushing, she straightened and withdrew her hand, but not without a pang of reluctance.

"I particularly liked that large landscape of the Alps," she told him, turning to safer topics. "Its vista is quite breathtaking."

"And just as hard to scale," he agreed, almost beneath his breath.

Marianne raised her brows, not sure she had heard correctly. What caused the shadow to cross his face? "Are you bored with the paintings, my lord? We can collect Louisa and return home."

"I should like to send Louisa—Miss Crookshank—to . . ." he hesitated, and she gazed at him in surprise.

"I should like her to be happy," he finished after a slight pause. "Which reminds me, I had something to tell you when we had a moment alone. I sent a man to Scotland to find out more about Alton Crookshank. My hireling has just returned."

Marianne felt her heartbeat quicken. "And?"

"And he was unable to arrange a meeting—he was told that Mr. Crookshank had journeyed to London for an extended stay."

"Oh, dear." Marianne stared blankly at the crowd in front of them, the large, milling crowd, and realized that she had allowed her own desire to see the exhibit to overrule her first impulse for caution. What was she doing, allowing Louisa to mingle in such a crush?

"We must find Louisa and take our leave," she suggested with a rush of guilt.

The marquess nodded, and they rose.

Louisa spent a pleasant few minutes chatting with Miss Talbert, comparing notes about the best dressmakers and the cunning shop full of ribbons and other notions that she had discovered tucked into a side street. When the other young lady and her mother said good-bye and moved on to finish their viewing of the exhibit, Louisa felt a pang of disappointment. She should return to the marquess now. She did not want him to feel neglected. But she was becoming a bit weary of her chosen good deed. As much as she laughed and teased and cajoled, he never seemed to match her gaiety with any spirit. Oh, he answered her, of course, and he was always polite, but the spark of fun that she and Lucas—well, that she and a friend had once shared—she did not feel it at all. Was this what marriage to the marquess would be like?

It was a lowering thought, and Louisa had to steel herself before she could smile again and turn to find Lord Gillingham and her aunt.

But a familiar face caught her attention before she had completed her about-face.

"Lucas!" she exclaimed in surprise. "What are you doing here?" Really, she had gone a whole week without stumbling over him, she should have known . . . "I mean, how nice to see you, sir." She looked about, but could discern no accompanying young lady clinging to his arm or hanging on his coattails.

For a delicious moment she thought he seemed glad to see her, but then his expression reverted to the cautious mask she was so weary of. The handsome hazel eyes were guarded, but she admired the smooth forehead and the adorable lock of hair that strayed from his careful brushing—she had once been free to push it back, but no longer. Louisa felt the pain of their parting as if for the first time, and she swallowed hard.

"Miss Crookshank," he said formally, giving her a slight bow.

She responded with a graceful curtsy, which gave her time to pull her thoughts together. She must not look so happy to see him. She had some pride left, even if his face still troubled her dreams at night.

"I agree, most of London seems to be here. Are you enjoying the display?" he asked, his tone no more than polite.

"Very much," she agreed. "And you?"

"Very much," he echoed.

She was goaded into replying, "I do not remember that you enjoyed artistic exhibitions. When we went to see that traveling show of Spanish landscapes, you said too much artwork could drive a fellow to drink."

He looked a bit self-conscious. "I was only a boy, Lou—Miss Crookshank. I have matured since then."

"No doubt," she said dryly.

"People change," he pointed out. "I am simply trying to broaden my cultural horizons, add a bit of town bronze, don't you know."

"Not to mention broadening your social horizons," she snapped. "Since you seem to be escorting a different young woman every time I see you."

He seemed ready to return an angry answer, but, almost to her disappointment, he mastered his first response and answered, with immense dignity, "I am endeavoring to meet young ladies, yes. I plan to marry soon—I am getting past the age of childish indulgences."

"I see." Louisa sustained her restrained pose with some difficulty. She wanted to cry, but she, too, could practice self-control. "Very mature of you."

"Besides, you're always with that ill-favored lord what's-his-name."

"It is rude to speak poorly of a person's looks, Lucas," she answered. "And Lord Gillingham is a very worthy man."

She put a slight emphasis on the last word, and perhaps it was that which caused her old suitor to remark, "Yes, no doubt, even if he is old enough to be your sire."

"Don't be ridiculous," she argued. "He is not old!"

"It hardly matters. With a lofty title, a no-doubt handsome estate and plenty of blunt, I suppose age makes no difference."

She gasped. In all their times together, Lucas had never been deliberately cruel. What had come over him?

"I am not allowing the marquess to court me because of his title or his money," she flashed back, putting aside any memory of her earlier interest in her fiancé's exalted rank. Besides, she hadn't really been serious. "He deserves better than the disdain that too many curious, ill-mannered spectators bestow upon him. He cannot help the scars of an old illness. Anyhow, it is the qualities inside him that make him a man to be admired."

"Doing it too brown, Louisa!" Sir Lucas suddenly seemed to lose all shreds of his much-acclaimed maturity.

"You expect me to believe that you really care for this man? He is not your sort, at all."

"Just because he is willing to accompany me to art shows and theaters? Because he will stroll with me through the park, which you used to find too tame? He is a man of taste and sophistication . . . He is a man, not a boy!"

"And I am not?" Lucas's usually merry eyes narrowed in anger.

"I did not say that, only—"

"If he is indeed a man of taste, he deserves better than a selfish hoyden who will desert him at the least provocation!"

"Oh, unfair!" Louisa blinked against the sudden tears that threatened to slip past her lashes.

"Sir Lucas?" A petite young lady with reddish-blond hair and delicate good looks had appeared at Lucas' side. "I'm sorry I took so long."

He was here with a companion, after all. Hadn't he said he was looking for a wife? Louisa felt this was the last straw. She struggled to master her unruly emotions before she was disgraced forever.

Sir Lucas's expression was almost comical as he wrestled with conflicting feelings. After a moment he managed a polite—only slightly twisted—smile. "Miss Romney, Miss Crookshank, an old acquaintance from Bath."

Louisa sank into a curtsy, bending her head to hide her face. She murmured some kind of greeting, later she could not have said what, and added, "Please excuse me, my friends will be missing me."

Then she turned and, almost running, pushed her way through the crowd. She had no idea where the marquess had gone, or her aunt; the mass of people made it hard to pick out any individual among the press. But she caught a glimpse of the door that led out to the street, and she had a sudden longing for escape. If she burst into tears right here, in front of a curious, staring mob, she would never live it down. Hadn't she already experienced enough social disgrace, after her blunder in the park, to blight her entire Season?

She pushed past a group of gossiping matrons and was able to slip through the doorway, pausing a few feet on to the pavement.

She must conquer this heartache; obviously, Lucas no longer cared for her. And if all she had to look forward to was comforting Lord Gillingham's reclining years, which left her feeling heavy with melancholy, so be it. At least Lucas would grow to see that she could be mature, that she was not as selfish and despicable as he was determined to think. And as for his own much-vaunted maturity, a really mature person would give a friend another chance, she thought, biting her lips to hold back the tears. But if only—

He had not always been so harsh. A sudden memory of Lucas tenderly taking her hand and pressing her lips with her first kiss was her undoing. The tears began to fall. Oh, folly, she could not be seen like this! She would find the marquess and her aunt and tell them she had a headache—

She took a few unseeing steps and collided with a solid object.

"Pardon, miss," a rough voice said.

She blinked and saw a street vendor with his cart.

"Not at all," she managed to say. "It was my fault." But the tears were sliding down her cheeks in earnest now. She turned in the opposite direction and almost walked into a stout lady who gazed at her in concern.

"My dear, are you well?"

Embarrassed, Louisa managed to nod. All she wanted was to get out of here. Where was her aunt? And, oh, what would she say to the marquess if he saw her like this?

While Louisa squeezed her eyes shut and tried to think of an excuse for her distress, she heard a familiar voice.

"Louisa, what is wrong?"

It was Aunt Marianne, and she sounded concerned. And, of course the marquess was with her. He came forward now with a speed that, in any other mood, would have pleased Louisa no end. But now she only blushed more deeply and tried to push back her tears.

"It was that rough man—I think he was about to assault the poor girl," the woman who had spoken earlier insisted.

"I saw him accost her, and it was very frightening. No wonder the poor child is upset."

"Oh, no," Louisa said. No doubt, the woman was only trying to help, but she had it all wrong.

"Where is the man?" Lord Gillingham demanded.

Louisa looked around but saw no sign of the street vendor. Thank goodness, she could not allow an innocent man to suffer any recrimination. But neither did she want to explain the reason for her silly nerve storm here in this public place.

"I never! He just slipped away," the too helpful matron said.

Aunt Marianne exchanged a glance with the marquess, then took Louisa's arm. "I think it's time we took our leave."

"Oh, yes, please," Louisa agreed. "I would like to go home."

In the carriage her aunt tried gently to question her, but Louisa only shook her head and gave her an appealing look until Aunt Marianne gave up.

By the time they reached home, Louisa had managed to compose herself, and when she said farewell to the marquess, she thanked him nicely for the expedition.

"I deserve no thanks, since I took such poor care of you that a stranger was allowed to frighten you," he said, his tone grave.

She blushed. "It was nothing, really," she murmured. "But thank you for your concern. I do feel safe when you are nearby."

She made her curtsy and hurried upstairs before anyone could question her again.

Once in her room she shut the door firmly and fell upon her bed. And the ready tears surged. Sir Lucas was lost to her forever, and it was her own fault. Perhaps she really was as superficial and selfish as Lucas believed. She should have been more mindful of his injury, on that fateful day in Bath, which now seemed so long ago. She should learn to think more of others. She considered the marquess, perhaps not as much fun as Lucas, not as lighthearted and playful, but a good man and determined to look out for her welfare. Marriage to him would not be so bad, surely.

And she would not turn aside from his courtship over any consideration of his looks or his sometimes brusque manner. She would not be selfish, this time, she would prove that she had matured beyond her girlhood shallowness, and in the end, she was certain she would learn to love him.

And then the tears overwhelmed her, and she lay her head upon the pillow, free at last to indulge in hearty sobs.

Downstairs, Marianne was frowning. "Do you think it was another attack on Louisa?" she asked the marquess. "We must find this Alton Crookshank."

He wanted to kiss away the worry lines that furrowed her brow, but he could not. How base she would think him if he tried to court her now. If he had more social graces, if he had not been in such a hurry to find a mate so that he could retreat from the prying eyes and painful social gatherings of a busy city, he would not have mired himself in such a dilemma. Her eyes troubled, Marianne gazed up at him, and he wanted to gather her into his arms and—he had to push the thought away, despite the surge of need that flowed through his whole body and made him ache with a longing he had never felt so urgently before.

"Marianne—Mrs. Hughes—" he said impulsively.

"Yes?" She stared at him, and his courage failed him. No, he could not speak, not now. If he could end the threat to Miss Crookshank, perhaps he could then manage to disentangle himself from the bonds with which he had ensnared himself.

"We will find the man and determine if your niece is in danger," he promised her. "I will not rest until I know."

She smiled at him, such a tempting lifting of her lips that again, he felt the ache deep in his belly. If he could only lean forward and taste that full lower lip, how sweet it would be, how much it would ease the passion in his blood.

Yet even as he thought it, he knew it was a lie; kissing her luscious mouth would only lead to more kisses, on the slender pale neck, on the swelling bosom he had only the barest glimpse of beneath the neckline of her silk gown. The heat gathered in his groin, and he could do nothing to tell her, to show her, how much he yearned for her touch, for her love . . .

She touched his arm lightly, making him jump—it took a palpable effort to keep from pulling her into his arms. She was speaking; he tried to make sense of the words.

"I am so thankful for your help, my lord. Otherwise, I would be at my wit's end."

He could only pat her hand, like some gray-haired grandsire whose blood ran as cool as his presently ran hot. He mumbled his farewell and wrenched himself away.

The footman held open the door, and John made the mistake of glancing into the looking glass as he passed. The scarred, unsightly face that met his gaze sent a rush of icy reality through him, effectively dousing any thought of love or desire.

What woman would choose to love a man with such an aspect?

He hurried out and into his hired carriage, anger at his wretched fate overcoming any other emotion. He knocked on the panel to send the carriage moving forward, and, alone, was able to scowl as deeply as he could wish at the empty seat opposite him.

What woman of sense would wish to marry him? True, Miss Crookshank had accepted him, but he suspected that his title and his estate might have influenced her ability to ignore his disfigured countenance.

Why did that bother him less than the thought that Mrs. Hughes might make the same bargain? Because he did not think that she would. She seemed to accept him with an easy friendliness, true, but he had not suggested more than friendship.

What if he did try to kiss her? He dreaded the thought of seeing her shrink away, repelled by such a gruesome visage leaning close to her own, like the last village girl he had been tempted by when his body's hunger became too urgent to ignore. But the girl's look of fear, of repulsion, had ended the suggestion of any tryst before it had well begun. He had sent the poor girl home and retreated, as always, to his study and his books, pulling the curtains to dim the lights and hide himself from view.

Miss Crookshank was younger and might be even more repelled, although he had never yet tried to kiss her. And somehow, it mattered less to him that she might be steeling herself to allow him the pleasure of her company.

Because she was not the woman he wanted, as by now he knew too well. And he could not dare to test Mrs. Hughes's forbearance, much less the faint chance that she might feel some attraction to him, until he had made sure of Miss Crookshank's safety. Then, he would try to untie the tangled knots he had woven through his own folly, and then, and then—

It was impossible to conceive. Muttering a few words which no lady should hear, he tapped on the panel again. But, caught in the usual London traffic, the barouche could move no faster.

Gritting his teeth, John leaned back against the cushions.

Eleven

Unlocking a man's true emotions can be as arduous
as opening an oyster with a toothpick.

—MARGERY, COUNTESS OF SEALEY

$\mathcal{T}$*he man John had hired to make inquiries*
about Louisa's mysterious missing relative turned up
early the next morning. He had been recommended by
John's landlord. The innkeeper had not seemed to find it
unusual when his titled guest had requested the services of
a dependable, respectable-looking man to make discreet
inquires, and if he seemed to assume that the matter involved a lady—there was some truth to that.

John put down his cup of tea and waited for the report.

Hat in hand, Mr. Compton looked as meek and unre-
markable as always in his somewhat threadbare brown coat
and wilted neck cloth, but there was a suppressed air of tri-
umph beneath his quiet appearance that made John feel a
surge of anticipation.

"I have found him, my lord!" he said.

John drew a deep breath. "Well done!" His investigator
already knew that there was a handsome bonus promised
for this information, so John added only, "You have earned
your commission. What is his address?"

The man told him, and John made careful note of it.

When the agreed-upon sum had changed hands, the little man took his leave, still looking most pleased with himself, and John ordered his carriage. He had a call to make.

The next day Louisa looked pale and wan, and begged leave to stay home when Marianne went out for a luncheon with female friends. Marianne felt real concern for her ward.

"Shall I stay at home with you?" she suggested, gazing at Louisa's pallid cheeks and woebegone expression.

"Oh, no, I just want to lie quietly. I have such a headache," the younger woman said, her tone earnest. "Please go and enjoy your party."

So Marianne left her with her lady's maid close at hand. Masters hailed a hackney, and when she arrived at her friend Therese's home, Marianne was pleased to find Lady Sealey among the guests.

"How are you, my dear?" the silver-haired matron asked. "You seem a bit abstracted today."

"You could say that," Marianne agreed, her tone dry, thinking of mysterious attacks and vague threats they could not seem to pin down. "It has been a tumultuous week. My niece is somewhat on my mind, and—"

"And?" The older woman asked, sipping a glass of sherry. "You have that look in your eye, my dear. Your niece, though a dear child, is not the only object of your thoughts. Has a man caught your fancy, at last? It's high time, you know."

Marianne found herself flushing. "No, no, I mean, I am only concerned with Louisa's happiness."

"And not your own?" Lady Sealey's look was pointed.

"I didn't mean that, exactly. Only that she is the one who needs a husband, not I."

"Miss Crookshank has plenty of time to find the appropriate mate, she's hardly more than a child. You should think about yourself for a change. You need to give matrimony another chance, dear girl. Or, at least, find an amusing lover."

Marianne blushed in earnest. Her older friend's views on love were a bit . . . Continental.

"Lord Gillingham is spending a good deal of time in your company, I've been told," the countess continued.

Marianne accepted a glass of sherry from the footman and took a sip, trying not to dissolve into nervous giggles. *She* was not a child, and she must not act so gauche. "No, no, he is courting my niece, who is in my care, so I am there, that is, we are often together, but it is only because of Louisa."

That sounded so jumbled that she was not surprised when the other woman raised her silvery brows.

"Are you certain? Sometimes it takes a man a while to realize what, or whom, he hungers for. He may think he craves lamb chops when all the time, it was really roast beef that he yearned after. Men are dear creatures, of course, but sometimes a little slow to realize their true feelings."

Marianne shook her head. "No, no, I'm sure you are mistaken. Although to be honest, I have had few intimate— I mean—personal conversations with the marquess. He rarely talks about himself. I know very little about his family, for instance, or his childhood, and I still wonder what has set the two brothers at such odds."

She lowered her voice and, knowing the older woman would be discreet, told the countess about her disastrous dinner party.

Lady Sealey looked thoughtful. "I think you should inquire of the marquess about an earlier love in his life."

Marianne blinked. "Oh, I couldn't. Whatever love affairs he has had, I would not wish to pry, and anyhow, it's none of my business."

"I meant a more important lady than any former amour," the countess insisted. "On some moment when the occasion presents itself naturally, I believe you should ask Lord Gillingham about his mother."

"But why?" Marianne asked in surprise.

Lady Sealey wielded her fan. "What he says might be revealing, or even what he does not say."

Marianne hesitated, not sure what to answer. And then they were called in to the luncheon, and she ended up seated on the other side of the table from Lady Sealey, so there were no more shared confidences about Lord Gillingham and his secrets. But that did not prevent her mind from repeating the brief conversation over and over, worrying the snippet of dialogue as a dog would a bone.

What should she ask about his mother? Why did the countess think such an inquiry would help explain—what? Perhaps she should just stop worrying about it all and help Louisa plan her wedding and be done with it.

And that was such a depressing thought that even her excellent cock-a-leekie soup lost its savor, and she put down her spoon with her bowl still almost full.

John took his carriage to the modest set of rooms where Alton Crookshank was said to reside during his stay in London. The building was neat but a trifle run down and seemed to indicate that Mr. Crookshank might, indeed, be in need of more funds. Whether he was willing to commit murder to achieve a more comfortable lifestyle was the question.

But when John rapped on the door of the second-floor flat, no one answered. John frowned and tried again, knocking harder.

Still, nothing. John swore, then heard a slight creak, and the back of his neck prickled; was he being watched? He turned and detected someone peering at him from behind the slightly open door across the hall.

"Do you know where I might find Mr. Alton Crookshank?" John demanded without preamble.

He thought the door was going to shut in his face, then it opened a few more inches. He was able to make out the slight form of an elderly woman, her expression a comical mixture of curiosity and alarm.

"Are you a bill collector?"

John bit back another oath. Had he acquired his expensive new wardrobe for nothing? "Do I look like a bill collector?"

She considered him, then shook her head. "Suppose not. Just don't wish to do Mr. Crookshank an ill turn. He's polite to me, which is more than I can say about most young things. And he does not use bad language!" She frowned in disapproval.

"My apologies," John told her. "I did not know anyone was listening, much less a lady." Young? That did not sound like the man he sought. But taking a harder look at this ancient lady, John supposed that anyone south of threescore years would look young to her.

"I only wish to pay my respects to Mr. Crookshank," he told her.

"You are acquainted?" She still looked suspicious.

John shook his head. "No, but I know one of his relations."

She considered, then said slowly, "He's at the Academy. He's giving a lecture this morning. He's a respected scientist, you know." She said it proudly, as if Mr. Crookshank's presence added some cachet to their shabby building.

John raised his brows. This was unexpected. "Then I certainly would not wish to miss such an important event," he said gravely. She was persuaded to tell him the address; then John thanked her and set out again.

This time, he had more success. After some persuasion he was admitted to a small office, where he found a gray-haired gentleman seated behind a desk, shuffling several piles of papers.

John's heart sank. This man did not have the appearance of a potential assassin. He looked as inoffensive as anyone could. Did they have the wrong man?

"The marquess of Gillingham to see you, sir," the doorman who had led John in announced.

The older gentleman looked up. "Are you here for the lecture? It's not until ten, and I must go over my notes first."

John shook his head. "I will not keep you long, sir, I assure you. I only wish to ascertain if you are the great-uncle of Miss Louisa Crookshank. Her father's name was Thomas."

The man took off the pair of spectacles with which he had been peering at the papers in front of him and gave John a harder look.

"I am, although I have had little communication with that side of my family for years." He paused for a moment. "Not their fault, really. I was a wild young man, and my father was incensed with some of my behavior. It led to a breach."

John nodded.

"So why would they be searching for me now, and what connection do you have with the family?" the other man demanded.

"I am a—ah—friend of Miss Crookshank's. She is in London for the Season and will be making her coming-out soon. She and her family wondered if you would be interested in renewing contact."

The man stared at him for a moment. "They wish to extend a flag of truce, so to speak? I would not be amiss to that, certainly. Our falling out happened long ago, and much has changed since then. I have not seen my nephews for years, though I read about young Louisa's father's death, a sad thing to die before his time."

"Yes," John agreed, even as he swallowed his disappointment. This could not be the man who had attacked Louisa. Which meant they had to start anew in their search for an assailant or accept that the accidents had been just that, unrelated and unplanned.

"I will pass on to her family your willingness to receive an invitation," he said. "I regret that I cannot stay for your lecture."

Mr. Crookshank rose. He looked over John's well-cut coat and seemed to come to a decision. "A marquess, you say? The Academy is always in need of endowments, my lord, if I may be so bold as to suggest it. If you should feel inclined to sponsor some of our scientific surveys, my own research would benefit greatly."

"I will certainly consider it," John agreed, offering his hand as if in apology for his earlier suspicions.

But when they shook, John was surprised by the firmness of the man's grip. Crookshank might be past fifty, but his frame was hard and lean, and his strong grasp spoke of a still healthy vitality. His brown eyes were unexpectedly shrewd, and by his own admission, he was in need of funds.

Perhaps John had been too quick to judge, and this man was not as harmless as he'd first appeared. . . .

When Marianne returned home, she had hardly entered the vestibule before there was another knock at the door.

"Lord Gillingham," her footman announced. His tone was suitably impassive, but Marianne knew her servants well enough to detect a tiny hint of complacency. At least her small staff were impressed with having a marquess calling so often, she thought, hiding her amusement.

And she could not dwell on the fact that her own dark cloud seemed to disappear as if a brisk spring breeze had swept it away. It was merely proper to give him her hand and to smile in welcome.

"I came to see if you—if you both are recovered after yesterday," he said, holding her hand a moment too long. "And I have news."

Marianne hated to break that slight contact, but Masters was waiting to show the guest to the sitting room. She stepped back but glanced at her footman. "I will show the marquess up," she said.

After he departed, she said, her voice low, "What have you learned?"

"I have met Alton Crookshank," the marquess told her. "My agent located him, and I made a call this morning."

Marianne put one hand to her throat. "And? Does he admit—no, I suppose he would not, even if he were guilty. What did you think of him?"

Lord Gillingham described the encounter, and Marianne frowned, trying to puzzle out what it all meant.

"So he seems innocent on the surface, and yet—" the marquess hesitated.

"Yet, you are not sure we should let down our guard? I agree, not when so much is at stake. It's Louisa's life we are speaking of!" Marianne sighed. "And speaking of Louisa, she had a headache this morning; let me see if she feels like coming down. I know she will be pleased that you called to check on her," Marianne said. "Excuse me for just a moment."

She hurried up the steps, and when she reached Louisa's bedchamber, she tapped lightly on the door. There was no answer. Marianne turned the knob and looked in. Louisa lay beneath a light coverlet, her eyes closed, her breathing even.

Should she wake her? Louisa would be disappointed to miss seeing the marquess. On the other hand, she had really not looked herself this morning, and perhaps she needed the rest.

While she tried to decide, Marianne heard a rustle of skirts and turned to see Eva, Louisa's young maid, in the hall.

"How is your mistress?" she asked, keeping her voice low.

"She had a dreadful headache, ma'am," the servant answered. "She only just dropped off to sleep a short time ago."

Marianne made up her mind. "I shan't wake her, then." She paused in her own room to take off her bonnet and glance quickly into the looking glass, then she descended the steps.

But the marquess was not in the sitting room. He could not have left without saying good-bye; that would be inexcusably rude. Where was he?

After Mrs. Hughes ascended, John started to follow her toward the staircase. But as she climbed the steps, something caught his eye, and he paused.

A door was ajar—it led into a small room across from

the dining room. He had never been in it before, so an impeccably mannered visitor should have ignored the unusual sight within and continued up the staircase.

Not being burdened with perfect manners, John pushed the door open and stepped inside. The room seemed to be a tiny study, crowded with shelves of books and artifacts. He moved closer to inspect the object that had caught his eye. Made from polished wood, it was a carving of an elephant with trunk upraised. Its style was unusual. Behind it a framed print revealed a woman in an Asian-style dress with slanted eyes and a mysterious smile.

He crossed to the bookcases and glanced through them. He saw histories and poetry and books of travels; an assortment of journals written by visitors to exotic lands. Not the usual sort of reading favored by ladies of the Ton, he suspected.

A Persian rug on the floor was bright with color, and in addition to the books, the shelves and two tables revealed half a dozen small curiosities. This was a side of Marianne Hughes he had not discerned before, though he thought he had had hints of her far-ranging interests.

These objects could have belonged to her late husband, of course, or been handed down from some other relative, but John had a strong sense that these were Mrs. Hughes's particular treasures. The books, the prints, and the artifacts all revealed a lively curiosity about a world bigger than any she had been able to glimpse in person. Yes, from the things she had gathered around her, he sensed her longing for more than the polite world of London Society. She had a bigger spirit than could be encompassed in a tearoom or even a fancy-dress ball. In this small room, he thought, he had been granted a glimpse of her heart.

He heard a hushed sound and turned. His hostess stood in the doorway, her expression difficult to read.

"Forgive me," he said. "The door was open, and I wondered about the—ah—elephant." His statement sounded foolish, and he hoped he had not angered her.

Her eyes were very bright, but he still could not decipher her emotions. Her voice was cool when she spoke.

"You have never seen an elephant before, my lord?"

"Not in a lady's chamber," he told her frankly. "I see that your interests are wide, indeed, Mrs. Hughes."

"You are surprised? You have never wondered about continents beyond the sea, where people live so differently than we do?" She came into the room and lay one hand on the carving with a touch so light it was almost a caress.

For one insane instant he envied the inanimate creature.

She did not seem to note his intent gaze. "Where there are marvelous creatures very different from those who inhabit our native woods and moors . . . brightly colored birds that outshine our drab sparrows, unusual creatures who seem put together from odd bits left over when God was finishing his creation?"

She picked up a book from a table and turned its pages. "Look, is this not a fascinating beast?" She held up the drawing for him to see.

It was a monstrosity, he thought, its awkward form looking like something out of a nightmare. "What is it?"

She smiled at his amazement. "A giant anteater, it lives in Africa. And there are so many more, unusual to our eyes but perfectly at home on their own native shore. Have you never wished to see more than the country in which you were born and bred?"

This time there was no mistaking the feelings that colored her tone.

"You have," he said slowly, moved by this glimpse into a side of herself that she usually kept hidden. "You are an explorer at heart, Mrs. Hughes. Would you really travel to those countries if you could? Brave the dangers of wild lands and savage peoples?"

She smiled, and it lit up her whole face, giving her a glow that made him long to pull her into his arms and grant her every wish.

"Oh, yes," she said simply. "To hear the lions roar at sunset on an African savanna, to glide down the misty canals of Venice and admire the churches and artwork in Florence, to marvel at the wild glory of the Alps, or study the ancient temples of Greece with all their mysteries, who would not wish to enjoy such adventures? I used to dream of such voyages, as a girl. I was going to don my traveling cloak and traverse the world, explore the fabled pyramids in Egypt and its wide trackless deserts! Would you not like to ride a camel?"

He was surprised into a laugh. "The idea had not occurred to me."

She had mentioned traveling to foreign climes before, he remembered, but he had not taken her seriously. Now he saw that this was more than idle conversation.

"Why did you and your husband not travel abroad?" he asked before he remembered that this might be too personal a question.

"When we first married, there was the war," she explained. "And later, when there was talk of peace, Harry wasn't interested. Even though we had spoken of it when we were young, planned safaris across Africa and sailing trips to the Orient, he said those were childish dreams, and now that we were grown up, not worth taking seriously."

Her voice was so sad he wanted to weep for her.

"As long as there were horse races and cockfights and bare-knuckle matches nearby, Harry was content. He had his male friends in London, and his clubs." She glanced down to veil those lovely and too revealing eyes. Her tone was matter-of-fact, now; perhaps she felt she had divulged too much.

But John was swept by a rush of anger.

"And what did you have?" he demanded. "I can see that your husband was perfectly content in the city." And if he thought the young man a churlish insensitive lout, John could hardly say so. The other man was dead and could not defend himself, though from the sound of it, he would have been amazed to have been called to do so. "But what about you?"

She would not meet his gaze. "I had teas and lunches and balls, theater parties and walks in the park, the usual sort of amusements with which ladies entertain themselves."

Except that she was not usual, in any sense of the word.

She was unique and extraordinary, and it was a tragedy that her thoughtless young husband had known her so little. What a waste, John thought, for such a woman to be condemned to the empty chatter of boring people.

"There is no need to feel pity for me," she said suddenly, glancing up at him.

John felt a jolt of surprise. He was the one too often fending off pity; to be on the other side gave him a new understanding of how helpless an onlooker could be, to see an unfortunate twist of circumstances and be unable to right it.

The irony was inescapable.

"I have had a very pleasant life," she went on, sounding defensive. "Fortunately, when my husband died, I was left with a comfortable income, though not enough—" She paused, and he finished for her.

"Not enough to travel, now that Napoleon is in exile, the world at peace, and the seas once more safe to journey on."

She shrugged and gave the wooden elephant one last gentle touch. "Indeed. So I enjoy strange sights through books and artwork—it could be much worse."

He saw the emotion that swirled beneath the serene face she showed to the world. Saw the longings that she would take to her grave, unfulfilled. How had he not glimpsed it before? Such a woman should not live with dreams never satisfied. She had a deep curiosity inside her, a zest for a bigger world, a passion just waiting to be fed.

But imagining her passion led back to his own . . .

Without any conscious decision, he took a step closer.

She looked up at him in surprise, and her eyes widened slightly. He gazed into their smoky blue-gray depths, like the color of deep ocean waters. If only he could bring the gleam of joy back into their somber hues. He could make out each dark lash which fringed her lids so becomingly, the faint flush on her cheeks and the soft luster of her ivory-hued neck. Her chest rose and fell a little too quickly, and he knew that he, too, was breathing fast.

He wanted her. He felt his blood surge and his heart beat faster, and the ache inside him made him weak with longing. He wanted this woman to be completely his. He wanted to show her what a man's love could do to brighten her eyes and deepen the throaty laugh she was sometimes surprised into giving. He wanted to make her laugh, wanted to thrill her, wanted to make her blood heat even as his did, right now, though he had not so much as reached for her hand.

But the air between them seem charged with energy, like a sultry summer day when lightning threatens and heavy clouds hang low on the horizon. He took another step till they were almost touching, and he could see her bosom—its delightful generous swelling making his palms itch to hold the sweet curves—rising and falling as she breathed more quickly. It seemed inevitable now that he lift his hand and—

A slight sound from the doorway made him freeze.

The footman stood in the hall, regarding them with an impassive expression. "I have brought the tea tray to the sitting room, ma'am, as you bade me."

John bit back a curse at the untimely interruption. He should thank the man, no doubt, for preventing an improvident action, one they both might have regretted—

Hell, no. He would take his chances on regret. The disappointment he felt now—could it be mirrored in Mrs. Hughes's lovely eyes? If so, she glanced away quickly.

"Yes, thank you," she said. She turned and brushed past him, leaving a hint of her rose scent in the air to tease him even more, to make the taste of discontent in his mouth even more bitter.

Reluctantly, he followed her out of the room, waiting while she closed the door firmly behind them, shutting her dreams away once again.

He climbed the steps without speaking, trying to think how to bring up the subject he really wanted to discuss, but he was stymied once more. When they reached the sitting room on the next level, they both paused in surprise.

Louisa had reappeared. Her hair was a bit tousled, as if she had dressed it in haste, and her eyes still heavy lidded, but she had found her usual bright smile. "My lord," she said. "When I woke, my maid told me you were here. I am so sorry I was still abed. I had a wretched headache this morning, but it's much better now."

"I'm glad to hear it," John was forced to say, when what he really wanted was to curse. He could already sense Marianne Hughes withdrawing, as she always did in the presence of her niece, so as not to interfere with his pursuit of the younger woman. Damn his courtship, his ill-advised, too hasty courtship.

He was forced to take a seat and accept a cup of tea, which Miss Crookshank poured. He drank it, as usual, without sugar, and if it tasted more bitter than usual, it was his own disgruntlement that ruined the flavor. He listened while the young lady chattered, and if both he and Mrs. Hughes contributed little to the conversation, Louisa did not remark upon it.

At last he found that he could sit no longer. He put his cup down with a clatter of the saucer and stood. Miss Crookshank looked up at him, her disappointment seemingly genuine.

"Must you go already?"

John frowned, but at himself, not her. He thought of the self-centered young husband whom Marianne had endured and told himself he could not be so unmindful of his actions. He forced himself to smile. "I thought you might enjoy some fresh air," he said, although it was a belated inspiration, and one that did not excite him. But for once, he would not think of himself. "Perhaps you would feel better for an outing, perhaps an easy drive in the park?"

She brightened at once. "Oh, I would love it. Let me fetch a shawl." She rose and crossed the room to ring for her maid. John had the chance to turn to Mrs. Hughes.

"I trust you will join us? I think that it is safe enough— we will not leave Louisa alone or allow her to wander through the crowds."

She always accompanied them as the girl's chaperone, but he hoped for more than a token agreement. After the unexpected revelations in her study, he wanted to give her the world, and all he could offer was a sedate ride through Hyde Park.

Marianne Hughes smiled slightly. "Of course."

She rang for her maid to fetch her gloves and hat, while Louisa made similar preparations. But it was Marianne he watched covertly as she adjusted the ribbons of her bonnet and pulled on her gloves, then picked up a light parasol.

They descended the stairs. In the front hall, he accepted his wide-brimmed hat from the footman. As he adjusted his hat, John was conscious of the irony. He had to brace himself simply to drive among the crowds in the park; Marianne Hughes was ready to brave a tropical jungle filled with lions. Perhaps he did not deserve to aspire to her hand, even when he was free of any other commitment. What could he offer her, when all he really wanted was to retreat to his own house, with its dim rooms and walled garden?

Grim-faced from such a quelling thought, he avoided gazing into the gilt-framed looking glass on the wall, although the ladies took a quick glance to check their hats before they went out the door and down the steps.

Instead, he helped them into his barouche and took his place on the opposite seat, then remained silent as his coachman slapped the reins and the vehicle moved into the usual London traffic.

Marianne Hughes deserved better than he could offer. And that thought kept him tight-lipped through much of the drive.

When they reached Hyde Park, they found it already bustling. Pedestrians strolled along the paths and carriages of all description followed the looping drive around the park.

His coachman had put down the top so that they could enjoy the pleasant mild air and the pale sunshine, mottled by passing clouds. The spring flowers were blooming, and it was no wonder that a large portion of London's elite seemed to have taken themselves to the park, even though it was not yet the fashionable hour for meeting one's friends.

For a few minutes they rode at a sedate pace, the ladies chatting and John sitting in silence, contenting himself with an occasional quick look at Marianne Hughes, watching her eyes gleam and her lips lift when something amused her. If only she could always look so at ease. More, if he could stir her excitement, what a delight it would be to watch her feelings play freely across her face. If she trusted him, she would not always keep her expression guarded, as happened too often, and her eyes would lose their sometimes sad look . . .

A childish voice interrupted his musings. "Lord Gillingham!"

Astonished—so few people here in London knew his name—John turned. In a moment he found the source. A stylish chaise was pulled to the side of the park road, and a girl leaned out its half-opened door, waving to him.

Without reflecting, he called to his coachman to pull up. Who was this child? Then he remembered. That angular face and the straight brown hair pulling free of its ribbon— it was his sister-in-law's rather peculiar younger sister, what was she called? An odd name—Circe—that was it. It was she who had stared at him so intently during his one disastrous dinner at his brother's house. Why was she hailing him so loudly in a public place? Had she been taught no manners at all?

Marianne had turned to stare at the child, too, and now she was frowning. "Something is amiss," she said quietly. "Louisa, stay here. My lord, if you would?"

So of course he helped her down and followed as Marianne picked up her skirts and hurried across to the other carriage.

Circe did indeed look agitated; her cheeks were flushed and her eyes had a suspicious glint as if she blinked back tears. "Please, my sister is ill, and I cannot support her out of the carriage all alone."

Then why stop on the side of the park road? John glanced at the team that pulled the carriage and saw that one of the horses had lifted its hoof and stood three legged. It had thrown a shoe, he thought, and likely come up lame.

But he had not time to consider the horses—he helped Marianne into the carriage.

Inside, his fair-haired sister-in-law looked very pale, and he saw at once that, as much as she might try to maintain her composure to avoid frightening her sister, she was gravely distressed.

"My lord, Mrs. Hughes, I am so pleased to see you. Forgive our lack of ceremony. We sent our coachman to get help for the horse, and while we waited I began—I began to feel unwell. So I sent our groom off, too, but he has not yet had time to return, and I think—I think that time is of the essence."

Marianne made a small sound of distress deep in her throat, then turned to him. "Give me your coat, please."

He did not understand, but he obeyed at once, shrugging off one of his new tailor's fashionable creations and handing it over. Not until Marianne wrapped it around Lady Gabriel's waist did he see the scarlet stains on the skirt of her pale-hued dress.

She was with child, though she had barely begun to show a gentle swelling. He had heard the ladies whispering about the happy event the night of the dinner party. Something was very wrong.

It was awkward in the cramped space of the closed carriage, but with two adults to bear her weight, they eased her out. Then he swept up his sister-in-law into his arms and carried her over to his own open barouche, where it was easier to place her carefully onto the rear seat. By now she had gone even paler, if that was possible. Several people on the walkway stopped to gawk at them, and one woman called out, "Here, what's this, then?"

Intent on the matter at hand, John ignored the query.

"Who is your physician?" he asked Lady Gabriel quietly.

"Sir William Reynolds," she told him, wincing. Putting one hand to her stomach, she told him the doctor's location.

He handed Mrs. Hughes back into the carriage, where Louisa was looking anxious—young Circe clambered in without waiting for any assistance and sat down close to her sister. He beckoned his groom, handing over some coins and repeating the street address.

"Take a hackney and fetch Sir William Reynolds. Tell him to come to Lord Gabriel Sinclair's home at once. His wife is very ill."

Then, so as not to crowd the women, nor embarrass his sister-in-law any more than was necessary, he swung up beside his coachman and told him where to go. "And hurry," he said tersely.

The man flicked the reins and did what he could to make haste through London's always crowded streets, but their progress seemed woefully slow. Never had John cursed the traffic as he did today.

Would she lose the baby? He had no experience with such things, but the pallor of her skin, not to mention the obvious signs of bleeding, did not bode well. And could the mother die, too, if it were impossible to check the flow of blood? It must be possible; whether it was likely, again, he had no clue.

He thought of his own earlier jealousy, his envy of his brother's happily married condition, and felt a deep sense of guilt that almost bordered on despair. Never, never would he have wished such a calamity upon anyone, not even his wretched sibling.

After an eternity they at last reached the handsome town house where his brother and family resided. John swung down to the pavement almost before the carriage rolled to a stop. He pulled open the carriage door and reached in to gather up his sister-in-law. He could tell that the bleeding continued; the coat wrapped about her would now be fit only for the dustbin, but he cared not at all. His mind was focused on more weighty concerns.

Lady Gabriel put her arms about his neck, and he carried her carefully up to her own front door. Circe had run ahead of them and pounded on the tall door.

A footman opened the door, only to gawk at them.

"Out of the way, man!" John said, in no mood for ceremony. "Circe, where is your sister's chamber?"

"Up here," the child said, running up the wide stairs and

calling, "Simpson, come quickly! My sister needs you."

Mrs. Hughes followed them into the house, with Louisa beside her. John did not pause to explain to the bewildered-looking butler what he was about. Instead, he followed Circe up the staircase.

When he reached the right floor, John carried his sister-in-law into the spacious bedchamber the child indicated and laid her carefully onto her bed. "The physician has been summoned. He should be here soon. Try not to worry," he told her.

Under the circumstances it was an inane statement, yet what else could one say? Circe was in tears again, but reinforcements had arrived. A grim-faced lady's maid of middle years hurried into the room. When she saw the blood, she threw up her hands.

"Oh, my lady!"

John hoped she would not fall into hysterics and make the situation even worse, but thankfully, she pulled herself together.

"We must send for Sir William!" she exclaimed, apparently too flustered to ask John who he was.

"I have already dispatched my groom to fetch him," John told her. "I hope—I trust he will be here shortly."

She nodded. "Circe, tell the footman to fetch hot water and clean linen, and then take yourself to the school-room—this is no place for you."

"I want to be with my sister!" The girl sounded truly frightened, and for once, she seemed a child in her manner, not strangely mature as she usually did.

Lady Gabriel leaned back against the pillows. "Circe, dearest, listen to Simpson. The doctor will be here soon. Send one of the footmen to fetch Gabriel, I think he was having luncheon at his club, then you can keep watch for him from the drawing-room window."

"I shall go to the attic; the view is better," the girl declared with more of her usual self-assurance. "I can see more of the street." But then a sob seemed to surprise her, overcoming her brief attempt at composure. "Only, I cannot lose you, too, Psyche!"

"I will be fine," Lady Gabriel said, reaching out one hand and allowing her sister to cling to it for a moment. "But you must go now."

The girl nodded and headed for the hallway.

The effort seemed to take the last of his sister-in-law's energy. She shut her eyes, and her face was as white as the linen sheets she rested on. John worried that she had swooned. The maid glanced at him, and he became aware that this was no place for a man, even one slightly related.

"I will leave you," he said.

The maid nodded, then looked past him. John found that Marianne Hughes had come into the room behind them.

"I am a friend of Lady Gabriel's," she said quietly to the servant. "And I have been in attendance when my sister-in-law had her babies. I think I should stay until the doctor arrives."

Simpson showed a flicker of relief. "Thank you, ma'am. I admit, I have no experience in birthing. Or with this—"

It was much too soon to deliver a living child, but John had the sinking feeling that his sister-in-law had begun her labor in earnest, and not even London's most esteemed physician would be able to stop it.

It was an ill day for his brother, John thought, feeling an unaccustomed flash of sympathy.

He retreated downstairs, and, when the butler stared at him, announced, "I will wait in the drawing room. The doctor should be here presently. I hope."

The servant gaped, but he showed him into the elegant chamber. Then the man retreated to the hallway, perhaps to listen for the door.

John was listening, too. He sat down on the edge of a rose-cushioned settee and wished for a glass of brandy, or at least wine, but was in no mood to summon another servant and witness more distress. Lady Gabriel seemed sincerely liked by her staff.

He thought of his own household, where his servants were most likely taking an unauthorized holiday while their master was away. His absence was such a rare occurrence that he suspected the hearths were going unswept and the beds unaired, and he only hoped his cook was not drinking up all the best wine. John had no heart to summon up any anger at the suspicion. He had no idea what his servants really thought of him, although at least he did not toss bottles at the footmen when he was annoyed, as his late father used to do.

It suddenly occurred to him to wonder what had happened to Louisa. As if his thought had summoned her, she appeared in the doorway, looking unhappy.

"I tried to help, but Aunt Marianne sent me away," she explained. "I only wanted to be of assistance."

He nodded. "That was good of you," he said gently, aware that she had been ignored by all of them. "Perhaps you could go up the schoolroom."

She frowned. "My lord!"

"I meant, to keep the child, Circe, company. She should be there, or perhaps in the attic. Ask one of the servants. The girl is most anxious about her sister, and I fear she has reason. Perhaps she would welcome some company."

Louisa sighed, releasing her indignation. "Of course, you are quite right. And she seems to be all alone. I will see if I can find her."

She left the room again, and John found that he could not sit still. He jumped to his feet and paced up and down. What was happening in the room a floor above him? And how could he leave Marianne Hughes to face such a trying crisis alone, with only the servants to help her tend to a woman so gravely ill? Yet what did he know of such matters? He could do nothing to help, and he knew she would send him away if he tried to rejoin them.

When the knock came at the front door, John hurried to the doorway of the drawing room. He heard the butler murmur a few words, and the answering sound of the physician's voice, then saw the man, bag in hand, hurry up the steps behind the servant. Thank God for that.

Presently, a footman appeared with a bottle of wine and a glass.

"Would you care for a glass of port, my lord?"

John nodded and accepted a glass, throwing back the

wine in one gulp. He was not usually much of a drinking man, but if ever there was a fitting occasion for strong drink, it was today. The footman showed no surprise but refilled his glass, then John dismissed him.

"You may go, but leave the doors open, if you please."

After his first moment of relief it seemed as if something should happen now that the physician was here, but whatever actions were occurring upstairs could not be heard below. Silence reigned in the house, and the tension could be felt, hovering in the air like a rainstorm on the horizon.

John wiped his brow with his handkerchief and found himself pacing again. There was little hope for the unborn child, but pray God the mother would not be lost, as well.

After a time the door downstairs slammed open, and he heard a heavy tread as someone ran up the stairs. A male voice spoke, its tone angry and alarmed, and then came a murmur in answer, but though John strained to hear, he could not distinguish the words.

John was not surprised to see his brother soon appear in the doorway of the drawing room.

He had seldom seen the normally debonair Gabriel so disheveled. His neck cloth was loosened, and his dark hair awry as if he had run his fingers through it. His deep blue eyes held a fierce light in their depths; he looked drunk, but John sensed he was only very afraid, and thus very angry, and so just as dangerous.

Gabriel glared at his older brother. Was his thank-you sticking in his craw, John wondered, feeling his moment of pity ebb. It was hardly a surprise.

But Gabriel said nothing at all. Instead, he charged across the room and, before John could react, grabbed him by the throat.

Gasping for breath, John tried to push the slimmer man off, but his brother seemed almost mad and thus stronger than any mortal had a right to be. For several long moments they struggled mutely, wavering, pushing each other back and forth and sending chairs and tables sliding and crashing all about them.

Gabriel seemed truly crazed, and his grip implacable. Within moments John found the room going dark around him. Stars glittered at the edges of his vision, and he could not see. One last time, he tried to pry off his brother's choking fingers, but his strength was fading. . . .

"No, Gabriel!" someone called from what seemed a long way away. "He came to our aid. I asked him to help, Gabriel, stop!"

It was the child, Circe. For just an instant Gabriel's grip loosened, and with one last burst of desperate energy, John was able to push the other man back. John gasped for breath. The room whirled, then settled into place.

Looking alarmed, Circe stood in the doorway, and beside her, Louisa, eyes wide as she gazed at the two men and the shattered tables and shards of broken glass that littered the carpet. The decanter of wine had overturned, and the dark liquid puddled on the floor. A waste of a tolerable wine, John thought in some corner of his mind.

But his attention was focused on the immediate threat. His brother's hands were still outstretched, as if he regretted letting go of his victim's throat. Gabriel's lips were drawn back, and he almost snarled. "One of my acquaintances sought me out in White's and told me my wife had been accosted in the park, carried off in that gawdy barouche you've been renting. I knew at once it had to be you. And a woman in the park told him that Psyche appeared to be injured. I did not think even you would stoop so low!"

"Gabriel," Circe tried to interrupt. "It's not like that at all—"

"Be silent!" John shouted, one hand to his bruised neck. Or at least he tried to shout; with his throat aching from the assault, the sound came out more like a wheeze.

He had been brutally attacked by a man who owed him gratitude, and now a child had done what he had not had the power to do. His own father would have said that children should be seen and not heard, certainly not a girl child. His father would have caned her for such forward manners. John had felt the lash of his father's stick often enough. He pushed aside the dark memories; he had never lifted his hand to a child, and he had no wish to do so now. But neither had he any desire to be rescued by a slip of a girl. Perhaps his pride was as sore as his throat.

"Do not speak so to my sister!" Gabriel shot back. "You have no right to speak at all—you will not open your mouth in my house while my wife lies above us, fighting for her life. The doctor would not even permit me to stand by her bedside and hold her hand. He had barely time to speak to me. And you—you have cost me my child—you deserve to die for that, alone. If I lose Psyche, too—" Gabriel swallowed hard. "Losing my birthright was nothing, compared to this."

Perhaps he might have felt compassion again, if his throat did not throb from his brother's agonizing grip. But John was done with pity.

"Gabriel, please listen," Circe pleaded.

But the two men were too intent upon each other.

It hardly mattered that he was innocent of the charge, John thought. This anger had been building between them for years. Childhood quarrels aside, the real seed of enmity had been planted when Gabriel had been disowned by his father—by his whole family. He had left England to roam like a gypsy, earning a precarious living as a gamester, his name dishonored, his relatives aloof. Since that day, the animosity between the brothers had grown apace. Meeting Gabriel's enraged gaze, he knew his brother understood, too.

"Just for the record, I am not responsible for your wife's situation," he said, trying to pull up some shreds of dignity. He was the eldest; he could show his maturity, even if Gabriel was still bitter over his family's rejection. "But you have attacked me, and I demand satisfaction."

"My lord," Louisa protested from the doorway, though her tone sounded uncertain. "No, indeed, please do not. Dueling is illegal, and this cannot serve to help the situation."

Neither of them heeded her. Gabriel smiled, a chilling lift of the lips that was more grimace than good humor.

"Nothing could please me more," he agreed. "Although my only regret is that we cannot finish this matter here and now."

"Now, I agree," John snapped. "Here is perhaps not the best or most appropriate place." He gestured toward the two females watching, their expressions appalled and apprehensive, and to the shattered mess the brothers had already made of the carefully furnished chamber.

"Then we will repair to the park in the middle of the square," Gabriel suggested, pulling off his coat. "Mason," he called to the butler, who had appeared behind the women. "Bring me the set of dueling swords that are on the wall of my study. They are antiques, but in good order, I think you will find, and no doubt hungry for blood after all these years of vain display."

"But you have no seconds," Louisa tried to argue. "Even if you must fight, this is not proper conduct at all."

"We need none," John put in, for the first time in accord with his younger sibling. "There will be no reconciliation for them to attempt, and the meeting place is set. And as for other formalities, there is a doctor at hand."

"Not that we will interrupt him from his more essential duties," Gabriel shot back.

"No, indeed. I suspect that when we are done, he will have little left to do," John concurred, his tone a grim promise.

Gabriel narrowed his eyes. "I could not agree more."

The butler, his usual impassive demeanor still showing signs of distress, reappeared with two slender blades in his hands.

Gabriel nodded to his brother to take the first choice.

John loosened his neck cloth and tossed it aside. He walked across and selected one of the swords at random, lifting it to feel the weight, carving an *s* in the air to judge its balance. One of the women gasped. Perhaps this was indeed a very old sword, but it was finely crafted and had not suffered for its long inactivity. "It will do," he said.

Gabriel picked up the other and motioned toward the door. "We will go out," he said, "and not disturb the ladies.

Mason, if you hear any news about Lady Gabriel, inform me at once. The doctor said it would be some time before he knew—" Gabriel's voice faltered, and his eyes shut for an instant. He had to clear his throat before he finished, his voice husky, "Before he could judge the outcome."

"Yes, my lord," the servant agreed.

Both of the females tried to protest, but they drowned out each other, and John walked past them as if they were not there. If Louisa tried to catch his eye, he ignored her effort. Instead he strode down the wide staircase and out the front door, across the avenue to the fenced park and the greenery within, aware that his brother followed a pace or two behind him, his step just as eager. For how many years had they waited to resolve old scores?

At least the heat of midday had driven any children and their nursemaids back into their respective homes; the park appeared almost deserted. One elderly woman sat on a bench beneath a tree, book in hand, and gazed at the two men in surprise.

"You may wish to go inside, Miss Strickland," Gabriel told her. "My brother's death will not be a pleasant sight."

She closed her book and stood, retreating to the gate, but hesitated there, her curiosity palpable. A servant from one of the neighboring houses had come out to the street to see what was happening, and a passerby hesitated just outside the fence. So be it. It was impossible to be totally private in the middle of the city.

John didn't care. He lifted his sword and made the customary salute.

Gabriel followed suit. "En garde," he breathed, meeting John's hard gaze with an icy glare of his own.

Then Gabriel's sword swung through the air with a speed that made it almost invisible. John raised his weapon to meet the attack, and metal rang against metal. The force of the impact made his blade vibrate in his hand, and he kept his hold only with effort.

He heard the older woman gasp, but could pay her no mind. She had been warned. Anyhow, he needed all his attention for the conflict.

He feinted, but his brother was not deceived; he was ready to meet John's thrust when it came.

Gabriel followed his block with a slashing attack, coming down hard against John's sword. Although John stopped the thrust, his brother's weapon managed to slide off his blade and slit his shirtsleeve.

A woman shrieked.

John felt the slight prick, but ignored it. Gabriel might have picked up some tricks during his time abroad, but if he became too confident, John would have him. His attack just now was so wild and frenzied that it was hard to predict, but he was bound to slow, eventually.

John set himself to meeting each slash, each driving blow, and biding his time for the best opportunity, the moment when Gabriel would drop his guard, when there would be an instant of weakness, and a killing blow could be delivered.

He had a dim awareness that Louisa and Circe and several of the servants had flocked out to observe the fight, joining other onlookers along the park's edge. But he was beyond caring, beyond even his earlier concern for the life-and-death struggle going on inside the big house. He had his own life-and-death conflict here, and it demanded all of his attention.

Gabriel was fighting to kill, and John would meet him with equal determination.

For long minutes they thrust and blocked and slashed, moving lightly across the grassy sward, with nothing here to hinder their movements. A bird flew away from a bush, alarmed by the tumult, but neither man gave it so much as a glance. The swords swept through the air, met and clattered and rang, steel against steel, and their forging held true.

The swords endured, but John found that he had to pace himself if he was to outlast his younger brother. He knew that his own physical condition had to be just as good; he had not paced the length of his property so many times for nothing. But he had not had his hand on a sword in years, and it took all his concentration to match his brother's frenetic attacks and to give back as good as he got.

In truth, some part of his mind acknowledged, they were well matched. But mostly he had no time to think of anything at all, only the thrust, the parry, the lethal dance of the swords as the two weapons met and circled and struck again and again.

Gabriel had settled down now into a more controlled fight. John made several attempts to break through his guard, each blow potentially lethal, but his sibling blocked each one. Gabriel's own thrusts were just as deadly, but John pushed them aside. Only once, when Gabriel slipped on the grass, did John have the chance to push his sword to his brother's throat, and, to his chagrin, he found himself hesitate, just briefly.

He would not win this match through an accidental weakness, he told himself. It must be a clear victory, a win due to greater strength and greater skill; nothing else would satisfy him for the years of humiliation, the countless slights and wounds known only to himself that he had endured because of his brother.

No, this would be the final accounting, and it must be clean and decisive, with nothing later to reproach himself about.

So he allowed Gabriel to regain his footing, lifting his sword until his brother's weapon was back into play. Then the swords clashed again.

He had no idea how long they had fought, but presently he thought that the sun had shifted the slant of its rays, and he could feel the fatigue dogging his arms, his shoulders, his whole body. But there would be no halt, no apologies. He had waited his whole life for this, and he would have his revenge upon the upstart boy who had so troubled his life . . .

The blades met again, rang again, and again, neither man could hit his target.

Then at last, John saw his chance. Gabriel lifted his blade a little too high, and the vital area of the chest was exposed. All it would take would be one clean, swift thrust—

John began his move, but a clap of thunder threw off his aim, and he felt a sting, as of a bee, but harder, knocking him a little off center.

Someone screamed.

Expecting Gabriel to take quick advantage of his loss of focus, John cursed and tried to lift his sword again, but his arm did not seem to work properly.

Instead of moving forward, Gabriel stood and stared at him, his expression perplexed and his own weapon lowering. What?

John dared to take his eyes off his brother and glance down; his shirt was damp with a widening scarlet stain, and now he felt the pain spreading through his arm and shoulder. His fingers were going numb. Although he tried to keep his grip, he felt his sword slide out of his grasp, and he groaned with frustration.

Gabriel's blade had not touched him—what had happened?

Only when Gabriel turned to gaze about the crowd did John at last comprehend.

He had been shot.

Twelve

After a moment of shock he glanced around. Where was Louisa? She could be in grave danger. Another bullet might find its true mark—and from whence had the shot come? He looked about, surprised to see the cluster of people outside the park's low fence—when had they collected such a crowd? He located Miss Crookshank standing beside Circe, her hands to her mouth in stunned amazement.

"Get the women inside!" he barked at Gabriel, frowning over the hoarseness of his own voice.

Gabriel turned. "Circe, go into the house at once, and take our visitor with you. Send a footman here to help."

Circe had the wit to obey. Pulling on Louisa's hand, she ran back toward the house. When John saw them slip through the doorway and out of view, he relaxed and looked back at his own arm.

The bleeding continued. He would need something to stanch it, and he must dress the wound. Just his luck to stop a bullet meant for someone else. Ironic, too, as this whole thing had started with blood flowing. For the first time in a while, he thought of the struggle being fought inside the house.

What had happened to his sister-in-law?

His sword lowered, Gabriel came closer.

"Do you not intend to finish me off?" John demanded. He felt no fear, only an overwhelming sense of frustration that their fight had been interrupted before—before what? Before he could kill his own brother? Some of his anger, dulled by the shock of the bullet that had come out of nowhere, had faded. Perhaps, just perhaps, it had been a good thing they had suffered an untimely interruption.

Gabriel lifted his lips, appearing wolflike for once despite his cursed good looks. "I, too, would have wished to complete our fight. But an unkind fate has intervened. Come along."

"If you can't kill me, no one else will be allowed to?" John suggested, his tone wry.

"Precisely," Gabriel agreed.

John tried not to lean upon his brother as Gabriel put one arm about his shoulders, but he found his legs trembling. Gritting his teeth and accepting as little as he could of his brother's support, John walked slowly toward the house. Muttering, the crowd fell back, their expressions reflecting a blend of disapproval and vicarious excitement.

A footman hurried outside to assist them, trying to take John's wounded arm and sending pain flooding through the whole side of his body.

"Bloody hell!" John muttered.

"Damn it, leave off," Gabriel echoed. "Make yourself useful and collect the swords. I do not wish to lose them."

The servant hurried to the park, and they continued toward the house.

The short distance seemed to have grown, but at last they were inside the door. Rather than attempt the stairs, Gabriel led them into the library.

At other times John would have appreciated the leather-covered chairs and well-filled bookshelves, but just now, his pain was increasing. He hobbled toward a chair.

There was a sound in the doorway. Glancing back, John saw Marianne Hughes standing there, her expression somber; she looked as if she had been weeping.

Without ceremony Gabriel released his hold on his brother's arm and allowed him to collapse into the nearest chair. Looking white about the lips, Gabriel hurried across to greet Marianne.

Wincing from his own pain, John watched Gabriel grip her shoulders.

"How is she?"

"My lord." Marianne spoke slowly, her eyes dark with sadness. "I regret to be the one to inform you that the child is lost. It was a son. I'm so sorry."

Pain darkening his face, Gabriel nodded. "And Psyche?" His voice was low and so hoarse that John could barely make out the words. "For God's sake, how is Psyche?"

Marianne gave him a wan smile. "She is very weak, but holding her own, my lord. The bleeding is stopped. Sir William believes she will make it, and that she will have a fair chance of bearing a child again, someday."

Gabriel made a strangled noise deep in his throat. He wavered, looking as if he might fall, too. She reached for him, even though he was taller and heavier, as the release from unbearable fear almost sent him to his knees.

Again, John felt a mixture of emotion as he watched. Happy, of course, to hear that his sister-in-law had not died, and yet . . . he could not separate the confusion of feelings inside him.

As she braced him, Gabriel pulled Marianne into an impulsive hug, then released her as quickly. "I must see her!"

"Only for a moment, my lord, the doctor wishes her to be untroubled. She needs to rest," Marianne warned him. For the first time she looked across at John, and her face blanched. "My lord—what has happened?"

"Oh, he needs the doctor's services, too," Gabriel flung back as he bolted for the stairs. "But only if my wife can spare him."

"Thank you so much," John muttered.

Marianne Hughes had already hastened to him. Dropping to her knees beside his chair, she reached to inspect his wound.

"How were you hurt?" She looked up to see the footman hanging the dueling swords back on their hooks against the wall. "Oh, no, you could not—tell me you two idiots were not fighting?"

He found he did not wish to meet her reproachful gaze. "Ah, an exchange of pent-up emotions, you might say."

"Lord Gabriel did this?"

This conclusion hurt his pride even more than her gently probing fingers hurt his shattered upper arm. "No, indeed! It is a bullet wound, and where the missile came from, I cannot say. From the angle, probably from the top end of the square, but there was no time to see who held the weapon."

To his great relief, she paused, her hands still. "Louisa?"

"She is untouched. If the gunman was aiming at her—she was standing behind me in a group of onlookers—he was not successful."

Marianne bit her lip. "This is worse and worse. Perhaps Alton Crookshank is just as villainous as we first supposed. At any rate, we cannot risk her life any longer. First Season or no, I shall have to take her home at once."

John felt a pang deeper even than the ache caused by his wound. Louisa would leave, and so, too, most likely, would her aunt. He would not see them again, perhaps for months. He tried to consider.

"Do you think she will be any safer in Bath?" he asked, thinking aloud.

"But what else can I do? She is too exposed in London."

"I agree. I think she, and you, of course, should come for a visit in Kent. At my estate we will have much greater control over who may approach her, and any strangers will be immediately obvious."

Marianne considered, and while he held his breath for her answer, they were interrupted by the physician.

"What's this?" The renowned doctor looked tired, but he became businesslike at once as he pulled up a chair to sit beside John and consider his injury. "Who has been lobbing bullets at you, my lord?"

"That is the question," John agreed dryly. Mrs. Hughes stood and made way for the doctor, but it was her face he watched. She must agree to his impulsive plan. He could not lose her, not now, when he had made no progress on securing Louisa's safety and working toward a disentanglement of his matrimonial intentions.

The physician slit open his shirt and pressed a clean cloth against his arm to slow the blood, forcing John to suppress a groan.

"Whoever delivered it, this bullet must come out, my lord. Fortunately, it seems to be a small bore."

Large enough, from John's viewpoint. He gritted his teeth as the man reached inside his bag and found a long metal instrument, which John eyed with distrust.

"Perhaps," he said, seeing Marianne still in the background. "You would excuse us?"

"Yes, my lord, if the doctor has no need of me." She glanced at Sir William Reynolds, who nodded.

"You have done good work this day, dear lady, and I am happy you were here. But this I can manage alone."

So at least she would not see him cry out in pain, John thought, beads of sweat popping out on his forehead as the doctor probed. God!

The room dissolved into a reddish blur as the pain overtook him, and if there were hoarse groans, he was not sure who made them . . .

Later, when at last the bullet had been removed, the wound dressed and wrapped in clean cloth, he was able to sip a glass of brandy and try to make his eyes focus.

"I would recommend not moving him for a while," Sir William was saying.

To whom was he speaking? John tried to answer, but his tongue seemed thick.

"We will see to him. And thank you again, sir." It was

his brother's voice, heavy with fatigue, grief, and the aftermath of great fear.

Damned if he would be beholden to his brother! John tried to protest, but he found that the doctor had left the room, along with Gabriel. He seemed to be alone.

He tried to get to his feet and was disgusted to find his legs wobbly as jelly. He fell back against the chair and heard Gabriel speak from the doorway.

"Poetic justice, that you should be the puny one, now, eh? And left in my charge? It makes me want to laugh."

John flushed. "What do you mean? I have no intention of troubling you."

His brother came closer and ignored the comment.

"When I was small, you were the one who tormented me. Could you have forgotten? I never will."

John frowned. "I did what any older brother does. So we had a few spats, why should that shadow you still? You're a grown man and doing well enough with your life, from the looks of it. Get over it, man."

Gabriel scowled at him. "You are lucky to be unable to stand. Otherwise, I would knock your teeth back into your head for your impertinence."

John shut his eyes for a moment. He had no strength left to quarrel. "Just help me to my carriage."

"In your condition? Neither my wife nor Mrs. Hughes would ever let me hear the end of it. I shall summon two footmen to help you upstairs and into bed."

"No!" John objected. "I must get back to the inn."

"You think a second-rate inn will offer more comfort than my household can extend?"

John tried not to snarl. "I have someone—something— I need to attend to."

"Who?" Gabriel demanded, still sounding as if he enjoyed having the upper hand, damn his hide. "Don't tell me you have installed a light-o'-love in your rooms even as you court a virtuous young lady?"

"Of course not." John glared at him.

"Our father could have done it, why not you?"

"I am not our father." He had to grit his teeth. Nor did he wish to tell his brother the real reason he needed to return. He had been ridiculed enough.

"He has a dog," a light voice said from the doorway.

"What?" Gabriel turned to look at Circe, who watched them from the threshold. "Impossible."

"He has dog hairs on his trousers and a dusty paw print on one leg that his manservant failed to brush off," she pointed out as if it were evident to anyone.

John bit back a groan. If she were not careful, this child would be burned as a witch.

"It must be a dog from the inn," Gabriel argued. "Our father never allowed dogs in his house—he could not abide them."

John drew a deep breath. "I have a dog, and the servants might forget to feed her or neglect to let her out for her run. Or worse, allow her into the street to be trampled."

Silence. His brother gazed at him, his expression impossible to read.

"She is not used to London traffic," John tried to explain, trying not to sound defensive. "What the hell is so hard to understand about that?" *Remember Circe's presence,* he reminded himself. He wished he could take back the expletive, then gave it up. If his brother's household maintained any of the proprieties, the child would be up in the schoolroom.

"You can't have a dog." Gabriel still stared at him. "Our father—"

"I am not our father!" John repeated.

The two brothers gazed at each other, and the air was heavy with unspoken emotion. A pity they had not finished that duel, John thought.

Gabriel wheeled and headed for the door. "I will send a servant to fetch your dog and your clothes, and pay your charges. The barouche has already been returned."

"My bills are paid," John snapped. "And I am going back to the inn."

"The footmen will help you upstairs," Gabriel went on as if he had not spoken. "The doctor will see you tomorrow when he comes back to check on Psyche. And I believe he left you something to help you sleep. Please take it."

"Your solicitude is most gratifying," John said through his teeth.

"I just wish to shut you up," Gabriel told him, his smile twisted. "Circe, you may leave now before you hear anything else unsuitable."

"Interesting, you mean," Circe said.

Gabriel raised his brows in silent warning.

"Oh, very well." The child turned and left his sight.

Two large footmen came to lift him, and John found he was too weak to prevent his brisk transport up the stairs and into a guest chamber, or the removal of his clothes, or the passing of a borrowed nightshirt over his head. Then there was a vile concoction to swallow, and then, indeed, he slept.

He woke, some hours later, feeling muzzy headed and feverish. The sheets had become twisted with his tossing about. Worse, he found he had an urgent need for the necessary. But a bossy valet—just what he hated about those servants—appeared at once and would not allow him out of bed. The manservant straightened the sheets and tried to sponge off his forehead.

John frowned and waved the sponge aside, then used his one good arm to try to raise himself. The other arm and shoulder were swathed in heavy bandages.

"The doctor said you were not to be up, my lord."

"But I need—"

The man brought him an earthenware jug and motioned to explain its use.

John swore. Allow another man to help him piss? Not likely! If only his legs were not still weak, and his head did not whirl like an eddy in a brook. The thought of flowing water made his bladder ache even more.

"Would you rather I summoned your brother, my lord?" The man seemed to have no idea how much that grated the patient's nerves or blew away his last vestiges of forbearance.

John cursed again, but what choice did he have? His body had failed him, and he had never in his life felt like such a weakling. His need too urgent to ignore, he allowed the man to hold the jug, but that was all.

"Just keep your hands to yourself!"

He thought he saw amusement in the servant's eyes, but the man kept his expression impassive. "As you say, my lord."

When John's bladder was empty, the valet took away the jug and gave him another dose of the foul-tasting medicine. Soon the heaviness descended once more, and he shut his eyes.

The next time he woke, he felt cooler. He was pleased to see Runt curled up on the rug at the side of the bed. When he moved, the little dog whined and lifted her head.

"So, you are here after all. I hope you bit a plug out of my brother. Not that he would have gone to fetch you himself, of course, so no hope there."

The animal wagged her tail in answer.

"Yes, I know you would have done so if I had bade it," John agreed. He felt a little less alone in the enemy's stronghold, as ridiculous as that reaction was. He shut his eyes for a moment and wondered where Mrs. Hughes had gone to. He hoped she had not left for Bath, to take her niece home.

"Does it hurt much?" a by now familiar voice asked.

John looked up quickly.

The child stood in the doorway, and the door was half open.

Aware that he wore only the borrowed nightshirt, John . pulled the bed linens up to his chin. "You should not be here."

"I know. Gabriel told me not to come into your room. I am not in the room—I am in the hallway," she said in her usual dignified tone. "But my governess, Miss Tellman, and I have been taking your dog for walks three times a day."

"Oh, thank you," he forced himself to say. He hated being in this house, but he could not take it out on her. "You should send a servant—"

"But you were concerned about her, and I have been most careful to keep her out of the road. She does heed my commands nicely—you have trained her well. What's her name?"

John shut his eyes for a moment, then opened them to see that his dog had run across to push her nose into the girl's hand. *Traitor,* he thought, unreasonably.

"Runt. For obvious reasons."

"Yes, she is quite small, and the ear—well, it lends character to her face. I have made a quite successful drawing of her for you when you are well again. She has a sweet nature, and she's most loyal, obviously devoted to you."

"Dogs usually are." He refused to act sentimental over a mere animal.

Runt ruined his attempt at rationality by running back to the bed, standing on her hind feet and whining.

John put out his right hand, pleased that he felt a little strength returning to his limbs, and rubbed the dog's head. Her tail wagged furiously.

"Down," he ordered, keeping his voice brusque. "You will tear the linen."

Runt licked his hand one more time, then sat obediently.

"My lord, how are you?"

Marianne Hughes stood behind the girl.

John felt such a rush of relief that she had not left the city that he almost forgot to be self-conscious. Then he remembered his ridiculous plight, not to mention his undressed state—damn, but if he had been whole and strong, he would have had a whole different set of feelings—and tried not to color. He rubbed his face, feeling the stubble that covered his scarred chin and cheeks and felt even more chagrined to be seen in such a condition.

Fortunately, she did not come closer, but stood in the doorway. "I did not wish to disturb you. I only wanted to see how you were feeling."

"It was only a slight wound, not worth this much fuss,"

he said, his tone gruff as he tried to conceal his delight at seeing her.

"If it had hit a more vital area, it would not have been slight at all," she suggested. "I am thankful that you are able to dismiss the wound, and that Louisa was not hit."

With a twinge of guilt, he remembered his fiancée. "Yes, indeed," he agreed. "I think—" He paused and looked at the child.

"Miss, um, Sinclair?"

"Miss Circe Hill," she explained.

"Miss Hill, I suspect that Runt would appreciate a walk, if you would be so kind."

The dog, who had been lying quite sedately on the rug, wagged her tail at the mention of her name. Nor did Circe look convinced. "We have only just returned from a stroll around the park," she pointed out. "But since you want to talk privately, I will take her out again."

Mrs. Hughes was trying not to laugh.

John tried to hold on to his dignity; he had little else to clothe himself in at the moment. "Thank you."

Circe called to the dog and led her away.

And they were blessedly alone. "Miss Crookshank sent down to the flower stalls herself and arranged a bouquet for you," Marianne Hughes said. "The footman is putting it into water and will bring it up."

"That's very kind of her," John said, feasting his vision on the lovely shape of her face, the blue-gray eyes, the well-shaped curving brows now drawn together with, could it be, concern over him? "Really, I will be up again very soon. And I hope you will contemplate my suggestion about us all removing to my estate."

"I admit, it does make sense," she said slowly, and his pulse leaped that she was considering it. "Although I do not wish to be a charge upon your staff."

"Nonsense, it will be good for them to have visitors in the house, and I will be especially delighted," he assured her.

"And I suppose it would be a good thing for Louisa to have a look at your—and her future—home," Marianne went on.

He hadn't thought of that, and his heart sank. "Um, yes, I suppose." Would this just convince Louisa that he meant to keep his pledge? Hell. But the thought of having Marianne close at hand pushed that worry away. He would deal with it later.

"And I should like to be there—that is, it would be as well for you to have someone there to keep an eye on you as you heal. I'm sure your servants are attentive, but that is not the same."

The idea of himself as an invalid was so repellent that he shook his head automatically. "No, no, I would not trouble you with such a burden."

"How could it be a burden?" She actually took a step inside his room, and he thought that her voice warmed. Could it matter to her how he fared? Could she, possibly, care about him?

His body responded, even in its less than hearty state, and he was glad that the coverlet was thick enough to conceal the surge of blood to his groin. "Mrs. Hughes," he began, then hesitated as a footman appeared, with a vase of flowers to place on the table near his bed.

They both paused until the servant withdrew, then Marianne added, "Your brother lent me a footman to help see Louisa safely home, and we went in his closed carriage instead of the barouche."

He had a sudden vision of Marianne shielding Louisa with her own body, and it made the hair on the back of his neck stand on end. Thank God she was not the one who had stopped a bullet!

"You must take care," he said, his tone urgent. "The attacks are becoming much more dangerous, and I do not know what may happen next."

Marianne nodded. "She has promised to stay inside until I agree that she may go out. But she cannot live her life cowering indoors. We must discover who is behind these murderous attempts."

"About Mr. Alton Crookshank—"

Marianne nodded. "Your agent and my footman are now taking turns watching his rooms, at my instructions.

My footman says that Mr. Crookshank's landlady tells us he was out most of the day yesterday. But where he was, we have no way of knowing. It means he would have had the opportunity to fire the weapon which wounded you. Yet he seems to lead a quiet life, going to his lectures and his studies, and shows no outward signs of murderous intent."

"He would hardly trumpet it to the world. As soon as I am out of bed, perhaps tomorrow, I will escort you down to Kent, and we shall have some breathing space to consider what should be done next."

"Poor Louisa." Marianne sighed. "She was so happy to be free to taste the delights of London Society, at last, and now she is a virtual prisoner. At least this visit to your estate will give her something else to think about."

John gazed at her. Would Marianne ever forgive him if he jilted her niece? She seemed most devoted to the younger woman. Yet how could he marry one woman, lovely and sweet-natured as she might be, when he yearned for—when he adored—another? He shut his eyes for a moment, then was frustrated to hear his visitor say, "I will leave you to rest, my lord. I do not wish to stay too long and tire you."

"No," he said quickly, but when he looked toward the doorway again, she was giving way to the doctor.

"I shall call again very soon," she promised, and John had to be content with that.

Her absence was more painful than even the doctor's probing. The man changed the bandages on John's upper arm and announced the wound was showing no signs of infection.

"I wish to leave for my estate," John told him. "Soon. Tomorrow."

Washing his hands in the china basin and drying them on a clean linen towel, the physician looked thoughtful. "Some fresh country air would no doubt be good for you, my lord, instead of London's dusty heat. But not tomorrow, perhaps in a couple of weeks or so."

"No," John argued, unable to explain how intensely he wanted to be free of his brother's house. "This week!"

They compromised on the end of the week, if John continued to heal without complications. The doctor repacked his bag, and a footman took away the soiled bandages and blood-tinged water.

"And how is Lady Gabriel?" John inquired, aware he should have asked that question earlier.

Sir William, who had turned, paused to answer. "She is very weak—she lost a great deal of blood when she lost the child. But she is also showing no indication of infection, my lord, an excellent omen. If she can get through the week without a fever, we may hope that she will in time regain her usual good health."

"I am most glad to hear it," John said, and meant it.

The doctor bade him good day, leaving John to his thoughts. He must send a note to his housekeeper to prepare the house for company; God knew what the state of the guest wing was; he hardly dared to imagine. He had never *had* visitors before, and if his father had ever entertained, John could not recall it. So this should at least give his servants a new challenge. He hoped they would not disgrace him.

"I need writing paper and pen and ink," he commanded when a male form entered the edge of his vision.

"I see you are making yourself at home," came the dry reply. Instead of the footman returning, it was his brother who came into the room.

Leery of any more unprovoked attacks, John watched him approach.

However, raising his brows, Gabriel merely regarded his sibling with a critical gaze. "I think you need a shave and a wash, first. Unless you enjoy such a state of dishabille?"

"Of course not!" His shoulders tense and his wound still aching, John tried to fold his arms and found, with one arm in a sling, it was not possible. He saw that his good hand was clenched and tried to relax it.

"Then why did you send my valet away this morning, when he has been so kind as to offer his services in nursing you?"

John frowned. He had no idea the manservant had volunteered for such a sorry task; why would he do that for a stranger when one of the underservants could have been directed to carry the slop jar and bring up his trays?

Gabriel seemed to read his thoughts. "He is very loyal to me—I think he did it for my sake. But you have given him little thanks. I wonder, if you treat your own servants so, that you are able to keep any. Our father had similar troubles, as I recall."

"I do not throw empty wine bottles at their heads!" John snapped. Why was Gabriel so determined to compare him to their late father at every turn?

"That is a start," his brother agreed, his eyes glinting with humor, which John could not help but regard as mocking. "And where is your own man? The innkeeper said you brought no personal servants with you."

John felt trapped. "I don't care for valets," he muttered, looking away from the cynical gleam in his brother's deep blue eyes.

"So one might judge from the usual state of your apparel. Although you do seem to have spruced up a bit for the city. Do I detect a civilizing feminine influence, Miss Crookshank's, perhaps?"

John opened his mouth to deny it, then remembered Mrs. Hughes's advice on a new tailor. Unwilling to be lectured on fashion by his always elegant brother, he changed the subject abruptly. "What about my groom and coachman and my own carriage?"

"They are still at the inn—I had no room for another vehicle in my carriage house. The barouche I have sent back, thinking you would not wish to pay for its daily hire while it sat unused."

John nodded. "Thank you," he said, although it took some effort to utter the words, adding more easily, "I am happy to hear that Lady Gabriel is recovering."

Gabriel's expression softened. "Yes, thank God! And I have been informed—lectured most severely by more than one female, in fact—that I misunderstood the incident in the park. But you realize that I was told—"

"And you had no trouble jumping to the wrong conclusion," John finished for him, happy to have the upper hand for an instant. "I do appreciate your faith in me, that you would believe that I could be capable of assaulting an innocent woman, much less my own sister-in-law."

"I remember your bullying when we were children. And I am aware that you still hate me," Gabriel said, his tone flat.

"I don't hate you," John said before he thought.

Gabriel looked unconvinced. And indeed, John was not sure why he had bothered to deny the statement. It was all too close to the truth. He went on to safer topics.

"If your valet still has any interest in attending me, you may tell him that I shall be appreciative of his efforts," John said. "A wash and a shave would indeed be welcome. If he does not wish to do it himself, send up one of the footmen, if you will. My shaving kit should be in my trunk, if you have brought over my effects from the inn. Plus, if the footman does it, you can always hope that an unpracticed hand will be more likely to cut my throat."

Gabriel's lips lifted, and again, he looked even more dangerous when he smiled. "Oh, no, brother," he contradicted, his tone soft. "If anyone does that, it will be me."

Thirteen

John slept off and on through most of the day.
After his brother left, the valet had reappeared, armed with John's set of ivory-handled razors, all carefully whetted—John noted with only the slightest whisper of unease—to their sharpest edge. If his brother wanted to rid himself of his hated sibling by staging an accident—

No, nonsense. Gabriel would never delegate a task he would so much enjoy performing himself, John told himself grimly. So he allowed the man to shave him, trying to keep his face impassive—and very still—and the valet performed his task expertly, without inflicting so much as a nick. And if, somewhere behind that mask of impersonal efficiency, there still glimmered a flicker of amusement, John did his best to ignore it.

A sponge bath followed, then a clean nightshirt, his own, this time, and he was at last allowed to lie back against the pillows and shut his eyes. Even without the cloying medicine, sleep came quickly.

Later, John managed a little soup for his dinner, then had a restless night. When he opened his eyes as the first faint signs of dawn lightened the darkness, he looked about him at the dim outlines of the chamber, frowning as he remembered where he was.

Runt lifted her head from where she lay at the side of his bed. Jumping up, she ran to him and whined.

"You shall go outside presently," he told her. "I cannot take you myself, just yet, and no one regrets that more than I."

Her dark eyes doleful, the dog sat down again. John wondered if he looked as woebegone himself as he contemplated his present lack of freedom. He wanted out of this house, he wanted an end to these unpleasant dangers at every turn, he wanted to be free of his nuptial entanglements.

He missed Marianne Hughes.

He missed her mellow voice, he missed the light scent of her rose perfume, he missed the pleasing aspect of her serene expression and her expressive eyes with their smoky blue-gray hue. He missed the chance to covertly observe the womanly curves that so inflamed his senses and the occasional opportunity to touch her hand as he helped her into a carriage or down a set of steps. He wanted her here, and he wanted to be free to court her openly.

And he could not attempt that until he identified and stopped the would-be assassin. Frustrated, he tried to push himself up in the bed and winced when he put too much strain on the wound in his arm.

If he could not find out the answer to the attacks, none of his other desires would be fulfilled. He lay back against the pillows and tried to think.

Presently, earlier than he had expected it, a light knock sounded on his door.

"You may enter," he called.

The door swung open, and Circe Hill peeked around its edge. "I've come to take Runt out," she explained.

"You're up very early," he said. Her hair had been hastily pulled back, but a few brown strands strayed from beneath the ribbon; he suspected she had done it herself.

"The morning light is the best," she explained. "For an artist."

She was indeed the strangest child he had ever encountered.

"I have no experience with such things," he told her politely. "But I shall not contradict you."

"It would be foolish to do so," she agreed, her matter-of-factness robbing the statement of much of its rudeness. "Since you acknowledge you know nothing about art."

"And you do?" he asked, his tone dry.

"Oh, yes, though I am only a student, of course. I should like to apprentice formally, but females are not generally accepted. But when I am older, I shall find a way around that." Her tone was confident, and her statement sounded somehow not as ridiculous as it should have, coming from such a slip of a girl.

"I rather think you will," he agreed, then shook his head a little that he should be speaking to her as if she were an adult. She had that effect on a person, John realized; it was hardly worth fighting.

"Come along, Runt," Circe said.

The dog had jumped up when she had appeared, and now the little spaniel hurried across to follow her outside.

"You are not going out alone?" he demanded, recalling the dangers he had just been mulling over.

"No, Gabriel has forbidden it. Just now, I shall take her only into the back courtyard," she assured him. "And the grooms are at work in the stable, and the maids are carrying up water and laying the fires. Later, when Telly is up, we shall go across the street into the park."

He nodded and watched them go. But then he felt more alone than ever. Why was he being such a baby? John thought, annoyed at himself. It was bad enough his body should betray him with its weakness, but if he could not even control his own thoughts—he missed Marianne. God, how he longed for her presence!

To distract himself, he sat up further and tried to swing his legs over the edge of the bed. They obeyed him, although they were a bit wobbly when he put his weight on them. But, with one hand on the bed, he was able to walk up and down the room until some of his strength returned, to take himself to the chamber pot tucked discreetly into the wooden commode, and to reassure himself that he was slowly coming back to his usual state of energy and command.

When the valet appeared with warm water, he stared to see his patient up on two, albeit shaky, legs.

"Do not overexert yourself, my lord."

John nodded, but he added. "I shall wish for some clothing today."

He half expected an argument, but the servant bowed. "Yes, my lord. Let us check the bandage for any bleeding—Sir William Reynolds will be back later in the day—and then we shall see about your attire and your breakfast."

Since the valet insisted that he must return to bed, and indeed, John was ready to rest, they compromised on a shirt and trousers, without the tight-fitting coat and neck cloth that would have made lying back on the pillows awkward.

John realized he was as hollow as an empty shell washed up on the seashore, and his stomach rumbled at the promise—he hoped it was a promise—of real food.

And indeed, when the tray arrived, he found ham and eggs and bread and pudding, a substantial spread after more than a day of fare limited to watery broths and thin soups. He enjoyed each bite. When a footman arrived to tell him he had a visitor, he allowed the servant to take away the tray while John looked eagerly toward the doorway.

He could barely hide his disappointment when it was Louisa Crookshank who swept into his room, her pale jonquil muslin gown the perfect showcase for her fair good looks.

"My dear Lord Gillingham, how are you feeling?" she demanded, her eyes wide with sympathy.

He found himself wanting to snap at her and controlled his irritability with some effort. "Quite well, thank you."

"When I think that you may have taken a bullet meant for me, oh, my lord. Such devotion—I really do not deserve it!" She clasped her hands together and gazed at him soulfully.

He could not think of any tactful way to remind her that his sacrifice had been totally accidental; he'd hardly seen the bullet coming and stepped into its path. "It was nothing," he said, hoping she was not going to burst into tears; she seemed nearly overcome with the force of her gratitude. "I am mending rapidly."

She smiled sweetly. "I am praying for nothing else. I assure you, my lord, I shall never forget your amazing dedication to my health and happiness."

Oh, wonderful. This was just what he needed, more reason to tie her to his side. John shifted a little on the bed. "Umm, I thank you again, but really, you should not be in my bedchamber alone. I do not wish to see any aspersions cast upon your good name."

"It is so typical of you to think of me first," she declared. "But I insisted on a moment alone to express my gratitude. And do not worry about any harm to my reputation, my aunt is just down the hall. Aunt Marianne, you may come in, now."

John wondered if he could repeat the summons, with even more urgency. *Please come in,* he thought. *I need you, Marianne, my love.*

Although when she appeared, she was veiled in the perceptible wall of reserve she always affected when she most wanted to efface herself. He was sick of it, John realized. Marianne should not be the one who remained on the sidelines, should not be the one who remained silent when someone else took center stage. She deserved every attention. Would he ever have the power to insist upon it?

"Aunt has told me of your very kind invitation," Louisa was saying. "It is so thoughtful of you. I am quite looking forward to seeing your estate for the first time."

"Indeed," he said again.

She chattered on for a few minutes, while John wondered why on earth he had ever been attracted to her; she was sweet and pretty and as empty-headed as a bandy hen. No, that was not fair, and he knew it. He had simply found someone else, a woman with more depth and maturity with whom the lovely young woman who tried so hard to engage his attentions could not hope to compare.

He felt sorry for Louisa, and for himself, too.

"I shall write to my butler today and warn him—inform him—that we shall be coming down at the end of the week." And to hell with the doctor if he did not agree, John thought. "In the meantime, I hope you will stay indoors, close at home."

Louisa's face fell. "If you insist, my lord."

"I'm sure your aunt agrees with me," he said, and Marianne nodded. "As irksome as I know it is, we must take every precaution." To him, the prospect did not sound irksome at all. In fact, John wished he could be at home unbothered by the city's din and crowded streets, but he knew that Louisa would not share his views.

His fiancée agreed to his and her aunt's urging, but with a decided lack of enthusiasm.

When the housekeeper appeared, announcing that tea had been sent to the drawing room for the ladies, Louisa followed the servant. To his delight, Marianne stayed for a moment. But it seemed she only wanted to discuss the mysterious assailant.

"I have made more inquires about Mr. Alton Crook-shank's movements," she told him quietly. "My footman has learned that he spent the day of the shooting at his office at the Academy doing research."

"So he is accounted for," John said, knowing he sounded as glum as he felt. Why could he not see the way clear to finding the hand that had held the gun?

"Not at all, the building has more than one exit, and he is not the most noticeable of men. He's quiet in his habits, the doorman told my man, and no one remembers just where he was or when he left." She looked quietly triumphant.

"Oh, well done," he told her, enjoying the glow of her cheeks as she relished his admiration. "I have been thinking about our—Louisa's—situation."

"And?"

"If she has been threatened in Bath and in London, there is no guarantee at all that going to Kent will shake off her attacker or guarantee her safety," he said slowly.

"Then you think we should not go?" She looked disappointed, but he was not sure if her disappointment came from his conclusion or the potential cancellation of their trip. He only hoped it was, at least in part, the latter.

"No, I'm sure that we should. Perhaps, with no crowds to hide in, the man can be identified more easily."

"But that means we are using Louisa as bait," she objected. "Like a bleating goat tied to a tree to lure the tiger from the jungle."

He smiled slightly at the anecdote culled from her store of travel books. "I doubt she will bleat, exactly. And she will be in no more danger there than here. Less, I devoutly hope."

"Yes, you're right," Marianne agreed, but she pressed her lips together for a moment. "I simply feel that if something happens, it would be my fault."

She had been carrying too much responsibility alone for too long, he thought. He wanted to lift that furrow of worry from her forehead, caress the smooth skin until all care was gone. Oh, bloody hell, how he wanted to touch her!

He pulled his thoughts back to Louisa. "The first attempt occurred before you took over her care," he reminded her.

"Yes, but she is in my custody now." Marianne met his gaze squarely, and he knew she would always look reality in the face. He felt a moment of pride in her courageous spirit. Amazing how much that delighted him, but perhaps everything about her did.

"I will be beside you," he promised.

And surely something leaped in her eyes at that simple vow.

Someday, he would be beside her always—he would find a way.

With the prospect of not only his removal from his brother's roof but the delightful anticipation of having Marianne Hughes, and Louisa, of course, staying in his house, the rest of the week went by with tantalizing slowness.

At last the day came when John saw his trunk repacked, and not one but two carriages prepared for the trip. In addition to his own black carriage, which somehow looked faded indeed compared to his brother's spruce equipage, Gabriel had added one of his own chaises to accommodate all the ladies' luggage and the two maids who would accompany them.

John rode in his own carriage, and Louisa insisted on riding with him, which meant that, although John winced at the thought of all the cosseting she would inflict upon him—she had already added two cushions and a hot brick for his feet—Marianne, as the girl's chaperone, would be included in their vehicle, too. The two maids and the extra luggage rode in Gabriel's chaise.

The footman tried to put Runt into the maids' carriage, but the little dog objected so loudly that she was switched to John's carriage, instead.

Louisa looked a bit askance when the small spaniel, panting slightly, curled up at their feet.

"Just think of her as a foot warmer," Marianne suggested, a twinkle in her eyes.

His brother had decided to ride, so he would canter beside them. John tried to tell his brother that his presence was not necessary. "I know you wish to be with your wife."

"What, not anxious to spend more time in my company?" Gabriel raised one brow. "I would rather be here, yes, but the doctor assures me that Psyche is out of danger. A friend has come to stay with her, and Circe is very mature; they have promised to send a special dispatch for me at any sign that I am needed. And I do not plan to linger— I will return to London shortly."

John had no doubt of that; his sibling had no wish to expend one more moment than necessary in this enforced family reunion.

"But my wife wishes me to see Miss Crookshank and Mrs. Hughes safely delivered, and I do not want to cause her any anxiety."

So they set off, after only two last-minute delays, as

Louisa forgot one of her bonnets, and then Sally, a curvaceous lady of very fashionable appearance, came out with a final message from Lady Gabriel. At last the coachman cracked his whip and the carriage moved forward.

It was a fair day, and John felt his spirits rise as they soon left London's busy streets behind and rolled through the countryside. From outside the chaise, he heard larks warbling as the birds soared high in the cloudless blue sky, and in the green fields new lambs scurried beside their dams. England in the spring . . .

John could almost have burst into song, himself. Even if Louisa kept talking—did the girl never shut up?—he could covertly admire Marianne from the corner of his eye as he nodded absently in answer to his fiancée's ceaseless chatter.

They arrived at the edge of his estate by late afternoon. John was pleased to see his brother, his expression approving, look over the well-kept acreage and neat farmlands.

"Have you tried the new method of cross-fertilization?" Gabriel surprised him by riding close enough to ask as the carriage paused at the gatehouse while the gate was opened and the coachman got down to check one of the horses in their team, whose harness seemed loose.

"Yes, I have found it an admirable system," John answered.

They had a brief but quite civil conversation about farming methods before the coachman climbed back up to his perch and flicked the reins. Then the chaise rolled forward again, with the other carriage following.

Within a mile they rounded the final bend and the house came into view. This time Gabriel had no comment to make, John noted, observing his brother covertly through the chaise window. Gabriel looked grim, as if old memories had been revived. But Louisa broke into extravagant praise of the large building. John waited, more interested to hear what the other lady had to say.

Marianne regarded the large mansion thoughtfully. "It is a handsome building," she agreed, "with noble proportions."

He smiled, relieved that she approved.

When the carriage drew to a stop, a footman stood ready to open the door and hand the ladies out. John regarded the servant with some jealousy; John would not have the pleasure of helping Marianne down. When he himself eased his wretched arm, protected by its sling but a little sore from the jolting of the journey, out of the chaise, he found the servants lined up to welcome him.

He spoke pleasantly to them as Runt sniffed at the shrubbery, but it did not escape his notice that the housekeeper looked anxious, the cook hungover, and the butler, Pomfroy, even more glum than usual. Oh, hell, he hoped the house would not be found to be in disorder, the one and only time he had brought guests, and guests whose good opinion he so much craved.

When they entered the front hall, John saw his house with fresh eyes. What he observed made his heart sink. Obviously, a frenzied last-minute effort had been made to neaten the place, and just as obviously, it did not make up for years of neglect.

The marble floors had smears where rag mops had missed their mark, and the tall ceilings were shadowed by an occasional cobweb. Even when they went into the drawing room, where at least the dustcovers had been removed from his mother's furniture—he never used the room himself and it was usually kept shut—he could see that dust darkened the edges of the carpet and the air smelt musty.

Thankfully, Gabriel remained silent, but his controlled expression did not totally hide his contempt.

John felt a deep sense of chagrin. "I'm afraid my staff has been somewhat lax," he murmured to Marianne, who smiled in reassurance.

"I think that you need a mistress of the house," she pointed out, her eyes warm as she gazed into his.

I need you, and for much more than overlooking the household, John thought, but he could not say the words aloud.

She glanced toward Louisa, who was looking about the room and apparently trying hard to find something to admire. "The—umm—draperies are very handsome," the younger woman declared.

For the first time in years John took a good look at the tall windows and their brocade dressings. "They were once, but they are sadly faded," he admitted. "It was my mother who chose these fabrics, and she has been dead for some time. It all needs replacing—I will have to see to it."

How could he have thought of bringing a bride to a house in such neglected condition? He himself had lived a hermit's life, going from his bedchamber to his study to the dining room and back again, and it had never occurred to him to worry about the dust or grime that was outside his immediate path.

"Men are not made to be housekeepers," he heard Marianne murmur to Louisa, as if in reassurance. "As Lady Sealey says, they enjoy a well-kept house, but they have no idea how to bring such a state about."

John could hardly argue the point. The housekeeper appeared in the doorway to show the ladies to their rooms, and a footman guided his brother to a guest chamber. John drew a deep breath, hoping the beds had been aired and the linen had no holes.

He went up to his own room and found the butler waiting to help him out of his coat. "Dinner will be served at six, my lord," the servant told him. "We did our best on such short notice, but two of the maids 'as quit, and the cook's complaining again about the chimney needing sweeping."

"So why wasn't it done?" John demanded. "Pomfroy, has the cook been dipping into the best port again? I told you—"

"Oh, no, my lord," the man protested. "I kept a close eye on the port, I did. He's been into the brandy, instead." He sighed.

John felt a surge of anger. "I have warned him before. You may inform the man he is on notice. As soon as I can find a replacement, his employment will be terminated." He could at least do this much to spare his future bride, whomever she might be, John told himself grimly.

Pomfroy's dour expression seemed to lengthen his long face even more. "Yes, my lord," he agreed. "But if I may suggest?"

"Yes?"

"You might wait to inform him until we actually have a new cook, my lord, and Corey's not—umm—mixing up our food?"

If his own cook poisoned him, he would not have to worry about outside assassins, John thought, not sure whether to laugh or groan. "A good point," he admitted. "But send out inquiries at once, if you please."

The man nodded.

"Come back in an hour, and I will change for dinner. Be sure that my guests have hot water and all that they need."

John lay down upon his bed and shut his eyes, but found it impossible to rest. How could he have been blind to the state of his home, and why had he not taken better care of his inheritance? True, he had only had the house a little over a year since the death of his father, but John could have spent more time seeing to its refurbishment. Perhaps most bachelors did not consider such things, he tried to tell himself, but he worried that the ladies—that Marianne—would receive a poor impression of the place, and he was sure that his brother was smirking, even if Gabriel did not show it openly.

Bloody hell.

When a footman came up to fill his copper bathtub with hot water, John gingerly—the doctor had warned him to avoid getting the wound wet—lowered himself into the half-filled tub and managed a quick bath. Then, drying himself awkwardly, he dressed, allowing the butler when he reappeared to help him into shirt, coat, and pantaloons. He usually tied his own neck cloth, but with one hand it was impossible, so Pomfroy, his expression intent, managed the job. Between them all, John was eventually made ready to go down to the drawing room and greet his guests.

He found the atmosphere in the big room less musky. Someone had directed the windows opened, and the light evening breeze was pleasant as it aired out the room.

After the ladies rejoined him, he found out who had given the order.

"Oh, how nice," Louisa remarked, looking about her. She sank into a chair; the brief rest and change of clothes seemed to have revived her usual cheerful demeanor.

"I hope you don't mind that I told the servants to open the windows, my lord," Marianne Hughes murmured after he had bent over her hand.

"Please, consider yourself at home and give any order that you think best," he told her, with more truth to the words than she could imagine. "I'm afraid housekeeping is not my strong point, as you have already suggested."

Her cheeks pinked. "It was wrong of me to imply it," she said, although her eyes still twinkled.

"If you had seen the house when my mother was alive, it would have looked very different," he told her.

Gabriel had entered the room in time to hear his comment.

"Indeed, our mother kept the place spotless," he agreed. "And she kept bowls of lavender in each room, so that the house always smelled sweet."

John felt a sudden surge of memory. "So she did. I should revive the practice."

"You will have to plant fresh lavender, then," his brother noted, his tone tart. "I see that my mother's gardens are sadly neglected."

John bit back an angry retort, keeping his voice level. "You have been for a walk, then?"

Gabriel didn't answer.

He had been to see their mother's grave, John realized. It was located at the end of the gardens in a private family graveyard. Some of John's anger faded. At least, his brother would have found the grave site well tended; that was one task John insisted was always performed regularly. But Gabriel's expression was brooding, and his eyes seemed dark.

Perhaps it was as well that the butler appeared in the doorway. "Dinner is served, my lords, ladies."

John was forced to offer his arm to Louisa, while his

brother took in Marianne. The table looked well with its white linen, the family china, and silver and crystal. Perhaps the silver could have used more polishing, and the flowers in the center looked a bit droopy. He would have to look into the state of the gardens, he realized, hating that Gabriel had seen the estate at less than its best.

When he took over total control of the estate and had finally had a free hand, John had been shocked once again at the disarray and neglect in which his father had kept it. John had applied his attention to the pastures and farmland and the sad shape of his tenants' cottages. He had not yet had time to think about the formal garden, but he should have thought to look over the flower beds his mother had planted. What else could go wrong with this visit?

When the first course arrived, his question was answered. The soup was watery, the pudding hard as any rock dug out of the slighted flower beds. The vegetables were overcooked, and the jellies wobbled.

When the fish course followed, it was tolerable, but the beef that came next was too brown, and the chicken dry and stringy.

His guests did not comment on the dinner's deficiencies, of course, good manners forbade any obvious criticism, but no one ate very much, and John was afraid even to look at his brother, sure that any expression of scorn would spark an instant argument. He would not spar with his brother, verbally or otherwise, with the ladies present.

It did not help his temper to hear, beneath the constant chatter of Louisa, who was seated on his right hand, that Gabriel was regaling Marianne with stories from his travels abroad, making her laugh with anecdotes of Trinidad markets and Greek islands, making her eyes brighten with tales of beautiful lands that John had never seen. Anger curled inside his belly and tightened his shoulders.

Damn his brother with his beguiling charm and his angelic—or devilish—good looks. What business did he have making Marianne looked so entranced? Who could compete with him for a lady's affection? Not John, not now, not ever.

The footmen entered with the last course, an array of sweets whose taste and texture were best not remarked upon. John took one bite of the peach tart and almost choked on a pit. What the hell—he put down his spoon.

The cook would have to go, as soon as it could be arranged. This was intolerable.

When Marianne collected Louisa's attention with a glance and then stood, he saw that the ladies, as was the usual custom, were going to withdraw and leave the gentlemen to their stronger after-dinner drink and male conversation.

A prospect neither he nor—he would wager—his brother relished.

When the door shut behind the women, the silence in the room seemed to echo.

"I shall be leaving with the first light," Gabriel said at last. "If I do not see you in the morning, my thanks for your hospitality."

"Judging by this abysmal dinner, not much to be thankful for," John answered, his tone just as gruff. "I owe you much more, for caring for me after my injury."

Gabriel waved away any expression of gratitude, no matter how tersely expressed. "Have you any idea yet who fired the gun?"

John shook his head. He had promised Marianne not to mention their theory that the gunman's true victim had been Louisa. The girl did not need to incur further gossip.

"I have had enemies, sometimes lethal enemies, in my time, but I always knew who they were," Gabriel remarked. "Have you harmed someone recently?"

John shrugged. "The trip to London was my first foray off my own land in years, and I hardly had a chance to do anyone any disservice there, other than trodding on a few ladies' toes, perhaps."

"Close to home, then. Turned a tenant off his farm?"

"After which he would follow me to London in order to attack me?" John couldn't help sounding skeptical. "No, I have not. I am about to fire my cook, but he's drunk too often to shoot me, especially before the fact of his dismissal."

Gabriel shook his head. "I don't know, then. I shall bid you good night and retire to my chamber."

It was early for bed, but John knew his brother had no wish to enjoy his company any longer than necessary, and he felt the same.

"Good night to you," he said.

But in the hallway Gabriel hesitated. "Do you still have grandfather's books? I might borrow one to peruse before I sleep."

John motioned down the hallway. "You know where to find the library."

Gabriel accepted the tacit invitation and walked down the hall. For no particular reason, John followed. A footman hurried ahead of them to light candles.

Inside the room the air felt cold and a little damp. Could his servants not care for the house for a few days without his supervision? This was not good for the collection of books that lined the walls. Still, he would have to show the library to Marianne tomorrow, John thought absently. She might find some new titles she would enjoy.

Gabriel stood with his back to him and surveyed the shelves. "I see you have added some of your own volumes to our grandfather's collection," he said, his tone polite.

John grunted; the answer was obvious. He knew that Gabriel was making an effort, but beneath the surface politeness, he suspected his brother's temper was growing as short as his own. *Pick a damn book and go to bed,* he thought, but he kept his mouth firmly shut.

And perhaps they would have ended the day with the same brittle politeness, except that his brother pulled open the glass door to reach for a volume on an upper shelf and hesitated.

Then he picked up, instead of the book he had intended, a small oval frame lying facedown on the shelf. His face went dark.

John tensed.

"I know this miniature . . . I remember sitting for this, although I must have been no older than three," Gabriel said as to himself. "My mother bribed me with sugar drops to be still enough for the artist to paint us. How very odd that the glass is broken and the frame cracked!"

He turned, and John braced himself. "It was an accident," he lied, remembering with a tinge of guilt the day he had knocked the small frame across the shelf.

Gabriel's lips curled. "I'm sure," he said dryly. "I am only surprised you did not throw it out."

John saw, uneasily, that his brother's grip on the small portrait did not relax. "I have few pictures of my mother," John said. "My father cut up most of them after she died. Mother kept this one—" he found the words hard to get out, but he persisted "—beside her bed. Her lady's maid hid it from my father's attention when he was destroying so much of her things. The woman gave it to me later."

Gabriel nodded, but he regarded the miniature with an expression in which both grief and anger mixed.

John remembered how his brother had brought a gleam to Marianne's eyes over dinner, and his indignation rose again, mixed with other, even darker emotions. He found his fists had clenched. He took one step closer to his brother, who regarded him with wary hostility.

"Take it, damn you," John blurted. "She would have wanted you to have it."

Gabriel walked to the door without answering, but once he had started, John could not seem to be still. "You had her heart," he muttered, "as you do with any female you glance upon, with your damned beautiful face and charming ways."

In the wide doorway, Gabriel paused and looked back, raising his brows. "I have no control over the face I was born with. Why should you hate me for that?"

"Because I could not compete with it!" John was too angry, perhaps too anguished, to control his words. "Because she loved you!" He followed his brother into the hall, and then paused, his feelings raw as an open wound, certain he had revealed too much.

"She loved you, as well," Gabriel said, his voice quiet. "I remember her sadness when our father would stalk in and take you away when she had gathered us inside her arms in the nursery ready to read to us both, or sing us to sleep at night. 'You shan't pamper my heir,' he yelled at her once, 'You shan't make him weak.' ''

John felt a strange conflict inside him. "I don't remember that," he said slowly. "No, perhaps I do. Mostly I only recall that you were always at her knee, and I seemed to be kept at a distance. And yes, I hated you for that." He drew a deep breath.

"She loved you," Gabriel repeated. "And so did our father, and he could not abide me, as you well know. You had the affection of both—why should you resent me?"

"But she was the loving one. Father might have required me to stay near him, but he was more apt to give out blows than hugs. I think you had the best end of the bargain . . ."

Gabriel looked scornful. "As I did when he threw me out, denied me my birthright, ordered me never to set foot in this house again? My only satisfaction at making this trip is that he must be tossing in his elegant crypt."

John looked away from the searing glance. "I did not know that he had turned you out till later," he said, though he knew it was a weak excuse.

"And then you tried so hard to find me?"

"No, and I should have done so, I should have made sure you were not starving and alone." For a moment guilt stirred inside him, then it was replaced by a darker emotion. "Though you seemed to have done well enough," John pointed out, his tone hard again, "judging from your colorful tales at the dinner table."

Gabriel eyed him with a too searching gaze. "So it's like that, is it? I suspected as much. When you look at Mrs. Hughes, your heart is in your eyes. So why did you propose to the other one?"

"I didn't, exactly," John said bitterly. "She thinks, however, that I did."

Gabriel gave a short laugh, and John took a step closer.

"I wouldn't," his brother warned. "You have only one good hand, and you made little progress with two, the last time."

"I almost caused your last breath!" John retorted. "And I

should be happy to take up where I left off, one hand or not!"

There was a slight sound from the other end of the hallway, and he glanced around to see Marianne Hughes regarding them both with a reproachful gaze.

They paused, although it was impossible to disguise their antagonistic stance. John lowered his good hand, and Gabriel, still holding the miniature, bowed to the lady.

"Good night, Mrs. Hughes. I hope you have a pleasant stay." Then with no further word to his brother, he headed for the stairwell and ascended out of sight.

"I came because I was worried what might happen when the two of you were left alone," she said to John as she came closer. She looked at him anxiously.

"It's that obvious?" he asked. Anger lingered inside him, but he felt the draw of her presence, and his morose mood eased a little.

"Oh yes," she said. "Dare I ask what has renewed your quarrel?"

It was impossible to tell her the truth, of course, so John was astonished to hear himself saying, "He found a portrait of my mother and himself as a babe . . ."

"And you argued over that?"

"I—the glass was broken. He thought I had done it deliberately, out of spite."

"Why would you do such a thing?" Her quiet tone was not accusing, but he winced, anyhow.

"Out of jealousy, I suppose. Gabriel was her favorite, and we both knew it. It was natural enough, he made a beautiful child." John tried to sound offhand, but was not sure he had succeeded. He braced himself against pity.

To his astonishment, she moved closer and lifted her hand to cup his cheek. He flinched, afraid she would feel his scars and draw back in disgust. But Marianne's touch lingered, and his blood leaped at her nearness, at the soft touch of her hand.

"And you felt unloved?" she suggested. "Gabriel spoke a little of your mother at dinner. I think she must have been a warm and affectionate woman . . . I am quite sure that she loved you, John. You were her first child, her first son. How could you not have been special?"

He could not answer. His throat seemed to have closed, and the rush of emotion inside him dissolved a few layers of icy despair. He put his hand over hers, wishing he could hold it there forever, hold her so close for all time.

To his infinite regret, she stepped back, although her voice sounded husky when she spoke. "Louisa will wonder if I do not return to the drawing room. But, my lord, please do not quarrel with your brother. Your mother would be grieved by it. Family ties are precious, you know, and should not be easily squandered."

She walked swiftly to the staircase and was gone before he could answer.

But he felt compelled to do her bidding. He would apologize, even if the words choked him. So he followed his brother's path up the stairs toward the guest wing. To John's relief, he did not have to knock on the bedchamber door; his brother was still standing on the landing, looking up at a large portrait of their father, the late marquess.

"He was a brute, you know," Gabriel said, as if their conversation had not ended minutes before. "He made my—our—mother's life hell."

"I know," John admitted. "He made everyone's life hell. In some ways, you had the better bargain, even if it came at a price. I had to stay and deal with him."

"I heard you had taken up residence in one of the smaller properties, keeping away as much as possible in the last years," Gabriel pointed out.

John nodded. "But I had to come by now and then, if only to try to keep the estate from falling totally apart. I had responsibilities."

"Oh, yes, the elder brother."

"And his heir. At least he had one. Mind you, I do not blame our mother, you understand—"

Gabriel turned suddenly. "For what?"

"For giving birth to another man's child."

Fourteen

*T*he silence seemed edged with ice, and Gabriel looked just as frozen.

"You knew that," John protested. "You had to know that."

"Not being present at the conception, in any conscious form, how would I have known that?" Gabriel's voice was tight with the self-control it took to maintain an even tone. But his face seemed turned to stone.

"But I had thought that Mother would have told you . . ." John's voice faded.

"You should not give credence to our father's rants," Gabriel snapped. "He was livid with jealousy, mad with it. Why else did he keep our mother a virtual prisoner through most of their marriage? Why did he spend his last years alone, holed up here and rejecting any company?"

"He didn't care for society," John pointed out. "And he suffered from occasional bouts of gout, which didn't help his temper."

"His ill temper needed no aggravation!"

"Perhaps," John agreed. "I admit that his soul was

twisted—that is one reason I do not blame Mother for seeking comfort elsewhere. And as for the other—well, no matter."

Gabriel took a step closer, and this time he was the one who reached out his hand. John took an instinctive step backward and almost slid down the staircase. Gabriel caught him by the lapel and halted his fall, but his brother's grip was savage.

"What? Tell me what you are inferring!"

"I came into her parlor once, and she tucked a letter away, out of sight beneath the cushion of her chair."

Silence. Gabriel's blue eyes met his own darker ones, both gazes intense with repressed emotion.

"How can you slight our mother's honor over such a trifle? That means nothing!"

"In itself, no. But after she died, after our father died, one of the maids, while cleaning, found a secret hiding place in a wall panel of her bedchamber. When I came to investigate, I found letters and a few other trifles hidden away."

"Letters? From whom?"

"A man. A gentleman, and he signed them with his 'eternal love.'"

"And you read them?" Gabriel's face contorted with anger and disgust.

"I did not! I burned them. She had the right to her private feelings."

Gabriel's face flamed. "I still do not believe it."

It was hardly surprising that his brother refused to credit the truth of their mother's affair. It made him a bastard, destroying in one blow what he thought he knew about himself, John thought. He should have rejoiced to see his normally urbane brother distraught, should have enjoyed witnessing Gabriel's always controlled and polished demeanor shattered by one secret from the past.

Instead he found that his own anger, nourished with bitter resolve over the years, fed with embers of childish jealousy, seemed to weaken, as if the fuel for its flame had been scattered. Only the dying coals were left, and he had been admonished to beat them into cold ashes, as well.

And because it was Marianne who advised it, he would try although he was not sure if he could find the words. He drew a deep breath and surprised himself.

"Perhaps I was wrong," John said.

Gabriel's gaze was suspicious. "You do not believe that."

He was new at reconciliation. Lying was not his strong suit, either. "No, I do not," he admitted, his tone even. "But you may believe it if you wish, and I shall not argue the point. She is dead. She was our mother, the bond that joined us. She loved you . . . I hope she loved me. Let her rest."

Gabriel released him and put one hand to his face, as if to hide the emotions that flitted across those perfect features. John felt himself almost wishing to put out an arm to offer solace, but he made no such move. Gabriel would likely knock him down the stairs.

Yet, was that not what big brothers were supposed to be? Mentors, protectors, comforters if need be? He had been miserably lacking on all accounts.

"I am sorry I failed you as a brother," he said.

Gabriel's eyes widened, but John felt almost as amazed. He had not willed the words to come; they had slipped out from some place deep inside him.

"You admit it?" Gabriel spoke slowly.

"Yes." He could have tried to explain that at first he was too young to understand his own behavior, and later he had been influenced by their father's bitterness and resentment. But none of it excused what he had done, and what he had failed to do, to protect his younger brother.

John would not have been surprised to have his apology, years overdue though it was, thrown back into his face. Silence stretched between them, heavy with emotions never before drawn into the light.

Then Gabriel nodded slowly. "Very well."

It was more than John could have expected, more than he deserved. He watched his brother turn and ascend the steps, but Gabriel paused at the top of the flight to look back. "I have another miniature of our mother, of herself alone, which the housekeeper kept for me and gave me after her death. Circe has made me a larger copy in watercolors, very nicely done. I will send the original to you, since you have—ah—allowed me to take the other portrait."

"Thank you," John said gruffly, glad that his brother turned away. He would not wish Gabriel to see the moisture that flooded his eyes.

Perhaps he had had his mother restored to him, today. It was a fanciful thought, and yet, he thought he might now gaze at her portrait without remembering the pain of the slights he had long imagined. Slights his father had encouraged him to feel, John realized. He would not allow his father's hand to reach out of the grave and control him still! If his mother had loved him, it meant—it meant he was not, after all, unlovable.

Taking a deep breath, John descended the stairs and headed for the drawing room. The ladies had been neglected long enough. He paused at the entrance and rubbed his face to make sure that no evidence of emotional confrontation remained. Then he nodded to the footman to throw open the double doors, and he entered.

The two women were seated at the far side of the room. Darkness had fallen outside, and the windows had been shut and the heavy curtains drawn. But the room looked better in the candlelight, the long years of neglect harder to distinguish. The butler had already brought in the tea tray.

"My lord," Louisa said, jumping up. "We were wondering where you were. Is Lord Gabriel not joining us?"

"He was fatigued after riding so far and has retired to his bed," John explained.

Louisa looked disappointed, and Marianne's glance was concerned.

He sat down, allowed Louisa to fuss about him and put an unneeded pillow at his back and then pour him a cup of tea.

It was Marianne who remembered to add a little cream, just as he liked it.

He listened to Louisa chatter for several minutes and did his best to respond. No need to make her suffer, too, from slights real or imagined. Somehow, John seemed to be acquiring a better understanding of how much small ac tions, or the lack of them, could linger in a person's heart.

Eventually, Marianne suggested that Louisa play fo them, and even though the pianoforte was sadly out o tune, the younger woman did her best, playing and singing with her usual sprightly cheer. It gave him the freedom to sit beside Marianne and enjoy the illusion of being—al most—alone with her. While applauding Louisa at the ap propriate times, he managed to steal covert glances a Marianne.

"I have apologized to my brother," he told her very qui etly, under cover of Louisa's music-making.

The approving glance she gave him was more than enough reward for the effort it had cost him.

"I am so glad. I'm sure that there is brotherly love there still, and in time, perhaps you both can recover from the in juries of the past."

"Perhaps."

"At least you have tried," she assured him. "And Lord Gabriel seems an honorable man."

She seemed to assume, without speaking the words, tha John's intentions could also be trusted.

And while he sat in her presence, John could believe that he, too, was an honorable and civilized gentleman, no the brute he had always feared he might be—his father' son at heart—never to be worthy of a lady's love, even be fore the maiming illness had struck him down.

As Louisa rattled her way along the ivory keys, Mari anne gazed at him with trust, and he felt bigger, better be cause of it.

It was such a difference from the corrosive suspicion hi father had emanated. John felt as if the very walls of the house seemed to breathe more easily, releasing their decades accumulation of poison, allowing it to ebb away, ready to be replaced by more positive, more healthy emotions.

When Marianne suggested that it was time that the ladies retired, too, John felt a sharp pang of regret. He did not wish to let her go. He could have sat up all night—if propriety did not allow a closer connection—just sitting close to her, enjoying her presence.

But he hid his regret, bowed over their hands, and allowed both ladies to depart up the stairs to the guest wing. He was no Mongol, who could throw a lady over his steed and decamp, as he had once wished he could do when he had first come to London and was decrying the necessity of a long and awkward courtship.

Now he thanked God he had stayed; he would never have met Marianne, else.

And that thought carried him up to his bedroom, reasonably content. Runt frolicked about him as the butler helped him out of his clothes and into his nightshirt, and then the servant was sent off to his own bed. John washed his face sloppily with his one good hand and, while the dog took her usual position on the rug beside it, threw himself upon his bed, thinking with rising need about how much he wished for Marianne to lie beside him, to turn willingly into his arms. Or would she turn away in distaste?

He thought about how she had touched his face, and his whole body tingled with desire. If he could just hold her close—

He had to put these thoughts away, or he would not sleep at all tonight. He wondered what she was doing in the guest wing, if she could possibly be thinking of him? He could so easily rise, go down the hall—

And what? Ravish his guest in his own house? In the chamber next door to the one occupied by his fiancée?

A most honorable man that would make him!

Groaning with unfulfilled desire that left his groin aching and his whole body tense, John pulled a pillow over his head and tried to think of something dull and unexciting, like the list of repairs needed for his house.

The next morning John rose early. He had slept little, but he was too eager to see Marianne again to linger in bed.

In the hallway he found Gabriel, already in his riding coat about to depart.

"I hope you supped—and I devoutly hope you found something on the buffet edible?" John asked.

Gabriel gave a wry grin. "The toast is tolerable, if you scrape off the black edges. I would not recommend the kippers."

John shook his head, then turned to matters of more import. "Thank you for all your assistance and for seeing me safely home. As for last night—I suppose you found my change of heart hard to credit, but my words were sincere."

His brother nodded. "I, too, have been lucky enough to find a woman who believes in my honor and my decency despite all the sins I committed earlier in my most wanton days. And as a result, I have found that I must live up to her beliefs, be the man she trusts me to be. I am not surprised to find that you feel constrained to do the same."

Silent with surprise, John found no answer.

"I hope you untangle your love life soon," Gabriel added, his smile now tinged with wicked humor. "Unslaked desire makes for unsettled nights."

John bit back an oath. Was it so obvious? But he found it in himself to offer his hand, and somewhat to his surprise, Gabriel accepted it.

"Our father is dead," his younger brother pointed out. "Let us leave him in his grave and not reenact old roles inflicted upon us in childhood."

"Agreed," John said.

He walked outside with his brother and watched Gabriel mount the handsome beast the groom brought up for him. The horse tossed his head and took a few restless steps before his rider tightened the reins and settled him. Gabriel's chaise was ready to follow, but his brother still preferred to ride.

"Safe journey," John said and was conscious of the unspoken irony of his words. Both he and Gabriel had come a long way over the last two days. Perhaps someday his brother would be able to visit his childhood home without the oppressive weight of bad memories, and perhaps John could shed some old nightmares, as well, and accept that his mother had loved him after all.

He raised his hand in a farewell wave and was even able to smile at his so-long-hated sibling. Whatever was the truth about the identity of the younger man's sire, Gabriel and he shared a mother, and she was the better part of their heritage. Perhaps Marianne was right about family ties.

Which reminded him, how soon could he expect to see the woman whose face now haunted the few scraps of sleep he had managed to obtain? He had a vague notion that upper-class women did not rise early, so he might have to wait. But just knowing that she was under the same roof gave him enormous pleasure, as well as—he had to admit—a constant rippling of desire that he was forced to keep in check.

He hurried back inside and found a footman hovering in the hallway. "Let me know as soon as Mrs. Hughes is up and about," he told the servant.

The man shifted his feet. "But she is up, my lord."

"What? I didn't see her in the dining room."

"I believe she is—ah—upstairs in the laundry room, my lord," the servant murmured, but for some reason, he did not meet John's eye.

John blinked. "What the devil—never mind; I'll see for myself." Had his wretched excuse for a household staff ruined one of her dresses? Fearing more catastrophe, he hurried toward the staircase.

On the first landing he paused, aware of unusual activity in the drawing room. A footman stood on a ladder gathering up armloads of faded brocade, and in the corner where the dust had been the thickest last night, a housemaid could be seen on her hands and knees, scrubbing hard with brush and bucket.

John gazed at them, then decided this could wait. He had to check on Marianne first, make sure she had not been inconvenienced in some way he might remedy.

He continued up the stairs. When he reached the upper level, he realized he had no idea where the laundry room was, but fortunately he ran across a maid hurrying on some errand, and although she looked flustered, she was able to direct him.

When he found the right chamber, which was pleasantly redolent of starch and drying linen, he was perplexed to find Marianne in the middle of the room, directing several of his female staff.

"Now, first, make a list of all the bedroom linen that needs to be replaced. Put the sheets that can be mended in this pile, and the ones that are beyond hope and should go into the rag basket over here." Marianne looked up and met his startled gaze. She crossed the room quickly.

"Mrs. Hughes, do I owe you an apology? Have you had a problem with my staff or the service?"

"Not at all," she told him cheerfully. "And I fear I am the one who owes you an apology, my lord. It is a poorly behaved guest who takes over the direction of the servants, and I regret to say that I have done just that."

He struggled to conceal his bewilderment. "My dear Mar—Mrs. Hughes, I assure you, you may give any orders that you wish. I want to ensure your every comfort, and I fear I have not done a very good job of it."

She grinned. "You had best wait to hear what I have done, my lord, before giving me carte blanche. And I should certainly have talked to you first, but—" Perhaps aware of the servants who had to be listening intently, although they flashed only covert glances toward their master and his unexpected guest, she paused. "Perhaps we should discuss this downstairs?"

John hastened to agree. He had not meant to inflict household chores onto his guest; she would have a poor opinion of him, indeed. And he could not tell her what a flood of warmth and longing flooded through him when he saw her so at ease even in such a pedestrian setting, as if she were the mistress of the house in truth as well as in his deepest dreams.

He made a gesture for her to precede him, then followed her down to the morning room, which was so far untenanted by servants. Marianne led the way into the room, then turned to face him, but she did not sit.

"I gather you have given some direction for cleaning?" he suggested.

She bit her lip, for the first time looking uncertain. "I know it is the rankest incivility for me to take charge of your staff, but—"

"Mrs. Hughes, you do not have to pretend that we are not both aware of my household's deficiencies. If you choose to offer my staff guidance, I will be grateful, although chagrined that you should be put to such trouble."

"It's no trouble," she said quickly, her face clearing. "Only, I did not wish to embarrass or anger you. You have obviously kept your land in good order; I heard the discussion between you and your brother. But the house—I do not expect a man to be aware of all that a well-run household needs."

He grinned slightly. "I thank you for your forbearance."

"Now, I said I was sorry—" Then she paused, as if aware that he was teasing. "You reprobate! I have never found a mere male to be aware of when the sheets need to be replaced, or how well or how ill the housemaids are doing their jobs. But Louisa put her foot through her sheet last night, and I thought that the linens must be sorted out right away, in order to save your reputation as a good host."

His smile faded, and he could not bite back the beginning of a curse in time. "Oh, bloody—I mean, I am sorry to hear that."

"Not to worry, but the next time you have guests, perhaps Lord Gabriel and his wife, your guest rooms will be better stocked. And I think he will return," she added. "I happened to be on the landing when you said good-bye, and I was happy to see the two of you shake hands. I am proud of you, my lord, for making peace with your brother. I promise you, you will not regret it."

Warmed by her words, he wasn't sure how to answer. "Much of the fault is mine, so it was right that I take the first step. I have not been the best of brothers," he told her, his tone gruff.

"But there is always time to change that," she suggested.

"Perhaps. I'm not sure I know how. Nor do I know if I

can be a good husband, though perhaps I should not confess that."

She lifted her hand for a moment to touch his cheek, the same light touch that had inflamed him yesterday, a memory that he still held close to his heart.

"With the right woman, I'm sure that you will, my lord." Her voice was husky.

Except that Louisa was not the right woman, and they both knew it; he was sure that Marianne understood how much he wanted to put his arms around her and pull her close. The spark that always lay ready jumped between them, and he held his breath. He saw the awareness in her eyes, and the slight flush to her cheeks, and he hoped that beneath the respectable neckline of her blue dress, her heart was beating as hard as his own.

Oh, God, how long could he contain these surging desires? And could she, would she—even if he were free—be able to return his passion? He was still not the man that Marianne deserved . . . he was flawed in face and form as well as in his family heritage. He was the child of a savage father and a mistreated mother; if she knew the full truth, would she dare to risk her life, her heart, to him?

He hesitated, this time held back from more than just an awareness of the impropriety of any closeness when he was still promised, at least nominally, to another woman.

Walking more briskly than usual, his arms full of something John could not make out, a footman passed the doorway. Marianne stepped back.

He hated to lose the moment. "I think that perhaps a good many of my staff need to be replaced," he suggested, hoping to hold her here by any means, even a discussion of his servants' shortcomings.

She smiled. "I think most of them merely need better supervision. The cook, however, I cannot guarantee."

He gave a reluctant laugh.

"I'd best see if Louisa is up. I plan to give her the task of overseeing the pruning in the garden. She's actually quite a good gardener," Marianne told him.

He had to press his lips firmly together to repudiate any

suggestion of Louisa playing the role of mistress here. See-ing Marianne taking charge was one thing, but Louisa was a different story.

He had a task ahead much more difficult than bringing his servants into an awareness of how to correctly run a household. How did one break an engagement, even one somewhat accidentally embarked upon, with a young woman of gentle birth without breaking her heart in the process? Because not only did he have no desire to hurt Louisa, who was not to blame for this quagmire—if he had been both more focused and more cautious, this situation would not have come about—but hurting her would not en-dear him to her aunt.

He would rather have scrubbed the floors himself, John thought ruefully. But he followed Marianne Hughes to the dining room, where they found Louisa seated at the long table. She nibbled on a piece of blackened toast.

"Good morning, my lord," she said. "I hope you are not pained by your injury? You look as if you've had little sleep."

There was no looking glass in the dining room to check his face, so he had to accept her judgment.

"My arm is improving," he told her. "I hope that you slept well?"

"Oh yes," she said, though she looked away from his glance, toying with her breakfast.

He could not think of what else to say. "I have horses in the stable, if you enjoy riding," he told the ladies. "But I would not suggest going far afield. Until we learn more about the person who threatens Miss Crookshank, I think she should stay close to the house. I have instructed my male servants, inside and out, to be vigilant and on guard for any strangers lurking near the estate."

That was one way his father's paranoia could be of ben-efit, John thought. The house and its immediate grounds were surrounded by a high stone wall, and no one would find it easy to approach.

Louisa looked somewhat less than enthused by his sug-gestion, but she nodded.

"I thought after breakfast, you might wish to spend some time in the gardens," Marianne Hughes told her ward. "You have a good eye for landscaping, and some of the shrubbery is badly in need of shaping and pruning. If you were on hand to instruct the gardeners, I think the finished product would benefit from your excellent eye."

Louisa agreed. "I shall fetch my parasol," she said, looking a little more cheerful.

To John's disappointment, Marianne was ready to return to her supervision of the indoor staff, so, with Runt pattering behind him, he went to his office on the ground floor.

News had already gone out that he had returned, and two tenants were waiting to see him about a dispute over a cow that had gotten into a neighbor's garden. This somehow took a good part of the morning. Then he felt he should ride out and check on the progress of the hay and grain fields and also be on the lookout for any strangers in the area. He sent instructions for his favorite horse to be saddled, then walked outside into the sunlight, wishing he could show Marianne around the grounds, not leave her to boring tasks she should not have to labor over. He threw his leg over the saddle and mounted, but cast one more wistful glance toward the house before riding away.

Marianne saw that the draperies in the drawing room were given a good dusting and shaking out, and the windows were washed before the curtains were rehung. She had the faded but good quality rugs taken outdoors for a beating to free them of some of the years of accumulated dirt, and the floor scrubbed and the furniture polished with beeswax and oil.

Their dinner that night was quieter, without Lord Gabriel's stories and jests, and the food unfortunately not at all improved.

"I am looking for a new chef," John assured them both. He put his knife, not without effort, into a piece of over-cooked pork. "Looking hard."

Louisa giggled.

After dinner John showed both the ladies his library, which Marianne had not had time during the day to explore.

Louisa nodded politely, but Marianne gazed in admiration at the large, handsome room with its high shelves filled with books.

"That is wonderful, my lord!"

He smiled, warmed by her approval. "My father was not a reader, but grandfather liked a well-stocked library, and I have added to the collection. Feel free to borrow any volumes you would enjoy."

"Perhaps you have a nice adventurous novel?" Louisa suggested hopefully. "With lots of romantic dialogues, ghostly visions, and haunted chambers?"

"Perhaps," he agreed and directed her to one of the shelves. She picked up a volume to peruse, and he was able to cross to Marianne. She stood at the side of the room in front of the large globe on its mahogany stand.

"So you have contemplated a larger world, too," she murmured. "Do you read travel tomes, as well, my lord?"

He smiled ruefully. "Not as many as you, I think, but yes, I, too, have ventured abroad through the pages of a book."

"Then we have more in common than you have admitted." She smiled up at him, and only Louisa's presence held him back from pulling her into his arms.

Both the ladies chose books to take to their rooms. As for John, tense with frustration, he paced up and down for some time before he trusted himself to go quietly up to bed.

In her chamber Marianne found even a four-volume history of the Ottoman Empire, which she had selected, failed to hold her attention. Instead, she thought of John—it was harder than she had expected to have him so close and be unable to spend time alone with him—until at last she sighed and extinguished her candle. And even then, he found his way into her dreams.

It was best to keep busy. As the week went by, she continued to lead the household staff in an energetic attack on the dirt and disarray. After the drawing room, they tackled the guest wing; the beds all needed new linen, the curtains had rotted from the sun, and some of the paper on the walls had mildewed. She learned from one of the few servants who had worked under the late marquess that John's father had never allowed fires in any rooms except the ones he had inhabited. And he had never had guests, except for very rare instances, so the guest wing had been quite abandoned.

Sometimes John came to see what she was about, apologizing again for the house's disorder, worried that she felt compelled to do too much, that he was being a poor host. She finally forbade him to say another word, and he retreated to his study or disappeared out of doors, spending long hours on horseback, either checking on his farmland or keeping an eye out for intruders, she wasn't sure which.

In fact, overseeing the cleaning kept her from dwelling on the tantalizing reality of John's nearness. At least that was her theory; the truth was, she still had to pull her thoughts back a hundred times a day. And going through his house taught her more than he might wish about the bleakness of his early life, and the ignominies he had suffered living with such a deplorable father.

She heard more recent stories, too. When she noted aloud that there were no looking glasses in any of the public rooms, the housekeeper told her that none was allowed in the master's suite, either.

"Ordered 'em all out when he had the sickness, ma'am. Couldn't bear to see his own face, apparently. A sad thing, that was. He was never the looker that his younger brother was—face of an angel, that one—" She paused.

Marianne raised her brows, her tone a little dry. "Yes, Lord Gabriel is most blessed." How John must have tired of being always compared to his brother!

The housekeeper flushed and went on, her words a little too fast, "But our own lord was a nice sturdy lad, and many of the local lasses cut their eyes at him. Then, he caught the pox—his late lordship had not inoculated his tenants, as most of the neighbors had. They said a group of gypsies, traveling through, had the sickness, and some of the young men who had been down to try their hand at games of chance came down ill shortly after. My lord always tried to be a good landlord, even when his father was alive, and he went down to visit the sick and take them food."

"Oh." Marianne paused with a brush in her hand. To encourage their efforts, she was not above joining the servants in their herculean task. "He never told me that part."

"He wouldn't, ma'am. He's shy about his own good deeds," the housekeeper declared. "I think he's still trying to make up for his father, if I say it, who shouldn't."

She looked anxious, and Marianne nodded, offering no rebuke for such criticism of a high-ranking lord.

She felt a deep rush of compassion for John, suffering so much. She put down the brush. "I think this paper is hopeless; it will have to be replaced," she said. "I will speak to his lordship about it. We shall begin on the dining room, next."

The housekeeper nodded. Although flustered from all this unaccustomed activity, at least she did not seem to resent Marianne's directions.

"I know it's all in a sad shape, ma'am," she told Marianne, not for the first time. "His lordship's mother kept the house better, I assure you—I was only a housemaid at the time, but I remember it well. After she died, well, the old lord had a time keeping any servants at all, and he cared little about the house as long as he had his wine at hand, and something halfway cooked on the table at dinnertime. He was a fierce one, he was, if you pardon me for saying so. I only came back after he died."

"Quite understandable," Marianne agreed. "I think you are shorthanded, as well, in a house this size. If you can find any girls in the village who are interested in a post, I'm sure his lordship would agree to hiring more maidservants."

The housekeeper positively beamed. "Oh, yes, ma'am. That would be most helpful. I will send word. We've had trouble hiring servants in the past—such silly stories the girls pay heed to—but having visitors from London, well, it's much more normal, isn't it?"

Marianne wasn't sure she understood this, but it seemed indelicate to pry too far. So they had a discussion about which chores to tackle next, then Marianne went in search of Louisa, whom she found in the formal garden, directing two of the gardeners.

"Yes, and I think this bush is past its prime—is there anything in the greenhouse ready to transplant?" she was asking.

The man wiped his brow with a somewhat grimy kerchief. "Don't know, miss."

"Even so, I think it has to come up. If we must, we'll buy more from the market in the next town," Louisa said.

She sounded confident enough, Marianne thought. If she did become mistress here—and the thought gave Marianne a sharp pang, there was no use denying it—she would no doubt do a fine job of looking out for the estate.

Louisa took out her fan; despite the shade of her parasol, she looked flushed from the heat. "Oh, hello, Aunt, what do you think of this?" She motioned to the bushes they had been cutting back, and Marianne nodded in approval.

"It looks very well. Are you ready to go inside for something cool? At least, if not cool, wet. I tried to order some lemonade made up, but there are no lemons, so we shall have to settle for tea. I fear the cook has neglected his pantry stores."

"The cook has neglected everything else, as well, judging by the food we've been offered," Louisa retorted. For once, her good temper seemed to have failed her.

Marianne made no answer in front of the gardeners, but she followed Louisa inside and up to the morning room. Louisa flung herself into a chair; she did not look at all happy.

Marianne waited for the tea tray to be brought in, then

shut the door behind the footman and sat down in the next chair. "What is it, my dear?"

"Oh, Aunt, can we not go back to London?" Louisa blurted.

"Not yet. You know why we came, to provide you with a safe haven," Marianne pointed out.

"But I would like so much to go back to town!"

Marianne wondered uneasily how Louisa would fare spending most of her time here. This lack of contentment did not bode well in a location destined to be Louisa's future home. "We've only been here a little over a week," she noted.

"It seems much longer," Louisa complained. "Surely, we could be safe somewhere with more people and more things to do?"

Thinking of the marquess's wound, Marianne tried to keep her temper. "Louisa, you are not being logical. Lord Gillingham has already been hurt. You must see that we cannot risk returning to London. We must determine who is trying to do you harm. This is a serious business."

Louisa made a face. "I know, yet I'm so tired of having my movements circumscribed. It is so very quiet here. How many evenings can one spend reading or playing at cards with only three people?"

"It's a beautiful house, beneath its neglect," Marianne pointed out. "When you are mistress here—"

"I don't know if I wish to be!" Louisa blurted, then stopped, biting her lip.

Marianne drew a deep breath, willing her heart not to beat faster. "What do you mean?"

"I'm just—not sure." The girl would not meet her eye.

"Perhaps you need to speak to Lord Gillingham about your feelings, Louisa?" Marianne suggested, keeping her tone quite neutral.

"Perhaps, but not yet . . ." Louisa stared into her teacup.

They chatted a little longer, about less important matters, but her aunt seemed strangely preoccupied and soon left to check on the servants.

Left alone, Louisa drank her tea, which was the color of mahogany. Was there nothing this wretched cook could not ruin? She wished she could have lemonade, instead. Typical that the cook would not have thought to order lemons from the nearest market town. In London, such foodstuffs came into port every day, brought by ships from tropical climes. Oh, how she missed London! She had seen only enough to whet her appetite, and then to be dragged back into the country, into a place even more removed and sedate than Bath—life could be very hard!

Louisa wandered back out into the garden. One gardener had gone to check on the greenhouse to see what was available for transplanting, and the other was hard at work and did not seem to need her guidance. Louisa crossed out of the formal garden—its stone walls reminded her too vividly of her present state of near imprisonment—and headed for the orchard. At least here, she had some illusion of freedom, and beneath the trees, greening as the season's blossoms faded and showing the first signs of the fruits that would mature by autumn, she could wander in the shade and escape the heat of the sun.

She found a wooden bench beneath one of the apple trees and sat down. She had not meant to blurt out her doubts to her aunt—she had not really fully examined her feelings herself—and yet, somehow she felt better for it. Surely, no one could say that she had not tried to love the marquess. She appreciated all the kindness he had shown her, but still—she could find nothing inside her but gratitude and friendship. And that seemed a barren field after the excitement and emotion she had felt for her first admirer.

If only she had not pushed Sir Lucas away . . . Sighing, she removed her bonnet and lost herself in memories, idly twirling her bonnet by its ribbons.

And when she heard the sharp ping of a twig snapping, for a moment it did not register. Then she tensed, aware that someone had approached her bench, someone who came up quietly without speaking. She was aware that a form loomed behind her, and fear gripped her throat.

She was out of sight of the big house—no one would know if the threatening stranger had reappeared.

Drawing a deep breath, Louisa gathered all her courage and prepared to scream.

Fifteen

"*L*ouisa?" *A familiar voice whispered.*

His slender, handsome form seemed to have stepped out of her musings. She gasped, then jumped to her feet and, before she thought, ran into his arms.

He caught her and pulled her to him, holding her very tight. For a moment she lay her head on his chest, feeling relief weaken her knees. Not a stranger trying to shoot her, but the person she most wanted to see in all the world. Yet, despite the first flush of joy that she felt, she must try for more self-control, not like the heedless girl he had been so quick to reject.

"Lucas?" She had been ready to shriek and trying to change her tone made the word sound like a frog's croak. With regret, she stepped out of his embrace. "What are you doing here?"

"I was worried. You disappeared from London so abruptly. And then I heard rumors about a shooting—they mentioned the marquess and that ladies were involved—and I remembered what you had said about an attacker.

I should have paid more heed to your fears, Louisa, forgive me." He looked unusually grave, and she tried to compose her own features. It would be unseemly to reveal the elation she felt at seeing him again.

"I'm glad you cared," she said simply.

"Of course, I care! And I wanted to check on you. I've heard some odd things about the marquess—do you know that he's called the Black Beast hereabouts? Even if he does have a great title, I could not allow you to be mistreated, Louisa."

"Oh no," Louisa argued. "Really, he's a most honorable man, kind and considerate of me in every instance."

"Ah, I am happy to hear it," Lucas said. He did not sound happy. His expression seemed strained, and his eyes had gone somber.

"I did not mean to defame him, especially to you, since you are betrothed. I do not wish to cause you any distress." He took a step back, and she reached out to him despite all her intentions.

"I'm not," she blurted, then, as Lucas stared at her, went on more slowly. "I mean, I will soon not be betrothed. I am going to tell the marquess that I cannot marry him. Truly, I have tried my best, and the marquess is a most worthy man, but I have decided that I cannot feel for him what I felt—what I once felt for you, Lucas."

"Louisa—" His expression was so twisted that she looked away, not willing to be rejected yet again.

"I know you no longer care for me in that way," she murmured, "and you have formed other attachments since our parting, but—"

"No, I haven't," he interrupted. "Not that I didn't try to. I was angry and hurt, Louisa, and I thought I could forget you, but no other young lady seems to quite compare. They all seem a bit quiet and dull after your company. I've missed you. You have such a happy spirit, not to say so much beauty and grace."

Louisa thought she might burst from sheer happiness. "Oh, Lucas, it was all my fault. I was indeed too selfish and too concerned about myself. I have changed, really I have, and I am trying my best to be more understanding and considerate."

He shook his head. "It was not all your fault. I was too easily wounded in my feelings and my pride. I should not have castigated you so severely. I don't want you to change, dearest Louisa. I love you just as you are."

She lifted her head, and he bent to meet her lips. Louisa felt the thrill of his touch through her whole being. Here was the spark, the joy that she had never managed to find with Lord Gillingham, that she had not even been able to imagine. She pressed herself closer to Lucas and their kiss grew and deepened, until she was dizzy with unaccustomed sensations.

At last, he pulled back, though she could see the effort it took.

"I shall speak to your uncle about a formal engagement," he said.

She nodded, then paused. "Not just yet, Lucas, please."

"You don't wish to marry me?" He gazed at her, looking more perplexed than angry, and she quickly stretched to give him another kiss. By the time they broke apart this time, she felt even more giddy, and she had to content herself with simply holding his hand between both her own.

"Of course I do! But we must consider the marquess's feelings. I have not yet even decided how I shall break the news. And I don't think we should disclose our understanding, not yet. I do not wish to wound his pride more than we must. We should wait a few months before the announcement is made. We will know that we are betrothed, but let us not broadcast it, not just yet."

He gazed at her in obvious admiration. "You have grown, Louisa. You're right, though I will chafe at any delay that keeps you from becoming my wife."

"Sir Lucas and Lady Louisa," she murmured, delighted at the sound of it.

"Not much, when you could have been a marchioness," he reminded her.

"It is everything I wish for," she told him. "Just as you

are everything I wish for. But, Lucas, do you think we can come up to London occasionally? I know your home is in Bath, and I will reside there all year if you wish it, but—"

"To be sure," he agreed. "I find London most diverting. After we are married, I think we will look for a town house to purchase, so that we can come up for the Season every year."

Louisa's smile widened. "Oh, Lucas, you are so good to me!" She leaned against his chest again and felt something scratch her cheek. She raised her head and found that a leaf clung to his lapel. And that reminded her—

"Lucas, how did you get here?"

"I rode down." But his expression was too innocent.

"No, there is a large wall about the estate, how on earth did you get over?"

He grinned. "I should say it's big! Didn't make it over the first time." He lifted his arm and she saw the rip in his sleeve. "Had to go back to the village and buy a ladder. And then my horse objected to the thing on his back, so I had to walk back, pulling the ladder, and dashed heavy it was, too. Wouldn't do that for just anyone, Louisa."

She laughed aloud and flung her arms around his neck.

When it was time to change for dinner, Marianne reviewed the dining room and prepared a list of chores that needed to be done. If they stayed here long enough, she would have the marquess's house in good shape, she thought ruefully. And at least, the work gave her some release from her own frustrations. She thought of Louisa's complaints and wondered if this engagement would really come to marriage. She could not picture Louisa here. And yet, would the girl really give up such an advantageous match?

Marianne bathed and changed into a simple black dinner dress. When the dinner gong sounded, she went out into the rose garden, but saw no sign of her charge. Pausing a moment, she stopped to admire a newly opened rose. The velvety crimson petals held all the promise of ripe and mature beauty yet to come. Marianne leaned closer to breathe in the richness of its scent. This was what love should be, she told herself, a blossoming of trust and affection and—yes—passion as sweet as the rose itself. Invariably, that thought led to an image of John, but she shook her head to dispel the vision in her mind's eye. No, she could not dwell on forbidden joys.

Coming back inside, she met Louisa on the landing. The younger lady looked a little flushed from her time outdoors.

"Did you take your parasol with you into the garden?" Marianne asked. "Your aunt Caroline will scold me if I let you become unfashionably bronzed from the sun."

Louisa laughed. "Oh no, I'm sure she would not be so unkind."

At least the girl's mood had lightened. She was quite merry at dinner, and it was the marquess and Marianne herself who spoke little as they ate.

The meals were the one thing Marianne had been unable to make any improvement in; the food was still uniformly bad. The chicken was stringy, the fish underdone. Marianne picked at a limp strand of French bean with her fork; how had the marquess not wasted away on such an insipid diet?

She was relieved when it was time for her to gather Louisa's attention with a glance and withdraw. The marquess stood as the two ladies headed for the drawing room.

But in the hallway she met the butler, his doleful expression looking even more dire than usual. "A special courier with a letter for you, ma'am, from Bath. I trust it's not bad news."

Marianne took the thick packet—what on earth was this?—and sat down, breaking the seal and scanning the contents quickly. Her expression must have altered, because Louisa leaned over her shoulder, her voice anxious, and asked, "Is Aunt Caroline all right?"

"Yes," Marianne answered slowly. "The family is well. But—"

She paused. The marquess had followed them to the drawing room; had the servant told him about the late arrival of the letter? "I wrote to your uncle, Louisa, about our concerns for your safety, and he has proposed a solution I had not considered."

"What? Can we return to London?" Louisa asked eagerly.

"No, rather the opposite. He thinks we should go to France," Marianne explained, knowing her voice sounded flat. "At once. He has sent along the necessary paperwork for our travel; lawyers are efficient in that way."

"Go abroad?" Louisa's voice squeaked.

The marquess frowned, then turned and gazed at the fireplace. Marianne read the letter again, still feeling stunned.

"He says we must keep you safe, and until we know who poses the danger and how to avert it, a quiet sojourn in a country village in the south of France might do the trick."

"A village? Not go to Paris, but to a village!" Louisa bit her lip and fell silent, and the marquess also said nothing.

Say something, Marianne thought, glancing at his silent form, his face hidden as he bent over the hearth as if inspecting the small fire within. *Tell me you do not wish me to leave!*

But when he spoke, he said only, "You would realize one of your dreams, then." His voice sounded gruff, but then it often did.

"What?" Marianne felt befuddled; she did not grasp his meaning.

"Seeing the French countryside," he reminded her. "One of the places where you wished to spend time, if I recall. And if the journey will keep Louisa safe . . ."

"Of course," she murmured. Her brother-in-law Charles was Louisa's legal guardian; he made the final decisions. Nor could she abandon Louisa now. She would have to go . . . she had no choice, and the marquess was not even going to protest her absence.

Louisa looked at them both, her expression now calm, but she said nothing.

"I suppose we should go up and begin packing, then," Marianne told her charge, trying to sound content with the new plan.

"I will have a carriage ready for you after breakfast," the marquess said. "We are not that far from Dover; passage will be easily arranged. I wish—"

Marianne held her breath, but he paused and did not finish. There was nothing for her to do but say good night and go up the stairs, with Louisa coming silently after her.

In her bedchamber, Marianne told her maid to begin packing the trunks, leaving out only a traveling costume to don in the morning, and the usual necessities for grooming.

She gathered a pile of shifts and folded them absently while she tried with less success to sort out her feelings. It was true, what the marquess had said. She had wished to visit France, but now, somehow, it was all different . . . she could find no elation at the thought of new vistas and picturesque landscapes . . . because John would not be with her.

When she and Hackett had put away most of the clothing and the trunk was nearly full, Marianne told her maid to leave the rest for morning. She donned her nightgown and got into bed, sending her maid off to get some sleep.

But for Marianne, sleep would not come. Leaving John . . . it was a bitter blow. Yet, her brother-in-law was no doubt correct about Louisa's welfare, and she had no logical answer for his arguments. She must leave, for Louisa's sake.

But not like this . . . with so much left unsaid.

Marianne rose and, drawing a wrapper about her shoulders to cover the thin nightgown, paced restlessly up and down the room. She had been bound to silence by his engagement to her niece, but increasingly, Marianne found it hard to believe that Louisa was really in love with the marquess, or that she really meant to see this engagement through to marriage. And to leave John so alone, so abandoned—

Pent up for too long, her own emotions could be constrained no further. Like a rain-swollen torrent bursting a dam, her feelings surged beyond her control when she imagined their parting.

Despite his scarred face and his scarred soul, his past haunted by a vicious father and a sad, lonely mother, she loved this man, loved him with a depth and an intensity she had never felt before. She could not allow John to retreat into his lair again like a wounded beast, to live alone and unloved. Would he avoid the society of his fellow men, lock away the restless curiosity and the passion she now knew he possessed? It was such a waste, such a travesty.

She would not allow it.

She had a vague idea where his bedchamber was located, and even though it was a scandalous—more than scandalous—thing to do, she had to speak to him. She marched to the door of her bedchamber and eased it open.

Louisa slept in the next chamber. Although its door was shut, listening hard, Marianne thought she could detect the girl's soft, even breathing.

The hall was quiet and dark. Marianne tied the belt of her wrapper more firmly about her, picked up her candle from her bedside table, and slipped into the hallway.

At least there was no sign of any servants. Hopefully, they were all in their rooms, sleeping soundly.

But when she reached the landing, Marianne lost her nerve. She could not simply march up to his bedchamber and rap on the door. He would think her the most dissolute of women, totally lacking in any feminine modesty or sense of honor.

No, this was no way to go on. Taking a deep breath, she sighed. She would have to go back to her own room and wait out the night. Tomorrow, she would somehow find a quiet moment before they departed, and she would tell him—what? She wasn't sure.

But just now, the hours stretched ahead like years. With her emotions in such a state of flux, there was no way she could sleep. A book, she thought, at least she could go down and find a new book to peruse. Even though she doubted she could concentrate, it might distract her enough to pass the long night.

So she turned and went down the steps very quietly, heading this time for the library. Her slippers made little sound on the carpets as she made her way through the wide shadowy halls, and she was so absorbed in her thoughts that she had opened the door and stepped across the threshold before she realized there was already light in the room. Candles burned on the tables and the large desk, and someone sat in a leather chair turned toward the empty hearth.

Startled, she hesitated, lifting her candle.

The marquess jumped to his feet. He was dressed in a heavy brocade dressing gown, and his hair was delightfully tousled.

"Marianne! I mean, Mrs. Hughes, what—"

"I came down to get a book." She flushed as she felt his gaze scan her state of deshabille. "I—I couldn't sleep." She took a step backward. She had longed to find him, and yet, now that he was here, she seemed to lose her tongue, not to mention her sense of purpose.

"Please, do not allow my presence to perturb you. If you wish to be alone in order to choose a book—"

He actually approached the doorway, and though his tone was formal, his gaze was—she thought—hungry. And it heartened her. Some of her courage returned. She set her candle down on a nearby table.

"My lord, what were you about to say to me tonight?"

"Say?" He stopped and then came a little closer.

She felt the vibrance of his nearness, the unconscious appeal of his wide shoulders and well-muscled limbs.

"Only . . . only that I wish you did not have to go," he said, his voice very low. "But I cannot say what else I wish until Louisa is safe, and I can tell her . . . well. It may not matter. Many women have drawn away when they obtained their first close view of my face . . ."

Marianne could not bear the pain in his voice. She put up her hand and touched his cheek lightly, smoothing over the faded pockmarks. How could anyone think these so very bad, and how could any female fail to see beyond them to the strength and the goodness and the virile male power of this man? They would turn him down for such a trifle?

"They were fools, then," she said.

He looked at her in surprise. "I am not blaming them," he told her, his voice husky. "I know that I am a sight unfit for delicate eyes—"

"No, no," Marianne interrupted again. "You cannot think so!"

He put up his own hand as if to hold her fingers still, then instead turned away. Marianne stared at his back as he braced his arms and leaned against the heavy library table.

"The first time I left my bed, still shaky from the illness and the long feverish days, I took a walk about the grounds. Everyone except my old nurse and my mother, who insisted on tending to me while I was ill, had been kept away from me because of the danger of contagion, but there was a kitchen maid in the back courtyard tossing out potato peelings to the chickens. She was only fourteen or so and newly come to the household. I came upon her before I realized someone was there, and when my shadow fell across her, she turned, startled. When she saw my face, she burst into tears of fright."

The heaviness in his tone tore at her heart. "My lord—"

He continued, his tone dogged. "I know that I am unsightly, Mrs. Hughes. I hardly dared to hope that any lady would be able to accept me as husband. But I wanted an heir badly, and your niece was kind enough to agree to my suit, even if I didn't precisely offer—well, never mind. But I suspect she has lost her enthusiasm for the match. And since I no longer feel the enmity for my younger brother that I did, perhaps the urgency of my desire to set up my nursery has faded. I admit, I have lately had dreams that a woman might love me, might feel for me what I felt for her—"

Oh, heavens. He was in love with Louisa after all? Marianne felt the pain constrict her chest. If it hurt him this badly, she would hound the girl into accepting him! Although what that would do to her own heart, she dared not think.

"But perhaps I have been fooling myself. Mayhap I am meant to live alone," he finished.

"Nonsense," she said, too loudly.

At least it broke through his musing; he turned to look at her again. "I don't wish to inflict myself—" he started.

Refusing to listen, she shook her head, "You are no ogre to frighten children and repel ladies of delicate constitutions."

"But—"

"I know, you startled the kitchen maid. But you were just beginning to heal then, my lord, the marks on your face were likely still red and inflamed. They have faded over the years, you know. I find them barely noticeable."

He shook his head. "You're very kind. But how can I forget my unsightly appearance when people stare at me in the street?"

"Then they are rude and unmannerly! One of my friends has red hair. She is sometimes stared at, too—that does not make her a monster." Marianne came closer to him, determined that he should not impose such an unjust sentence upon himself.

"And do you think that a woman—that a woman like you, for example—" he paused.

Marianne thought her heart pounded so hard that her chest must reveal its tremors. "My lord?"

"I do not wish to disgust you, nor hurt Louisa, but I fear I will not be able to marry your niece."

"Why?" Marianne almost whispered.

"Because I love another woman," he told her simply. "If she will have me, one day, when I am free, I will tell her just how much I wish to have her in my life."

Marianne had to clear her throat to make the words come out. "And who is this woman, my lord?"

He reached for her hand and lifted it to kiss, very gently. "I think you know."

She had not dreamed it, after all, those times when the air had seemed to vibrate between them, when she had felt it almost impossible to resist coming nearer.

Now she did not have to resist.

He swallowed hard. "But my blemishes . . . they are not slight."

Marianne lifted her hand and touched his face. "Slight," she insisted, running her fingers lightly down his cheek, over his chin. "Very slight."

She heard him take a ragged breath. He covered her fingers with his own, pressed her hand against his face.

"Marianne!" But then he paused again. "You don't know the whole of it, my dearest. And if I repulsed you, I don't think I could bear it. Perhaps it's best not to put it to the test."

"I will not allow you to hide behind your fears," she said, her voice firm. He stared at her in surprise, but she felt almost as much astonishment at herself. Who was this woman so determined to force them both toward the moment of truth? She thought of her protestations of contentment with her single life, and how she had disavowed all interest in remarriage, in a lover, in any affair of the heart.

But she had not met John, then.

"You must give me more credit than that, my love," she told him.

He hesitated, then, without speaking, he pulled open his robe, and she saw he wore no nightshirt beneath it. And, as he turned toward the candlelight, she also saw what she was meant to see.

The scars did not stop at his face, of course. The pox had covered his whole body, and his chest, hard with muscle, also showed signs of the deadly sickness. The scars were deeper here, if perhaps more widely scattered, and no doubt, his arms and legs were also marked.

She touched his chest and felt the quiver of response run through him. She looked up at him so he could see that she smiled, that her gaze was open and untroubled. Then she bent and kissed the nearest pockmark, kissed it gently as if she could heal him with her caress.

"Oh, my love," he said, his voice hoarse with emotion and desire. And suddenly, despite his still healing wound, he swept her up into his arms.

She had a momentary qualm about his arm, covered now only by a small strip of bandage, but John seemed untroubled by her weight. She put her arms around his neck

and allowed him to carry her to the settee, settle her gentl
there, and bend down to kiss her.

His lips were firm and sure, and she answered the kiss
and the hunger that she felt beneath it, with her own ur
gency. She had waited so long for this, not even knowin
she was waiting, until the right man triggered her long
buried thirst. Like a woman wandering so long in th
desert that she has forgotten the taste of cool clear water
she pressed her lips against his in elated surprise, surren
dering herself to every impulse, while her body responde
in ways she almost did not recall.

Her breasts pressed hard, nipples erect, against the wa
of his chest as he leaned against her. He kissed her lips, he
throat, her eyes, even the dark curls that edged her brow.

It had been too long. For weeks she had watched hir
court Louisa, when all the time she had wanted his hand o
her arm, his lips on hers, his body inside her to incite her t
passion more intense than the short interludes she had onc
shared with her boyish husband.

Thinking of her husband, she felt a moment of guilt, bu
she pushed it aside. She was no longer Harry's wife. Sh
could not harm him, nor was she constrained by any vov
Death had parted them, ended the marriage contract, an
she was free to love again.

Indeed, her marriage seemed a lifetime ago. She wa
another person now, older, more sure of her feelings, mor
womanly of body, and perhaps with a larger heart an
more capacity for both love and desire.

Certainly she had never felt this rush of yearning tha
left her almost trembling. She pushed her wrapper aside
hoping he would do the same.

And John lifted himself enough to discard the heav
robe. She had a brief look at the long lines of his leg
the well-made chest and abdomen, even the private mal
areas that she had not glimpsed since the advent of he
widowhood.

And it made the ache inside her leap, the fire grow. Sh
tried to pull off the thin nightgown and found that John'
hands were helping tug the cloth over her head, freeing he

breasts at last and leaving them ready for his hands to clasp and stroke while she moaned with the desire every touch only seemed to inflame. He caressed her breasts, rubbing her nipples gently, and instead of satisfying her need, it merely augmented it. She pulled him toward her, and again their lips met, hungrily, almost painfully, so intense was the touch.

"Come to me," she whispered against his mouth. "Come, my love."

And he laid himself over her, slipped easily inside her, her depths liquid with the urgency of her need, and she felt the breadth and length of him with surprised delight.

This was nothing like—no, she could think of nothing but John, and how wonderfully they fit together, as if they were the first man and woman ever made, with no greater purpose than this union, this glorious sensation of him inside her, moving with a firm rhythm that sent ripples of delight through her whole body.

She was the ocean who enveloped him, and she was the one who was drowning in sensation, sinking into joy.

"Oh, yes," she murmured. "Yes, yes."

And he lifted himself and pushed harder, harder, and every motion was tinged with pleasure so intense that she uttered small inarticulate sounds low in her throat. She moved against him, with him, lifting her hips so he could push himself even deeper, and again, the pleasure only seemed to grow.

There were no words for it, no terms she could frame in her mind; only her body ruled, now, only the feelings, the sensations that rushed over her again and again.

And when he surged deeper, with a hoarse sound of released passion, when she knew that he had spent himself inside her, she felt tears suddenly form in her eyes.

It had been so good. How could she bear for this magical interlude to end?

For a few moments they lay entangled together on the settee, which was not broad enough to hold them, but did, though John's legs and hers hung over the side. Because their bodies were moist with a light sheen of sweat, and her

hair was damp against her face, she thought he would n
notice the idiotic tears. Yet he did.

"Marianne, my dearest, did I hurt you?"

She shook her head, not trusting her voice.

"Then if you regret this joining, if I have rushed yo
into something rash and dishonorable—oh, God, I wi
hate myself for it," he told her, his voice almost breaking.

This forced her to speak, despite the tremor in her ow
voice. "Oh, no, my darling," she told him, stroking th
clean lines of his jaw, the slight cleft in his chin. "Oh, no.
was a miracle. I think I brushed the threshold of heaven i
self. I just—I can hardly bear that it has ended."

His expression cleared, and he leaned down to kiss he
gently, kiss the damp tear tracks on her cheeks. He smiled
"Then," he told her, "we will simply do it again."

And before she could grasp his meaning, he had lifte
her into his lap and begun to stroke her still sensitiv
breasts until she gasped with the intensity of her response

"And this time, I will not be so hasty," he promised.

That was hasty? Marianne smiled back at him, suddenl
aware that, brief marriage or not, there was much of thi
lovemaking business she did not know. And what a deligh
her education was going to be!

"This time," he told her, with a new timbre of happines
shading his deep voice, "this time, we must make sure
push you past the threshold and through the golden gates.

So he caressed her bare breasts until she shivered, an
when he put his lips around the rosy nipples, she gaspe
aloud. The quivers of feeling reverberated through he
body, and the only thing better was when he left one brea
to kiss and fondle the other, his tongue touching her nippl
and making her tremble with delight.

Then, he ran his hands over her arms, down her thigh
and ankles and lightly rubbed her feet. She had neve
dreamed that her feet could be a sensitive area. It was a de
licious sensation as he massaged her toes, and sole, an
arch, careful not to tickle. She gazed at him in wonde
"How do you know so much?"

"As you have noted, I have an extensive library." H

grinned at her, looking as free as a boy, as wise as a man. "And I have had weeks to dream of this, to think just what I would like to do to you."

"Weeks?" She swallowed hard as his sure touch moved up, again, up her shin, up her thigh, stroking the inside of it gently, with tantalizing slowness.

"Weeks," he assured her.

Now his hand moved onto the curly mass of dark hair above her thighs, and she trembled. He rubbed the curls gently for a moment, and then—when she was ready to jump with impatience, his fingers slipped inside.

Marianne made a small inarticulate sound. The pleasure was almost too much to bear. She moved against him while his hand stroked and curved and thrilled her, sending waves of heat that radiated through her, over and over. He went on till she could not sit still and moved toward him, wanting—not to end the wonderful sensations but to replace them with something even better.

She could play this game, too, even if she was just now learning the rules. She touched his chest, kissed its hard layers of muscle, kissed the old scars, kissed his flat nipples, touching them lightly with her tongue. She was gratified to hear him inhale deeply, although all the while he moved his hand inside her with delicious, easy strokes. So she ran her own hand down, down his groin. He tensed, and when she circled him with her hand, stroked the cause of so much pleasure, he moaned deep in his throat.

Marianne almost laughed out loud. She, too, could give pleasure. So for a few long minutes she caressed him as he stroked her, until she said, gasping, "Now, John, now, please."

So he pulled her onto his lap, and she settled onto him, delighted at the new posture and the amazing sensations it evoked. She was already so heady with desire that his thrusting sent her beyond speech. She knew that small sounds of pleasure came from someone's throat, but she hardly seemed to know who uttered the cries.

This time he moved slowly at first, with more control and less frenzied passion than the first time, but every

movement inside her induced waves of sensation, of plea
sure, of delight. She was enveloped in the joy, she was par
of him, body and soul, seeing in his rapt expression the
same intensities of feeling and emotion as she enjoyed
She moved her hips against his, and still he rose and fell
and she gripped him with her innermost self and moved
with him, and they were surrounded by joy unfolding in
layer after layer, like a rose unfurling to the morning sun
And all the while the deepest most intense pleasure still lay
ahead, while she floated and spun like a dust mote in a
golden beam of sunlight, and her body taught her pleasure
she had never known, until at last they reached the core, the
heart of ecstasy itself.

And this time, this time, she soared with him, peaked
with a height of sensation that stopped her throat and
drenched her soul with surprise and awe and exquisite de
light. John held her tightly, and she felt his spasm, felt he
own body arch and tighten and her cry ring out, and then he
kissed her again, once, twice, and at last they lay still.

She rested her head against his chest, and John wrapped
his arms about her. She could not speak. It was enough to
lay her head against him and feel his chest rise and fall a
his heart slowed from its tumultuous beat. She marveled a
what they had shared.

She hadn't known it could be like this. She felt weak
with the aftermath of love, warm with contentment, de
lightfully languid. She could happily remain here, nestled
in his arms forever.

No, she thought drowsily, that would mean they could
not do it again. And she certainly intended to love this man
many more times.

For the rest of her life, she hoped.

After what seemed like hours of contented silence, John
brought her hand to his lips and kissed it with a gentleness
made even more poignant by her awareness of the latent
strength in his grip.

"I feel I have been reborn," he told her. "If I can make
you happy, if we can be so good together—perhaps, after
all, I am not such a beast as I had feared."

The light in his eyes lifted her heart. "Never," she said simply. "You never were. You belong in the sunlight, dearest, not the shadows."

John thought this newfound joy might shatter him; it was almost too much to contain. He tightened his grip, and they lay sprawled together, and it did not matter that the settee pressed too hard against his back, or that his healing arm ached a little from too much exertion. He had the best, most wonderful prize he'd never dared to imagine, and he would not release her until his body went numb from lack of movement.

Only, as he drifted into a light sleep, did he remember, with a piercing pain, that she still had to leave on the morrow . . .

Sixteen

Marianne woke early the next morning. Even before her eyes opened, she found she was smiling. Why did she feel this unaccustomed joy? As she stretched, feeling pleasantly sore in ways she had not experienced for years, memory rushed back. With it came a rush of elation. How wonderful it had been—the stolen hours of lovemaking! But her first emotion was followed quickly by a wave of guilt.

If she was wrong about Louisa, about her lack of feelings for John, how would she ever face her?

And they still had to leave.

The pain of that thought was almost too much to bear.

Marianne sat up abruptly. Glancing at the pale light seeping past the draperies at her window, she realized that it was early yet, but she knew she could not go back to sleep. Sighing, Marianne rang for her maid and went to wash in the tepid water left over in her ewer.

Later, when she had sipped a cup of tea, eaten some toast, dressed, and her hair had been pulled back into its usual loose knot, she asked Hackett, trying to keep her voice even, "Is Miss Louisa up yet?"

"I don't believe so, ma'am," the dresser answered. "Her maid is still abed with a toothache, but Miss Louisa hasn't rung for another maid to help her dress."

Marianne nodded. Very well. Best to get it over with. They would get on the road, and later, she would have a heart-to-heart talk with her ward. Summoning her resolve, she went to Louisa's bedchamber across the hall and knocked on the door.

When she heard no sound, she knocked again. Still nothing.

Was Louisa sleeping so soundly? Marianne reached for the doorknob. When she opened the door, she was shocked to see that the bed was empty. Was the girl in her dressing room?

But a quick inspection revealed the room and anteroom were both unoccupied. Where was Louisa?

Then Marianne saw the folded sheets of paper on the mantelpiece. Taking quick strides to snatch up the missive, she saw her own name on the outside. Marianne felt as if her heart skipped a beat.

"Oh, dear lord," she muttered beneath her breath. Did Louisa know—could she have possibly known—about last night?

"Hackett!" she called, hearing the alarm in her own voice. When her maid looked into the room, Marianne said, "Summon Lord Gillingham, at once!"

The servant disappeared. Taking a deep breath, Marianne picked up the sheet and began to read.

"Dearest Aunt Marianne," the letter said in sprawling script that revealed the writer's agitation, "I hope you will not hate me. I have tried, really, I have, but as much as I honor and esteem Lord Gillingham, I find I cannot marry him. He is a most worthy and kind man, and I appreciate all he has done to protect me. I do not wish to disappoint him or make him feel slighted, but I find I cannot feel for him what I had hoped.

"I know I have done badly to accept his suit and then reject him, but I can't become his wife, and I don't know how to tell him. And I don't want to go to France, if you please. I am going back to London and from there on to Bath, so that I can talk to my uncle and make him understand. I tried to write it all out in a letter, but it's too hard to explain. Please forgive me and tell Lord Gillingham that I am sincerely sorry to have caused him hurt."

The last words were smudged from haste and the—no doubt—strong emotion that had made Louisa's hand shake. It was hard to read the ending, something about "don't worry" and "all for the best."

Marianne felt a sinking in the pit of her stomach. How had her niece rushed out into deadly peril, all because she could not tell them her misgivings face-to-face? Marianne wasn't sure if she most wanted to hug Louisa or shake her!

Then she heard a knock at the door and looked up to see John gazing at her through the doorway.

"What is it?"

She hesitated, not sure how he would react to this abrupt ending of the engagement. Of course, he had not wanted to marry Louisa, either, but still—

Something in her face must have warned him because he held out his hand. She thought of trying to soften the message, but his expression was imperious and his eyes grim. Biting her lip, she allowed him to take the letter and scan it quickly.

Silence stretched as he leaned against the mantel.

"Ironic, isn't it?" he said quietly. "I was concerned about how to break the news to her that I did not wish us to wed . . ."

"John—" Marianne began.

He waved aside her concern. "Never mind. I have news, too, and it is not good. One of my gardeners has found the marks of a ladder in the dirt outside the stone wall, near the orchard."

"What?"

"And a trail where it has been dragged through the grass—I was just about to investigate."

Marianne stared at him, knowing her eyes had widened. "Louisa! She may have walked out straight into the killer's arms. We must find her, John, at once!"

"Indeed," he agreed. He turned and strode toward the staircase, and she ran after him.

On the ground floor several of the male servants waited. John had already sent out a summons, it seemed. He gave them brisk orders masking his inner unease with his usual air of command.

Marianne found her own anxiety harder to hide, but she tried to compose herself. Falling into hysterics would hardly help Louisa.

"I will look for any tracks," he told Marianne as the servants hurried to do his bidding. "I'm sending servants out to the western and eastern edges of the estate, and one will check the guardhouse at the end of the front lane. I have not yet questioned the gatekeeper, but—"

"I will do that!" Marianne said quickly, relieved to have something useful to do.

"Go with the footman," he told her. "I do not wish you to be alone."

She nodded and, with the youngest of the manservants hurrying to keep up, she ran out the front doors and hastened down the long driveway.

At the end, after the last curve of the lane, the small stone gatehouse came into view. The man who kept the gate was an ancient, retired servant, gray of head and hard-of-hearing, which was why the marquess always knocked very hard on the outer gate when he needed the gates opened or had the coachman blow his horn.

As usual, the gate was closed. They rapped smartly on the cottage door, and when the old man hobbled to open it, he gazed at them in surprise.

"Have you seen anything of Miss Crookshank?" Marianne demanded without preamble.

The man stared. "Eh?"

"The fair-haired young lady who is the marquess's guest," she added, speaking slowly and clearly. "Have you seen her?"

"Yes, ma'am," the man answered at last. He seemed to need time to get his words from his somewhat befuddled brain down to his thin-lipped mouth. "Went out for a walk she did, early this morning. Asked me real nice, like, to open the gate for her."

As simple as that. Marianne drew a deep breath. Where could Louisa have been headed? She would hardly expect to walk back to London.

"Does the London coach travel this road?" she asked the gatekeeper, who peered at her, blinking, and did not answer.

Frustrated, she turned to the footman, who was more knowledgeable.

"No, ma'am. The nearest the coach comes to his lordship's estate is through the next village; it's a good five mile up the road to Little Brookside."

Marianne made a decision. "Go back to the house and send word to Lord Gillingham about what we have learned; then get a chaise and driver with all speed. We must go to the village to see if there is any sign of Miss Crookshank. I will wait here for you to return with the carriage."

"Yes, ma'am." The footman turned and hastened back up the driveway; it would take him a few minutes to retrace their steps and order a vehicle made ready, but it would be faster than trying to get to the village on foot. Marianne paced up and down, trying to think.

"Would you open the gate for me, please," she directed the gatekeeper. The old man shuffled forward and unlatched the iron gates, pulling them open.

As she glanced about, she noticed for the first time a faint trail, barely discernable among the trees across the road. She looked around for the elderly gatekeeper, who had taken a seat on the front step of his cottage and was stoking a pipe.

"Is that a pathway?" she asked.

"Yes 'm," he agreed.

"Where does it lead?" she said, exasperated. The man was as forthcoming as an oyster determined not to yield its pearl.

"Shortcut to the village," he explained, puffing on his pipe.

She stared at him. "The same village—Little Brookside? It's shorter this way than by the road?"

He nodded.

"How far is it on foot?"

"'Bout two mile," he said. "If'n you wade the brook."

"I don't suppose Miss Crookshank asked about the path?"

"Yes 'm, she did that," he agreed, his voice placid.

Marianne bit back a shriek of exasperation. "Why didn't you say so?"

He looked surprised at the question. "You didn't ask."

"Listen to me carefully," she said, curling her hands into fists so that she would not shake him like a willful child. "When the footman returns, tell him I have taken the path in case I can catch up with Miss Crookshank. Tell the footman to take the carriage and go on to the village in case Miss Crookshank is already there. He must watch for the London coach, if it has not already passed through."

He nodded, though she wondered how much of the message he would remember.

"Oh, what time was it when you opened the gate for her?"

He glanced up at the sun. "Early," he said.

Marianne took a deep breath. What did she expect? The man likely did not own a clock.

Crossing the road, Marianne plunged down the narrow path and into the woodland. Almost at once, she left behind the bright sunshine and found herself in dappled shade. She smelled the rich musky odor of decaying leaves and the fresh scent of new greenery, blending in the snatches of breeze that forced its way through the forest.

Golden light flickered through heavy layers of leaves, which rustled in the wind, and the shifting patterns of light and shadow made the uneven path deceptive. She wanted to run, to rush ahead, but she did not wish to twist an ankle on an unseen root or a loose rock, so she minded her steps and made the best speed that she could.

Birds called overhead, sometimes flying up in alarm when she rounded a bend or stepped on a twig that cracked too loudly. Squirrels ran up wide trunks at her approach, and she saw the flicker of a fox's red tail displayed behind it like a banner as the animal darted across the path and out of sight into the trees.

Breathing hard in her haste, Marianne wondered if this whole pursuit was futile. Louisa was likely already at the village, might have already boarded the coach for London. But they would find her, and please God, before anyone who meant her harm.

And then Marianne would tell Louisa exactly what she thought of such a harebrained scheme!

Trying to catch her breath, Marianne hurried on. She was just thinking that surely she must be nearing the village when she turned another crook in the path and saw two figures ahead of her.

Pausing, Marianne hardly trusted her own eyes. Louisa!

And—she felt a cold wave of fear rush through her—a man, his form cloaked in shadow as he stood very near to Louisa. He seemed to grip her hand.

Louisa had risen early in the soft darkness just before sunrise. She donned her clothes without help—she had bidden her young maid to stay in bed this morning and plead toothache. Louisa knew Eva was loyal, but she did not trust the girl to keep silent about the details of her mistress's plan. Besides, she wasn't sure both of them could slip out of the house undetected.

Last, Louisa pulled on a lightweight woolen cape, tiptoed down the stairs, and unlatched the front door. She hurried down the driveway, the back of her neck tingling with the fear that someone would look out a window and see her, but she heard no outcry. The air was cool upon her face, and the sunlight grew brighter with every minute.

When she rounded the first bend and was hidden from sight by the tall trees, Louisa stopped to catch her breath. She went to the side of the road and retrieved from behind a tall oak the small carpetbag and hatbox she had packed last night, and which her maid had hidden for her.

Supplied with a change of gown, a nightdress, tooth-brush and tooth powder, a hairbrush, and small mirror, Louisa felt ready to face the perils of the world.

The iron gates at the end of the drive were only a minor obstacle. A smile and a polite request to the gatekeeper, and the gates were opened. Thanking him nicely, and ask-ing about the best route to the village, she slipped through.

She looked up and down the road. No sign of anyone. So she crossed the narrow lane and made her way into the woods.

The grass at the edge of the barely noticeable path was wet with dew; the hem of her skirt was soon soaked. But despite the occasional rustle in the underbrush that made her jump, or the startling caw of a crow that caused her heart to beat faster, Louisa felt as if a great weight had been lifted from her heart.

She was not going to marry the marquess; if they had not found her note by now, they would soon. And she was cer-tainly not going to be interred in some out-of-the-way French village.

She paused, hearing the snap of a twig. Someone was coming this way. Holding her breath, she waited for the man to come into view. And then she ran—and threw her-self into his arms.

Feeling close to panic, Marianne looked about her for a stone to cast at the male silhouette—anything that might distract him and allow Louisa to escape. But the forest floor seemed ridiculously unlittered, not even a fallen branch with which she might attempt to cudgel the man.

Then Louisa looked up and caught sight of her aunt. Her face brightened.

Marianne waved her hand, trying to signal the girl to re-main silent. Louisa's captor had not yet seen the new ar-rival, and she did not wish to lose the element of surprise.

But Louisa called out, in a voice that sounded quite

normal, "Aunt Marianne, you have come. Are you seeking me?"

Of all the inane questions . . . Marianne hurried forward, then paused a few steps away. She knew this young man, and it was not whom she had expected.

"Sir Lucas!"

The young man reddened in confusion when he saw Marianne. Louisa released his hand so that he could give the new arrival a bow.

"Of course. Are you very angry at me, dearest Aunt?" Louisa asked, her tone cautious. Her cheeks seemed a bit flushed; otherwise, she looked quite serene.

"Angry? I should like to strangle you!" Marianne snapped, then sighed when the girl's face fell. "No, Louisa, I am only so relieved that you are safe. How could you leave the estate so foolishly—and then to find Sir Lucas here—Louisa, you are not eloping?"

Sir Lucas gaped. "Running off to Scotland? I say, of course not."

"We are going back to Bath, just as I said," Louisa assured her aunt. "We do plan to be married later, but suitably. I would not give up a proper wedding to jump over the broomstick—and without a real wedding dress?" She sounded aghast at the thought.

"Proper?" Marianne said, incensed beyond the bounds of temper. "You talk about proper? You're going off alone with a man—"

"I have hired a village girl to travel with us as Louisa's maid," Lucas assured them, sounding almost prim. "Really, we have considered the proprieties."

"And what about the danger?" Marianne demanded. "Have you considered that?"

Louisa looked stubborn. "I don't think that it's so great," she argued. "Perhaps it was all a series of accidents, after all."

Marianne drew a deep breath, but the girl rushed ahead.

"I'm sorry, Aunt Marianne, but I don't wish to go to France just now, and certainly not to some dull little village. It would be just like here, only worse, because my

French—despite my governess's best efforts—is not very good."

"Louisa, what do you think this will accomplish? Your uncle Charles will be most displeased with your behavior!"

"But that is why I must speak to him in person," Louisa said, as if it were all self-evident. "I'm sure I can make him forgive me—he must be made to understand that what I really want is to go back to London."

"If you think I shall take you back with me, after this!" Marianne frowned. "Louisa, this is beyond the pale."

Louisa looked contrite, and stubborn, at the same time. It was quite an accomplishment, and if Marianne had not been simmering with annoyance, she might have admired it more.

"Lucas says his aunt might very well be willing to extend an invitation to me to visit her in London. I'm really a very good houseguest, Aunt, wouldn't you say?"

She smiled sweetly, and Marianne found herself truly speechless.

"We must go back to the house," she told them when she could find her voice again. "The marquess must be told that you are safe."

But a bird called, and Marianne paused at the sight of a thin gentleman striding jauntily down the path toward them. He carried something long and slim under one arm, draped in some kind of concealing cloth.

Not a gun?

Marianne's anger faded, replaced once more by apprehension. She motioned to the two young people to retreat.

But the stranger came closer and greeted them first. "Good morning, is this the right way to the marquess of Gillingham's estate?"

Marianne stared at him. "May I ask who needs the information?"

"I do," the man said simply. "I am a connection of his future wife—my name is Alton Crookshank."

Seventeen

Marianne drew a deep breath. *"I cannot—
that is—you should not—"*

But his expression stern, Crookshank raised one hand in
admonition.

"Do not move," he warned.

She stopped, afraid he would hurt Louisa if she did not
obey. The girl had gone pale. *Oh, dear God,* Marianne
thought. *John, where are you?* Louisa had walked straight
into the path of the man who wished her harm.

Young Lucas balled his hands and seemed ready to
launch himself at the older man.

But instead of pointing the long object at Louisa,
Crookshank, moving with surprising speed, pulled off the
cloth and waved the pole high above his head, then dipped
it swiftly toward the ground.

Lucas had taken one step, but now he paused, looking
confused.

Eyes wide, Marianne watched. Crookshank bent to
twist what she now saw was a net so that the small object
inside would not escape.

"A very nice *Celastrina argiolus*," he said, his tone reverent. "How fortunate I brought my net with me."

"What are you doing?"

"I am a collector, of course. Only, now I must get this specimen fixed as soon as possible; I do not wish it to damage its wings by fluttering against the strings."

Marianne wondered if they had all gone mad. What was the man talking about? Then she looked closer and saw that it was a small silvery-blue butterfly imprisoned within the net.

"But what are you doing here?" she demanded.

"Ah, the marquess has kindly offered to fund some of my research. He came to see me in London, you see, but when I asked at his house in town, they told me he had gone into the country. Fortunately, his country seat is listed in one of the books detailing the noble families."

So much for their retreat from the public eye, Marianne thought.

"If you will excuse me, I must return to the inn now. I shall have to call upon his lordship a little later."

Holding his specimen carefully, Alton hastened back down the path.

Marianne hurried to Louisa. "You are all right?"

"Of course," Louisa said, although she reached to lean upon her swain's arm.

Sir Lucas still stared after the man. "I think he's light in the head. Chasing about after butterflies?"

Marianne felt such a wave of relief, she didn't know whether to laugh or cry. "You are more fortunate than you deserve, Louisa. He could have been the villain we feared."

Then she stopped, rigid with shock. If it was not Alton who had fired that bullet in the square in London, or who had spooked the horse that had almost run down Louisa in Hyde Park, who had?

She felt cold.

"The gunshot hitting John was not a mistake!" Marianne exclaimed. "You've walked calmly through the woods, and no one harassed you. It was John who stopped a bullet. Oh, God, what if we have been wrong all along? Perhaps it is not you, Louisa, who is the target?"

She felt her heart beat fast.

"I am returning to the house," she told the couple. "Lucas, escort her back, please, instead of running away like errant children. We shall work this all out. Lord Gillingham has no wish for a reluctant fiancée. But I have no time to argue about it just now. I believe the marquess may be the one in danger!"

Then she picked up her skirts and ran.

The distance seemed to take forever to traverse. She had to stop once to catch her breath, then she walked and ran and walked until she approached the estate once more. When at last the house loomed up before her, Marianne rushed inside.

"Has the marquess returned?" she asked a startled housemaid.

"No, ma'am." The servant looked bewildered.

"We have to find him," Marianne said. "He may be at risk. Is there a back gate to the wall?"

"Yes, ma'am," she said. "At the west end of the orchard."

"Come with me."

She hurried outside, remembering John's plan. How far could he have gotten? They ran past the formal garden, past the rose garden at the side of the house, then the kitchen garden, with its neat rows of vegetables. At last, panting, Marianne stopped and pressed her side until she caught her breath. There, just ahead, was the orchard that lay at the back of the grounds. And he was there! John stood next to a tree, his posture somehow too stiff.

And there was someone else.

Marianne felt a chill sweep over her. What she saw left her silent with shock.

Instead of the brawny—and male—assailant she had feared to see, Marianne made out a much more surprising sight.

A young woman stood beneath an apple tree, in a slightly mussed but perfectly respectable brown traveling outfit. She did not appear to be a servant, and her ashen face was unfamiliar. Her expression was twisted, and her eyes—her eyes were big with strain and distress. And in her hand, she held a gun.

"She has a pistol," Marianne murmured to the maid, whose eyes were also wide. "Go and bring help!"

The servant nodded and set off at a lope. The stranger did not seem to notice; her stare was fixed on John.

John had detected the new arrivals, and he felt his heart sink. He saw Marianne hesitate, just beyond the girl's range of vision. If the stranger turned her head at all—

Go back, he thought, *my love, go back!* But Marianne did not withdraw, and in his fear he spoke quickly, trying to hold the young woman's attention.

"I could not think, at first, why I knew your face," he told her. "But I met you when I first came to London. You are Sir Silas Ramburt's granddaughter—I came to pay a call, and you said he was ill."

She didn't answer, but he did not wish her to turn her head, so he continued as another memory flashed through his mind. "I've seen you since, though I did not remark upon it at the time. You were in the park when—when the horse ran away and almost trampled Miss Crookshank."

The young woman watched him, as if waiting, and beneath that fixed gaze, John put the pieces together.

"It was you." John took a step forward, and the girl lifted the old-fashioned dueling pistol a little higher. "You're the one who startled the horse. You meant it for me. And then when it failed—was this the pistol which fired the ball that pierced my arm?"

She nodded. "I was aiming for your heart."

He was the focus of her strangely blank stare. It was he who was the target upon which the gun centered, he had always been the target.

To his dismay, Marianne stepped forward. The young woman turned, pointing the gun for an instant in her direction.

Marianne paused a few feet away; she seemed to have

realized the answer, too. "It's not Louisa; it was never Louisa. She has been attacking you, John! But why?"

"Why do you wish me harm?" John asked, keeping his voice controlled. "Why would you wish me dead?"

He did not think she would respond, then something sparked inside the dull-eyed stare, and she spoke with more passion than she had yet shown.

"It's too good for you, a fast and easy death," she told him. The gun in her hand trembled, but at least it was pointed, again, toward him and not Marianne.

For a moment he could hear the savagery that was so at odds with the girl's prim facade. He wondered if she had gone totally insane.

"My grandfather was granted an end much less easy than a quick gunshot . . . he was spared not one moment of agony, not until he drew his last breath two weeks ago. When I buried him, no one was there but me and the vicar and a few of the servants."

"I'm sorry to hear that," John began. "If you had sent me word—"

"Could you think that I would have wanted *you* there!" She laughed, and the peal held a quiver of hysteria.

"I think the strain of your grandfather's long illness, the responsibility of looking out for him, nursing him, may have affected your judgment," he suggested, keeping his voice gentle.

"You have no idea what I have seen, or how badly he died. Death should be clean and quick and simple—I was granting you that much. You should have thanked me."

"But why should he die, at all?" Marianne demanded, her face flushed with anxiety. "This makes no sense."

"Because he is his father's son, and I cannot murder a man already dead," the girl declared, her voice dulled by years of pain and rage.

Once again, his father's shadow had reached out to touch him, soil him, John thought. He shook his head to brush away the notion.

Miss Ramburt seemed to take the movement as a dispute, because she went on, her voice louder. "I know it was he, my grandfather said so. He told me—well, he talked, perhaps not to me—when he was in his deliriums. He re-lived the days of debauchery when he followed your father, the infamous marquess, into every gaming hell and tavern and brothel in the direst streets of London. And it was there that he contracted the pox."

"He had the smallpox, too?" Marianne asked.

The other young woman, who must be much the same age as Louisa but who had faced agonies Louisa had never dreamed of, shook her head. "No, you fool, the pox, the French disease."

The disease of sad-eyed whores and rakes who shared their beds—syphilis the physicians called it, John thought in a sickening wave of understanding. A fearful disease without a cure, and one which took years to kill as it grad-ually destroyed the body and the mind. And this girl—only a child when her grandfather had begun to fail—had been there to watch as her last surviving family member died inch by agonizing inch. No wonder her wits had been ad-dled. Out of the years of shared pain, she had apparently plotted a plan of revenge.

"You wanted to kill my father," he said slowly. "And when you found that he was already dead, you chose me to murder in his place?"

"Someone had to pay!" The hand holding the gun trem-bled.

"You cannot do this!" Marianne raised her voice, as if trying to break through the girl's strange air of befogged concentration. "Even if that account is true—and your grandfather was a grown man who made his own choices, you know—even if it had anything to do with the late mar-quess, it was not John who led your grandfather into those lairs of vice and disease."

"Miss Ramburt, consider what you are about to do. I do not think you can truly wish me dead," John added.

Except he thought perhaps she did. He wondered with a sickening emptiness deep in his stomach if he would lose all the joys he had only just found, all the love he had waited his whole life to claim. If she killed him here—

He pushed away the despair that might paralyze him; whether he died or not, he had to get Marianne safely out of this.

"When I saw that you were scarred, disfigured, I was happy," the young woman murmured. "I thought it only fair—but it's not enough. You're still healthy enough to live your life, to dine and wine and visit with lady friends. Look at you, at ease in the gardens. You cannot be allowed— someone has to pay for what my grandfather suffered."

"They will hang you for it," Marianne said, perhaps trying to shock her into clarity. But Miss Ramburt still seemed to float in her own fog of despair.

She had dark shadows beneath her eyes, lines of worry etched into her forehead, and if she was Louisa's age, she looked ten years older. What an unkind hand Fate had dealt her, John thought.

"You cannot have enough bullets in that gun to kill us both," Marianne continued. "And there are servants all about. Someone will survive to raise the alarm. You must not do this—you have already lost your childhood—surely you do not wish to give up the rest of your life, too. Your grandfather is dead. Let him rest—at last—in peace, while you reclaim your own life. If you need funds, we will help you. Allow yourself time to mourn and then heal and be happy. But first you must put aside this quest for vengeance!"

Marianne had stepped forward again, and the gun wavered for a moment in her direction. He could not allow her to risk injury. So John stepped forward, too, and the gun swung back to face him.

"I know about families and how twisted the loves and hatreds can become," he told her. "I have been influenced by my father, as well, and not for the good. Do not allow your grandfather's hatred, or his madness, to destroy your life, Miss Ramburt. You must choose a better path."

She blinked and lifted the gun. He thought that her finger tightened on the trigger, but for just a moment, she hesitated.

Then a small shape shot forward, growling, and the girl jumped, turning toward the new arrival. John seized the moment, lunging toward her to grab the gun and push down the muzzle.

The explosion of the gun's blast was like thunder. The flashing powder burned his hand. He swore softly. Marianne called out his name, her voice frantic, and then one of his servants rushed forward.

A footman helped him hold the girl, who struggled against their restraining arms. The little dog was still trying to bite her leg.

"Down, Runt!" John said. "You have done good work today, but enough."

Looking disappointed, the dog sat, panting.

"No, no, I must, I must—" And then suddenly her unnatural, masklike solemnity dissolved, and the young woman sobbed, loudly, like an infant who wakes to find itself in a strange and unfamiliar place.

Marianne rushed to him, touched his face, his good arm, as if to reassure herself that he was still whole.

"I am unharmed," he murmured. "The bullet has gone into the dirt." His hand stung, but the burns from the powder were not serious.

Marianne shuddered, then put her arms about Miss Ramburt and allowed the young woman to cry into her shoulder as she patted her gently.

Now several more servants rushed up, alerted by the gunshot, and he nodded toward two footmen. "Here, take her inside and summon the doctor. She should be attended to as soon as he arrives."

"Fetch my maid," Marianne added. "Tell her I said to sit with this lady. On no account is she to be left alone, not even for an instant, do you understand?"

The servants nodded, although they looked bewildered, as well they might. John said, "She is not in control of her faculties, so take the greatest care. But treat her gently and with respect."

They led her off, and Marianne looked so pale herself that John put his arm around her.

"I thought you were going to die, and I've only just found you," she whispered. "Oh, John, if I were to lose you, too!"

"I am here," he told her, kissing the top of her head. "You will not be rid of me so easily, my love. But just now, let us go inside." He offered Marianne his good arm, holding the gun carefully with his other hand. They walked toward the house.

"Did you find Louisa?"

Nodding, she told him the story.

"We will send the young fools back to London in my chaise," he said, shaking his head. "I know I have scared off many a fair maid, but this is ridiculous."

When they reached the house, Marianne went upstairs to check on the unfortunate Miss Ramburt, and John waited in the drawing room until she joined him. Sir Lucas and a somewhat pink-cheeked Louisa had returned, and he sent them to the dining room for a belated breakfast.

The food they found there would be punishment enough for their foolish schemes, he thought.

When Marianne returned, he poured them both a glass of wine.

"I suppose she fell apart under the strain of nursing her grandfather," he said. "I'm afraid she was right about my father—his early life was full of unsavory conduct."

Marianne sighed. "What a sad life she has had."

They sat quietly together for a time until the doctor was announced. John went out to greet the man, whom he had known for years, and gave him a quick explanation of the circumstances. The physician was a stout man with a comforting, matter-of-fact air, and when he entered the guest room where Miss Ramburt was lying on a bed, he spoke to her gently, looked into her eyes, and took her pulse. The doctor took powders from his bag and mixed her a soothing draught to drink, which he promised would make her sleep.

John left them. Later, the doctor came outside the bedroom and shut the door. "Her mind is certainly clouded," he agreed. "I do not think she should be left alone. She might try to injure herself. She has lost the certainty of her goal and is now slipping into a deep sorrow that has been, I suspect, long deferred."

"Will she recover?" Marianne, who had come up to hear his prognosis, asked.

The doctor pressed his lips together for a moment. "I cannot say, ma'am, my lord. Only that she will have to be supervised, day and night, for her own safety as well as that of others."

John thought of the gun the woman had already wielded twice, and he nodded. He gave orders to his servants, then walked downstairs with the doctor, who bathed and bandaged his burned hand while Marianne went into the bedroom to check on Miss Ramburt. Then the doctor departed, promising to return on the morrow.

Presently, Marianne rejoined John in the library, where he sat at his desk, but with the estate business on its surface untouched.

He had been holding something in his hand, and he looked up when she entered. Her expression was distressed.

"What is it, my dear?"

"John, if she does not improve, you will not have her sent to Bedlam? I have heard awful stories about that hospital. They say it is a most distressing place."

He nodded in understanding. *Hospital* was perhaps too kind a word for the overcrowded facility for the insane, which was renowned for its lack of either oversight or basic comforts.

"No, I would never consign her to such a fate; she has been through hell already," he agreed. "If her inheritance from her grandfather's estate is not sufficient to ensure her welfare, I will see that she has private nurses and guardians. We will find a secluded cottage for her, perhaps by the seaside, a serene and peaceful place where her mind might be able to heal."

Marianne's frown eased, and she came to lay her hand upon his shoulder. "That's very good of you," she said. "Oh, John, I was so frightened."

He put his hand, now lightly bandaged, over hers. "As was I," he agreed. "I do not think I will forget this day for a very long time."

"In her madness, she has put you through a great deal."

She sighed, but he shook his head. "On the whole, I think it has been for the best."

Marianne looked at him in surprise. "What do you mean?"

"I have been thinking of what Miss Ramburt said. Poor old Sir Silas, moldering away, a prisoner of his failing body and mind. And I—I have made myself a prisoner almost as effectively. No more. You have places you wish to see." He lifted what he had been holding, and her eyes widened as she made out the open book with the illustration of an Egyptian statue.

"But—you are uncomfortable amid crowds. I would never ask you to endure the painful stares of strangers," she protested. "As I said before, you have brought the world to you through your library. I can be content with that, too."

"Why should you have to be?" he asked. "And why should I care about the approval of strangers when I have you beside me every day? As long as I see myself in your eyes, witness your love and acceptance, why should I fret over anyone else's opinion?"

Her expression startled, she gazed at him. "Are you certain, my love?"

He nodded. "When I first contemplated setting out for London, it was like a great weight on my shoulders. I dreaded every moment, every hour; all I longed for was to retreat to my own house, withdraw into my library where I could pull the draperies shut, open a book, and find my usual refuge, forgetting the rest of the world.

"But now—now when I consider traveling with you beside me, I think only of how much I will enjoy seeing the marvel in your eyes when we stroll together down the Gallery of Mirrors at Versailles, or venture into the dim tunnels of one of those ancient pyramids. I think we should start our honeymoon in Paris and then—we'll just keep going, my love, wherever your fancy takes us. As long as you are with me, I know I shall never feel ill at ease."

"Oh, John! You are marvelous!"

"Just don't tell me how much you admire and esteem me," he warned. "Or I shall expect another jilting."

Laughing, she hugged him so hard that he winced. Looking contrite, she pulled away at once and caressed his almost-healed arm. "Oh, you must get well, my love, we have such plans to make. I shall go through all my atlases and travel journals—"

"And the wedding, first," he reminded her, grinning. "That needs a little thought, too. I cannot bear to be apart from you an hour longer than is necessary. And you'll find someone else to chaperone your lovely niece? Because despite her—"

He hesitated, and Marianne put in quickly, "Her sweet nature?"

"Yes, that among other things. . . . Despite all her good qualities, I confess that if she is with us every moment, I may be tempted to strangle her just to stop her chatter. In any case, she cannot come with us on our honeymoon!"

Chuckling, Marianne gave him a quick kiss. "Louisa is hatching her own schemes, and she is welcome to them. Besides, she may end up with a wedding to plan, too, and must return to Bath long enough to see to the arrangements. Anyhow, if it comes to that, the banns will have to be read there, as both she and Sir Lucas have their homes in Bath."

"True." John blinked as he considered the necessary formalities, and recalled just how many Sundays the banns had to be read. "We, on the other hand, shall obtain a special license. It's much more speedy, and we've waited long enough!"

She kissed him again, and he pulled her into his arms, wounds be damned. And this time, their embrace was not in the least hurried.

Turn the page for a special preview of
Nicole Byrd's next novel

Vision in Blue

Coming in February 2005 from
Berkley Sensation!

*T*he letter arrived on her birthday.

Big-eyed at being entrusted with such an important errand, one of the first-year girls intercepted Gemma on the second floor hall on her way to the music room.

"Thank you, Mary," Gemma murmured as she took the letter. It was larger and heavier than the usual quarterly note. Hope leaped, unbidden and unsought, from the place deep inside where she usually crammed it down.

"Yes, miss." The little girl dipped a curtsy as she would to one of the teachers before trotting back to her classroom.

Gemma hid a sigh. She was as old, in fact, as some of the instructors and to the younger students, she must look much the same. Although officially now a parlor-boarder, she sometimes helped out with the children, listening patiently as they played scales on the pianoforte or checking their spelling on ink-blotted essays, remembering when she had been this small. At such an age, the brick walls of the school had seemed a fortress, protecting and succoring her. Lately, they sometimes appeared more like a prison.

Today, she turned one and twenty. Many girls her age were already married, were mothers even, and she occasionally received correspondence from friends she'd gone to school with, friends who had left three years, four years ago to go on to the real business of life. Of course, they had somewhere to go.

She might have that chance, too, to fall in love and marry, create a family and defy the emptiness of her life, if she only knew if she had the right to wed a respectable man.

Gemma looked at the thick packet. The outer sheet, with her name: *Miss Gemma Smith, Miss Maysham's Academy for Select Young Ladies, Yorkshire*, was penned in the tiny, precise writing of the solicitor who had, for years past, forwarded her quarterly allowance, along with a few impersonal lines noting that her school fees had been paid. But she had had her allowance only a few weeks ago; what was this about? She was not expecting birthday greetings; certainly, the man had never written anything personal in all the years he had handled her affairs. Was it possible that—

She broke the wax seal and read the first sheet with increasing incredulity.

"Dear Miss Smith: Two decades ago, I was instructed to forward you this missive on the occasion of your one and twentieth birthday. I remain, your servant, Augustus Peevey, Solicitor."

The inner packet, which was labeled only *Gemma,* had a wax seal, too, unbroken, though she could not make out its impression. The paper was of fine quality, and this script was more delicate, with larger loops and swirls. Somehow, it suggested a woman's pen. Gemma's heart beat fast now, and she felt her breath coming quickly. Trembling, she broke the seal and scanned the letter, then—not believing her eyes—read it again, and yet again.

Then she pressed the sheet to her chest and felt behind her for the wooden bench at the edge of the hall. Her knees were weak, and Gemma collapsed—rather than sat—onto it.

Her world had suddenly expanded outward, and nothing would ever be the same.

❧

No doubt about it, money had its uses.

Miss Louisa Crookshank straightened the seam of her new navy blue traveling costume and smiled, careful not to appear smug. She was known in some circles as the "Comely Miss Crookshank," and she knew that appearing satisfied with one's self did not generally serve to enhance one's natural beauty.

But the fact remained, being in possession of a comfortable fortune made all the difference. Since she had achieved her one and twentieth birthday during the final days of winter, she was at last in possession of the fortune she had inherited from her father. True, her uncle Charles still nominally controlled her funds, but her uncle was a dear, and it usually took little effort to coax him into agreement with her latest scheme. Which was how she came to be sitting in her own newly purchased and elegant chaise, on the way to her most cherished goal: London.

At long last!

She had tried last year to have a proper London Season, a coming out long delayed by the sad fact of her father's death and the resulting year of mourning, then by other family problems. But when she had arrived in London, nothing had gone according to plan. Remembering the disasters that had brought her brief sojourn in the capital to such an abrupt and unhappy end, Louisa shuddered. But this year, it would be different, this year—

The carriage jolted to a stop. Louisa clutched the seat to avoid being thrown onto the floor. On the other side of the carriage, Miss Pomshack, her hired but very respectable lady companion, had been dozing. Now, the older lady jerked awake and gave a small shriek. "What is it, Miss Louisa? Are we attacked by brigands?"

"Of course not," Louisa retorted, trying to make out a familiar form through the rain-streaked window, but torrents of liquid obscured her view. She pushed open the door just a little, ignoring the wet gusts that dampened her skirt and the draft of damp, cold air that swept through the carriage. Miss Pomshack screeched again and pulled her shawl closer about her thin shoulders, but Louisa persisted. In a moment, she had found him.

Her fiancé, Sir Lucas Englewood, brown hair plastered to his head—the wind must have knocked off his hat again—rode his steed closer to the carriage. He had insisted on riding—and although Louisa had invited him sweetly inside the carriage when the first drops began to fall, he had scoffed at her suggestion. "A little rain never hurt a fellow," he had said gaily.

He did not look so happy now. "It's no use, Louisa," he told her. "The rain isn't letting up, and the road's turning to soup. The team can barely pull the carriage. There's a decent-looking inn just ahead. We're going to have to stop and wait for the weather to improve."

Louisa bit back a protest. She had so wanted to end the day with her long-awaited arrival in London. But, gazing at the sheets of rain that cloaked any view of the countryside, she nodded reluctantly and shut the door.

In a moment, the carriage moved again, lurching as the team pulled hard against the grasping mud. Bracing herself, Louisa sighed.

Perhaps money couldn't accomplish everything.

When they hurried into the inn, heads bowed against waves of water that drenched them thoroughly before they reached the protection of the building, she found they were not the only travelers to take shelter from the storm.

Inside, the innkeeper bowed and smirked and was as obsequious as the most demanding member of the Ton could require, but the fact remained, there was no private parlor to be had. "But the travelers from the stage is a nice, quiet bunch, miss, and I'll make sure that no one bothers you," he said. "And me wife is cooking up a grand dinner, which will lift your spirits no end."

Sir Lucas frowned as he escorted Louisa to a seat in the

corner of the room and helped her shed her sodden cloak. She would have preferred to be closer to the fire, which Miss Pomshack also eyed with longing, but Lucas was, as usual, more concerned with the proprieties.

The public coach, it seemed, had also had to make an unscheduled stop. Several men crowded around the leaping fire, lifting their coattails and drying rain-soaked coats and broad backsides all at once, talking in loud voices about market shares and the price of wool. The whole room smelt of damp wool, the scent mingling with smoke from the fire, as well as the fumes from one particularly noxious pipe that an elderly man sitting by the hearth had clamped between thin lips.

On the whole, Louisa decided she preferred her distant corner.

"At least I was able to obtain a bedchamber for you and Miss P.," Lucas told her.

"We have to share a room?" Louisa demanded, though she kept her voice low. Her companion was shaking out her pelisse and didn't seem to notice the quiet complaint.

"It's the last one," Lucas told her. "I'll have to camp out in the parlor with the other men, so count your blessings."

Sighing, she nodded. "Thank you, Lucas, for looking out for me so well." She smiled up at him.

His chest seemed to swell visibly. "I promised your uncle I would see to your safety, didn't I?" he told her, his tone dignified. "You will not come to any harm this year!"

Not wanting to discuss last year's perilous adventures, Louisa frowned. Her near-escapes were now only painful memories, and she had no wish to relive them.

The innkeeper brought them all steaming cups of mulled wine. Louisa held the hot pewter cup carefully, glad she had not yet removed her gloves, and sipped.

A pleasant warmth spread through her, and some of her disappointment ebbed. She was on her way to London; this was only a momentary delay. Very well, not momentary, exactly, but still brief.

Lucas excused himself to check on the carriage and team to be sure the horses, including his own handsome gelding, were properly rubbed down and fed. Left alone with Miss Pomshack, who seemed interested only in her cup of wine, Louisa glanced around the room. This time, she noticed one lone female sitting a bit apart from the group of men.

What was a woman, who was—Louisa noted—dressed most respectably if not richly, doing alone on the coach? This woman, who looked not much older than Louisa herself, kept her gaze down and seemed to be doing everything she could to avoid contact with the other passengers. Did she have no one to travel with her?

Louisa's ready curiosity stirred. Besides, she was bored, and there was a long evening ahead with no one to talk to except Miss P., who was not much of a conversationalist, and dear Lucas, who would probably spend hours in the stables until he was sure that all the horses were seen to. Acting on impulse as she often did, Louisa stood, and before her companion could protest, marched across the room.

She paused in front of the other woman, who looked up at her in surprise.

"Forgive me," Louisa said, her tone cheerful. "But you seem to be alone. Would you not like to share some wine with us?"

The young woman flushed. She had dark hair tucked beneath a somewhat soggy bonnet and unusual eyes, of a blue so dark and rich that they put one in mind of ocean depths on a sunny day. Her skin was fair, and when she spoke, her voice sounded educated and genteel.

"I would not wish to intrude," she said, looking unsure.

"Not at all. I know this is not precisely a proper introduction, but I am Miss Louisa Crookshank of Bath, but just now on my way to London for the Season."

The stranger still hesitated. "It's very kind of you, but are you sure your mother will approve?"

"Oh, Miss Pomshack is my companion; my mother died years ago," Louisa explained matter-of-factly. "I had no female relatives available just now to chaperone. I have aunts, but one has a new baby and isn't interested in the

Season"—she shook her head at such madness—"and the other is newly married and taking an extended honeymoon around the world. I get letters from the strangest places, I assure you. She was riding camels and exploring pyramids the last I heard. However, she does send the most delightful gifts. I have a Persian shawl—light as air but very warm and such colors—that is utterly divine."

The other woman smiled. Louisa was glad to see it; the stranger had been looking rather downcast. Mind you, Louisa's bubbly good spirits usually had that effect on people. "Come along," she coaxed. "A more congenial group is just what you need on such a miserable day. And you can eat dinner with us, instead of with the men on the coach, which would be much more to your liking, I'm sure?"

The light outside the rain-streaked windows was fading, and the group at the fireplace was growing noisier.

The young woman seemed to make up her mind. She stood and gave a small curtsy. "Thank you, you're very kind. I am Miss Gemma Smith, for several years a student at Miss Maysham's Academy for Select Young Ladies, just outside of York. I have only recently left."

Louisa led the way back to their corner, where she introduced Miss Pomshack and beckoned to the landlord to bring more wine.

Soon they were comfortably settled. Miss Smith removed her damp bonnet and attempted to push her hair back into order.

"Are you traveling to London for the Season, or to visit family?" Louisa asked politely, trying not to sound too inquisitive.

The other young lady hesitated. "It is for family reasons, yes," she agreed, taking a long drink from her cup.

This did little to enlighten Louisa. She decided to explain some of her own circumstances. Perhaps this would put Miss Smith more at ease, and more apt to share her own situation.

"I am traveling with my companion and my fiancé, Sir Lucas Englewood," she told the stranger.

"Oh, my congratulations," the other girl said.

"Thank you. Lucas wanted us to be married this spring, but I have so wanted a real London Season first—I've never even had a proper coming out—that I saw no reason to rush into matrimony, as dear to me as Lucas is. Not to mention—" Louisa lowered her voice in respect. "After the sad death last fall of Princess Charlotte in childbirth, well, it somewhat lessened my eagerness to rush into the married state."

Miss Smith nodded. It had been a national calamity. The princess had been very popular, unlike her volatile father, the Prince Regent, and her loss had been genuinely mourned. The prince had been most cast about at losing his only child, or so it was rumored. But the prince was a fun-loving man, and Louisa was privately hoping that this spring's Season would not be too much subdued by the tragedy.

"Do you have a home in London?" the other lady asked, trying to rub away the water spots on her gray traveling costume as it slowly dried. "Or are you staying at a hotel?"

Louisa smiled. "I have rented a very nice house in west London; it is fully furnished and comes with servants, at a quite reasonable rate," she explained. "Lucas has taken rooms for the time being; he's feeling very proper just now and doesn't think it would be suitable to stay with me, even with another lady to chaperone. But after Lucas and I are married, I hope to purchase the house or one like it. My uncle handled the lease, and I have not yet seen the residence myself, but he assures me I will be pleased."

"How lovely." The other girl sounded a bit wistful.

"And I suppose you are going to stay with family? You will have to call on me once you are settled," Louisa suggested. She liked the look of this girl, with her intelligent blue eyes and her reluctance to put herself forward; her manners were very nice. "Were you in London last year? I have the feeling I have seen you before."

For some reason, the girl flushed. "No, this is my first visit. I do have family in London, but—um—they are not yet aware that I am coming."

That was unusual, but it would have been bad form to remark upon it. Generally, a lady did not set out until she was sure she had a safe haven at the end of the journey; big cities—as Louisa's aunts were only too eager to tell her— could present many dangers for young ladies on their own.

"Perhaps your letters have passed in the mail," Louisa suggested, trying to sound as if this were not an odd situation.

"I'm afraid it's more complicated than that." The other girl took another sip of her wine and avoided Louisa's gaze. "But I do have a brother who lives in London. If you have been in company there, you may have met him?" There was the slightest question in the way her voice rose.

Curiosity inflamed once again, Louisa looked up. "Perhaps, though I did not go about in Society last year as much as I would have liked. What is his name?"

The other young woman hesitated, then said slowly, "Lord Gabriel Sinclair."

Louisa gave a start of surprise. "But I do know him! In fact, my aunt is newly married to his older brother. I can tell you some really scandalous gossip—not that I would share it with just anyone, but if you are family, you should really know what he has been up to, if you don't already— and of course, he's a most charming and devilishly handsome man, and his—your—family is most well connected, so I imply no censure. No wonder you looked familiar— the shape of your eyes and that unusual dark shade of blue, and your fair skin and dark hair. Oh, how nice to meet another one of the Sinclairs!"

She hesitated, suddenly remembering that the stranger had given her surname as Smith. Fortunately, before the pause became too awkward, a serving girl approached with a large tray full of dishes. She pulled a table closer to them and set down the food. No one spoke as the table was laid.

But Louisa's ready interest was again at full alert. Was there some mystery or intriguing family scandal here? When the servant retreated, Louisa added, as delicately as possible, "I admit I did not know Lord Gabriel had a sister."

"Actually—" Again, Miss Smith did not quite meet Louisa's eye. "Actually, he doesn't know it, either."

Dear Reader,

We hope you have enjoyed *Beauty in Black,* the continuing adventures of the Hill/Sinclair families. Since the books have been printed out of sequence (not the fault of our publisher but rather of our incurably impulsive Muse, who grew so enchanted with Circe after the first book that she insisted on plunging ahead and letting Circe grow up in order to give her her own romance), we thought we should list the chronological order.

Here it is:

Dear Impostor
Featuring Lord Gabriel Sinclair and Miss Psyche Hill,
and introducing Psyche's younger sister, Circe

Beauty in Black
Featuring Gabriel's older brother, John Sinclair,
marquess of Gillingham, and Mrs. Marianne Hughes, a Merry Widow,
and introducing Louisa Crookshank

Vision in Blue
(On shelves early 2005)
Introducing Miss Gemma Sinclair and Captain Matthew Fallon

Lady in Waiting
Featuring David Lydford, earl of Westbury,
and Miss Circe Hill

We have also begun the Merry Widow stories, about a group of courageous young widows making new lives for themselves, which includes *Beauty in Black* and:

Widow in Scarlet
Featuring Charles Needham, Viscount Richmond, and
Mrs. Lucy Contrain, and
introducing Margery, countess of Sealey

We hope you enjoy them all!

Cheryl and Michelle
aka Nicole Byrd

www.NicoleByrd.com

NICOLE BYRD

Widow in Scarlet
0-425-19209-1

When Lucy Contrain discovers that
aristocrat Nicholas Ramsey believes her
dead husband stole a legendary jewel, she
insists on joining his search.
Little does she know they will be drawn
into deadly danger—and into a passion
that neither can resist.

Praise for the romances of Nicole Byrd:

"Madcap fun with a touch of romantic
intrigue...satisfying to the last word."
—Cathy Maxwell

"Irresistable...deliciously witty,
delightfully clever." —*Booklist*

Available wherever books are sold or
to order call 1-800-788-6262.